THEY ARE NOT WHOM YOU EXPECT. . . .
THEY ARE CLOSER THAN YOU KNOW. . . .

THE FATHER—The awesome power at the center of a conspiracy reaching into the highest circles of America's government—the secret leader of all who play "The Game," a plan that will make his twisted dreams . . . and our worst nightmares . . . come true.

JEFF—The tough reporter on the trail of a story that will rock a nation—a determined man whose newly aroused feelings for a woman drive him toward a desperate fight for his country, his family—and his life.

SANDY—The passionate young widow unable to give up the conviction that her "murdered" daughter still lives—an electrifyingly beautiful woman whose fierce desires plunge her into a maelstrom of love and danger.

TAMI—The exceptionally intelligent child, long missing, long thought dead . . . like all the other special children no one can find—a little girl chosen for a terrifying destiny, one of those now trapped . . .

WITHIN THE WEB

Also by Melvin Weiser

THE TRESPASSER

WITHIN
THE WEB

MELVIN WEISER

A DELL BOOK

Published by
Dell Publishing Co., Inc.
1 Dag Hammarskjold Plaza
New York, New York 10017

Dell ® TM 681510, Dell Publishing Co., Inc.

ISBN: 0-440-19718-X

Printed in the United States of America
First printing—September 1984

Dedication

With love to Isabelle,
who has always believed

Acknowledgments

My appreciation to the following
people for their generous assistance in
getting this novel into print:

In New York—*my dedicated agent, Roberta*
Pryor; a truly patient and astute
editor-in-chief, Susan Moldow;
and my gifted editor, Jeanne
F. Bernkopf
In Phoenix—*my friends, Charlene and Alan*
Jeffory, Sheila Paige Roth,
Marilyn Adler, and Jeanette
and Phil Gilbert
In Los Angeles—*George Chasin, agent*

1

There are 206 separate bones in the human body; 158 of his bones were either broken or crushed.

Idaho newspapers gave the accident a few lines. The lengthiest coverage appeared in the *Lowman Eagle*:

> A lone driver, Edgar Lee Baliston, 33, of Los Angeles, was killed last night when his Ford pickup went out of control and fell into rugged terrain near the Crooked River.
>
> Sheriff Lyman Parling of Boise County stated that although there were no witnesses, it was clear from tire evidence that a blowout sent the vehicle into a skid from which the driver never recovered. The car left the mountain road near Katchatee Cross, plunging 228 feet into the canyon below.
>
> The presence of camping equipment suggested that Mr. Baliston may have been returning from a fishing vacation in the Sawtooth Range.
>
> Efforts to locate next of kin have been unsuccessful.

The reason authorities had failed to find a relative was that the only next of kin for Edgar Lee Baliston was his eight-year-old son, Daniel, who had been right there with his father—until violent hands had torn them apart.

They were in the woods not fifteen yards from the gentle glow of the Baliston campfire. They were watching. A man. A woman.

Encased in the darkness of the August night. Infinitely patient.
Without so much as the movement of a finger. Watching. Waiting.

"Dad," Daniel Baliston murmured. His voice was soft, and the word seemed to curl into the licking sounds of the fire.

"Hmmmm?"

"This is great."

"Hmmmm." Unqualified agreement.

They were on top of their sleeping bags. The boy was on his stomach, chin resting on the back of his hands, eyes locked on the flickering flames; the man was on his back, palms under his head, thoughts meandering among the stars.

"I'm gonna catch a fish tomorrow that'll make Santiago's look like a guppy," the boy promised lazily.

"Who's Santiago?" It was a murmur.

"You know . . ."

Silence.

". . . the fisherman."

More silence.

"In Hemingway's *The Old Man and the Sea*."

"Hmmmm."

Eddy Baliston smiled. Well, if that's what Danny wanted, that's what Danny would get. They'd come home from this trip with a fish so big, the monster would have to be strapped to the side of the pickup! Danny deserved it. He deserved anything he wanted because he was a special child. A bright, sensitive, and loving human being. And he'd had more than his share of trauma this year, more than enough for a lifetime.

For a long two minutes, night sounds filled the silence between father and son. Insect voices. The gentle conversation of leaves. Then Danny spoke. "I wish they could have been with us." It wasn't said in torment. Just with a whisper of wistfulness. But it was enough to make Eddy Baliston's breath catch.

His wife, daughters, and parents had all been killed recently in one terrible, freaky, Hollywood Freeway accident. The loss had almost destroyed Eddy. Imagine what it must be like for the boy, he had thought when he was finally able to think again. That thought had led to this vacation. He had hoped that he and his son would enjoy each other and take their first steps in the creation of a new life—far from Los Angeles, near a quiet stream, under a star-studded sky.

Now the boy's wish made Eddy abandon his stargazing and turn on his side. He studied his son. "You all right?" he asked gently.

"Yeah . . . I was just thinking."

There were a few moments of silence.

"That's okay," Eddy finally whispered. "They're always in my mind, too."

Danny rolled over suddenly, his right arm flying up, the back of his hand coming to rest on his forehead. A muffled sob troubled the air.

Eddy ached for his boy.

After a few more moments, the small voice, husky and trembling slightly, went on. "Sure is a beautiful sky," Danny said.

It was a glorious effort, one that almost choked Eddy Baliston with pride and love. "Mountain skies and ocean skies always seem to have more stars," he commented softly to help his son.

The two in the darkness rose as if some mysterious signal had prompted the movement. The woman started directly toward the campsite; the man circled to its opposite side. They closed in soundlessly, without the snap of a twig or even the crush of grass.

Danny pulled himself to his elbows. He studied the night. "There's the Pleiades," he said, pointing.

"The what?"

"Pleiades. See that bunch of stars over there? Over near that big one?"

Eddy couldn't distinguish one cluster of stars from another, but he answered, "What about them?"

"They're part of the Taurus constellation. There are seven of 'em, but we can really see only six with the naked eye. According to the Greeks, there was this giant whose name was Orion. He was a great hunter, and he wanted the seven daughters of Atlas. I guess they were pretty."

"Did he get them?"

"Nope. Zeus turned them into those stars."

"What happened to Orion?"

"He was killed later by another pretty girl. Her name was Artemis. It was an accident, and Artemis felt so bad, she turned him into a constellation of stars, too. He's right up there near the Pleiades.''

"Well, it's too bad he had to die, but at least he's always near them, right?''

Danny nodded seriously. "I think that's what they call the fatal attraction of beautiful women.''

Eddy exploded in laughter. Jesus, he thought, the things that come out of that kid's mouth! He felt better now. It's all going to be just great, he told himself, just great.

"Good evening." She stepped into the clearing.

Her voice and sudden appearance were a shocking surprise. Danny sat up quickly; Eddy jerked to his knees. His attention darted around the campsite in search of others. He saw no one; her partner was still concealed.

"Didn't mean to scare you," she said with a smile.

"What can we do for you?" Eddy asked, standing. He continued to look around suspiciously. What could a young, attractive woman be doing out here all by herself? Innocently strolling through the woods alone at this hour? Not likely. California newspapers had been reporting acts of vacation violence all summer long. He had read of three camping incidents just last week, and now his heart raced.

"Just want to join you," she said pleasantly. "My name is Andrea." She started toward him.

"Hold it.''

She stopped.

"You alone?" Again he glanced about quickly.

"Eddy, don't be so difficult." She laughed.

The sound of his name snapped his head in her direction. "What?''

As he croaked his surprise, her partner stepped from the dark woods, saying crisply, "I'm over here, Eddy.''

He had made his appearance behind Danny. His sharp voice startled the boy to his feet, and the leveled gun in his hand made Danny leap toward his father's protective embrace.

Now all of them stood in the center of the clearing: father and son, waiting; determined strangers, closing in on both sides.

"What do you want?" Eddy asked. "Money?''

They didn't answer. They merely stopped some four feet away.

Eddy reached into his back pocket. He fished out his wallet. "Here . . . a hundred eighty bucks . . ." He tossed it.

The man made absolutely no movement to catch the billfold. It struck him lightly on the chest and fell to the ground.

"Equipment?" Eddy tried again. "Take it. Take it all."

"You leave my dad and me alone," Danny warned.

Eddy squeezed his shoulder. "Shh . . . easy, Dan."

"Step away from the boy," the man ordered. He had a razor-voice: cold, keened through a tight larynx.

Danny Baliston clutched fearfully at his father's waist.

"What is it you want?" Eddy demanded. He pulled the boy closer and struggled to control himself for his son's sake. "Take it, I told you. Take it all. The truck, too. Go ahead. The keys are in the ignition and—"

"Step away from the boy," the man cut in.

"No, Dad . . . please."

"Look, we haven't done anything to you," Eddy argued.

The woman spoke. "No one's going to be hurt if you do what you're told."

But Danny shouted, "*You'll* get hurt if you don't leave us alone. You leave us alone, you hear me? You leave us alone, or I promise *I'll* hurt *you*!" Sobs quavered in his impotent threat, and tears began to course down his cheeks.

"Don't be afraid, Danny," she said. Her sounds were soothing, strangely sympathetic.

Eddy demanded, "How do you know our names?"

"Danny, I wouldn't hurt you," she continued, ignoring the question.

"You been following us?"

"Come here to me, Danny . . . please."

Danny held tighter.

"I'll help you, you'll see," she promised.

The boy was almost in a panic. He clung to his father, shaking pathetically.

The man suddenly spat, "Step away from that boy!" He leaped forward, hand darting, as though to grab Danny's arm.

Eddy shifted instantly, twisting between his son and the threat. But the moment had been carefully orchestrated, and just as Eddy moved, the woman charged from behind and tore Danny loose with one swift powerful motion. It happened so quickly that Eddy Baliston was standing there alone before he even realized what had happened. He heard his son's cry, and like a helpless beast, he moaned in torment and rage.

The gun was pointing at his heart. The tight, razor-voice was threatening, "If you want to stay alive, don't move!" Eddy held his ground.

Danny was screaming and kicking in the woman's arms.

"Get him out of here," the man ordered.

She started from the clearing, carrying the boy with an ease that belied her small appearance.

"Where are you taking him?" Eddy cried.

"On your knees," the man ordered. *"On your knees!"* The gun zeroed at his brains.

Clumsily, Eddy Baliston dropped to his knees, begging softly, "Don't hurt him, please . . . please . . . don't hurt him."

Meanwhile, Danny was thrashing about wildly, his cries cutting the night. The woman's left hand came up abruptly and smothered the sounds in his throat. He didn't feel the hand clamp over his mouth; he didn't even feel her little finger slip accidentally between his lips because if he had, he would surely have bitten it off, all of it, or rather all that was left—because one joint was already missing. All he felt was helplessness and terror.

In the clearing, Eddy Baliston waited on his knees, his head turned in the direction of his abducted boy. "Where are you taking him?" he pleaded, pulling his attention back to his captor. "What do you want? For God's sake, what do you want?"

The man said nothing. He just waited. Waited until they both heard the sound of a car's engine turning over in the distance. Then he moved. With infinite care, he began a slow encirclement of his victim. All the while that reedy, gelid voice muttered only one word. "Easy . . . easy . . . easy . . . easy . . ."

Eddy's mind was a welter of thoughts. Fragments of desolation. "Danny . . . safety . . . gun . . . Danny . . . loss . . . cries . . ." His body ached with the tension of desperation. He heard the man's word. Heard him circling. He even heard the motor idling somewhere in the woods. It was as though everything had jumbled into one swirling mass of sensation, crying to be separated by action. He must do something. He must!

"Oh, dear God!" he moaned, and he fell forward to his hands.

The man jumped back a step.

"God . . . God . . . God . . ." he repeated endlessly, tossing his head from side to side as his fingers clawed at the soft earth.

The man resumed his slow circling.

Suddenly Eddy Baliston screamed. He fell to his back. A huge handful of sand clouded the air. His legs kicked crazily at his attacker.

The man dodged quickly, but not before a boot struck the hand that held the gun. The gun went flying.

Eddy was on his feet in an instant, lunging like a maddened, wounded animal.

It was all for nothing, though. The man caught him on the charge and sidestepped nimbly. He crashed a powerful forearm across Eddy's shoulder blades. He kneed him deftly and broke his ribs. And then, with perfect timing, he punted Eddy Baliston's head like a football.

It had taken only seconds. Eddy lay with his face in the sand, moaning on the edge of consciousness.

The man leaned forward to whisper in his ear, "I'm sorry about this. I really am." Then with one sharp jerk, he broke Eddy Baliston's neck.

The man stood. He sighed and retrieved his gun. He collected all of Danny's clothes and equipment and carried everything through the woods to his car.

After placing it all in the trunk, he came around to the woman. A look told her of Eddy's death. "I'll meet you," he said quietly. He reached in and took a long-handled flashlight from the dashboard.

"I'm being good," Danny offered timidly, trying to look up at him through the driver's window. "Andrea said if I'm a good boy, you won't hurt my daddy. I'll be good, I promise."

The woman turned and stroked his cheek. "It's all right, Danny," she said with great tenderness. "Don't you worry. Everything'll be all right."

"He won't hurt him, will he?"

The man bent and looked in at the child. "I wouldn't hurt your daddy, son. Don't you worry about a thing." The words were as gentle and reassuring as the strange voice would permit.

"Okay." The boy shrank into his seat again.

Nothing more was said. The woman put the car into gear. The man turned and made his way back to the campsite.

There he stuffed the wallet into Eddy's rear pocket without removing any of the bills or cards; he placed all camping matériel into the pickup; he covered every trace of campsite existence,

smoothing sand, burying embers. Finally, when he was satisfied
that everything seemed normal again, he settled Eddy Baliston's
body into the cab of the truck and slid behind the wheel next to
him.

He drove the pickup to Katchatee Cross. Leaving the motor
idling, he pulled the emergency brake on the crest of the hill. He
jumped from the cab and hauled Eddy over to the driver's side.
After that he knelt at the left front tire. Using a small but
powerfully pressurized cannister that he had removed from his
belt, he pumped in a few quick jets of gas. Quickly he squeezed
in next to the lifeless body. Then, leaving the driver's door open
as he released the hand brake, he threw the vehicle into gear.

The pickup started down the hill. It accelerated rapidly. There
was a small explosion: the left front tire blew.

He jammed on the brakes and burned skid marks on the road.
He leaped from the truck, tugging the wheel sharply to ensure the
vehicle's going over the cliff.

At first the pickup sailed into space like a glider. Then it
dropped sickeningly and smashed off the mountain walls, spinning,
bouncing, plunging.

It didn't explode or burst into flames. It lay unseen in the
darkness of the starry night.

Miles away, some backpackers heard the crash. They were
concerned. But the hour precluded investigation. Their concern
soon became wonderment; their wonderment, indifference; their
indifference, sleep.

The man now walked the quiet mountain road. He felt strangely
disturbed. This had been his eighth killing. As with all the
others, everything had gone almost exactly as planned. Then why
wasn't he feeling elated? He had a terrible thought: Was he
beginning to feel for his victims? After all, he *had* whispered
regret into the ear of tonight's loser, something he had never
done before. Perhaps it was time for him to rest. Yes. He
would have to request a change of assignment. Yes. Before
he did something foolish or rash that would jeopardize The
Game.

Four miles down the road, he reached the woman and the boy.
They were waiting in the car on a partially hidden spur. He
settled into the driver's seat.

"Is my daddy all right?" Danny asked anxiously.

The man started the motor. "Everything's fine, Danny," he answered. "Everything's just the way it's supposed to be."

The car vanished into the night.

The disappearance of Daniel Baliston didn't remain a secret, of course. Although the first Idaho press statements hadn't mentioned him, later police investigation in Los Angeles revealed that he had left home with his father. Then a massive hunt was undertaken in the mountains surrounding the wrecked truck. The campsite was eventually discovered, but the boy was never found. Nothing else was ever heard of him.

The date of these crimes—Eddy Baliston's murder and his son's kidnapping—was Saturday, August 16, 1975.

2

"It's the brass—it's always the miserable, self-serving brass."

Jeff Rader, syndicated columnist of the *Los Angeles Voice*, was grumbling over a half-empty mug that was cupped in his hands.

"But why are you letting this get to you?" she asked.

He ignored the question. "Really, Annie, if incompetence were music, some administrators would be Beethovens."

She smiled. Not too bad. She'd accept that. He was always good for at least one breezy metaphor each time they met. This would satisfy today's minimum requirement. "Thank you." She laughed. "And it's only eleven A.M."

The response stopped him. A *non sequitur*? That wasn't like her. He cocked his head and lazily raised an eyebrow.

"Not your best metaphor, but considering the handicap of your present state of mind, not bad."

He slumped.

She couldn't see his face as it hung over the mug in his hands. She came around to him with the Silex in her hand and touched his shoulder. "More coffee?"

He straightened and settled back against the kitchen chair, showing a weary grin. "Annie . . . Annie . . . what would I do without Annie?"

She stroked his hair once and bent to kiss him on the crown of his head. Then she refilled his mug.

He reached an arm about her waist.

Her stomach was a seven-month balloon, pressing his face now. He poked a finger at it and made a popping sound that caused her to slap at him playfully and to pull away with a chuckle.

Her name was Ann Kroft. She was thirty-four years old. She was a pleasure to look at, a joy to be near. She was married to a successful accountant, Stanley Kroft. And she was Jeff Rader's younger sister.

Theirs was a warm relationship, one in which concern and care were openly and freely expressed.

Jeff gulped a mouthful of the hot, black refill and grunted. Then, settling back into his seat and pointing at his sister's bulging belly, he asked, "Soooo, you sure you want to bring that lovely little child into this crazy world?"

She smiled, but her concern was evident. "What is it, Jeff?" she asked with chiding gentleness. "You haven't been right for some time now." She sat again and faced him across the table.

He rubbed a hand over his eyes and sighed. "I don't know," he admitted. "Just getting roasted a little; that's all, I guess."

"You've been roasted before, my brother. That's not it. So come on and tell Mother-confessor Kroft, and you'll feel a whole lot better."

He couldn't tell her. He wasn't quite sure what it was himself. But he knew she was right: It wasn't the roasting he was getting now for his series on unsolved crimes. It had started long before that.

"I like your new series," Annie offered by way of brightening his mood. "Especially yesterday's on the missing Baliston boy."

He looked at her. "It's coming," he breathed. "Like shit through a straw—but it's coming."

"But the Baliston one's not really an unsolved crime, is it?"

"I see you've been talking to the Honorable Harold Durkin."

"What do you mean?"

"That's what the roasting is about."

"He came after you?"

He nodded. "Our illustrious police commissioner spoke to Tom Pendleton this morning. Well, he didn't actually speak to him. It was more like a phone-burning session. Told him if he was any kind of city editor, he'd have stopped this series before it even got into my head." His voice became a mimicry of

officialdom. '' 'Unwarranted accusations of police ineptitude!
Dangerous to the credibility of effective law enforcement!
Demeaning, headstrong, destructive journalism that does nobody
a service!' ''

"You did accuse them of—"

"Dropping the case. That's all. There are still unanswered
questions and a missing person."

"But does that really make it a crime?"

"Of course not. The crime is the police department's unwilling-
ness to find the answers to those questions."

She opened her mouth to respond.

He held up a hand and stopped her with the gesture. "I
know—there are thousands of felonies being committed in L.A.
every year, and we can't expect an overworked police force to
handle all of them satisfactorily. True. But I think we *should*
expect them not to close the book on something merely because
they've lost their appetite for that particular dish. I'll tell you
what the trouble is with this Baliston thing: There's nobody left.
Nobody. Nobody to season the meat, nobody to turn on the
burners, nobody to generate heat. So the dish goes stale and cold,
and the L.A.P.D. dumps the whole thing into the garbage can of
closed files."

She was grinning, fighting back audible pleasure.

He rubbed his eyes and sighed. "You can bet your unborn
baby's bib that if our noble police commissioner were a Baliston
instead of a Durkin, this little case would still be open and
there'd be one hell of an ongoing investigation until those questions were either answered or that boy's skeleton found. Police
commissioner. Meathead, that's what he is."

Now she was laughing. Eyes sparkling. Palms applauding.
"Beautiful! I love it!"

He stopped. He stared at her for a moment and then smiled
sheepishly and dropped his head. "I do go on," he mumbled.

"I love it when you get off like that, and you know it," she
answered, grinning at him.

He took a cookie from the dish in the center of the table.
"Well, showtime's over for today, baby sister." He stood. "Gotta
get back to the laborin' mass." He groaned comically and started
for the front door.

She followed him. "What's going to happen now?"

"With what?"

"The series."

"Tom told me to go easy for a while. Can't make an adversary of the police department. Too helpful to us."

"Is that true?"

"Truth is, it is. Police leads can be invaluable."

"But when the cops are wrong, they're wrong, right?"

"Uh-huh."

"So what are you going to do?"

He shrugged. "Go right on doing the only thing I know how to do, I guess."

She kissed his cheek and beamed at him with obvious pride. "Go get 'em, Tiger," she whispered.

And he would. Because what Jeff Rader didn't realize at this time was that he was already inseparably bound to the Edgar Lee Baliston murder. Bound by an incident about which he knew very little—something that happened three full years before this day's kaffeeklatsch with his lovely sister, Annie Kroft.

3

It was a morning with a hangover, dull and gray, one that had barely recovered from the night's binge of cold and chilling rain.

But it wasn't enough to discourage Oliver Porter. He had recently met a magnificent machine. Her name was Jill Kinnerly. She was tall and sleek and she owned a twenty-six-year-old pelvis that rolled and jerked with breathtaking abandon. She was his Dream Machine. And after Saturday night's encounter, he was absolutely determined to prepare his body for all contingencies.

At best he was a reluctant athlete. Morning sleep-ins had always been more attractive than morning workouts. But having enjoyed Jill Kinnerly once, he was a man now who would have raced naked through a blizzard for the mere touch of her skin.

She had suggested jogging.

So there they were at 5:00 A.M. on Ohio Drive, near the cherry trees south of Buckeye. And though his eyes were only half open, he could see that even at this insane hour she looked simply fantastic.

They were going to jog north along the Potomac, past the Ericsson Memorial up to Roosevelt Bridge and back. When he actually saw the distance, his brain puckered, but he grinned with phony bravado and challenged, "Let's go."

For a while he found her pace invigorating. Then, troubling. And finally, somewhere near the pier where summer tourists crowd the boats for their sight-seeing jaunts, Oliver Porter's pizzazz spluttered and dimmed and fizzled out completely. Burning lungs and creaking joints had forced him to a dead stop.

Jill Kinnerly returned, bouncing brightly on the balls of her feet.

"You okay?" she asked.

"Oh, sure . . . sure. I just . . . thought . . . I saw something . . . out there . . . that's all," he lied cheerily. He waved a hand vaguely at the Potomac River.

She looked at the gray water while he almost collapsed behind her. "Where?" she asked, still bouncing like a bubble.

"Out there . . . out there . . ." he gasped.

She stared at the river; he played for time.

Then she said, "Oh, yes. I see it. What do you think it is?" She turned to him.

He straightened quickly, not wanting to be caught. "I . . . I don't know. It . . . just looked . . . strange to me . . . so I thought . . . we ought to . . . stop . . . for a minute."

Her attention went back to the river. Soon her bouncing slowed. It came to a halt. She was troubled. "Y'know," she said very quietly, "I think it looks like a body."

Her obvious sincerity made Oliver Porter scan the water for his own lie. Then he saw it. To him, too, it resembled a body—only there was something distinctly odd about the way it lay in the water. Clumped. Swollen. As though it had a camel's hump.

"Come on," he murmured, his lungs and joints forgotten, his eyes now locked on the thing. Silently the two joggers walked the shoreline, watching the object drift closer and closer to the parkway.

Soon it washed into the angle of a jutting retaining stone; they saw it clearly now.

"Je-sus," he whispered. "There are two of them . . . tied together."

Jill Kinnerly's murmured horror matched his own. "Oh, my God—the top one looks like . . . a child."

They were identified as Adam Clark Wilkenson and his four-year-old daughter, Tami.

The medical examiner's report established the following facts: Deaths had occurred at approximately 9:00 P.M. the previous evening; the cause in both cases was strangulation; both bodies had then been subjected to fire; the adult corpse was barely recognizable; the child had no recognizable features at all.

A partial fingerprint led to the man's identification, which was corroborated by his military dental records. The child's identity was established by means of clothing threads still adhering to parts of the charred flesh and by a gold bracelet on her right wrist and a ring on the middle finger of her right hand.

It was a grisly double homicide. Strangulation. Incineration. Piggy-backed bodies. It offended even the most hardened of the capital's police. From the outset, they went after the killers with more than their customary zeal.

Something else kicked the investigation into even higher gear: It was the discovery that Adam Clark Wilkenson had been the first assistant to the U.S. Secretary of State.

All of Washington, D.C., was shocked.

"He was a marvelous man," a close friend said. "I don't know of a single person who disliked him. Not one. He was a rarity. Why, he could disagree with you completely and do it in such a way that you simply had to listen and come away feeling that . . . well, maybe there was more to the subject than you had been willing to admit. You know what I mean? What a loss, what a loss."

Another friend choked. "I've known them ever since Tami was born . . . that poor, darling sweetheart . . . four years old but . . . bright as a star, and. . . ." She hadn't been able to continue. When she recovered sufficiently, her thoughts veered. "How's Sandy? Mrs. Wilkenson. Is she all right? They won't let any calls through."

The pieces were quickly assembled:

Sandra Wilkenson was now the only surviving member of her family. Four days before the death of her husband and child, she had had an accident. Her Cuban housekeeper, Maria, had inadvertently bumped into her while they were on the upper level of her house. The protective railing hadn't saved her. She had tumbled over it and crashed to the living-room floor. The housekeeper was of no help; she had panicked. Fortunately, the arrival of two friends at the moment of the accident had brought immediate medical attention. After being admitted to Georgetown Hospital, she was told that the fall had only broken the femur of her left leg. The postsurgery prognosis was excellent; her spirits were high.

Two days later, Maria left the household, saying, *"Yo no puedo quedar aqui más . . . porque cada vez yo pienso de lo que yo he hecho, yo empiezo a llorar."* I can't stay here any longer . . . because every time I think of what I've done, I start to cry.

It took Adam a few moments to understand her despite his command of Spanish; her tears and sobs had mingled into a gargled lament. But when her decision to leave became clear to him, he was shocked. My God, who would care for the house? And Tami? Who would feed her? Get her ready for school? Be there when she returned? He forgot his annoyance with the maid for her part in the accident. He begged her to stay. He assured her that no one in the family blamed her in the least. But his efforts were wasted.

Her departure was sad. Tami wept; Maria wept. After all, she had been with the Wilkensons for eight months, and she had been especially kind and attentive to the child.

Once she was gone, Adam accepted her absence stoically and even convinced himself that an adjustment to the new circumstances would be simple. There were other Marias; the agency would just have to find one, that's all. Until then, he'd forgo lunch and leave his office by one o'clock every day. In that way he'd be home and have dinner going before Tami was even delivered by the day school's big, yellow station wagon.

Saturday, he had brought Tami with him to the hospital. They had cheered Sandra Wilkenson until 4:00 P.M.

They had done the same on Sunday. This time, however, they had stayed with her long past her dinner, the weather being so vile that they'd even joked about remaining overnight.

The following morning, their bodies were found in the Potomac River by Oliver Porter and Jill Kinnerly.

The District of Columbia police moved fast. But when a telephone call was received at headquarters from Henry Bayard, the President's closest friend and most trusted advisor, and he made it clear that he was calling because the President was deeply upset by this heinous crime, the investigation took on the momentum of a downhill racer.

The entire pattern of the Wilkensons' family life was laid bare in only two days.

Within this pattern, the thread was found.

At first it seemed far-fetched. Then the FBI offered its own files, and the conclusion became undeniable: Adam Clark

Wilkenson and his daughter, Tami, had been the victims of an assassination.

Alpha 61 was a fanatical Cuban nationalist organization. It had a bloody history of anti-Castro violence. Any person, Cuban or not, who was believed to be working against its aims was a candidate for its hit list. It had marked the Wilkenson family for death after Adam's return from Havana. There he had helped to negotiate an agreement for the return of all future airplane hijackers. According to Alpha 61's leadership, any agreement with Havana represented acceptance of Castro's authority, which had to be discouraged at all costs.

Strongly supporting this official conclusion was information about a recent social gathering in the Wilkenson home. At that party, Adam had spoken for an ongoing dialogue with the Castro government. Such contact, he had argued, could only lead to greater successes than his own hijacker agreement. Overheard by Maria Gonzalez, his Cuban housekeeper, that argument was to become his family's death warrant.

Sandra Wilkenson escaped assassination only by the lucky appearance of two friends at the moment of Maria's attack. But Adam and Tami soon became Alpha 61's grim warning to the United States government.

The warning failed. Local and national government joined forces to answer this political insanity. The full weight of Washington's official power came crashing upon the organization. Hideouts were instantly raided, leaders rounded up, indictments handed down, trial dates set, convictions obtained. It was a beautiful sweep, accomplished swiftly and neatly.

Only one person escaped—Maria. The police were never able to locate her. The loss of one small fish didn't bother them, though. The organization had been broken, and that was all that really mattered. There would be no more killings by Alpha 61.

There were only two things wrong with all of this: Alpha 61, though guilty of many atrocities in the past, had been perfectly innocent of this one; and though Adam Clark Wilkenson had been identified quite accurately, that four-year-old child found tied to his back was someone other than his own sweet daughter, Tami.

4

Jeff Rader had just finished the next day's column. It had been an agony to produce. The words hadn't come, he felt spiritually enervated, and even his feet hurt. He had removed his shoes and stared at his desk for a full ten minutes before starting. "What the hell's the matter with me?" he had muttered. Then his years of professionalism had asserted themselves and slowly, torturously, the column had taken shape. He'd worked his self-anger into a diatribe. It was a white-hot poker. He felt weak after completing it—weak and only morbidly satisfied—and he thanked God that it was finally done. The column revealed the pressure being put upon the paper. It named the name. Castigated the castigator. In short, it not only burned the butt of Police Commissioner Harold Durkin, but, Rader hoped, it might even shut the asshole up for good.

He cleared the screen of his ET/960 computer. Then he swallowed a final mouthful of coffee from that ever-present mug on his desk and bent to put on his shoes.

"Jeff . . ." His name cut straight to him from the middle of the city room. "Jeff Rader, you here?" It was his editor, Tom Pendleton.

Jeff straightened and signaled a hand. "Yeah, Tom. Over here."

The editor made his way toward him. When they met, he

didn't speak. He merely put a hand on Jeff's shoulder, jerked his head, and cut off in another direction. It was obvious that he wanted to be followed.

The conference room near the *Voice*'s library was usually reserved for high-level discussion.

Jeff Rader now settled into the biggest and best chair in the room.

The city editor closed the door gently and sat opposite him. A few moments of silence passed. He was staring at his paper's most successful columnist, wondering just how to start his discussion. Finally he decided to wade right in. "I'm killing the column," he said.

"What?"

"The one you just put in the slot."

Rader leaned forward. "Wait wait wait. What do you mean? I just finished that a few minutes ago, and you're telling me you've already read it?"

Pendleton understood the implications of that question. The computer stored the whole layout of every edition; unquestionably, other articles, stories, columns, items had preceded Jeff's into the bank. Why would the city editor have read his so quickly if he were not being singled out and watched with special concern? Tom Pendleton's silence answered that question.

"I'll be damned," Rader muttered as he snapped his head sideways in a flash of anger.

"Now take it easy," the editor cautioned.

But Rader wouldn't be mollified. He stood, and his voice began to rise. "What's going on, Tom? That's the first time since I've been with this paper that one of my stories has been killed."

"Listen to me—"

"I've written hotter things than this, and nobody's ever made an issue of them."

"This is different—"

"What's so different about it? Son of a bitch. Not you, Tom—the system. A lousy commissioner screams because his skin is too thin, and the *Voice* begins to censor—"

Pendleton cut him off. "Nobody's censoring anybody."

"Then what do you call it?" Rader flashed back. "I file a story, and you're telling me it's dead—"

"You're on weak ground, God damn it!"

"That series is as solid as steel, and you know it."

"Not if the Baliston part is any indication, and you know *that*!"

Jeff Rader pulled back. An argument with his city editor wasn't going to get him anywhere. He took his seat again. "Look, Tom," he said, his voice trembling slightly with the effort to control himself, "that Baliston case may have been more than just a lost kid and a distraught father who dropped into a canyon. It could have been murder, couldn't it?"

"Yes. But it could also have been as innocent as it appears, and that's the point. The *Voice* can't take on Commissioner Durkin unless you've got more to go on than speculation. That's what's really burning him: One of the most thorough investigations in police history was conducted before that case was closed. Vice-President Frazier was governor of California then, and because the victims were from Los Angeles, he personally begged and got the Idaho authorities to let the L.A.P.D. in on the case. Everything that could be thought of was done, and now Durkin doesn't like our paper saying that police anywhere are inept or indifferent. And you want to know something, I can't blame him!"

Silence filled the room after that rush of words. The editor fished a cigarette from his shirt pocket. He lit it and dragged deeply.

Jeff Rader sagged back into his chair. He felt drained. He gathered his emotions. Finally he said softly, "It took the police nearly two months to find a lead near the Baliston camp. By that time, the weather had obliterated all but one very faint tire track. But that was enough. A plaster cast of the track matched the tread on the pickup, and that led to the uncovering of the site. Notice I said *uncovering* . . . because that campsite had been covered. Not by nature, but by human hands. The fire, everything. Now if you had lost your son somewhere in the Sawtooth Range of Idaho, Tom, and you were rushing for help, would you have taken the time to erase all signs of the campsite before getting into your truck?"

Tom Pendleton heaved a troubled sigh.

"That's all I did with that story, Tom, and you know it—just raised that question and suggested that the absence of outside

muscle to force further police effort was what really caused the
authorities to let that investigation die.''

The editor jabbed his cigarette into a nearby ashtray. He
looked directly into Rader's eyes. ''It's dead, Jeff,'' he said
flatly. ''Not only tomorrow's column, but the whole series.''

''What? *Why?*''

The answer came simply: ''Because Police Commissioner Harold Durkin and our publisher are boyhood buddies.'' The reality
of that relationship ended all further discussion.

Now it was dilemma time.

Jeff Rader was on the downhill side of thirty-nine. He was a
one-paper newsman who had joined the *Los Angeles Voice* while
he was still in his senior year at Hollywood High. He had worked
his way through every menial city room assignment the paper had
thrown at him to reach his present position. Today 128 papers
around the country ran his column. The one thing he had enjoyed
above all the other benefits of his trade was the freedom to write
about anything of his choice, exactly as he wished to present it.
Now that freedom was being restricted.

Dilemma. Dilemma. What does a man on the downhill side of
thirty-nine do when the most important pleasure of his work is
being threatened? Swallow it? Say ''What's the difference? That
series isn't going to change a damned thing anyway''? Or does
he keep his challenged integrity intact and just walk out?

The questions ran through his mind in an instant and created a
moment of terrible despair.

Tom Pendleton caught it. He saw Rader's eyes dull; he heard
that single, short but sharp exhalation. ''Don't do anything rash,
Jeff,'' he urged quickly and gently. ''Look, I know something's
been bugging you lately, and it's not the series. You've got six
weeks' vacation coming to you. Take 'em. Go someplace. Relax.
Sort things out.''

There was another silence as Rader seemed to study his editor's
face. Then he sighed deeply as though shaking himself back into
the present, and he rose from his chair. ''I'll be in Downey's''
was all he said. He strode quickly from the room.

''You remember Katy Maguire,'' Mike Gavin was saying,
''and the time she was doing that piece on rest homes?'' Some of
his listeners were nodding and grinning; the rest wore the happy
expressions of expectancy. ''She asked this ninety-four-year-old

geezer out at Sunny Acres if there were any interesting activities in the home. And he answered, 'Only sex.' And Katy laughed and said, 'Do you participate?' 'Not very often,' sighs the ol' coot. 'At my age, it comes only as a gift, an' there ain't many gift-givers around.' Then he looks straight at her boobs and cackles, 'Say, missy, how'd you like to play Santa Claus?' ''

The group roared.

"Oh, she was a good-lookin' woman, that lady," someone piped over the laughter.

"Indeed she was," he agreed.

They were in Downey's, a marvelous old bar and grill on Broadway, where the sawdust was changed every day and where big, shiny spittoons spiked wooden floors, where turnstile fans rotated lazily in summer and winter and the daylight refracted crazily through stained-glass windows. It was a journalists' watering hole. A sweet place. And they were there now, swapping stories.

Mike Gavin had been the *Voice*'s city editor before his retirement nine years ago. He was a rough old bird. Stocky. Florid. With white bushy eyebrows, pale-blue eyes, and a whiskey voice that sounded like the idling of an old Mack truck.

"Michael, remember the earthquake in sixty-nine?"

"February twenty-seventh, near Palmdale, four point three on the Richter," Gavin shot back. He had a computer's memory.

"I was in the john when it hit," the teller, a no-nonsense female, told the group. "I tell you, I flew out of there so fast, my drawers were still around my knees. And that whole building was shaking like a mound of Jell-O in a hurricane. Well, I got back to the newsroom in a flash, and I could see things flying off the desks, bulletin boards crashing off the walls, windows cracking and everybody too scared to move—except Michael Gavin here. He's standing on his desk, a World War I Red Baron's helmet on his head, a big, white scarf around his neck, and that God-damned unlit Havana sticking out of his face . . . and he's yelling, 'Canby, cover the hospitals! Russell, check the seismo center! Rader, see if the dams are holding! Martin, handle the police and fire departments! Move it! Move it! MOVE IT! We're gonna beat the *Times* an' *Examiner* on this one or you'll wish t'hell this God-damned building *had* fallen on you!' ''

The crowd erupted again.

Mike Gavin bobbed his head happily, a big, shy grin plastering his broad Irish face.

Jeff Rader entered Downey's just in time to hear a young voice weave enthusiastically through the merriment, "And did you beat the *Times* and *Examiner*?" and Mike Gavin's good-natured growl, "God-damned right we did." The reaction escalated into cheers and applause.

"What am I missing?" Jeff Rader asked. His voice was subdued.

"Whaddayasay, kid?" Gavin offered his usual, gruff greeting.

"Michael." Jeff acknowledged simply with a nod.

"Whatsa matter, kid? Bad day?"

Jeff shrugged his eyebrows and called out to the bartender, "Jack Daniel's, Charley. Make it a double."

Gavin had his answer.

He excused himself from his circle of friends and crossed to a small, secluded table at the opposite end of the room, whispering to Jeff as he passed, "Bring the drink over there."

Rader followed. As he slid behind the table, he breathed a long, throaty grunt.

"Well, it can't be your writing because that's just as bad as ever," Mike Gavin teased. It was the correct scalpel. It opened Jeff Rader quickly. At first, only his feelings seeped out; but then came the blood of his dilemma.

When the entire problem had been exposed to him, the old city editor leaned back in his seat and murmured, "It isn't the killing of the series, kid. Hell, there are things in this business you can't fight, and you know that. Sure they hurt. But they're not gonna put us in our graves, and we get over them eventually, even though they leave some scars. No, it's not the series." He paused here for a moment. His expression changed to one of deep regret. There was true compassion for Jeff Rader and a sense of personal loss in what he said next. "I think you've got it, kid," he offered softly.

Jeff felt his breath catch. He didn't answer.

"Take Tom's advice," Gavin urged him gently. "Pick up your vacation time. Find some quiet spot. Sort things out."

I think you've got it, kid. The words echoed within Rader's head. Je-sus, no. And yet deep inside his being he knew he had suspected as much all along; he had just been resisting the thought, that's all—afraid to face the unmentionable. Maybe he should get away for a while. Find that quiet spot and think. Yeah—that made sense. Someplace far away.

But where? Then he thought of the little village of Hana on the island of Maui in Hawaii. He'd always wanted to visit it. Well, maybe now was the time. . . .

"Mr. Rader?" Her voice was soft, uncertain. She was looking from one man to the other.

Gavin pointed a finger at Jeff.

"They told me at the paper you'd be here," she explained, turning toward Rader. "My name is Sandra Wilkenson."

She was a trim woman. About five nine in her three-inch heels. Her hair, black and fine, was cut short, combed back over her ears and up off her forehead. She had deep-brown eyes, a straight, delicate nose, and full, sensuous lips. Attractive. Very. I'd say she's about thirty-three, Mike Gavin guessed, finishing his appraisal. Then because she seemed a bit unsure of herself, he judged her business with Jeff Rader to be of a personal nature. He excused himself and started to rise.

"Wait a minute . . . where are you going, Michael?" Jeff asked quickly. "Don't leave now."

"I'm—I'm sorry. I-I seem to be interrupting something," she apologized.

"Well, actually, you are." Jeff tried to make it gentle, but he failed.

"I'm sorry," she replied. "I'll—I'll come back another time."

A flicker of her eyebrows didn't escape the old city editor, though. He saw pain there. "Hold it, miss," he said. He leaned on the table and murmured to Jeff, "One of the things you're not supposed to do now is worry about yourself. Speak to her, kid. We'll talk more later." He eased away from the table.

Rader watched Gavin leave, a silent protest still lodged like a lump in his throat. Finally he glanced back at the young woman. She hadn't moved. One hand still gripped the shoulder strap of her stylish bag. The other still clutched a ten-by-thirteen manila envelope. Her posture was still straight, her attention still riveted upon him. She made him feel uncomfortable.

"Sit down, please," he muttered. He was frowning as she slid appreciatively onto the chair opposite him.

"Thank you," she murmured. She fidgeted with the edge of the envelope for a while before she spoke again. "I-I knew I had to talk to you the moment I started reading your new series."

The mention of his series stirred ugly feelings again. He didn't want to discuss anything related to those articles now. "Miss . . ." he groped for her name.

"Wilkenson. Sandra Wilkenson." It was offered quickly. Eagerly.

"Look, Miss Wilkenson, I don't mean to be rude, really I don't, but—"

"My husband and little girl were murdered three years ago, Mr. Rader," she cut him off. It was said softly, so gently and yet so insistently that it had the effect of a low-current electric charge.

He looked quickly at her eyes. They were pleading with a strong, quiet urgency. He felt a bit helpless. "Why tell me?"

"I don't know. . . . I really don't," she faltered, "except that your story on the Baliston family—"

"Please, Mrs. Wilkenson," he cut in, "I'd rather not—"

"Nobody will listen anymore. You, listen to me, *please*." It was a desperate whisper.

He studied her for a moment. "Okay," he relented. "Go ahead; I'm listening."

The grateful smile that flashed was remarkably beautiful. She began. She told him everything she knew about the killings: about Maria, her own hospitalization, Alpha 61, the police conclusions, the trials, the convictions. A receptive ear seemed to be all that she needed. Her hesitancy disappeared. Her feelings poured out.

Rader listened silently. He recalled some of the particulars; after all, it had been one of the fairly big stories to come over the wires. But after a while, he began to wonder why she was taking his time. Before she could conclude, he stopped her with: "I'm sorry, but I don't see the connection. What has any of this got to do with the Baliston case?"

She hesitated, unnerved by the challenging note in his voice. "Well," she replied, "there are unanswered questions . . . just as in the Baliston case. Why should my family have been selected by Alpha 61 when my husband wasn't the senior member of that delegation? He was only an assistant, only a translator in this instance. He didn't do the negotiating. That was the Secretary's job. So if Alpha 61's intention was to punish someone for that hijacking agreement, why didn't they choose the one who was responsible—"

"Who can say why these crazies do what they do?" he interrupted. "Maybe they thought it would be easier to get at your family than at the Secretary, maybe they felt their point would be made regardless of who was killed, maybe they thought the public reaction would be worse if they hit the Secretary instead of your husband—"

"But it wasn't."

"They couldn't know that. They could have believed it would be."

She was becoming flustered. "Well, the authorities have closed this case, too," she offered, reaching for another parallel.

"Of course they have." He sighed. "They've got the killers, all except that Maria—"

"But it was all circumstantial. . . . They still swear they were innocent—"

"Lady"—he stopped her with an impatient, palm-up gesture—"if I were in their boots, I'd be screaming the same damned thing."

"There's more," she pleaded. "Please listen. For the past year, I've been researching—"

Again he cut her short. "Look, Mrs. Wilkenson, I'm not trying to be cruel. I know you've suffered terribly, and if I could do anything to ease your pain, I would. I really would. But I just don't see any connection between what's been in my column and what's happened in your life."

It was as though she had been punched. The finality of those words left no room for response. She inhaled, and her breath made a slightly quavering sound. Her eyes filled quickly. Then just as the tears were about to spill over, she rose wordlessly, turned, and hurried from Downey's.

He felt like a Class A son of a bitch. But that feeling wasn't strong enough for him to go chasing after her. Then resentment set in. He had enough problems of his own. His whole life was hanging by a thread. Besides, there was no connection. None! The Baliston boy was still missing; her daughter was found dead. The Baliston family was all gone; she was still alive and making waves. Anyway, even if there were a connection, there wasn't anything he could do to help her. He was just a reporter, for Chrissake.

He belted the remainder of his drink. Then he realized for the first time that she had forgotten the large manila envelope in her haste to leave Downey's.

In a corner, her name and telephone number appeared in neat, strong script.

It was close to 6:00 P.M. when he reached his apartment. He lived in Westwood, on Wilshire Boulevard, in one of those new, expensive high-rises. It was the only real luxury Jeff Rader permitted himself. "When it comes to calling someplace home," he had once joked, "he who flops softest lasts longest."

. Tonight, though, he was too troubled even to glance at the view from his seventeenth-floor living-room window. After closing the door, he crossed directly to his bedroom. There he dropped the manila envelope on the coverlet, threw his jacket over the arm of a chair, kicked off his shoes, and sagged to the edge of the bed. Then with his hands hanging limply between his legs, he just sat and stared. Not at anything in the room. At thoughts.

Everything's going flat . . . stale. . . . Everything's rotting. He shook his head. Have I really got it? Could Michael be right? Even as he asked himself the question, he knew that Gavin had never been wrong about this. He had seen it in too many others. He knows, Jeff thought. Yes, Michael knows. He fell back upon his bed and stared at the ceiling. I've probably got it, he thought, I've probably got it.

And what was this "it" that was so terrible?

Rader knew very well what it was. He had explained it to his sister, Annie, a long time ago when one of his closest friends on the *Voice* had been found dead, hanging from a beam in his home, a soured and lonely man. "It's the reporter's occupational disease," Jeff had said then. "It's a shriveling of the soul, and it comes from an overexposure to the ordinary ingredients of our daily news. There comes a time for some of us when the spirit sickens, when it just can't stand any more murder and rape and child molestation, when it's had enough of political games and deceit, when it can't look at another accident, robbery, or disaster, when it just can't endure any more suffering and despair. There's a point when some of us don't want to dig anymore for corruption behind someone's laughter, for a flaw in the heroic, for the crud within. And when that happens, the newsman is finished. Because that kind of digging is the essence of his work, and his work has been his life, and there's simply no way to start again. He's like the disenchanted cop. What does a cop do when everything finally gets to him? Where does he go? The answer is: He doesn't do anything, and there's no place he can go. He's sour and lonely and lost.''

And that, as far as Jeff Rader was concerned, was a devastating threat now. It's so insidious . . . the way it slips in, the way it infects, he thought. I should have faced it . . . should have tried to help myself.

Then he realized suddenly that he had tried. That he'd actually tried all the remedies, but that none had worked. For example, he had been drinking very heavily lately, trying to wash the dirty feeling away. It hadn't cleansed. A few times it had just made him a dirty drunk.

Women hadn't helped either. His last lady was an associate professor at U.C.L.A. She had been as eager as she was intelligent and good-looking. But that liaison had lasted only one week. His failure during their three nights together had scared him. Not only had his condition worsened as a result of this, but his desire to try other sexual forays had suffered, too.

The young stewardess before that hadn't been much more successful with him.

Or the executive secretary before that, either.

As for work—well, in all probability his series on unsolved crimes had been no more than a final effort to save himself through his column. Good as they were, he recognized, those articles had emerged like a breech birth. With great difficulty and terrible pain. He remembered when ideas used to dance through his typewriter with the grace of a prima ballerina. Oh, those had been glorious times! Now, though, he admitted to himself, it's as if the remedy of work is as diseased as the illness it's meant to cure.

"So"—he sighed aloud—"what happens now?"

His hands flew back to rest beneath his head. As if in answer to his question, his left elbow slapped against the manila envelope.

The heavy paper crinkled near his ear. He turned to see what it was. He had completely forgotten it. Reaching over now, he lifted the packet and glanced at it again. Her name and telephone number seemed to leap at him.

He struggled to a sitting position against the headboard and wondered about her. What's with this lady? She had been so intense while talking to him and so pained at his rejection. Sighing, he opened the envelope and turned it over.

Newspaper and magazine articles tumbled to his lap. They were all photocopied and neatly stapled together. Covering them were two sheets that listed the articles in chronological order. Each item on these cover sheets contained a two- or three-line identification of the article's salient points. What struck him immediately was that everything seemed to be on the same subjects: deaths and missing persons. There were exactly two dozen articles. The earliest was dated November 3, 1956; the latest, January 16, 1981. A span of twenty-five years.

"Now what's this all about?" he murmured.

Since he had nothing else to do, and he didn't want to dwell on his own misery anymore, he began to read.

The articles had been arranged to correspond with the chronology of the cover sheets: the most recent on top; the oldest, last.

On completing each one, he flipped back to the top sheet to scan the leading points that she had listed. It didn't take long for him to recognize the pattern: All the deaths had been the result of accident or murder, nothing natural; in each case, the deceased adult had been a parent; all the missing people were children— and, except for her own experience, the immediate family of every missing child had been completely destroyed. Finally, while not part of the pattern, he noticed that although most of this had taken place in the United States, two of the incidents had occurred in England, one in Japan, one in Brazil, and one in Israel.

He dropped the pack to his lap and creased his brows. What's she trying to do? He saw the similarities to the Baliston case, but why had she done this crazy research? Certainly families are being killed around the world, he told himself; it's not a unique disaster. And why shouldn't missing people be children? Adults have no monopoly on disappearance. Apparently, he thought, she's chosen certain articles so that she can build a pattern of similarities. But why?

He remembered her, sitting across from him at Downey's. Bright. Cultured. How could someone so intelligent have contrived so weak an argument? And the time it must have taken!

He shook his head sadly. Grief. That's the answer. Grief. It's a torture rack that twists and deforms the ability to reason clearly.

That conclusion seemed so true to him now that he felt another stab of guilt for having contributed to her pain.

He reached over and pulled his telephone to the bed. He would apologize for his abruptness, get her address, and mail this material back to her.

The instrument at the other end rang four times before it was answered.

"Yes?"

"Uh . . . Mrs. Wilkenson? Sandra Wilkenson?"

"Speaking."

"This is Jeff Rader."

"Oh, Mr. Rader!" Her voice cut him off with surprise and relief.

"You forgot your envelope this afternoon, and your telephone number was—"

"I realized that when I got home. Thank you for calling."

"Well, I just wanted to ask you—"

"Have you read the articles?"

He didn't want to respond to that, and he hesitated before answering. "As a matter of fact, I have." He had tried to make that noncommittal, but now there was a heavy, awkward silence.

"Well . . . what do you think?"

I should have known this would happen! he thought. He sighed. "Mrs. Wilkenson," he began a lie, "that's what I wanted to talk to you about."

"I'm glad." Relief again.

"Well, you see . . ." How to break this to her? How to break this . . . "Actually, Mrs. Wilkenson, I don't know what you're trying to do. I mean, I don't know what you really want—"

"Mr. Rader," she interrupted again, "the only thing I really want is to get my daughter back again." This time her voice was so calm and sincere that he felt the hair on the nape of his neck move in his surprise.

"But I thought—"

"She's alive."

"Didn't the police find her body with your husband's?"

"That poor little thing wasn't my Tami."

The tormented mother, holding desperately to an impossible hope, he thought sadly. Then he asked, "How do you know that?"

"I have proof." Again that rich, quiet sincerity.

Now a weighted silence.

"What kind of proof?" he finally asked.

"I'd rather not discuss this over the phone, Mr. Rader." This was no cool ploy. He could hear the soft pleading current of the words.

Now what if she's right? he asked himself. What if this were some God-sent remedy for the restimulation of his moribund juices? He had no idea what she hoped of him or how his column could help her, but in his own desperation he finally said, "Okay, Mrs. Wilkenson, maybe we ought to talk about this face-to-face." He could hear her breath escape in a sigh of relief.

"When?" she asked quickly.

"Well, how about lunch tomorrow at twelve? I'll meet you at Nate and Al's on—"

"I have a better idea. There's a contractor coming here around nine to give me an estimate on some remodeling, but he won't get in our way. Suppose you come here, and I'll make a good breakfast . . ."

"That won't be necessary."

"Please. I'd be a wreck, waiting until lunchtime."

He noted the lovely, charming tone of the offer.

"Okay," he acquiesced. "Nine A.M., your place."

She recited her address, and he jotted it onto the envelope.

After he slipped the receiver back into its cradle, his eyes wandered back to her handwriting above his own. He stared at her name. Sandra Wilkenson. Now what does she mean, she has proof? he thought. What kind of proof? And why the hell has she collected all these articles? He inhaled deeply. Well, maybe . . . just might turn out to be something. Suppose the kid is still alive, and I could help get her back to her mother . . . Even if it were my last story, it'd be a great way to go out.

It was the palest of hopes, but at least it was hope. Though it didn't generate outright happiness, it did make him feel a lot better than he had felt when he'd entered the apartment.

He left the bed now and crossed into the living room. There he sucked in his breath for a noisy sigh, and absently thumped his stomach with the palm of his hand. The action made him aware of a spreading softness and the fact that he had not had a regular workout in the past three months.

He had always been a vigorous, athletic person—a gymnast in high school and a student of karate from the time he was nineteen.

The karate started when Mike Gavin had told him that a reporter's ability to defend himself was as necessary as the ability to type. "No telling when some God-damned nut might try to throw you through a window for writing something he doesn't like." At first, Jeff had thought he was being conned by the older man. But the day after Haley Wingate was shot in the *Voice*'s newsroom by a God-damned nut for just that reason, Rader had raced out and registered for karate instruction at the Institute of Martial Arts on Pico Boulevard.

He had taken to it immediately. Its discipline, timing, and speed had helped to make him more alert and self-aware. Furthermore, the sense of accomplishment that each workout produced had sharpened his appreciation of the art. At thirty-nine, now, he was a fourth-degree black-belt *karateka*.

Yeah . . . getting soft, he thought, rubbing his stomach again. I'm falling apart. Then suddenly he decided to visit the institute. Not the following day or week. But right then. *Get out of this God-damned rut before I go crazy. Gotta do something to save myself!*

Yes, a good, vigorous workout might be just the thing to save him.

He had driven down Wilshire into Santa Monica Boulevard and then north on Beverly Drive. At 8:50 A.M. he was crossing Sunset Boulevard where he jogged left a bit to pick up Crescent Drive. Good area, he thought as he looked for Sandra Wilkenson's address. Smaller houses but north of Sunset is really the quiet, classy section of Beverly Hills. Well, she's certainly no pauper.

The house numbers along Crescent are not always clearly displayed. Jeff Rader had to park his old Ford along the curb and get out for a closer look. He discovered that Sandra Wilkenson's address was seven or eight houses farther along. He felt better this morning than he had in a long time—a bit achy from last night's workout but pleased that he had started an exercise program again. So, leaving his car where it was, he trudged up the hill the remaining distance. At a gently landscaped and particularly attractive house, he pressed the door button. A tinkling brush of bells came faintly from deep inside the house.

She opened the door. Dressed in slacks and a blouse of earth-tone shadings, she looked warm and bright.

"Mr. Rader." She sparkled, making his name sound like a delightful announcement. "Come in, please. Come in."

"Good morning."

"I'm making some waffles and eggs. That all right?"

"Fine," he said as he followed her through the front part of the house into the kitchen. The table in the dining area was set for two.

"Make yourself comfortable," she urged. "I'll have everything ready in a minute."

"Need any help?"

"No, I've got it." It was evident that she was nervous. But everything was arranged quickly and without mishap, and soon she sat opposite him. Looking directly into his eyes, she said quietly, "Mr. Rader, I want to thank you with all my heart for coming here this morning."

The unexpected directness of the statement threw him. "Well . . . that's okay," he murmured self-consciously. Then he recovered quickly with "You know, I think we ought to get this mister and missus thing out of the way, so from now on I'm Jeff and you're . . ."

"Sandy." She grinned.

"Sandy." He nodded.

"Jeff." She extended her hand, and they shook once over the table. "Now, let's eat."

"You say you have proof your daughter is still alive." He went right to the reason for the meeting.

"Yes," she responded quickly. Then she added with some hesitation, "To me."

He looked up from a forkful of eggs. "What does that mean?" His voice was edged with suspicion.

"No one else will accept it."

"Why?"

"It's a personal thing."

He put down his fork.

She became apprehensive. Something had slipped into his look. He wasn't going to believe her. Like all the others. "Please," she begged softly. "Please listen."

He felt her anxiety. He relaxed. "All right, Sandy, that's why I'm here."

Relief played across her face as she began.

"When they found my husband, the child's body that was

bound to him was burned beyond recognition. Identification was made only by some clothing threads and jewelry.''

"The threads did come from your daughter's clothing, though, didn't they?''

"Yes.''

"And the jewelry was hers, too, right?''

"Yes. But they had been transferred to this other child.''

"How do you know that?''

"That's the personal thing. You see, Tami—that's my daughter—had a bracelet and a ring. They were gifts from my husband and me on her fourth birthday. She loved them. She was so thrilled with them, she never took them off. Never. She wore them when she slept, she even kept them on when she bathed.''

"So?''

"Well, Sunday—the day my husband was killed—he and Tami visited me in the hospital. I had been injured in a—''

"I know. It was in one of the articles.''

"Oh . . . all right . . . well, that day the weather was absolutely horrible, and we joked about it, and Adam said that Tami had been responsible for it. When she asked why, he teased her and came up with a perfectly crazy reason: He said the weather was bad because Tami would only wear her bracelet and ring on the same hand. But if her bracelet were switched to her left wrist, then that would get rid of the storm.''

"Imaginative man.''

"He always played with Tami that way. She loved it. She knew it was play, but she always went along with it.''

"And what did she do this time?''

"Well, she nodded her head as though he'd said something very profound. Then she said, 'Y'know, Daddy's right. I guess I'm just a little troublemaker. But watch—I'm going to make everything all right again.' And she removed her bracelet for the first time and transferred it to her left wrist. We laughed, and we thanked her for making the world a better place. Then we all had some ice cream and cake to celebrate the imminent improvement of the weather. It was a wonderful day even though it was only two days after my leg operation and I was still in some pain. . . .''

She broke off, the memory choking her.

Jeff Rader waited patiently.

It didn't take her long to recover. "Tami was very pleased with the way she had cheered me. And the last thing she said before they left was: 'Daddy's fun. I know what makes the weather bad and it's not a bracelet, but I'm going to wear mine like this anyway until you come home again, Mommy, okay?' I kissed her and said, 'If that's what you want, then you do that, Angel,' and she answered, 'That's what I want.' ''

Now she stopped and looked directly into Rader's eyes. "Jeff," she said, "when they found the bodies the next morning, that child—whoever she was—was wearing Tami's bracelet on the wrong wrist."

Jeff Rader felt a slight flutter in his stomach.

She waited.

Finally he said very gently, "Listen, Sandy, I'm not saying that couldn't be significant, but there is a possibility that you're getting carried away by what you need to believe. So let's explore this further—and I'll play Devil's Advocate now to keep things in balance, okay?"

She nodded solemnly.

"First, how do you know which hand the bracelet was on when they found the bodies? You were in the hospital at the time, and no one would have told you that; it wouldn't have seemed important."

"You're right. It was in the police report."

"How did you get to see the report?"

She paused, trying to decide where to begin. The tip of her tongue teased the corner of her mouth, and her deep-brown eyes looked off to a side.

She began slowly. "I didn't get out of the hospital until long after the funerals. And when I did, I didn't care to go on living. My head was filled with thoughts of suicide. Friends offered to take me to the cemetery—my leg was in a cast and I was still using a wheelchair—I had no desire to go. But then one day—I don't know why—I had this terrible need to visit the graves. A neighbor took me and—"

Her narration was interrupted here by the bright, gentle rustle of bells. Inside the house, Rader noticed, they sounded even more pleasant: an audible breeze, running across the top of long, cool grass.

A slight frown puckered her brow. She didn't care to be stopped just then. "That's probably the contractor," she said, rising. "I'll be back soon." She hurried to the front door.

She was gone only two or three minutes.

"I'm having a new fireplace put into the living room," she explained as she returned. "He's preparing an estimate." She slid quickly onto her chair. "Now, I was telling you . . ." She resumed her story exactly where she had left off. " . . . I sat near the graves for almost an hour and cried myself sick. I thought I would die right there. . . ." She trailed off at this point and looked up from her fingernails. "I know what I'm about to say can sound like the raving of a grief-stricken wife and mother, but something—I don't know what it was—something made me think that Tami was still alive."

Jeff felt his heart sink. There it was—nothing. He had almost been hoping that she had uncovered some tangible evidence to support her belief. But a graveside feeling? Nothing.

She sensed his reaction and hurried to reassure him. "I know that's nonsense, but it did happen to me—not a voice telling me this in a mysterious tone . . . just a deep, deep *feeling* that that little grave before me wasn't Tami's."

He was looking at her noncommittally.

"Well, regardless of how meaningless that may sound," she continued quickly, "it did produce something more concrete: It made me want to recover. Blew away all thoughts of suicide. And when I was well enough to get around again, it started me on my own investigation into the murders. Jeff, Washington had been my home for many years. I had always been actively involved in the Washington scene. So I wasn't without influence. Well, I contacted all my friends and made an absolute pain in the ass of myself. Eventually I got my hands on the police files of the case, and that's how I learned about the bracelet and on which hand it had been found." She stopped for a moment before adding with charming self-consciousness, "Long-winded answer, but you should have the whole story."

He felt strangely relieved. He nodded, and she smiled gratefully. "Let's go on," he said. "Do you have any other way of proving the body in that grave isn't your daughter's? You see, Tami could have switched the bracelet back to the other wrist despite what she said to you in the hospital. There's no way of telling what Adam may have said to her on their way home, and if he made her change her mind in the first place, it's possible—I'm not saying he did it, but it is possible—that he could have made her switch back. Right?"

"I agree, and I thought about that while I was still in

Washington. So what I did was to try to get the body exhumed and checked through Tami's dental records, the way they had corroborated Adam's identification through his military dental record.''

"And?''

"The courts wouldn't approve the request without proof from the dentist that such records existed.''

"So you got the dentist's acknowledgment.''

"No, I couldn't.''

"Why not?''

Again she looked at him in that direct, strong way. "When I tried to contact him, he was gone. He'd disappeared.''

"Wait a minute, wait a minute—what do you mean, disappeared?''

"Gone. Vanished. Office closed. House vacated. His whole family—'' She made a short, sweeping back-handed gesture.

"You told the police, of course.''

"Certainly. But all they said was that he'd apparently given up his practice and moved. No warning to his patients, no provision for his records—not even a forwarding address.''

"That's crazy.''

"I thought so, too. So I hired a private investigator to find him.''

"And?''

"I got one report from him, saying he was following a good lead. And then a week later my investigator was found shot to death.''

Jeff Rader's skin began to crawl. "Where?'' he asked quietly.

"Here in California. That's what brought me west. He was found near Santa Barbara.''

"Ohhhh, yes. I remember the item. 'Private Investigator Killed in Accident.' ''

"Accident? A man with eighteen years' experience, one of the best of his kind, killed by his own gun—an accident?''

"Unusual, but it can happen, Sandy, it can. Let's get back to Tami, though. There's something else you have to consider, okay?''

"All right.''

"Let's assume she was kidnapped and that she's still alive. . . . Then whoever did it obviously took great pains to cover the abduction and to make it appear as though she's dead, right?''

"Where are you taking me?" she asked.

"Well, they had to have a replacement, a perfect one."

"I don't understand."

"Was the dead child four years old?"

"Yes."

"Same height and weight as Tami?"

"Uh-huh."

"Same hair coloring?"

"All the hair had been burned away."

"They should have detected something within the follicles."

"Wait . . . yes. I remember reading . . . the child had black hair. . . ."

"Like Tami's."

"Yes." Her voice had become a whisper.

"And the color of her eyes?"

"Brown."

"Like Tami's."

"Yes."

"So that had to take *careful* planning. I mean, obviously that substitute had to be very carefully chosen."

"I suppose so."

"Now, this is the point: If we add to all that care the fact that they were also *careful* enough to put Tami's clothes on the substitute before actually burning the child's body, and they were *careful* enough to put Tami's jewelry on it, too, then how could they possibly have been so care*less* as to have *put the bracelet on the wrong wrist*?"

It was a devastating question. It forced her to face the possibility that she had been all wrong. That the child in that grave was indeed her Tami. "I don't know . . . I don't know," she whispered.

Suddenly he felt like the world's worst bastard. Here he was destroying this woman's hope. Here he was dismantling her reason for living. What in hell did he think he was doing? What God-damned right did he have to do that? Just because he was miserable didn't mean he had the right to make others miserable, too. "Wait," he heard himself urge quickly, trying to fan that flickering life fire again. "Remember, we're just exploring this." And he reached for an answer to his own question. "If they were so careful, then, more than likely some kind of records were kept. I mean, careful people don't trust to memory or chance.

And furthermore, careful people don't collect details haphazardly. So let's say there had to be a main source of information, someone relatively close, someone who knew Tami well enough to be exact about her height, her weight, a little idiosyncrasy like wearing the bracelet only on the right wrist—''

"Maria?" she cut in.

"Possibly. Then if the substitute body were being prepared later from such a record, that record would *not* have included Tami's decision in the hospital to switch wrists. Then that kind of mistake would have been made not as a result of carelessness but, instead, as a result of very consistent *care*. You follow me?''

She brightened immediately.

"Whoever did it, then," he concluded, "had their own carefulness foul them up.''

She was smiling beautifully at him.

He felt much better.

"Now tell me," he continued quickly, "why did you collect these articles?'' He tapped the envelope near his plate.

She jumped to her feet and crossed to the kitchen where she took a sheaf of papers from a drawer. "There are more. I prepared only two dozen for you. There are thirty-seven more. And those are only the ones I've found. I mean, I don't know how many other cases I may have overlooked.'' She spread them across the table. Then quickly she sat next to him, their forearms brushing. "At first I was just looking for anything about my husband's death and maybe something about Dr. Einberg, the dentist. But as I read, I came across these other kidnappings. When I studied them, I began to realize that they all had certain things in common.''

He had been leafing through the papers. Sixty-one unsolved kidnappings! And all alike in so many ways. He didn't want to believe what was shaping in his mind. He tried to switch his thoughts to something else. Then the full significance of the articles hit him and he gasped.

He sat back and stared at her. "Do you know what you're suggesting here?" he asked quietly, holding the papers before her. A strange current ran through his words. "You're suggesting that murders have been plotted and deaths have been staged in order to cover an incredible number of kidnappings . . . and you're also suggesting that all the similarities were not the result of coincidence. Do you know what that means? That means there's some organization that's been masterminding all of this on an international scale for at least"—he riffled through the papers—"*fifty-nine years!*"

She seemed to shrink under his words. These conclusions weren't new to her. But to hear the words actually spoken by another person, to feel the weight of their sound . . . "I know," she whispered. "It's insane, but there it is."

"But *why?*" he pressed. "Why should any organization do this? What could it possibly want? Apparently, from your articles, the children have all dropped completely from sight. No contact has ever been made. No ransom has ever been demanded."

"I don't know," she answered. "I've thought about that, and the only conclusion I can reach is that they're selling the children. Something like a black market. But that seems ridiculous, too, because if it's money they want, there's certainly more to be had in ransom—except that, perhaps, collecting a ransom isn't as safe as a black-market sale. But then there's all this killing and the length of time it's all been going on. . . . I don't know, Jeff. I don't know."

The air seemed swollen with implication.

Finally Rader exhaled sharply. "Well, I really don't know what I think about all of this yet, Sandy," he began softly, "but if you believe your Tami is still alive, and my column can help—" He'd forgo Hawaii for a while.

"I don't want your column, Jeff," she said quietly.

He looked up.

"I want you."

He was taken aback.

"You're a syndicated journalist," she continued, the words beginning to rush. "You know how to dig. You have contacts everywhere . . . and where you can't reach, my friends in Washington can help. The police have closed the files—just like in the Baliston case and all these others." She tapped the papers on the table. "Jeff"—she leaned toward him and touched his forearm—"I need someone like you to look for her."

She was very moving. But there was no way in this world he could give in to that request, he felt. He wasn't a policeman. He was a reporter, and while all this discussion had been interesting, in the final sense it was all conjecture. In all probability her child *was* dead. In all probability the similarities in this nightmare of suffering really *were* a network of insane coincidences. In all probability—

"Mrs. Wilkenson—" The voice cut his thoughts. It came from a wiry man who stood squarely in the doorway of the kitchen.

Sandra and Jeff jumped at the intrusion.

"Ohhh . . . Mr. Wexler," she breathed in relief, "you startled us. I'd forgotten you were in the house. I'm sorry. Can't talk to you now, though. Will you leave your estimate on the table near the front door, please? I'll call you as soon as I've had a chance to study it."

"My estimate," the contractor said with an odd smile, "yes, my estimate. Well, I estimate that in about two minutes you and your friend here will be joining your late husband in the immense universe of the dead." Slowly from behind his back he brought up a silencer-equipped .36-caliber automatic.

Jeff's back had been to the doorway, but he had jerked around at the sound of the man's voice. His right arm was still resting on the table.

The sight of the gun brought a horrified gasp from Sandra Wilkenson; it was all the cover Rader needed.

His breakfast plate came up in a sweeping arc. It whipped like a deadly Frisbee straight for the intruder's head. At the same time, he pushed wildly at Sandy and dived for the floor.

She slammed into the back of her chair. The force toppled it and sent her tumbling into the kitchen.

The gun went off just as the plate smashed into the intruder's face. Rader heard the slug whiz past his ear and splatter the wooden table leg near his head.

"Get out, Sandy!" he screamed, and he was up, charging in an instant.

The edge of the plate had caught their attacker above the eye and sheared away a huge piece of scalp. He tumbled backward against a cabinet, and Jeff was on him before he could recover.

The gun!

Rader had the man's wrist in an iron grip, smashing the hand against the frame of the doorway.

Two more shots plowed into the ceiling.

Finally the gun flew out of broken fingers. It skittered under the dishwasher.

Sandy went diving for it.

Jeff felt a foot against his chest. It kicked and he went flying across the table. He bowled into the kitchen, pounding Sandy into a corner.

"Get out, Sandy!" he was shouting.

She was trying to crawl back to the dishwasher. "The gun!" she kept screaming. "The gun! The *gun!*"

The attacker was struggling to his feet, clawing at the river of blood that ran over his eye and down his face. He found his bearings. "Son of a bitch!" he spat, and he moved toward Jeff with a grim determination that screamed death.

Jeff whipped around to face him again.

The fingers of the man's good hand were hooked like the beak of a chicken.

Jeff understood. A *karateka!*

The man lunged. His arm swung in a deadly arc. The beaked fingers ripped at Rader's eyes.

Jeff's forearm shot up and smashed against the hand with numbing force. The parry became attack. His hand grabbed the man's collar and jerked him closer. As the intruder came pitching in, Rader rammed a middle-finger fist into his lower rib cage.

Ribs gave. The attacker screamed in agony. But even as he did, he spun and lashed wildly at Rader's throat.

Again the blow was blocked. And this time the followup was the heel of Jeff's hand slamming the side of the man's head.

An eardrum exploded. Hands flew up to tear at the pain. It was the final opening that Rader needed. He stepped in quickly and drove rigid fingers deep into the abdomen with all the power he had. It was a killing blow. If it had not been aimed slightly off center, the man would have died right then. But now a rush of air mingled with a cry that was more like a whimper. The would-be murderer collapsed like a sack of wet laundry.

Jeff stepped back. He was breathing hard. "Get the police," he ordered Sandy.

She scampered to her feet and raced for the phone.

As she punched buttons, Rader pulled their attacker to his feet and dumped him into a chair. "Now," he demanded as he ran his hands over the limp body in search of other weapons, "just who the hell are you, mister?"

But all he heard was a weak mumble in a gasping, cold voice: "Should have . . . taken me out . . . after Baliston. I told them. Should have . . . taken me out. . . ."

"What's that?" Jeff snapped. "Did you say Baliston?"

There was no response.

In the background, Sandy spoke urgently to the police, giving directions, pleading for quick attention.

"Answer me!" Jeff shook the groggy, battered figure. "What do you know about the Balistons?"

The man's eyes cleared. He almost smiled. And that frigid, strangled voice croaked, "You'll never find him. . . ."

"*Who? The kid? Danny Baliston?*"

"The police'll be here in a minute," Sandy announced, hurrying anxiously toward Jeff.

"See if you can get his gun."

"The gun!" She remembered. She dropped to her knees again and hunted under the dishwasher.

"He mentioned the Balistons," Jeff said.

In that brief exchange, their captive made one last move. He reached up quickly and pulled something from behind his good ear. His hand passed across his face and fell to his lap again.

Rader turned in time to see an odd smile touch his lips. "Now you tell me, mister," Jeff asked once more, "is Danny Baliston still alive? Do you know anything about Tami Wilkenson?"

The man's eyes rolled into the top of his head. His body twitched and jerked twice. He was still smiling.

"Are they still alive?" Jeff demanded. *"Do you know where they are?"*

". . . fah . . . thuh . . . wes . . . cose . . ." the man mumbled. And that was all. He was dead.

Jeff had leaned in close for those last words. He had caught them. But he had caught something else, too, something he was totally unprepared for: a faint whiff of almonds on the man's breath—the characteristic smell of cyanide.

5

While Sandra Wilkenson and Jeff Rader were talking to the police, two middle-aged men were winding up another important conversation in a nearby city.

"It'll work out beautifully, Ralph," the heavyset man was saying.

His distinguished-looking companion grumbled, "I'll never get used to this one, Jesse."

"Certainly you will."

"Believe me, I won't."

"Would you like a different name?"

There was a moment of thought. Then, "I suppose not," he muttered. "It's all one and the same."

"Don't take it so hard . . . please."

The distinguished-looking man gazed up from his fingernails. "Do you know, this will be the eleventh time for me?" he asked.

"I know," the visitor answered softly.

"Well, I guess I'll live through this one, too." The troubled man suddenly sighed. Then he said quickly, "I hear that Gerstead and Hamilton have been nominated for the Nobel prize."

The visitor nodded.

"They're good," the host murmured. He paused and pulled absently at his lower lip. "I could have gone for the Nobel. I had greatness within me, Jesse," he whispered.

The heavyset man nodded agreement. "Your life hasn't been so bad, though, has it?" he asked.

"That's not the point. The point is, it's never been what I know it could have been."

The visitor stood and crossed to him. He placed a hand on his shoulder. "The Game is coming to an end, Ralph," he said comfortingly. "That's exciting, isn't it? You're only fifty-one. You'll have your chance yet." He smiled, but it was clear that his host wasn't buying his optimism. "This change will probably be your last one. I'll stay close, I promise." He offered his hand as a signal that he was leaving. "Besides," he added lightly, "the move will end your idleness for a while, and that's good. Too much inactivity boggles the mind and prevents the person from grabbing his chance when it does come along. You don't want to become like that lazy mosquito who got so confused by opportunity that he bit a naked Dolly Parton on her elbow, do you?"

They both chuckled. After a few more words, the visitor left, finding his own way to the front door.

Alone in his den, Ralph Watson had just settled into his large leather armchair when he heard his wife calling him: "Ralph . . . Ralph, you in here?"

"Here, Phyl."

She came into the room, kissed the top of his head, and stood looking down at him. "What's up?" she asked. "What did he have to say?"

His smile wasn't exactly enthusiastic. "It's going to be Masden, next time—Thomas Masden."

Her shoulders slumped. She sagged to the hassock. "Not again." She groaned, and her upper lip curled in a comical sneer.

"Could have been worse." He grinned. "Could have been Percival."

"I was just getting used to Ralph."

"Me, too." He leaned over and stroked her cheek.

"What about me? Do I keep Phyllis?"

"Joyce."

"Joyce," she tasted the word. "Joyce Masden . . . well, that's not too bad. And the kids?"

"Andrew and Steven."

She smiled. "They'll like those. They won't like the idea of starting over again, but if they have to, they'll like it a little more as an Andy and a Steve." She studied his face. "Did he say why? I mean, we were just getting settled here, and—"

"I need a deeper cover."

"Trouble?"

He shook his head. "Just getting me ready for another assignment."

"Where?"

"Minneapolis."

She thought about that. "That's not too bad. Cold weather, but good cultural life. When do we leave?"

"Two weeks."

"Well, here we go again." She groaned in mock pain as she stood.

He stood with her. He took her shoulders. His expression as he looked into her eyes was gentle and sad. "I'm sorry," he whispered.

She grinned. "Come on, I'm only fooling. I knew exactly what it was going to be like when I decided to marry you."

"Has it been that bad?"

She touched his cheek. "Not really. Considering what some other CIA wives go through, I think my life has been almost normal."

He pulled her close. He held her tightly. God, how he loved her!

She leaned her head back. She studied his face. "Is everything all right?" she whispered.

He grinned quickly and lied again. "Perfect, Phyl."

"Joyce," she corrected.

"Whatever."

She matched his grin. "Perfect is just the way I like it," she said, "because that's how it's got to be for tonight's dinner. We'll make it special. I'll get a special wine from Girari's, and we'll toast a new beginning—"

"Another beginning," he corrected.

"Whatever."

They laughed, and he brought his hands up to cup her face.

She turned her head and kissed the palm of his left hand. Then the fingers, one at a time. Finally she planted a light and comical peck on the tip of his little finger, the one with the missing first joint.

She broke away with a leer. "I intend to make this a special evening right into daybreak," she promised in a throaty voice, and she left immediately for Girari's and that special wine.

Alone, Ralph Watson slipped a Vivaldi cartridge into his tape deck. He opened the Arcadia door of his den and stepped onto the sundeck. The ocean lay before him. He didn't see a drop of it, though; his thoughts were on the Nobel peace prize. It's all wrong, he told himself. I'm every bit as good as Gerstead or Hamilton. Even they know it. But they've had the opportunities while I've been selected only to help. Where's the justice in that?

Yet it had always been that way. Selections were made at an early age. The players' roles were set quickly. No one questioned— because it was all part of The Game, and The Game was everything.

He had been selected to be a Helper. The decision had been made only three years after his own abduction.

Well, maybe Jesse is right. Maybe The Game is actually going to end soon. Maybe there still is some kind of chance for me. I'll take a name then and keep it. I'll find a place and stay in it. I'll open myself and let this incredible feeling of power have its way. Then the lying will be over. Then that sweet woman won't have to believe I work for the stupid CIA. And I won't have to be doing sickening things anymore. Maybe, yes, maybe I'll find some kind of peace then.

That sounded good. He'd get into some kind of research. He'd settle somewhere up in the Northwest. Take a good name—Milton Einberg. Yes, he'd liked that name. He'd wanted to keep it. But the Wilkenson Move had made that impossible. The Wilkenson Move. Tami Wilkenson. He'd come to like her so very much while he was her dentist. A very special child, all right. He hoped she would be chosen for more than just helping or soldiering.

As Ralph Watson considered the circumstances of his life, his friend, Jesse, was driving back to Los Angeles in troubled thought. The meeting had not gone well, he felt. There had been resentment. Resistance and resentment. That is never to be tolerated. In lesser men it's merely unpleasant, but in someone of Ralph's enormous capacities resentment can jeopardize absolutely everything. And the end is so near!

As much as he regretted it, he would have to report this. He'd have to make his recommendation: Pedabine 23, presently Ralph Watson, has become extremely dangerous to the interests of The Game; he should be eliminated immediately.

6

The small, nondescript luncheonette was near the intersection of La Grange and Sawtelle in West Los Angeles. Not the kind of place he ordinarily visited, but he wasn't there for food. It was 3:00 P.M., and Jeff Rader was alone and waiting.

At 3:05 a tall, burly man with the face of an actor entered. He was Murray Fried, a long-time friend. He was also Lieutenant Detective Fried of the staff of Police Commissioner Harold Durkin.

"Murray."

"Jeff."

There was a brief handshake as the detective dropped with a low grunt to the other chair at the table. "I was gambling," he murmured. "Hoped you'd beep your answer machine today."

"You sounded urgent . . . but why'd you pick a place like this?"

"You're getting to be a bad item, my friend," Fried answered.

"You ready to order now?" the beefy counterman called from across the room.

"Two coffees and a couple of prune Danish," Rader called back.

"Gotcha."

Rader turned to his friend. "What's happening, Murray?" he asked.

Fried put his hands on the table and hunched forward. "You're happening," he started, "and you've got me worried." His tone was troubled. "Something's going on. I don't know what the hell it is, but I heard your name used three times today alone—and not in very flattering terms." He paused as though he were waiting for a reaction.

Rader watched him. "I'm listening" was all he said.

"It seems to be a few things, Jeff. First it was your series. I'm telling you, the commissioner's office went right up in the air over those articles."

"I know."

"And then that thing this morning—"

"Coffee and Danish," the counterman interrupted. He set the order down sloppily. "Anything else?"

Rader answered, "We'll let you know."

The counterman ambled back to his chair near the cash register. Jeff faced his friend again.

Murray Fried picked up his thread of thought with an insistent: "I want you to tell me what really happened in that broad's house, Jeff."

"That maniac tried to kill us—"

"And now *he's* dead."

"I just stopped him—"

"And that's what's got me worried about you."

"You're losing me, Murray," Jeff answered. "What are you getting at?"

In answer, Fried leaned in farther. "Listen, Jeff," he said, "that guy committed suicide, but you know that already. What you don't know is that we haven't been able to turn up a God-damned thing on him. Fingerprints don't check out anywhere; there wasn't a single laundry mark or manufacturer's tag in his clothing; no wallet, no credit cards, no money; his gun was untraceable; and his car was stolen. He's the God-damnedest blankest corpse I've ever seen."

"So?"

"So that kind of hiding has got to be planned. In other words, this was no burglar with a sudden urge to kill. This was a straight-out hit man. Somebody on a job. And that's why I'm worried about you. You're involved in this now, Jeff, whatever the hell it is. And whoever has that lady numbered has got to be thinking of you, too."

Jeff Rader's stomach sank.

"Now, for your own safety," Fried went on, "I want you to tell me what really went on in that house."

"We told the cops—"

"No, no," the detective cut in. "You tried to make it look like you were completely baffled by it. The both of you. But that guy was out to kill, and you've got to have some idea why. Now, what were you doing in that house in the first place?"

Jeff Rader looked directly into his friend's eyes.

Seconds passed.

Murray Fried's shoulders settled. His expression relaxed. "Jeff," he urged quietly, "we go back to the fifth grade together. I'm not playing cop now. I haven't even been assigned to this. I'm really, truly concerned about your safety, and that's why I called you to meet me. Look, that incident in the Wilkenson house was strictly a Beverly Hills P.D. matter. I mean, there should have been no reason why my office had to be brought into it. But it was."

"Her husband was an important man, Murray—" Rader interjected.

But the detective cut him off. "Bullshit. There are bigger people than that lady living in Beverly Hills, and when they get involved with the law, the Beverly Hills department doesn't go racing to telephone Harold Durkin."

"Then why—"

"They were *asked* to, that's why. She was under surveillance. And that request had to come from Durkin himself."

This was a surprise.

"So you see," Murray Fried concluded, "if it's not who the lady is that generates that kind of interest, then it's got to be what she's into—and whatever that is, my friend, you seem to be into it, too, now." He paused for a moment. His gaze was steady. "There's more," he suddenly said. Now his tone became even more troubled. "It's about the dead man. He died of cyanide poisoning . . . a capsule."

"I suspected."

"And you know where it was kept?"

"Where?"

"Behind his ear. Right back here behind the lobe . . . in a sac."

"In a what?"

"That's right. A little sac that was surgically created and

probably for that specific purpose—and furthermore, if it was done to one guy, it wouldn't surprise me if there were others like him.''

The significance of that remark jolted Jeff Rader. This was insanity. Could there actually be killers who were preparing themselves surgically for the possibility of suicide rather than capture? Why? What were they so terrified of revealing? Who was behind them? What was it they wanted? And why should they have tried to murder Sandy Wilkenson in her own house?

He didn't include himself in that last question. He was convinced that his own presence in the house had not been anticipated. The breakfast appointment had been made on the spur of the moment and only last night, and this morning his car had been parked seven or eight houses down the block from the Wilkenson address. The killer had probably been surprised to find him there, but since the assignment had called for the woman's death, an unexpected breakfast companion could easily be made to accompany her.

Jesus, what was he getting himself into? What was Sandra Wilkenson's part in it? Could the L.A.P.D. commissioner know what she had been researching? Could his office possibly be investigating the same thing? The same thing. That's it! he saw in a flash. That's why Durkin was so upset by my column. He didn't react until *after* he had seen the Baliston story. It wasn't the series; it was the Baliston case itself. I'll be damned. There must really be a connection between Danny Baliston and Sandra Wilkenson's findings. And Harold Durkin has been conducting an undercover investigation into the whole thing—one that even Murray here isn't entirely aware of. That's why he wants my series killed; that's why he's watching Sandy Wilkenson: We could both be jeopardizing his entire investigation.

The conclusion had sprouted in an instant, along with new-found respect for Police Commissioner Harold Durkin. Well, Jeff Rader was one reporter who wasn't intentionally going to complicate a police effort. He'd step aside. He'd get out of Harold Durkin's way. He looked directly at his friend now. "Thanks, Murray," he said warmly. "There's nothing to worry about anymore. I'll be all right."

He had made a decision. He didn't give a damn if this turned out to be the story of the century. He'd sit down with Sandy Wilkenson and tell her what he had just realized. He'd advise her to leave it all in the hands of the L.A.P.D. and Harold Durkin. He was out of it now; he was going to lose himself in Hawaii for six weeks and pull his life together again.

But the detective wasn't entirely satisfied. His gaze hadn't shifted a hair's breadth. "You make me feel better," he answered quietly, "but I still want to know what you and that broad *didn't* tell the attending officers."

Jeff smiled weakly. "It's too crazy, Murray," he said. "I don't know what it's all about myself—and either you already know and you're trying to pump me to see how much I know, or Durkin's keeping his staff in the dark about it, too."

"I don't know what you're talking about," Fried answered. His response rang with honesty.

Jeff studied Murray's face for a moment. His friend was truly in the dark, and he was asking to have the light turned on.

"The guy who tried to kill us," he started, "was probably part of an incredible operation." He paused.

"Go on," the detective prompted.

"Okay, but first let's talk about him. Apparently he was a trained killer—even to the point of being into martial arts."

"I know," Fried answered. "He had the usual markings: knuckles, heel of the feet, things like that." He smiled. "Like you, only he must have missed something once because he lost a joint of a finger."

"Yeah?" Jeff grinned in return. "I didn't have time to notice while we were going at it."

"Left hand. Little finger. First joint. Weird the way some doctor fixed it up, though."

"What do you mean?"

"They usually clip it straight at the joint, but this guy's little finger was cut on a bias, a very sharp angle, you know what I mean? So that even though the joint was missing, the finger came to a weird kinda point."

"Probably treated himself."

"No, this was treated by a doctor—flap, stitches, a very neat job."

"That *is* odd," Rader agreed.

"But then again, maybe not," Fried allowed suddenly with a grin. "Durkin's got a finger just like it, and if it's good enough for a police commissioner—"

Jeff Rader didn't hear a word beyond the first part of that sentence.

"Same hand?" he asked abruptly.

"Yeah, why? Same finger, as a matter of fact."

What's happening? Rader thought. If Harold Durkin didn't get upset until my Baliston story came out, and the killer knew about the Baliston boy, and the killer had a weird little finger, and Durkin's got a weird little finger—could there be a connection? Could it be a missing finger joint? Could that be some kind of organization mark? Could the commissioner of the Los Angeles Police Department actually be part of this whole unbelievable madness?

He went pale at the possibility.

Fried saw the change in color. He leaned in. "What's the matter, Jeff? You all right?"

Impossible, he thought. The finger's a coincidence. It's got to be.

He said, "Yeah, yeah, fine. Just had a paranoid thought, that's all." Jesus, he really did need a vacation. Well, that was it. That was the clincher. He'd speak to Sandy and beg off.

"I've got to see somebody, Murray," he said. "Don't worry, though, I'll tell you everything I know after I've spoken with her, I promise. But I've got to get this off my chest with her first."

Lieutenant Detective Murray Fried knew when it was time to stop pushing a friend. He eased back in his seat. "Okay, Jeff," he conceded, "we'll talk tomorrow." He paused. "You said 'her,' so I'm going to take an educated guess and say it's the Wilkenson lady."

"Good guess."

"Well, if you're planning on seeing her, there's a little problem."

"Like what?"

"Getting to her. She's been placed in protective custody. One attempt on her life was enough."

Rader felt those strange sensations again. "Who suggested the custody?"

"Durkin."

"Himself?"

"Uh-huh."

"Isn't that unusual? I mean, does the commissioner usually handle something like that himself?"

"No, but as you said, her husband was an important man."

"Where is she?" Jeff suddenly snapped.

"Can't tell you that."

"Murray, don't play around with me now," Jeff urged. He suddenly had a flash of her face with the pink tip of her tongue toying at the corner of her mouth and her eyes looking off to the side. A sense of her vulnerability swept over him. She was alone and totally unsuspecting. In protective custody, true. But just what if this anxiety about Durkin was justified? What if she was not being protected at all, but instead being set up now for what that freaky-fingered killer had failed to accomplish in her house? He couldn't abandon her now to—

"Where is she, Murray? Come on, Goddamn it, tell me!" he demanded with more vigor than he had demonstrated in a long time.

Fried was startled by Rader's stinging tone. "What is it, Jeff? What is it?" he asked.

"I don't know . . . I really don't. . . . But I think she may be in danger. Murray, please—where is she?"

There was only a beat before the detective trusted his instincts. "Century International," he snapped. "Come on! You'll tell me what this is all about on the way over."

Jeff Rader was on his feet. He threw some money on the table and raced for the restaurant door with Murray Fried hot behind him.

The new Century International Hotel is a sixty-four-story obelisk that looms over the southwest corner of Beverly Hills.

Halfway down Olympic Boulevard, Rader could discern the tip of its imposing outline. While he watched it grow slowly like some gargantuan erection, he kept his dialogue with Murray running at a fevered clip. He had amazed his friend with all that had happened at Sandy's house that morning. Now he was trying to learn all he could about the measures being taken to protect her. Their exchanges were staccato bursts of questions and answers, as though both men were caught in a race with their speedometer.

"How long'll it last?" Rader snapped.

"No telling."

"A week? Two? Three?"

"Till they get a fix on who's after her and why."

"How many watch her?"

"Four."

"Where?"

"Lobby, elevator, room door, and one inside."

"What floor?"

"Sixty-one."

"Why?"

"Puts her over nearby buildings. No chance of sniper fire or outside snooping."

"Room?"

"Sixty-one oh one."

"Any reason?"

"Corner. Cuts traffic and offers the best defensive position."

"Communication?"

"Radio all the way around."

"Do I know the men?"

"Two, I think: Duello in the lobby and Chavez outside her door."

"Good men."

"Best we've got."

"And Durkin assigned them?"

"Personally."

"Jesus."

Everything sounded right. So right, in fact, that Murray Fried looked sideways at his friend and quipped, "Too good a get-up for a setup, right?"

Rader agreed with a nod of his head.

"No way my boss can be part of this, Jeff."

The reporter was quiet. He was still troubled.

"We'll follow through anyway, though," Fried added.

"Thanks, Murray."

Fried watched the road, and Jeff Rader knew it was only his long friendship with the detective that was working for him now.

Inside the Century International, Detective Anthony Duello was crossing the lobby at a signal from the hotel manager.

"He's here," the manager murmured when Duello reached the front desk.

"Where?"

"My office."

The detective turned and strode quickly to a door near the desk. He opened it and entered.

A very ordinary-looking, balding man in a gray tweed suit turned to face him at the sound of the doorknob. He was unsmiling as he put out his hand. "Bill Milland," he said.

Duello crossed to him and shook his hand mechanically. "Tony Duello."

"I know."

"But I don't know you. Where's your ID?"

Milland pulled a wallet from the inside pocket of his jacket and flipped it open.

Duello studied the plastic card staring up at him. He glanced at the man. Faces matched. But he reached for the wallet. "May I?" he asked.

The wallet was released.

Duello extracted the ID card and turned it over. He searched the lower left corner for a tiny, inconspicuous green dot that could easily have been mistaken for an insignificant spot of ink. It was the mark. The difference between authenticity and forgery. It was there. The ID was genuine. Satisfied, he relaxed a bit. "You got here fast," he offered.

"Left the second we heard about this morning's attack."

"Why didn't they send guys from your L.A. office?"

"It's a very special case," Milland stated.

Duello waited; Milland offered nothing more.

"How many are you?" the detective finally asked.

"Two."

Duello's lip curled in resentment. "Shi-it," he muttered.

"What's the matter?"

"What makes you guys think two of you are as good as four of us?"

"I never said that."

"Well, somebody did," Duello spat. "You're here, ain't ya?"

Milland's expression grew colder. "I follow orders just like you, Detective Duello," he said flatly.

"Yeah, sure." But clearly he wasn't satisfied. "Where's your partner?"

"On the way up."

"They'll hold him at the elevator."

"They'd damn well better."

Duello looked steadily into Milland's unwavering gaze. His professional pride was being challenged by all of this, and he didn't like it one bit. "How're you going to handle it?" he asked.

"We'll both be in the room with her."

Duello smirked. "That the way they do things in Washington?"

The other man just watched him.

"Okay, Milland." The detective sighed heavily. "She's all yours."

The balding man walked out of the manager's office.

Alone, Anthony Duello pressed the collar of his shirt against his throat with one hand and a small button receiver deeper into his ear with the other. "Gans," he murmured.

One of his men answered immediately. "Yeah?"

"Chavez, you there?"

"Yo," the second responded.

"Mingus?"

"Here, Tony."

"Those Secret Service guys are here now."

"Got one by the elevator," Mingus said.

"Hold him. The other's on his way up." Then he couldn't resist a last touch of playful malice: "Make the fuckers show their IDs every step of the way."

"Right," they said almost in unison.

"See you downtown, men."

Detective Anthony Duello dropped his hands. He tapped a palm against his thigh in annoyance. Now why had federal men been brought into this—and all the way from D.C., too? Couldn't the L.A.P.D. be trusted to protect this Wilkenson lady satisfactorily? Oh, well, it wasn't really his business anyway. Durkin knew what he was doing. And it wasn't the job of a detective to go around questioning the decisions of the commissioner of police.

There are six levels of underground parking at the Century International Hotel.

Murray Fried ignored them. He screeched to a stop almost directly before the lobby entrance and flipped the car's sun visor down to reveal his police credentials.

"Now," he said, turning to face Jeff, "if it's all kosher, there's nothing special we're looking for, right?"

"I suppose so," Jeff agreed. "I guess I just want to see if it *is* kosher. Everything you've told me sounds right, Murray. But, still, I have this feeling—''

"Okay," Fried cut him short, "then here's how I see it: This is supposed to be a highly confidential operation, and covert activities and newsmen just do not go together. Not in the eyes of a police commissioner, at least. If this custody is legitimate, Durkin's going to fry my ass for blowing his secrecy—especially to you."

"And if it's not legitimate?"

"He'll come after me anyway, but then it won't matter because I'll probably be going after him, too. The point is this: I don't mind exposing myself when I'm sure there's something wrong. But since there's a lot of doubt here, I'm going to play this differently. Besides, if Duello sees you with me, he's not going to be very responsive or cooperative, anyway."

"So what are you suggesting?" Rader asked.

"You wait here. I'm going to check this out by myself."

"But I—"

"I'm going in there alone. I'll ask some questions, go up to see if the lady's all right, and come right on down. Won't take more than a few minutes."

"And if there is something wrong?"

"Then you'd only be in the way, my friend." With that, Murray Fried left his car and headed quickly for the hotel entrance.

When he entered the enormous lobby of the hotel, Lieutenant Detective Fried headed straight for the manager's office and asked for Anthony Duello.

"Yes, Lieutenant Fried"—the manager warmed after seeing his gold shield—"he usually stayed near the south escalators, but he's not there now."

"Do you know where he is?"

"No. He left the hotel about five minutes ago."

"All right, then, who's covering and where can I find him?"

"No one's replaced him to my knowledge, Lieutenant."
Murray was puzzled.

"At least in the lobby, I mean," the manager added.

"What does that mean?" Fried pounced on the implication. "Has he been replaced in another sense?"

"I believe so," the manager answered. Though he couldn't identify the new guards as agents of the Secret Service, he told Fried all he knew of the departure of the L.A.P.D. contingent.

"And there are only two on duty now?"

"Yes, sir."

What the hell was going on here? He had seen the assignment sheet himself. It had called for four men, not two. And why had Duello been pulled off? There was certainly nobody in the department better than Tony Duello.

Quickly, he asked if the custody rooms had been changed. When he learned they hadn't, he hurried with long strides for the express elevators.

He reached the sixty-first floor in only a few minutes. That helped his edginess. But stepping out, he immediately felt additional discomfort to find no one there. The hallway stretched a quarter of a city block. Empty. Funereally silent. He started down the long, thickly carpeted corridor. Unaccountably, his heart began to play those familiar little tricks on him. The faster beat. That pulse in his throat. Intuitive signals of danger. His fingers went automatically to his jacket button, and his coat slipped open to make his gun more accessible.

Meanwhile, in the car, Jeff Rader twitched like a man with a rash. He felt alone, separated from something important. A feeling. Just a feeling. But it was so strong that suddenly he knew exactly what Sandy Wilkenson had meant when she had told him of her graveside experience. Something was pulling him. Something intense and undeniable. He couldn't resist it any longer. He jumped from the car and made for the hotel. He'd avoid being seen by Duello, he reasoned. As for the men on the sixty-first floor—well, he'd worry about them later. Besides, if he wasn't actually with Murray, maybe no one would make the connection and his friend's integrity would be safe.

Integrity was the last thing on Fried's mind as he stepped up to the door of 6101.

Two men, he thought, and no one outside. Strange. Very strange.

He rapped lightly right under the number, his head bowed, listening.

"Who's there?" The voice on the other side of the door was strong and authoritative.

"Lieutenant Detective Fried, Los Angeles Police Department. That you, Gans?"

A pause. "What do you want, Lieutenant?"

"Open up. I want to talk."

A long silence.

Murray's heart raced a bit faster. He rapped on the door again. "C'mon, open it," he snapped.

"A minute, Lieutenant."

He heard it. A woman's sound. Soft. Muffled. Then the thud of something against flesh. And he moved fast.

His gun came out. His foot crashed at the door just below the knob. Wood cracked and the door flew open. It smashed into Agent Bill Milland, slamming him against the wall.

Fried charged into the room. He dived for the floor, catching a glimpse of Sandy Wilkenson's limp body being hauled toward the suite's bedroom. He rolled. Spun about for Milland. But he wasn't fast enough. A bullet ripped into his gut. He went flying backward from the impact. He rolled, whipped his gun up, and fired twice so quickly it was like one shot. The bullets tore into Milland's head, and he tumbled forward, dead.

The next slug caught Fried in the neck. He jerked around. Milland's partner had dropped Sandy. He was firing away. Fried caught another in the shoulder. But he twisted wildly and got off two more shots. They caught Milland's partner squarely in the chest and lifted him right off his feet.

Now there was silence.

An odd sense of separation began to pull at Murray Fried's mind.

But it wasn't over because Agent Bill Milland's partner struggled doggedly to his feet. With blood drooling from his mouth, he stumbled toward Sandy Wilkenson. He grappled clumsily with her unconscious form, and began to drag her into the bedroom.

Down the hall, some doors opened. Curious guests poked their heads out anxiously to determine the cause of the disturbance.

"What happened?"

"I don't know."

"Sounded like shots."

"Where?"

"Down the hall, I think."

"Estelle, call the manager."

"Are you crazy? Close the door. Don't get involved."

"Somebody ought to call the police."

That's what Jeff Rader heard as he stepped from the elevator on the sixty-first floor. It galvanized him. He went charging toward the custody suite, bumping, shouldering, knocking aside the few people who had ventured into the hallway.

"Hey!"

"Easy!"

"What the hell's the matter with you?"

When he reached 6101, the mayhem took his breath away. But he hesitated only a moment. The sight of his injured friend lying on the floor made Jeff race into the room, all thoughts of danger gone from his mind.

Murray's throat had been torn open. His eyelids were flickering weakly. Blood poured from his shoulder and stomach wounds.

"Murray . . . Murray, don't move," Jeff whispered. "I'll get a doctor. . . . Don't move."

The sound of shattering glass jolted him. It came from the bedroom. Loud. Repeated smashings.

Suddenly he remembered Sandy Wilkenson and felt a sweeping sense of danger. He reached for Murray's gun. Felt its reassuring weight in his palm. He moved cautiously toward the open bedroom door. What he saw there stopped him cold. The entire window of the room had been smashed out. Drapes around it were waving crazily like pennants in a wind. And kneeling on a desk right under the opening, blood gushing from his chest wounds, was Agent Bill Milland's partner, slowly and torturously trying to pull Sandra Wilkenson up there beside him. His intentions were obvious: He was going to throw her out that window!

"Stop!" Jeff shouted.

The agent looked up sharply. His hand went quickly for the gun that was lying near his knee.

Jeff Rader didn't know what moved him. He had never in his life killed a man. But, all at once, there he was on one knee. Both hands around Murray Fried's gun. Arms extended. The automatic going off. One. Two. Three shots.

They caught the agent. All of them. And he lurched backward, dropping Sandra Wilkenson as he pitched through the shattered window to fall sixty-one floors to the street below.

Jeff rushed to Sandy's side.

She was still unconscious. Bruised and cut but otherwise unhurt. He rubbed her hands. Slapped her face lightly. "Sandy," he kept repeating, "Sandy, are you all right? You all right? Sandy . . ."

She stirred. She opened her eyes and came out of it quickly then. "Yes . . . I'm okay I think," she mumbled.

That was all Jeff needed. He was up and away in an instant, rushing back to Murray Fried.

The detective was still breathing. Irregularly. His lids flickered open and his lips moved. There was a sound. It was little more than a bloody gargle.

"Don't talk, Murray," Jeff pleaded. "Don't talk . . . please."

But Fried tried again and tugged weakly at Jeff's sleeve to pull him closer.

With his ear virtually against his friend's mouth, Rader heard him ask: "The girl . . . she all right?"

"Fine . . . she's fine, Murray."

"Good . . . good. Now . . . check his . . . hand."

"What?"

"Check . . . hand."

Rader understood. He jumped to his feet and raced to the body of Bill Milland.

The agent had been left-handed. Despite the violence of his death, he still gripped his gun.

Rader tore the weapon free and stuffed it into his own pocket. Then he grabbed the hand and stared at it.

The little finger came to an oddly angled point; the first joint was missing.

He broke to Murray's side again. "It's missing," he whispered. "Murray, it's missing!"

The detective actually smiled. "Looks . . . like . . . you were . . . right," he strained to say. Then the smile vanished. "Get . . . him . . . Jeff . . . get . . . him."

"Don't talk anymore, Murray."

Sandy Wilkenson entered the room. "Oh, my God," she whispered at the sight of the carnage.

"Call the desk! Get a doctor, fast!" Rader ordered. He turned again to his friend. "Lie still . . . please. Everything's going to be all right, you'll see. . . ."

Lieutenant Detective Murray Fried had one more thing to say. He blinked his eyes slowly and mumbled into Jeff's ear, "Jeez . . . there are . . . so many . . . things . . . I haven't . . . done . . . yet."

Then he died.

Jeff Rader's eyes filled quickly with tears, but there wasn't time for grief. He grabbed Sandy's hand and pulled her into the hallway. "C'mon." The order was choked with such urgency that it discouraged any possibility of hesitation. He rushed her down the hallway. Not to the elevators, though. Police would soon be pouring out of one of them, and he couldn't risk meeting them. Not without knowing whose side they were on.

Two guests still hovered near 6101, pulling back quickly as he and Sandy charged past. It didn't matter to him that their flight was being observed. He was thinking as clearly as ever. He knew exactly what had to be done if they were to make it safely out of the Century International Hotel.

Into the stairwell. Down three flights. Leading Sandy. Pulling. Jumping. Two, three steps at a time. The fifty-eighth floor. A corridor again. Quickly. To the elevators. Great luck! The doors were opening. The down arrow burned red. A little girl exited. She didn't even see them. They were inside in a moment and alone. Until the twenty-fifth floor, the car was a local; below that, an express to the lobby. He touched a button: 25. The doors closed. Now pray: no stops . . . no stops . . . no stops. . . . Damn it! On the thirty-sixth floor, an elderly couple entered. Jeff moved Sandy into a corner. He faced her, covering her bruises, her dishevelment. The elderly couple watched the doors. Down again. Twenty-nine, -eight. The cubicle was heavy with silence. On the twenty-seventh floor, two more entered. Jeff covered Sandy again. The newcomers turned and stared at the indicator lights. Twenty-six . . . twenty-five.

"Excuse us, please . . . getting out."

They sidled past the other passengers. Deftly. Stirring no more interest than would be forgotten in a matter of minutes. They hurried to the local elevators. One was there, doors open. A young boy was waiting. Jeff punched the third-floor button as they went past him to a corner of the car. At the tenth floor, the boy left. At the sixth, a man entered; he ignored them. Five . . . four . . . three. The doors opened and they left. Then to the right. The stairs again. They were running now. Down steps. Leaping. Jumping. She blessed the low-heeled shoes she was wearing.

They reached the first garage level and kept on going to the second. He stopped there. They took a moment to compose themselves, to catch their breath, straighten their clothes, comb their hair. Then they stepped quietly into the garage and walked to the opposite end. His reasoning: If the police had been summoned already, they wouldn't use the garage; they'd pull right up in front the way Murray Fried had done, and if, by some quirk of behavior, they did pull into the underground levels, they would certainly not go below the first level. Since the main entrance to the hotel faced north, he and Sandy would leave by the garage's south ramp; in that way they would avoid the possibilities of both lobby and garage contact.

He led her up the ramps and into the street.

They had no difficulty finding an empty cab. He gave the driver an address near the Santa Monica Freeway. He signaled Sandy to be silent. Not a word was spoken throughout the drive. He paid the cabby at the corner of Hughes and Exposition, and when the car was no longer in sight, he led Sandy to a bus stop.

They rode down Exposition Boulevard a few miles and then left the bus and hailed another cab.

He was being extremely cautious. He knew that if Commissioner Harold Durkin were actually involved in the attempts on Sandy's life, every element of police machinery at his disposal would soon be activated to find her. An investigation would quickly locate the driver of that taxi, and he'd be able to identify his passengers and their drop-off point with little difficulty. Inasmuch as three killings had occurred at the Century International, guests on the sixty-first floor would be interrogated, and they, too, would be able to describe him to the police. Without a doubt, Rader assumed, an APB would include his name as well. There was also the very real possibility now that Durkin had already started a dossier on him because of Sandy's research activities and her meetings with him. If that were the case, the file would undoubtedly contain the locations of his favorite haunts and the names of most of his friends and acquaintances. That's how it was done, Jeff knew. So it was essential to be particularly circumspect, to cut off leads, to double-back, to avoid all known locales and associations.

Jeff Rader was a west-side man in his living and his tastes. Except for periodic trips to Dodger Stadium, he rarely visited the east side of the city for personal pleasure. However, his work had made L.A. his town, and he knew almost every corner of it. He was aware of places that under normal circumstances were alien to his interests and habits. He was heading for one of those places now, and he and Sandy would hole up there until he'd had an opportunity to decide upon some clear-cut course of action. He told the cabby to let them off at Figueroa on the other side of the Los Angeles River.

It was a seedy neighborhood. Full of bars and run-down stores. And off the main drag there was a small, garish motel.

No one would ever connect him with an X-rated flophouse, and no questions would be asked there.

Being careful to the very end, he and Sandy Wilkenson walked the last two blocks to the Eros Lodge.

They had been silent throughout their taxi and bus rides. Now, in the safety of their motel room, they faced each other.

"Now what?" she asked anxiously from the edge of a chair.

"I don't know," he said. He looked up at the ceiling and exhaled sharply. "My God, I've just killed a man!"

She was astounded.

"And my best friend is dead," he added, his voice cracking in anguish.

"Did you kill the one in the gray suit?" Her question was a whisper of surprise, of compassion, gratitude, and fear. He realized suddenly that she had no way of knowing what had happened, that she had been unconscious during the entire violent episode.

"No," he answered. "I think my friend shot him—but I'm not even sure of that."

"There were two men," she said. "They were Secret Service agents, but they—"

"Secret Service?" He remembered Murray Fried's last smile and the missing finger joint of the other man in the room, and his mind went into a spin. "No. That's not possible," he insisted. Then he spewed out all the particulars of the events in suite 6101—why he and Murray Fried had been there in the first place, what he had discovered on entering the rooms, why he had killed the man in the bedroom, what he had seen of Milland's left hand, what it meant in terms of the other assailant at her house that morning, how it all seemed to connect with his own story on Danny Baliston.

And in the telling, he glimpsed facets that he had never before considered. The enormity of this thing washed over him like a gigantic wave. For a moment he felt himself floundering helplessly.

If Sandy was right about her secret international organization of kidnappers and murderers, and he was right about Police Commissioner Harold Durkin, then this insanity had permeated the highest levels of local law enforcement. And if the man who was trying to throw her out of that hotel window was a partner of the one with the missing finger joint, and they were *actually* Secret Service agents, then there was a grisly connection between Los Angeles and Washington, D.C. Not only that, but if Durkin was responsible—as he undoubtedly had been—for the presence of those agents at the hotel, and he could get them only with the assistance of someone else within the Secret Service, then whatever this poison was, it had actually spread into the highest echelons of government!

He couldn't accept it. Yet it made sense. Then with a gasp he remembered his session yesterday with his editor, Tom Pendleton, and the way the older man had squelched all discussion about his column. "It's dead, Jeff," he had said. "The whole series . . . because Police Commissioner Harold Durkin and our publisher are boyhood buddies." Could the publisher of one of the most powerful newspapers in the world be part of this, too? Who else? And where are they? And why should such eminent people be involved in the widespread kidnapping of innocent little children?

Maneuvered on the table of discussion like pieces from a jigsaw puzzle, the thoughts had formed the frame of a crazy picture. Only the frame, but at least it was some kind of order for Jeff Rader and Sandra Wilkenson.

"So," Sandy murmured finally, "what happens now?" She knew where she stood: She would continue to search for her daughter, Tami, if she had to scour the country forever. What remained was for Jeff Rader to join her. But would he?

Jeff looked down at her—she was sitting on the edge of her chair again—and he sensed the depth of her need. He was looking at a very special person, he knew. One who had had soul-scarring experiences without being mutilated. Helping a woman like this would certainly be among the better acts of his life.

And then there was Murray Fried and the bloody gargle of his dying words: "There's so much I haven't done yet." Yes. So much. A beautiful man . . . extinguished so brutally. And for what? Rader didn't know the answer to that. All he knew was that he couldn't shake the terrible feeling of responsibility for the death of his friend. Murray had become involved in this solely because of him. Because of him and someone else, somewhere.

Somewhere—if his and Sandy's logic were valid—somewhere,
someone was busily manipulating ugly events, making cold decisions that extinguished warm lives. Murray couldn't make the
murderers pay for his own death, but, he, Jeff, could do that for him.
Revenge? Absolutely. Pure and clean. Murray had said it to him:
"Get him, Jeff, get him," and though he hadn't realized it at the
time, he knew now that he had been committed from that very
moment.

He knelt before Sandy and looked directly into her eyes.
"We're going to find Tami," he said with grim resolve. "We're
going to find her and Danny Baliston, if he's still alive, and
whoever's responsible for this whole sickening thing."

The corner of her mouth twitched ever so slightly. The firm set
of her expression eased into a look of relief and gratitude. Her
lips relaxed into a tremulous smile. She put her arms around his
neck and leaned in so that her cheek was against his and her lips
close to his ear. "Thank you," she whispered. "Oh, thank you,
thank you, thank you."

7

Michael Gavin was watching the six-o'clock local news. The attractive black woman and her equally attractive white male colleague were reeling off the day's disasters with an urbane charm that made him want to puke. "Sweet Mary, save us," he muttered. "The only time those two hyenas stop grinning is when they've heard a good dirty joke." It was said aloud, to the walls and to the furniture because Michael Gavin lived alone, without dog, cat, or even a goldfish to fill his life. It's not that he didn't appreciate pets; it was just that as a young man, he'd always believed it to be extremely unfair to make creatures dependent upon anyone whose career could not guarantee fixed schedules or permanent residence. After he had retired from the *Voice*, it was too late to change old habits. So he talked to the room, to the TV set and, best of all, to himself. "Oh, what's to become of us?" he groaned as he rose from his armchair to get another cold beer from the refrigerator.

He was delicately pouring an exceptional head when his ear caught the name: Sandra Wilkenson. He remembered her instantly as the young woman whom he had left with Jeff at Downey's. He hurried back into the living room and stood before the TV set:

. . . Mrs. Wilkenson was being guarded by two Secret Service men. Their deaths and Mrs. Wilkenson's disappear-

ance have the Los Angeles Police Department alarmed and
concerned. Also killed in the shootout was Lieutenant Detective Murray Fried, a member of the staff of Police Commissioner Harold Durkin. Observed running with Mrs. Wilkenson
from the scene of the killings was a man whom authorities
believe to be Jeff Rader, syndicated columnist for the *Los
Angeles Voice*. [Pictures of Sandy and Jeff appeared on the
screen.] We have been asked by the police commissioner's
office to alert all L.A. residents to the need for information
concerning the whereabouts of these two material witnesses.
If you know anything that could lead to their discovery,
please notify your nearest police authority. . . .

Gavin turned off the set and settled slowly into the softness of
his armchair again. "I'll be damned . . ." he muttered.

An hour later he was still struggling to comprehend what could
possibly have happened (he had called the *Voice* and several
friends at police headquarters without learning much more) when
his telephone jangled him out of a moment of troubled reverie.

"Gavin here." He answered a phone as though he were still at
his city desk.

"Michael, it's Jeff."

Michael Gavin came alive with a jolt that spilled his fifth beer
of the evening. "Where the hell are you, kid?"

"In trouble."

"I know that—"

"I need you."

"You've got me."

"Eros Lodge on Fortieth Avenue off Figueroa. Room twenty-
one."

"Be there in an hour, my boy."

Actually, he was there in forty minutes, and it would have
been sooner if he hadn't taken every conceivable precaution
against the possibility of being followed or stopped.

He eased through a carefully opened door, whistled deprecat-
ingly at the room's tawdry decor, and turned at once to the matter
of concern.

"What happened at that hotel?"

Jeff still gripped his hand. "Thank you for coming, Michael."

"Jeff says you're the only one who can help us, Mr. Gavin,"
Sandy added.

"Did you kill those people?"

"We'll tell you everything, Michael—everything. But first I have to let you know that you may be risking your life if you listen to what we have to say."

Gavin's scraggy face broke into a broad grin. "What life, kid? I'm seventy-four, and I've done it all. At this stage, whatever I let myself in for is gravy and better than the boob tube."

Jeff Rader closed his eyes and exhaled sharply. He had been praying for that kind of response.

Sandy Wilkenson sighed her own relief.

They sat around a cheap, mirrored table while Jeff and Sandy recounted everything they could think of concerning past events, suppositions, and recent conclusions.

Gavin said absolutely nothing while they spoke.

After completing their revelations, they watched him in a moment of breathless apprehension. Did he believe them? After all, except for the identification of missing finger joints, there was really nothing to link their experiences together. And if he didn't believe them, would he recommend that they give themselves up to the police? Or even worse, for their own sakes would he try to turn them in?

Michael Gavin's first words were a soft "Arthur Marquand's got a joint missing on his left little finger, and the angle of amputation is exactly as you've described the others."

Jeff Rader fell back into his chair.

"Who's Arthur Marquand?" Sandy asked.

"The paper's publisher," he whispered.

Now there were four: the "contractor," the police commissioner, the agent in the hotel, and the illustrious publisher of the *Los Angeles Voice*. Given all the other related circumstances, the deformity in that kind of tally could never have been coincidental.

Jeff sighed; it was a sound of trouble and relief.

"That's the cement, Michael," he murmured. "I guess that's all I've needed to hold this thing together for me." He turned to Sandy. "Since this goes back to Washington, and you lived there so long, do you have any other corroboration?"

"What do you mean?"

"Other people there with the same sign."

She looked off to the side, and her brows creased in thought. Again, the tip of her tongue played at the corner of her mouth.

"No," she finally answered slowly, "I don't remember anything like that."

"How about Maria, your housekeeper?"

"I never noticed."

"But you told me she lived with you for eight months—"

"She was help, Jeff, not family."

"Still and all—"

"It's not strange; you didn't know it about your own publisher."

Jeff stopped short. She was right on target. Apparently it was the kind of identification about which little note would ever be taken. He looked at his former city editor. "We're going to need a car, Michael."

Gavin reached quickly into his pocket. He removed a key and tossed the rest on the mirrored table. "You still have one for my house on that ring—just in case," he offered. "I'll get a cab home."

"My car's still on La Grange and Sawtelle," Jeff said.

Gavin cut the idea short. "Leave it. The cops'll find it and impound it, and that'll be better for everybody." He paused. A distant look touched his eyes. He rubbed a fingertip back and forth over his lower lip.

"What is it?" Jeff asked.

"I don't know," he answered. "There's just something about that finger business that bothers me. Like I've heard of it before." Silence filled the room as he probed his memory. Then he spat, "Damn!" and growled in his failure, "I'll get it, I'll get it." The old city editor suddenly grinned at his protégé. "Okay, what else can I do?"

"I'd like you to dig—into Durkin's background, Marquand's, the police reports on those agents in the hotel—into anything that'll give me some leads."

Gavin stood abruptly. "You've got it, kid. And look, I want you to use this telephone number to keep in touch with me." He scribbled a number on a little pad that he'd taken from the inside pocket of his jacket. "It's my brother's. Don't use my number; that may be too dangerous. But you call this one at least once a day, and when you leave a number where I can get back to you, always run the last four digits in reverse. Got it?"

"Got it," Jeff echoed as he rose and took Gavin's hand. "Be very careful, Michael," he urged softly. "Please. I don't want anything to happen to you."

The old city editor smiled. "Hell, kid," he mumbled in some embarrassment, "a person'd have to be out of his mind to mess with Michael Gavin." It was a charming bit of nonsense. It made Sandy Wilkenson go to him and kiss him lightly on the cheek.

He loved that, but he covered his feeling with a gruff "I better get out of here, kid, before this young lady becomes my slave."

All three laughed.

When the door had closed behind his old friend, Jeff Rader turned to look at Sandy once more. Would they ever see Michael Gavin again? They read that thought in each other's expression as though it were a neon light. She touched his arm, and he rubbed a finger over the back of her hand as an understanding response. Then his rhythms switched abruptly. "Come on," he said, "we don't have time to waste on worry."

Her adjustment was just as quick. "What do we do now?"

"While Michael's digging for leads for us," he said, "I want to start with two of our own."

She creased her brows questioningly. She hadn't been aware that they had anything specific to consider.

He explained: "We have a few things to work from. First, what that creep said before he killed himself this morning. I asked him where Danny Baliston was, and he grinned and gasped out, '. . . fah . . . thuh . . . wes . . . cose . . .' Well, if we tie that to the second point, to what your investigator told you before *he* was killed . . ."

She smiled faintly at his acceptance of her earlier suggestion of murder.

He continued, "He had a fix on Tami's dentist somewhere in the Santa Barbara area. That's *farther up the west coast*. And that's probably what the killer was teasing us with. So, Santa Barbara is one starting place for us, and that's our first lead."

"What's the other?"

"I'm not sure yet. First, tell me how that guy in your house knew you wanted to remodel. I mean, he was there supposedly to give you an estimate for the job. How did you come to his attention? Did you advertise?"

Sandra Wilkenson's face paled. "No," she answered.

"Then someone knew about your need and sent him to you."

She settled weakly on the edge of a chair. "Oh, no," she whispered.

"Who was it, Sandy?"

"I've got only one living relative, Jeff . . . a distant cousin in Mandeville Canyon." She was so shaken, she could barely be heard. "He was my only link to some kind of family reality when I came out here . . . so I looked him up. . . . He was married two weeks ago . . . and I told his wife about the remodeling at their wedding."

"No one else?"

"No. We were alone for a moment, and I was telling her how much I liked their house, and she said the living room was going to be done over, and I said I wanted to do something to mine, too . . . and then she said she'd send over their contractor. . . ." She trailed off and looked up at him plaintively. A silent question screamed in that seamy motel room.

Jeff Rader couldn't help but hear it. "It's even in your family," he answered her somberly. "Let's go. That woman is our starting point."

Myra's tremulous kiss pressed lightly over Gary's receptive mouth. They were alone for a moment. Their guests were in the living room and the kitchen, enjoying themselves immensely. Myra had caught Gary's eyes watching her, and though she was laughing heartily at one of the evening's cleverest stories, she was swept by a feeling of such intense love for this man that she simply had to touch him. At that very moment. She had to hold him. To kiss him in a special way that would not do for guests to see. So she had closed her eyes slowly in the signal that had become their sign of need, and he had slipped into their bedroom where she soon joined him.

There was fervor in the gentleness of that kiss. Deep, churning hunger. It was a tribute to her self-control that she didn't tear his clothes off and devour him then and there.

"I just had to hold you for a minute," she said with her forehead against his chin. "I never dreamed there was this much happiness. You're the best thing that's ever happened to me."

"You mean, even better than your award?" he teased.

She had just been voted "Woman of the Year" by the American Association of Women Authors. The awards dinner was to take place at the Beverly Hilton Hotel on Saturday.

Gary had prepared tonight's soiree to allow her the congratulations and pleasure of their closest friends. Something like a delicious appetizer before an elaborate entree.

She kissed him again. Much more fervently. Then she touched his face in the most tender way and whispered, "I love you so much, I can't find the words." And she led him back to their guests.

That was at 8:10 P.M.

At 8:25, Jeff Rader and Sandy Wilkenson were turning off Sunset Boulevard onto Mandeville Canyon Road.

Myra London was Sandy's new cousin.

Mandeville Canyon Road winds through trees and vegetation so lush in places it's difficult to believe a cosmopolitan environment exists nearby.

About a hundred yards past the London house, Jeff Rader backed Gavin's Chevy into a tight clearing immediately off the road. He snapped off the ignition and killed the headlights. The night's blackness swallowed them. Trees and shrubs enveloped the car. They were completely hidden from view.

"Now, I don't know what's going to happen back there," Jeff started, thumbing in the general direction of the house, "but we've got to be prepared for anything. So, in case we have to get away fast, I want you to stay right here behind the wheel of this car."

"I'd rather go with you."

"You'll be more helpful now as our insurance, provided, of course, you're a good driver—are you?"

"Damned good."

He couldn't see her smile in the darkness, but he heard her conviction, and he was satisfied. "Okay, now tell me everything I should know about her."

On the way over from Eros Lodge, they had set down the objectives of this gamble: to find out why Sandy had been marked for death; to confirm their belief in the existence of some kind of conspiracy; to learn if Tami Wilkenson was still alive; and to discover anything that might lead to an understanding of *why* all of this was taking place.

Now Sandy told Jeff Rader what she knew about Myra London. "You'll recognize her physically by her hair. It's red. Flaming red. And her eyes are a vitreous green. She's absolutely exquisite. She's about my age and tall and lithesome. Moves with the grace of a cat. I mean, she's really feline. A very unusual woman.

You'll spot her immediately." Then a thought flashed, and Sandy added, "But you probably know her already."

"Why should I know her?"

"Before she became Myra London, she was Myra Macon."

"The writer?" He was astonished. While he didn't know her personally, he certainly had heard of her.

Myra Macon was becoming an international figure. Her definition of feminism was shaping universal guidelines. The human soul is the starting place of all equality, she maintained. It had nothing to do with sex or culture. When we've clearly defined the nature of the human spirit, we'll have our reference for female activism. "Women must not be demanding the right to become as insane as men," she wrote in her latest book, *Moving Forward*. "We can shape a sane world where social equality clearly expresses equality of the human soul."

"She's brilliant," Jeff murmured in bewilderment. How could anyone as extraordinary as Myra Macon be involved in the madness to which he and Sandy were being subjected? "Sandy," he asked softly, "are you certain you didn't speak to anyone else about your intention to remodel your house?"

"Absolutely." The answer was subdued but insistent. "Myra sent me that contractor. He even told me that when he called for his appointment."

He flicked the light switch above them; the interior of the car would now remain in darkness as he opened his door. The pallid February moon barely washing the sky gave them their only light. Next he poked into the glove compartment and removed the heavy screwdriver he had transferred from the trunk before they'd left the motel. Then he reached behind himself and pulled out Agent Bill Milland's gun; it had been in his belt, nestling snugly against his spine. "I hope you won't need this," he said, "but if you do, don't be afraid to use it."

She hesitated for a moment. Then she took the weapon and placed it on the seat between them.

He pushed at the door and turned to leave, but she stopped him with a hand on his arm and a soft: "Be careful." More than apprehension was in the words. He heard a note of genuine concern. Something tripped within him, a light flip of warmth. He knew the sensation. No woman had been able to stir it for months, though. He was surprised and pleased by it.

He answered with a quick: "I'll be careful." Then his voice

gentled in explanation. "Sandy, I don't know whether this will work or how long it'll take. Once I get into that house I may have to wait hours before I find a way to get her alone. And even if I do get her alone, I'm not certain I can get any significant information from her. She could lie to me, she could make a scene bad enough to bring help, she could do any number of things—I just don't know. . . ."

"Then why are we here?"

"I guess what I'm really saying is—this might not work, and it's dangerous for you, too, but it's a lead and the reporter in me says it has to be followed."

"Jeff," she murmured, "you don't need a disclaimer for me."

Rader felt that warm flush again. "You just be ready and patient, no matter how long I'm gone," he said, and he was out of the car and into the thicket before his feeling could intrude upon his purpose.

He worked his way through the brush with great care. He had reasoned that if Myra Macon London were indeed connected with the attempts on Sandy's life, then she would now know about Sandy's escape. If she hadn't learned about it from the evening TV news, then she would certainly have been informed by Commissioner Durkin himself, or by her associates within the Secret Service. She'd know, too, that he, Jeff Rader, was in hiding with Sandy. No doubt he was now as marked as Sandy. Hunters who had plotted so carefully to kill would surely not be lax while their quarry was running around loose and armed.

He came to the edge of a clearing. Across an expanse of swimming pool, hot tub, redwood gazebo, and Japanese garden, he saw the London house alive with light. Remaining hidden among the trees, he circled toward the front. The sight of cars filling the driveway told him that a special gathering was in progress. A meeting of the clan? he wondered. He edged back toward the rear of the house. It's either business or social, he told himself. Either way, it presented unexpected problems. But, then again, it also presented unexpected opportunity. For one thing, if the house had an alarm system, it certainly wouldn't be in operation at this time; for another, the activity of the guests would probably be excellent cover for his entry.

He looked again toward the rear of the house. He singled out a large, sliding glass door. It was situated only five or six feet from the edge of the swimming pool. Now if there was no dog to alert anyone, his first task would be to get into the house through that door. He scanned the yard for evidence of an animal—toys, doghouse, excrement, anything—but the moon was so faint and the yard so dark, he could discover nothing.

He'd have to risk it. He eased from the protection of his hiding place and moved swiftly toward the house. His heart raced.

There was no dog.

He breathed more easily as he sidled up to the glass door. Then he heard music coming from the front of the house. Someone had started to play a piano. It was no tape, he knew, or no LP album because cheers, laughter, and applause greeted the pianist's comical introduction to Chopin's *Polonaise*. Good—attention was focused elsewhere; entry would be easier now. He tried to slide the door. It was locked. He had considered the importance of Arcadia doors to California architecture and had prepared himself. He pulled the heavy screwdriver from his rear pocket. He wedged it under the base of the door. He pressed down hard. The door lifted a full half inch off its runners. The hook latch was freed from its grip, and he slid the huge window open with ease.

He slipped around a velvet drape that ran the length of the wall and found himself in the house's master bedroom. He opened the drape slowly and quietly. Then he eased the Arcadia door wide open. He felt he might have to make a fast exit and he wanted nothing to impede that escape.

He went to the door and listened. Yes, a party, he told himself, confirming his earlier belief. That made him feel much better. Activity elsewhere in the house gave him an opportunity to consider his next move. He crossed to a far, dark corner of the room and, leaning against the right angle of the walls, wondered exactly how he was going to get Myra Macon London alone.

His problem would soon be solved for him.

Though Myra had nibbled at her husband's mouth a half hour ago, Gary London still tasted the fullness of his gorgeous wife's lips. He was thinking about them when he felt her eyes upon him. He looked up to see her staring and smiling at him with such naked yearning that his stomach churned with matching hunger. How he loved her! He grinned at her in return and slowly dropped his eyelids in their signal.

Her smile broadened. She would never ignore that signal. She slipped unobtrusively from the avid group around the piano. She would wait for him in their bedroom.

Jeff Rader stopped breathing when he heard the sound of the turning doorknob. He drew deeper into his corner.

She entered, closed the door gently, and went directly to the tall lamp on her nightstand. She reached under the shade. A quick turn of the switch flushed the room with soft, clear light. She straightened sharply, her attention gripped by the open Arcadia door and the drawn drapes. She turned quickly.

Jeff Rader was advancing from his corner. He had no difficulty recognizing her; she was as exquisite as Sandy had predicted.

"How dare you invade my home this way?" she demanded. Her voice was low and controlled. "You're a bigger fool than I had expected."

Rader felt his skin prickle. She knew him. It was an outright admission. There were no hysterics. There was no panic. She was just coldly arrogant and resentful.

There could be no oblique approach to someone like this. Directness was all she would understand. "You set your cousin up to be killed," he said flatly. "Why?"

"You're a dead man." The pronouncement was chilling. "And she's dead, too."

The incongruity of this stung him. Here was a magnificent-looking, brilliant, accomplished person enunciating death sentences with a coldness devoid of human sensitivity. It was like watching a beautiful painting crawl with maggots.

"You set your cousin up to be killed," he repeated. "Why?"

She didn't speak. Instead, with the flicker of a sneer on that full, ripe mouth, she started a slow, steady cross straight *toward* him.

He hadn't known what to expect before breaking into this house—but it surely wasn't this. He backed up a step.

Her hands were before her, waist high. She was toying with a large cluster ring on the middle finger of her left hand as she continued her catlike advance. "What is it you want?" she asked. Her voice purred now.

"Stay just where you are," Jeff warned. He found himself retreating, trying to stay out of her reach. Why? He didn't know.

"Is that all you want?" she purred, still coming on. "To know why she must die?" She kept touching the ring. "Because alive she can ruin everything."

"All she wants is her child back." It was a clever move: Instead of asking if Tami Wilkenson was alive, he was stating it.

"The girl's better off where she is."

"Why do you want to hurt a beautiful, innocent child?" he snapped.

"Hurt her!" She bared perfect teeth. "She's being *improved*." She laughed warmly.

The tilted sound of that laughter stopped Rader cold.

She stepped up to him. "She's become a Pedabine, you damned idiot . . . like *me!*" She said it with such fierce pride that her words exploded like a gun going off in an echo chamber.

Suddenly the bedroom door opened. It was Gary, coming for his wife.

Jeff's attention was momentarily diverted.

And in that moment Myra's hand came swinging up in a backhand arc toward his face.

His years of training sprang into automatic response. He saw the movement. Saw the hand. But he didn't parry the blow. Instead he jerked his head back, and his left hand flashed and gripped her wrist. High. Up near the palm. So hard, her fingers were forced wide open and she couldn't twist the hand to touch him. Then he saw the ring. A cluster of spiny needles, blossoming over the heads of rubies and emeralds, only inches from his face.

She was thrashing madly, kicking and straining to bite her way free.

At that same moment Gary London came flying across the room to free his wife from the grip of this mad intruder.

Jeff knew he was coming. Still holding her wrist, he tried to swing Myra Macon to block her husband's charge. But he was slightly off balance, and he could get her only partially around.

Her body twisted sideways. Her hand flew out and backward. The ring smashed into her husband's face, ripping his cheek open on that cluster of spiny needles.

Gary London's charge stopped abruptly. His eyes went wide. He clawed imploringly at the air. Then he croaked one word: "*My-ra . . .*" and pitched forward on his face—dead.

Myra London stared in disbelief and horror at the paroxysm of his almost instantaneous death. A harrowing cry surfaced from the depths of her soul.

Jeff Rader was almost moved to release her, but he understood clearly that oblivion lay in the touch of that ring. He yanked her hand up to look at the instrument of death. Even before he noticed the small spring that triggered the needles, his eyes locked on the mark that he had now come to expect—she, too, was missing the first joint of her little finger.

"Where's Tami Wilkenson?" he growled.

It was as though the question were an electric prod. She jerked from her misery and glared at him. She lashed out with her free right hand, but he snapped a handcuff of fingers around that wrist, too. Her eyes flashed. Her brows scowled. Her upper lip curled grotesquely, torturing the lovely mouth into a curve of hatred. He was staring at a mask of absolute malevolence. Then the mask suddenly screamed—again and again—waves of screams like a wild sea.

He was drowning in the sound. He had to get out. He turned sharply, swinging Myra London off her feet; at the same time, his foot came up and caught her between her breasts. Releasing her hands, he pumped his leg like a piston and sent her catapulting toward the door before she could touch him with that deadly ring.

Quickly, then, he spun around and charged through the glass door he had left open for his escape. As he reached the far side of the pool, he heard the frenzied sounds of guests responding to Myra's screams. He tore for the forest surrounding the property. Someone was after him. He heard the racing footsteps hit the pool's cooldeck and then muffle on the soft grass. The crack of a gun sent lead whistling past his ear to tear bark off a nearby tree. He ran among the trees to where he thought Sandy was waiting in the car. But no matter how he raced and dodged and twisted, his pursuer continued to gain on him. There were more shots. The misses were now near hits. Even in the darkness, even in the denseness of the foliage, his margin of safety was steadily disappearing. What kind of person was this hunting him?

Jeff's lungs began to ache. Bushes tore at his clothes. A switch of oak lashed the corner of an eye and almost blinded him. Suddenly he was out of the brush and on Mandeville Canyon Road. He had miscalculated! Sandy and the car were not there. He was off by a good fifty yards. He raced up the road as though all the demons of Hell were pursuing him, his ears filled with the sounds of his breathing, of his shoes slamming the asphalt, of the pounding feet gaining on him.

Then lights swept around a bend in the road, coming head-on. A car was tearing directly toward him, locking him in its beams.

There was no way out.

The vehicle was upon him.

He dived for the roadside brush. A fender nipped the heel of his shoe. But the speed of the car kept it going, arrow straight, and his pursuer was slammed off the road like a ten pin.

There were screeching sounds as the driver jammed on brakes. The vehicle was tearing in reverse, coming back for him, returning to finish the job.

He was through. He knew it. He didn't have strength to fight. Didn't have breath to run.

The car skidded to a stop. "Get in—fast!" he heard the clear command. It was Sandy Wilkenson.

He flopped into the seat next to her, slammed the door, and stared at her with a weak but admiring smile.

She didn't even look at him. Her attention was fully on their getaway. Mike Gavin's Chevy went hurtling down Mandeville Canyon Road toward Sunset Boulevard. However, she did manage to murmur, "Where do we go now?"

And his gasping response was "Santa Barbara."

8

On the southern edge of Santa Barbara, Pedabine 23, Ralph
Watson, raised a glass of delicate red burgundy to his lips. It was
a Volnay Santenots, vintage '67—that special wine his wife had
bought for their special dinner, but he gulped it with virtually no
awareness or appreciation. He was a deeply disturbed man.

His meeting with Jesse would go into a report, and that report
would detail the character of his resentment. He knew Jesse and
he knew Pedabine. Resentment was never to be ignored. It was
always a matter for the Discipline Committee, whose punish-
ments were consistently and terrifyingly severe.

Then as if this wasn't enough, the six-o'clock news had made
him gasp aloud.

Three Pedabines lost in one day. Catastrophic!

What made the matter even more startling, Watson thought,
was the fact that all three deaths had been related to Sandra
Wilkenson and this new compatriot of hers, Jeff Rader.

Turbulent, troubled thoughts.

"You haven't enjoyed your dinner at all, have you?"

She was sitting across the table, watching.

"Hmm?"

"It's the transfer, isn't it?"

He nodded his head.

"Don't let it bother you," she begged. "Please. I'm going to
love Minneapolis, and the kids will, too."

He studied her for a moment. "I'm really sorry," he said.

"Believe me, hon—"

"I mean, about the dinner."

She stopped short. She put down her napkin. Then she rose slowly and went around the table. Looking down at him and grinning suggestively, she made her voice exaggeratedly sultry. "Listen, buster," she growled, "if I can't get to your heart through your stomach, I know a few anatomical detours that are guaranteed to increase any man's pulse rate."

It was so unexpected he burst out laughing and then joined her game. "You sure the kids're staying late at Bundy's tonight?" He leered.

"I arranged that personally."

"Then you, my lady, are about to see a few anatomical tricks of my own." And he went for her.

Laughing, she broke away. "First the dishes," she promised. She grabbed two plates and spun gracefully toward the kitchen's swinging doors.

Actually, he was relieved. Sex was the last thing on his mind. Just then he wanted to get to his television set. A news update was about to go on.

The announcer started with the incident at Myra Macon London's house. According to Myra's statement, Jeff Rader had broken into her house and attacked her husband. Later, police added, he had apparently run down and killed a guest during an automobile escape. The guest's name was Arturo Hernandez, the Republic of Mexico's youngest multimillionaire.

Hernandez—Pedabine 148, the bridge to Latin America!

This was no Soldier. This was no Helper. This was a principal figure in The Game! Good God, Watson thought, the hierarchy must be in a state of red alert now . . . and all in one day, all because of one man.

It was then that the idea emerged. It made such perfect sense that Ralph Watson couldn't stifle a soft, joyous whoop. Certainly, that was it. He'd always known he was one of the most gifted of all Pedabines. Others knew that, too. But he'd been misused, wasted. And his resentment had finally been expressed. Now if Jesse's inevitable report should actually cause the Discipline Committee to move against him, then Jeff Rader would be his savior. It was simple—so simple and so beautiful. He would find Jeff Rader and Sandra Wilkenson! He would lead Pedabine straight to them, and in serving the organization so well, he'd not only appease the Discipline Committee, but he'd prove to everyone the justification of his discontentment! Yes, yes, yes.

He felt relieved. The enormous weight of the day's anxieties had been lifted in one brilliant moment. He slumped back into his leather armchair and grinned like a child anticipating a birthday present. Tomorrow . . . he'd start tomorrow, and there wasn't the slightest doubt in his mind that he would succeed. He was a master of ratiocination. His logic was faultless. All he'd have to do is isolate himself for an hour or so, and he would hand Jeff Rader and Sandra Wilkenson to Pedabine like two plump partridges for a Christmas dinner.

9

Santa Barbara is approximately an hour and a half's drive from Los Angeles.

As Ralph Watson formulated his plan, Jeff Rader and Sandra Wilkenson were already one third of the way there.

Except for the few clipped directions that Rader gave Sandy to get them safely to Highway 101, neither of them said anything for the first fifteen minutes of their getaway. The experience at Myra's house had left Jeff limp; he gulped air like a beached fish, struggling to regain his strength. The incident on the road had made Sandy weak; she trembled in the realization that she had actually, intentionally run down another human being.

When the silence was finally broken, Jeff's words were a question. "What made you come after me?"

"I heard the shots. They had to be for you because you'd left your gun with me. Then when they stopped getting closer, I guessed you'd made a wrong turn among the trees and would come out short of where I was."

"Good guessing"—he smiled—"but you scared the hell out of me, the way you came barreling straight down that road."

"He was right behind you, and I couldn't curve around to get him without crashing off the road. I prayed you'd jump."

"I heard the prayer." He looked at her and saw the quivering set of her mouth and the glistening tears at the corner of her eye. His heart melted. "I know how you feel Sandy," he whispered comfortingly. "It was terrible, but you did only what had to be done."

She nodded her head, but she was still unable to speak.

Later, with deliberate calm, he recounted every particular of his own terrible experience.

It took Sandy's mind off her anguish. She was appalled by the death of Gary London and the violence within the house, but at the conclusion of his narrative, she threw a glittering glance at him. She was thinking now of her daughter, Tami. "She's alive," she murmured.

"Somewhere," he said, nodding agreement, "somewhere."

Her question was quick. "What's a Pedabine?"

His shoulders jerked an eloquent shrug.

"I mean, have you heard the word before?"

"Never. But knowing it now takes us a giant step closer to who knows what."

They drove in silence for the next mile or two.

"All right, here's what we have."

"This is the way I see it."

They had spoken simultaneously.

"Go ahead," she deferred.

"No," he urged her, "you."

She smiled. Then, after a brief pause in which she collected her thoughts again, she began with a grim kind of enthusiasm. "Well, we're sure now that an organization of international kidnappers actually exists; it's apparently called Pedabine; it steals only children—for whatever reason, God knows, although it believes it's improving them through the kidnapping; it has some brilliant, accomplished people in it, all of whom have a common mark of identification—an amputated finger joint; and, somewhere, it's still holding my daughter, Tami, and maybe even Daniel Baliston. Have I missed anything?"

He stared straight ahead. His eyes squinted as he muttered the thought: "They're also murderers who seem to be making orphans of the kids they take. . . ." He saw a flash of Murray Fried's face in death. "Killers who've placed a death sentence on you and me because we're supposed to be dangerous to something that may have been shaping for more than half a century."

A pall of silence enveloped the car.

In time, Jeff continued. "Now let's see where all of this leads us: I was told that you have to be eliminated because you can

ruin *everything*. Obviously, that was a reference to the entire
Pedabine operation—an operation that includes people like the
commissioner, my publisher, and Myra Macon. But why? That
seems to be the critical question: Why have such talented, intelligent people become part of a program of child abduction?''
There was another heavy pause before he concluded, ''If we're
ever going to find out where Tami is, Sandy, I think we're going
to have to find the answer to that question first.''

The scope of what he was suggesting seemed enormous to
Sandra Wilkenson. In the darkness of the Chevy, he could actually feel her shrink a bit behind the steering wheel. He reached
over and touched her hand. ''Don't worry,'' he reassured her
with soft, but sharp-edged, determination. ''If that dentist is in
Santa Barbara, and he's connected in any way with this
Pedabine''—he had spat the word—''we'll find him. And when
we do, you can bet everything you own that before I'm finished
with him, we'll have at least part of the answer to that question.''

They came up East Cabrillo Boulevard along Cabrillo Beach.
They were at the southern edge of Santa Barbara.

''How do we keep from being recognized?'' Sandy asked.
''Michael said our pictures have been on the evening news.''

''Commissioner Durkin's being very clever,'' he muttered,
''but I don't think we'll have much to worry about here. Santa
Barbara's not only a beach city, it's an art colony as well.''

''What does that mean?''

''California beaches and art colonies are notorious for encour-
aging individuality. And when one place is both—well, you're
going to find a lot of strange people there.''

''I'm sorry. . . .'' She threw him a look of bewilderment.

''There's so much weird activity, involving so many oddballs,
what usually develops is a general indifference. What I'm saying
is that most people in places like Santa Barbara don't even notice
each other, let alone perfectly straight-looking strangers.''

She nodded her understanding. ''I hope you're right,'' she
murmured.

He grinned. ''I'm never wrong. I thought I was, once, but I
was mistaken . . . and that was enough to make me a very, very
cautious man.''

She smiled at his playfulness. Nothing more was said.

They searched for twenty minutes before Jeff selected a thirty-unit, cabin-style motel, two full blocks from the beach.

It was February and off season; VACANCY flickered invitingly in yellow neon under large blue letters that identified the place as the SEAGULL MANOR.

Sandy parked the Chevy at a distance from the office, deep in the cover of tall oleanders.

"Slip over to my side," Jeff whispered. "Then lie down and pretend you're asleep."

As she followed his instructions, he started toward the dimly lit office. On the way, he rumpled his hair and pulled his shirt collar askew.

It was 11:15 now. The motel management appeared to be asleep for the night. The door was locked. Only a faint light glimmered inside. But the night buzzer glowed clearly within a black-and-white plastic guard, and Jeff pressed heavily upon it.

Soon a door within the office opened. A bleary-eyed old man emerged, tying a rumpled flannel bathrobe. He shuffled to the office door and opened it. But he kept the screen door between them locked. He squinted at Jeff through thick glasses.

"Good evening." Jeff made his tone apologetic. "My family and I just got in from San Francisco. Saw your vacancy sign. Sorry to bother you at this hour, but we're bushed."

The old man unlocked the screen door. He pushed at it to allow his customer to enter. At the same time, he flipped a wall switch. The small room exploded with blinding light. "No need to apologize," he wheezed. "That's why we have a night bell."

Jeff entered. He winced at the attack on his eyeballs.

The attendant went behind the counter. He readied a registration card. "How many in your family?"

"Four . . . two kids, my wife, and myself."

"Y'gotta speak up. I'm a little hard o' hearin'."

Jeff smiled and repeated his answer a little louder.

"Got a cabin with two king-size beds," the old man said.

"If it's off in a corner, it'll be perfect."

"Corner . . . corner . . . let's see. Yep, got that, too. Cabin fourteen." He took a key from a panel of hooks. "How long you planning to stay?"

"One night. We're on our way to San Diego. Visiting my folks."

The manager looked at the registration card. "Timothy

Waddell.'' He pronounced it Waddle. "That'll be thirty-six dollars plus tax, Mr. Waddle.''

"Sure thing." Jeff pulled folded bills from his pocket.

The manager looked from the money to his face. His expression became pained. "Don't you have a credit card?" he wheezed.

Jeff's heart jumped. If he were to use a credit card, the name wouldn't coincide with his motel registration. He shook his head with a pleading weariness. "It's in my suitcase in the trunk of the car. What's wrong with cash?''

"Nothing, 'cept we put ours away for the night an' I won't be able to give you change."

Jeff nodded understandingly. "That's all right. You'll give it to me in the morning before we leave, okay?" He put two twenties on the counter.

"Okay by me if it's okay by you." Then the old man stopped abruptly and looked directly into Jeff Rader's eyes. His brows creased as though he were trying to pull something to the surface of his memory. "You ever stay here before, Mr. Waddle?"

Jeff tensed. "First time," he answered. "Why?"

"You look familiar, like I seen you before."

Rader forced an interested grin. "That's funny, I've seen you before, too.''

"You have?"

"Absolutely. You ever been up to San Francisco?"

"Not in fifteen years."

"Well, I've seen you before . . . and in San Francisco, too."

"I must have a double then."

"Maybe." Rader smiled. "Maybe we all do."

"Maybe we do"—the old man chuckled—"maybe we do. Well, have a good night's rest." And yawning, he followed his guest to the door to lock up once more behind him.

In cabin 14, Jeff Rader turned to Sandy Wilkenson and announced, "He recognized me, but he couldn't put it together."

"Who?"

"Either the owner or the manager."

"Should we leave?"

"No, I think it's all right. He'll go back to bed and forget all about it until he sees another newscast or reads a paper. We're safe for a while, at least—and, besides, after what's happened today, if we don't get some rest now, we're not going to be worth a damn tomorrow."

She was standing between the beds.

In the soft light of the room's lamp, he saw a tremor of concern flicker across her lovely face. It touched him. She had come through this horrendous day magnificently. In the whorls of extraordinary danger and adversity, she had been dependable, strong, resourceful. But now in the relative safety of the motel cabin, she was unable to conceal her fears. In that brief quiver of eyebrow and mouth, she had revealed a touching vulnerability. It affected him profoundly.

She realized how clearly he had seen her concern. She sank to the edge of the bed. Her hands lay on her lap, palms up. She looked absently at them. "I'm sorry," she whispered.

He went to her and sat opposite her on the other bed. "For what?" he asked quietly. "For being human?"

She looked up. Her eyes were misty with tears. "You've been so marvelous, and here I am . . ." The words trailed off.

He took her hands. "Here you are," he concluded with supreme tenderness, "a woman with more raw courage than an army of combat veterans, who feels she's failed me now because she's allowed herself a fleeting expression of anxiety. Well, if it's any consolation, I'm plenty anxious myself, so I guess I've failed you, too."

Her protest was quick and strong: "Oh, no!"

He grinned at her. "That's exactly what I mean."

She understood. Her responding smile was tinged with shy embarrassment, an embarrassment that dissolved steadily in the intimate locking of their eyes. "You're a very special man," she whispered. And she leaned forward to place her warm, moist mouth upon his lips.

He felt with infinite delight the soft tip of her tongue against his mouth. He touched it ever so lightly with his own.

The kiss was a suspended moment. It lasted only a brief while. It didn't sweep into lover's passion. It didn't explode into lustful groping. Anything more would have sullied it. Anything more would have perverted the moment and embarrassed both of them.

When they parted, they held each other in a warm, smiling gaze. Jeff clasped her hands between his own.

"And you," he whispered, "are a very special woman."

*   *   *

It was 5:30 A.M.

Half a mile away from the Seagull Manor Ralph Watson was slipping quietly from his bed. He was trying not to disturb his wife. They had enjoyed an evening of wonderful lovemaking, one of the most exhilarating in their long and happy marriage. His mind had been free of worry. She had sensed his happiness and responded like a newlywed. He would have liked to remain in bed. He enjoyed the pleasant weight of her knee upon his thigh. But there was an important task to complete, and comfort had to concede to priority.

He slid his leg from under his wife's knee. The movement caused her to stir, but he gentled her back to sleep with a soft sound and a tender touch of her hair.

After donning a Japanese-cut bathrobe, he went into the large bathroom and washed his face vigorously. He needed to be as alert as possible.

From the bathroom he went directly to his den. He switched on a light near his favorite leather armchair. Then, after easing gently into the chair, he placed his elbows on the armrests and cathedraled his fingers under his chin. He was ready. Thinking could begin.

First, he identified his facts and organized them into a sequential pattern. Next, he culled the insignificant details from the obviously important points. Finally, he structured the remaining considerations into a network of logical segments.

Point one: I was her daughter's dentist, and she hired a private investigator to find me; the private investigator was eliminated and his body (foolish error) was left in Santa Barbara; Sandra Wilkenson then appeared in California. Conclusion: She may have come west to complete the job of the private investigator.

Point two: There were two direct attempts to eliminate her yesterday; a newsman was with her both times; both attempts failed and resulted in Pedabine soldier deaths; she couldn't have effected that by herself. Conclusion: The newsman must have helped her and may now be committed to her objectives.

Point three: The newsman appeared at Myra Macon's house; he was chased but he escaped; another Pedabine was run down during the escape. First conclusion: She may have been with the newsman, aiding him. Second conclusion: They have transportation.

Point four: They're being hunted by the police, the Secret Service, and Pedabine; they do not burrow in or try to leave the city; instead, quite brazenly, the newsman appears at a Pedabine house. Conclusion: He is an assertive, aggressive man, a hunter even as he is being hunted.

Now, reversing the conclusions: I have an aggressive hunter with transportation, assisting someone who, in all likelihood, came west to complete the job of her private investigator. Undoubtedly, if the reporter is committed to her, he will assume the lady's objective, too. Since Sandra Wilkenson suspects the investigator had narrowed his pursuit of me down to the Santa Barbara area, the newsman will want to follow that lead. First conclusion: He will come to this city. Second conclusion: Since she's probably with him, she'll probably come, too.

Point five: Both of them are wanted by the Los Angeles police; since they have not turned themselves in, they're obviously trying to avoid apprehension; since they have a Santa Barbara lead, and since their experience at Myra's house has intensified police efforts to find them, they will probably believe Santa Barbara to be much healthier for them now than Los Angeles. Conclusion: They will want to leave the threat of apprehension in Los Angeles *as soon as possible* for the prospect of finding me in Santa Barbara.

Now, if this is correct—assuming they had nothing else to keep them in Los Angeles—and they left Myra's house last night at 9:00 P.M., according to the police report, then, because it takes an hour and a half to drive here from Los Angeles, they arrived in Santa Barbara at about 10:30. If I allow another fifteen minutes for evasive "side-street" driving until they reach the freeway, that will bring their arrival time to 10:45 P.M.

Once here, they'd need a place to stay for the night. They'd want to rest after their day's ordeal. So they'd either stay with friends or find a motel. If they're with friends, I'm finished. But in all probability they'd want a motel because one, they'd be reluctant to jeopardize the welfare of their friends, and two, they'd feel fairly safe taking a room at an hour when clerks are tired and not very attentive.

Now, what kind of place would they want? Something special. One not too large where many people could see them or too small where they'd stand out. A medium-size motel in an unobtrusive location. Very important point.

But where? Well, coming from Los Angeles, they would enter

Santa Barbara from its southern end. So the southern end is where they would probably look first.

Now, if I allow another fifteen to thirty minutes for them to find exactly what they need, that would mean they'd have signed into a motel—under an assumed name, no doubt—at 11:00 or 11:15 last night . . . and, in all probability, they're no more than a couple of miles from me at this very moment.

Pleased with his reasoning, Ralph Watson then crossed from his armchair to his desk. He opened a Santa Barbara Yellow Page Directory to the word "Motels." Quickly but carefully, he wrote down the name of every motel to be found in the southern end of the city. Next, he eliminated those that were directly on the beach or in prominent locations. After this, he scanned the Yellow Page advertisements and, guided by them, he drew a line through each name on his list that seemed to be either a particularly large or an especially small establishment. He was left with sixteen names. These he separated into two columns: one, under a capital *A*, listed the remaining advertised motels; the other, under a capital *B*, listed the unadvertised motels.

There were six names in column A. He planned to call them first.

He began to dial. His approach would be the same for each call. "Good morning. This is Sergeant Crowley of the Santa Barbara Police Department. I'd like to speak to whoever was on duty at eleven o'clock last night, please."

He learned there were no late check-ins at the first two motels on his list.

At the third, he was informed that an elderly man and his wife had registered at 12:45 A.M.

On his fourth try, a wheezing voice greeted him with: "Seagull Manor."

And his opening speech produced: "You're talking to him, Sergeant. Name's Sam Meadly."

"Morning, Mr. Meadly. Sorry to bother you at this hour, but we're doing a motel survey as part of an investigation, and I wonder if you can tell me if you had any late check-ins last night."

"Matter of fact, we did. Man and his family from San Francisco."

"How late did they come in?"

" 'Bout eleven fifteen."

"Did they ask for a corner room or one out of the way?"

"We have cabins, Sergeant."

"Sorry. Did they ask for a corner cabin?"

"Oh, yeah. Everyone likes to be off to the side. Gives 'em a chance to sleep late. Less morning noise there. Gave 'em number fourteen."

"How old were they, Mr. Meadly?"

"Only saw the man, Sergeant. He was in his late thirties, I'd guess." Then, suddenly, the old man became concerned. "Say, he ain't wanted for anything, is he?" he demanded. "I don't want any trouble around my place—"

"No trouble, don't you worry," Ralph Watson cut in. "We're looking for a couple of teenagers from Bakersfield, not a family from up north. Sorry to have bothered you, sir, and thank you for your cooperation."

"Pleased to have helped, Sergeant, pleased to have helped."

Ralph Watson called the twelve remaining motels on his lists. There had been late registrations at only two other establishments. In both the guest descriptions obviously did not fit either Jeff Rader or Sandra Wilkenson.

The telephone receiver lay nestled in its cradle. He tapped the instrument absently with a fingernail as he arranged his final thoughts. He kept returning to his fourth call. His fourth call: *Seagull Manor. Southern Santa Barbara, off the road, medium-size motel, 11:15 registrant. Man in his late thirties requests corner cabin . . . says he has a family, so that means he's not alone. This seems to have all the ingredients, but could it be a family from San Francisco? Could it really be that? Yes. . . . But it could also be a ruse, an effort to deceive, to cover tracks. . . . Yes, this reporter would, he would. . . . He'd be a fool not to, and events have shown him to be anything but a fool.*

Pedabine 23 allowed a grin of intense satisfaction to spread slowly across his face. *Yes, that has to be it.*

"Cabin fourteen," he whispered. "Gotcha!"

It was 6:18 A.M. now.

The process of locating his prey had taken Ralph Watson exactly forty-eight minutes.

She had fallen asleep almost immediately. Slipped under the covers and turned on her side with a sweet, languorous sigh. The Seagull Manor was an outpost of heaven, she was sure. The bed must certainly have been crafted by angels. For one swift minute, random pictures had bombarded her closed eyelids, and a thought had danced tirelessly through the kaleidoscope of images: *So much has been learned in just one day . . . and all because of him*.

There had been a flash of his warm gaze. And one of the curve of his lips.

Then a startling realization: For three years, no man had shared a bedroom with her. Not since Adam. And there she was now with someone she had known only one day. A stranger. But a very unique stranger. One with whom she felt perfectly safe, completely in harmony. And that really made him no stranger at all, didn't it?

The thought soothed and relaxed. It prompted the last flashing image: a man's hand reaching for her waiting, naked breast. Jeff's hand, she had realized. Wish projection. Shameless. But she smiled slyly at it just as the quiet blackness had overtaken her.

Jeff, too, had surrendered completely to sleep. And for not too different reasons. In his maelstrom of bizarre experiences as a newsman, he'd never known any as awesome as today's. Death had hounded him like a demented banshee. His nervous system had been assaulted without letup. His energies drawn almost to the point of bankruptcy. He had become enmeshed in a Pandoran nightmare. And all because of one person—that woman in the opposite bed. That woman. He should have resented her. But what was there about her that made him quiet at her glance? Yesterday he had felt wrenchingly sick in his soul. Today he had felt gloriously happy in her kiss. Something unusual was happening to him. Unusual and wonderful. But death and violence were no nutrients for the growth of that special feeling. If he and she should ever work their way through this labyrinth of terror, if he and she should ever survive this endless agony, then he'd find it very easy to love this lady, he told himself . . . to love her with an intensity and fullness that only yesterday he'd believed impossible to feel again.

His own images had drifted and tumbled through that minute before welcome sleep claimed him.

The night wore Mercurial wings.

It was 6:18 A.M. now.

Ralph Watson was preparing his next move.

And Jeff Rader and Sandra Wilkenson were still wrapped in the deep and unsuspecting sleep of the just.

Ralph Watson removed his Japanese-style bathrobe. Standing straight, he thumped his flat stomach with the palms of his hands and grinned broadly. He felt marvelous. Safe and vindicated. He was certain he had located Jeff and Sandy. However, before reporting to the Primary Council, he'd have to verify his conclusions. It would hurt him badly if he were to inform Pedabine of the whereabouts of Rader and Wilkenson and then be proven wrong. There was still a remote possibility that the residents of cabin 14 were a family from San Francisco.

It was 6:20 now. The city wouldn't be functioning fully for another two hours. Until then, drained by their experiences, his victims would probably allow themselves the luxury of much-needed sleep. While they were asleep, he'd find his verification. It would be in their car. The car would tell him everything.

He had to get moving now. Quickly, he slipped into a pair of shorts. Pulled up white athletic socks. Tied the laces of his Adidas.

The Seagull Manor consisted of separate cabins; he had decided against driving right in. Too conspicuous that way. Instead, he planned to park down the street and walk in confidently. Morning athletes are so common in Santa Barbara, he'd arouse no interest at all. Hurriedly, he finger-combed his full white hair. Then he picked his keys off the dresser. They jangled. He glanced at his wife. She was still sleeping soundly. Good. He wanted it that way. Get there and back without waking her. He'd telephone Jesse immediately, and then ease back into bed and make love one more time to this wonderful woman. What a great life it suddenly was! Pedabine would have to recognize his value after all. He had the feeling that things were finally turning around for him. Everything was going to be beautiful in just a few short minutes. Silently he thanked Jeff Rader and Sandra Wilkenson for coming into his life.

He was out of the house now, settled behind the wheel of his Peugeot and gunning toward the motel, only five blocks away.

He was there in minutes. He parked about a hundred yards from the entrance. He snapped all the locks except for the one on the driver's side. Then, leaving his key in the ignition, he slid out from behind the wheel. For a moment he thought of crossing behind the motel and coming in from the rear. But he rejected the idea. If anyone was to see him, it might look as though he was sneaking around. No. The best way was the bold way. Always walk into a place as though you belong, he reminded himself. So he strode briskly onto the grounds and past the office like a guest returning from an early-morning workout. His eyes, though, were taking in the numerical order of the cabins. He found what he was looking for quickly—14—off in a corner.

His heart did a sharp little trip; a car was still there.

Now it was truly gamble time. If he had actually found Jeff Rader and Sandra Wilkenson, he was safe only if they were still asleep. He had to examine their car, and he couldn't go skulking around. He'd have to walk right up to it, look speedily and effectively for what he had in mind, and get out of there fast.

He took an especially deep breath and shifted his gait directly toward Mike Gavin's 1984 Chevrolet.

Inside cabin 14, a clock was working. It was located in Jeff's brain. Its alarm had been going off automatically at 6:30 for years now. Not even exhaustion or the warm feeling of love could reset its deeply imbedded mechanism in one day. At 6:28, just as Ralph Watson had shifted toward the car, that alarm was clicking into the preliminary stirrings of consciousness. Jeff turned on his back, eyes still closed, the blanket of sleep thinning over his senses.

Pedabine 23 was only yards away now. He knew exactly what he was looking for. One of two things: either some indication that this was, indeed, a traveling family, or something to identify the car's origin. He reached his objective. Looking through the windows, he felt his breath catch excitedly. The inside was clean. No personal articles. No food wrappers, cups, bags. None of the multitude of things with which a family—especially one with two children—would ordinarily litter a car while traveling.

Light filtered through Jeff Rader's closed eyelids. He didn't fight it. For a moment he wallowed in the marvelous feeling that a good night's rest can produce. Then he remembered. He turned his head quickly and looked at Sandy in the nearby bed. She was still asleep, on her back, her left arm curved over her head, her lips invitingly parted. Rader smiled at the sight of her.

Only a few feet away, Ralph Watson walked around to the rear of the car. He tilted his body and peered downward. What he found jolted him. There it was! Big as a promise and twice as deadly. A chromium license-plate frame. And it bore the telling identity of the dealer's name and place of business. On top: *Bud's Chevrolet*; on bottom: *Santa Monica*. And as if this wasn't verification enough, there was also the unexpected gift of a bumper sticker lauding the *Voice* as L.A.'s leading newspaper, an old retired editor's gesture of undiminished loyalty. Everything was going so right for him! Ralph Watson wanted to shout his joy. But he controlled himself and, instead, merely threw a happy glance at the number on the cabin's door. "Gotcha, my friends," he murmured, "*gotcha*!"

"Need some help, mister?"

The voice rang with authority, and the question was so unexpected, it stabbed into Pedabine 23's brain like a needle. He jerked erect and spun around in momentary confusion.

"What? Huh? Oh . . . uh . . . no . . . no, I'm fine, thank you, fine."

Inside the cabin, Jeff Rader heard the wheezy question and the uncertain response. He jumped to the window and pulled a crack in the drawn drapes. He recognized the manager at once. But who was that tall, distinguished-looking man in the jogging outfit? The sound of voices immediately outside his cabin had been reason enough for alarm. But even more reason for concern lay in what he had heard. His trained reporter's ear had listened to thousands of answers in his long career; it was able to recognize evasiveness in an instant. Now it had heard uncertainty and insincerity sounding as loud as a Klaxon. That startled him. What could that stranger have been doing to cause him to respond with such sudden and obvious apprehension? The thought stung Rader into action. His senses became instantly alert; adrenaline rushed through his system; he was into his pants, socks, and shoes in seconds.

Kneeling at her bedside, Jeff touched Sandy's shoulder. "Sandy," he whispered, "wake up."

Her eyes opened instantly. She smiled at him, but the smile collapsed in the jarring urgency of his next words:

"Someone's outside. Get dressed—fast."

She leaped from the bed. She had slept in her panties and bra. It took her only seconds to get into the rest of her clothes.

All the while, from the moment he had heard the voices, Jeff Rader kept his ear tuned to the conversation outside:

"You're not a guest here, are you?"

Ralph Watson had recovered quickly. "No, I live in Santa Barbara." Now he was smiling engagingly. "Just out for my morning run." However, despite his apparent ease, he was careful to speak as softly as possible without seeming to whisper.

"I'm the manager here. Sam Meadly."

"Morning. I'm Howard Biggs."

"What were you lookin' in the car for?"

Pedabine 23's smile broadened. "Thought I'd take a shortcut through your property. Hope you don't mind."

"I don't mind that. But what were you lookin' in the car for?"

"Oh"—he chuckled—"just happened to see this Chevy. My boy's buying one exactly like it today, so I merely stopped to look at it. . . ."

"What? Speak up. I'm a little deaf. Can't hear ya."

God-damned old fool, Ralph Watson thought, but he smiled affably and repeated his explanation a bit louder. He had to get out of there. He had to get to a phone to call Jesse. He had them!

Inside cabin 14, Jeff Rader had heard every word of that exchange. It disturbed him. A sudden idea to take a shortcut? Across this particular property? On this particular morning? Past this particular cabin? Where he just happened to see a Chevy model that his son happens to be buying today? The thoughts raced through his mind as he forced Agent Milland's gun under his belt and thrust his arms into his jacket. Who was this guy? Was he alone? Was he a threat? Or had he, Rader, made a mistake? Had his ears deceived him? Could the owner of that refined voice really be telling the truth?

Fully clothed now, Jeff turned toward Sandy, expecting to see her rushing through the final movements of dressing. Instead he found her standing perfectly still, her fingers locked tightly on a button of her blouse. She was frozen by a chilling memory.

She had heard the voices, too. One of them had yanked her violently into the recent past. That soft, resonant voice. She'd never forget it. She had once told its owner, "You should have been a radio announcer. With that voice, you could sell sand in Saudi Arabia." And he had laughed appreciatively before turning his attention again to the cleaning of Tami's teeth.

"Sandy, what's wrong?" Jeff snapped.

She hurried to the drapes. She edged a side open and peered out. She turned quickly. "Jeff," she whispered, her eyes wide, "he's outside."

"Who?"

"Einberg. The dentist."

Excitement exploded within Rader. He charged across the room to the door, fumbling with the safety chain, swearing as he jerked the door almost off its hinges.

The old manager of the Seagull Manor was standing directly in his way. "Got a call a little while ago that woke me early, so I thought I'd bring over your change before—"

Jeff saw the dentist jogging now toward the driveway of the motel. He leaped past the manager, almost knocking him over. Sandy came running out after him. "The car!" he shouted, tossing keys at her as he went after the running figure.

Pedabine 23 heard that shout. He jerked around. The sight of Rader racing at him from the open doorway of cabin 14 sent him charging for the motel entrance, a man possessed.

Jeff came pounding across the property. "Get him," he kept repeating to himself. "Get him . . . get him . . . get him . . ."

He'd tie him in knots if he had to, but he'd find out now what this madness was all about! He swung past the office and turned onto the street. Only a few yards ahead, Ralph Watson sped over the asphalt like a sprinter half his age.

But Rader was gaining. He heard his breath quickening; felt his legs pumping, his arms swinging, his whole body charged and alive. He was gaining. He saw it. He knew it. He had him!

He hadn't anticipated the car.

Idiot! he cursed himself. Stupid, damned idiot! He had swallowed the whole jogging thing. He had believed the dentist had been entirely on foot. Now when he saw him pull at the door of the Peugeot, his heart sank. He poured on a final burst of speed, drawing strength from he didn't know where. He'd get him before he could start the engine. He'd get him!

Pedabine 23 fell into the driver's seat. His heart felt like bursting. His breath came in painful gasps. He yanked the door shut and hit the lock exactly as Jeff Rader lunged at the outside door handle.

The engine turned over in a second. With Rader hanging on and beating at the window, Watson floored the accelerator and raced down the narrow, quiet street.

Jeff went spinning. He fell. Rolled. Slammed into the wheel of a parked car. And all the while his thoughts were screaming: *Sandy . . . Sandy . . . where the hell are you, Sandy?*

As if in answer, Sandy came careening around the entrance of the motel. Jeff had tossed the keys at her wildly. They had flown into the shrubbery against the cabin. She had spent anxious moments pulling desperately at bushes and plants before she had found them and as she struggled, the motel manager had been trying to stop her.

The last thing she heard him yelling as she swung the Chevy around to follow Jeff was "You got no right to ruin a man's business! I'm calling the police! I'm calling the police!"

The Chevy came down the street almost like a jet.

Jeff was on his feet in an instant when he saw it, breaking across its path in order to be able to jump into the passenger's seat quickly.

Sandy jammed on brakes.

Jeff pulled the door open and lunged into the car. They were off even before he could get into place.

Up ahead, the Peugeot screeched into a corner turn. Barely missing a parked car, Ralph Watson tried to unscramble his thoughts as he hunched over the steering wheel. They were after him, and he was trying to lose them; that much was clear. But he didn't know what was going to be achieved if he succeeded. Even if he could alert Jesse now, they'd be gone before Pedabine could arrive. All of his deductions had gone for nothing. His hope of improving his position, ruined! Maybe he was wrong to run this way. Maybe he should just face them. Bluff it out. Impossible! These were dangerous people. Four Pedabines had been killed already because of their meddling. They had to be stopped. Jesse. Jesse. If only Jesse were there.

Sandy Wilkenson suffered no such confusion. She had only one thought in her mind: That man in the car ahead had almost certainly been involved in the abduction of her daughter; Tami was still alive; he would know where she was. She stayed on his tail like a pilot in a dogfight. Around corners. Up alleys. Across parking lots. The hour was still young; there was virtually no other traffic on the streets to get in her way. And she was closing in on him. No matter how he tried to shake loose, she held on, gaining inch by inch.

There was silence in the Chevy. Jeff said nothing. He saw the grim set of her expression. He knew exactly what was consuming her. And he knew, too, that any sound on his part would destroy her concentration. He just held tight, switching his thoughts to what he would do once he had his hands on that man ahead.

But Pedabine 23 had no intention of being caught. He had been racing away from his beachfront house, avoiding the main streets, working toward Sycamore Canyon Road and the foothills. Escape. The only thought in his mind had been escape. If he did manage it, he thought, perhaps the police would apprehend his pursuers later. After all, they were wanted by the law. But he couldn't lose them. Regardless of what he did, where he drove, they were staying right with him. Damn!

Then it suddenly occurred to him that escape was not the answer to his problem. Escape would solve nothing. Even if he should lose them and they were later caught by the police, he would still have a problem: They could do Pedabine unspeakable damage. And if they did manage to elude the law, they'd still be looking for him. He would still be exactly where he was before he had found them . . . with them *and* with Pedabine. He had been racing in the wrong direction. Figuratively and literally. He had to get back to his house. That was it! He had to lead them there. Draw them in. There in his house he had the means to survive! He pulled the Peugeot into a sharp turn and headed west.

Sandy whipped the Chevy around and went straight after him.

Pedabine 23 was less than a half block from his home when, suddenly, the sky before him split open with a brilliance that paled the early-morning sun. The air itself seemed to be ablaze, and an explosion of monumental intensity shook the entire area.

He saw it. Directly ahead. His house—atomizing, flying asunder. A huge, billowing fireball swirling and bubbling at its core like molten steel. But the color of this fire! Different. Not the pure reds and oranges of angry flame. No. Blue and green coils twisting and fusing into a bizarre and almost macabre purplish hue. He had seen that kind of brilliance only once before, but he didn't make the connection now. Now he couldn't think clearly at all. His house had disintegrated before his eyes. The horror of the sight made him slam on his brakes and screech to a desperate stop. All thoughts of Jeff Rader and Sandy Wilkenson were instantly expunged. Only one reality screamed inside his head now: *My family! God, my family!* Like a madman, he leaped from his car and ran in the direction of the blaze.

Jeff and Sandy, too, were appalled by the suddenness and intensity of the blast. As soon as they had swung into the last turn of the chase, Jeff had sensed that something was different. The careening had stopped. The evasive maneuvering had leveled into an almost straight-line run. They were heading now for a particular destination, he was sure. But where? When they had hit Carlysle Place, the ocean loomed in the distance. He could see only one house at the end of this lonely street. If they were going someplace special, that had to be it. But why were they being led there? It was a question Rader had no opportunity to consider. Now, when the sky lit up in that roiling column of purple flame and the shockwave seemed to slam the Peugeot up ahead to an abrupt stop, Jeff screamed an order for Sandy to stop.

It hadn't been necessary. She, too, had seen everything. The Chevy's brakes locked even before the words were on Jeff's lips. The car jolted and then rolled to a fast stop, swerving up against the curb.

"My God," Jeff murmured.

"Ohhhh, Lord . . ."

It was absolutely raining destruction, and Ralph Watson was running about insanely and helplessly within a slow-motion downpour of debris.

"His wife and sons must have been inside," Sandy whispered.

Something struck the dentist—a piece of door or furniture— and he went down like a blade of grass in a hailstorm.

Sudden fear gripped Sandy: What if it's killed him? I'll never learn where Tami is! She threw a glance at Jeff. He read her thought. He nodded once, and she moved her foot quickly to the accelerator. But just as she did, he grabbed her arm and snapped, "Wait."

A green sedan had burst onto the scene, seemingly out of nowhere, traveling an intersecting beachfront road. It skidded to a stop near the dentist as he rolled over and tried to get to his feet once more. A man jumped out.

Jeff was in a quandary. Less than a minute had passed between the explosion and the appearance of that car; nevertheless, firefighters and police would be there in moments; their quarry was standing again, apparently being assisted by the unexpected Samaritan of the Green Sedan. He and Sandy had to get that dentist away from here before the police could arrive, and they didn't have much time to waste. Did they dare charge in now with someone else on the scene and authority undoubtedly on the way? The sticking point was concern for that stranger. He could be injured or, perhaps, even killed if he were to get in the way.

While that thought flashed through Rader's mind, strange and angry words were erupting near the door of the green sedan.

Through his wild grief, through the chaotic numbness of having been drummed to the ground by the falling debris, Pedabine 23 saw the outlines of a familiar face sharpening before him. Jesse. His best friend, Jesse. He felt a laugh deep within his anguish. When he needed him—just when he needed him, he was there! Jesse . . . Jesse!

He fell against his Pedabine associate.

"Jesse . . . Jesse . . ." He was mumbling and weeping in misery and gratitude. "My family . . . my family . . ."

Then all at once the entire series of events locked into place. He saw a picture of shattering consequence. He shoved Jesse away. "The flame," he croaked, sweeping an arm in the direction of his devastated house, "the purple flame. . . ." He remembered where he had seen it before—*at a Pedabine demonstration*. Only Pedabine knew of it! His mind reeled. Because here was Jesse—on the scene—and there had been the flame, and that could mean only that he, Jesse, had set off the Pedabine charge. A Pedabine death charge! He had been charged to die. And that sentence could have been passed only by the Primary Council and the Father himself! But why? For what? Merely for saying he had been misused? It couldn't be. The Father would never do this simply because he had complained. Yet here was Jesse . . . and the flame . . . and the conclusions were incontestable.

Pedabine 23 now felt his resentment crest into anger and then into hatred. "He was my father," he shouted through sobs. "I loved him! I worshipped him!" As he spat his words of deformed devotion, he reached to his own throat and ripped away a delicately braided gold chain. Clutching it in his fist, he waved it angrily before Jesse's face. "I would have done anything for him," he ranted, "anything! But now you tell the Father, I'll be at the side of the Devil, waiting for him in Hell!" And he jerked around quickly and hurled the gold chain in Jeff and Sandy's direction with all the force of defiance his strength could command.

Jesse had been watching unemotionally. However, when Ralph Watson hurled the chain into the air, a look of consternation flashed across his face. "Good-bye, Ralph," he murmured quickly. "You should have stayed inside the house."

Watson saw the gun coming out of Jesse's jacket. He heard the last words as though he were in an echo chamber. Yes, he should have stayed inside the house. That would have been better than this hideous emptiness he was feeling. But he had been out trying to help his Pedabine. Out locating Rader and Wilkenson. Rader . . . Wilkenson. He had forgotten them. And they were on this street now! He'd intended to use them to save himself, but now he'd use them to destroy everthing. They'd avenge him. They would avenge him!

He lunged against Jesse just as the gun cleared the jacket. Then, turning, he charged up Carlysle Place shouting: *"The Father! The Father! Convocation! Get the Father!"*

"Move!" Jeff barked at Sandy; her foot hit the accelerator like a lead weight.

Gavin's Chevy leaped toward the sedan, the fire, the two figures.

Jeff and Sandy saw their quarry charging toward them. Heard him shouting. Saw his face explode in blood. Saw him tumbling, rolling in the gutter of Carlysle Place. They saw everything— even the cool, calm way in which Jesse had ducked behind the sedan and leveled the silencer-equipped .38 that had blown away part of Ralph Watson's head.

Jesse had seen them coming, too. He didn't know who they were. He couldn't discern details from that distance with the sun behind them. But whoever they were, they were an intrusion. He swore softly. He should have been gone from there long before this. He had triggered the electronic device from his car, believing the entire Watson family still to be asleep. Then, suddenly, almost at the moment of explosion, there was Ralph racing toward the conflagration. If Ralph had only been in the house— But then again, no regrets; it was luck to have seen him at all. Alive and free after the disposal of his family, Pedabine 23 would have become an extraordinary enemy. Well, now a car was bearing down the street. It didn't matter, though—even if its driver had seen the killing. He'd retrieve the chain—couldn't allow *that* to be found—and if it was necessary, he'd eliminate the occupant of the approaching vehicle, too.

Jeff and Sandy watched Jesse running toward them, the weapon still in his hand.

"Hold it," Jeff ordered, and Sandy brought the Chevy to a sudden stop again. "Down, fast." He pulled at her as he shouldered the passenger door open wide. Her body fell to his seat, safe below the windshield level, and Jeff slid out of the car behind the door. He had Agent Milland's gun in his hand, his wrist propped on the frame of the open window. He had seen the glint of the gold chain in the morning sunlight when Pedabine 23 had hurled it. Now it lay some fifty feet ahead of the Chevy. He didn't know what it was, but he sensed its importance because there was the dentist's killer coming for it now. Sirens sounded in the distance. The area would be flooded with people any minute. He and Sandy had to get out of there—but not without that object! He squeezed the trigger of his gun.

The crack of the bullet's impact on the asphalt only a foot away from Jesse brought a look of astonishment to the Pedabine's face. He stopped short. He dropped to a knee. His .38 came up, and four slugs spat around Jeff's exposed legs.

Rader had ducked behind the door. He was up fast. Three of his own shots went off so quickly, they could have been a cough. There was a cry. Jesse tumbled off balance. Rolled to his side. Staggered to his feet again. He'd been hit. Jeff saw him clutching his chest.

The scream of sirens was getting louder.

Jesse stumbled toward the green sedan. The highly secret detonating device was still in the car. He couldn't risk that being found. Son of a bitch! He hadn't expected this intruder to have a gun.

Rader dodged from behind the Chevy. He charged down the street and scooped up the gold chain. Then, swinging around, he raced back toward Sandy.

But Jesse had tumbled into the driver's seat of his own car and, looking up as he slammed his door, he saw Jeff clearly for the first time. *Recognition*.

The sirens were coming down Carlysle Place.

Rader was back in the Chevy. Sandy had gunned the engine, and they were heading straight for the green sedan. Behind them, fire engines were roaring in.

Jesse saw them coming. He saw the fire engines, too.

The Chevy seemed bent on collision. But ten feet from impact, Sandy spun the wheel and cut into the oceanfront street that intersected Carlysle Place—heading south, opposite to the direction in which the green sedan was pointing. At this stage of events, she had reasoned, the wounded killer wouldn't struggle to turn his car around to follow.

She was right.

Jesse stepped on the gas and raced north, weakening steadily from hemorrhaging.

Events had erupted with such force and suddenness that Jeff and Sandy'd had no chance to reason much of anything out. It had never occurred to them that Pedabine could kill Pedabine. Who the killer was, why he'd murdered Einberg were blurred thoughts. All they saw clearly was that their objective had been taken from them—and that the street would soon be glutted with firefighters and policemen. They'd had to get out of there now; that's all that mattered.

They cut in and out of the side streets, working their way to the foothills. Santa Barbara held nothing more for them, they believed. They were returning to L.A. The back roads of 192, 150, and 126 would get them to I-5, where they'd be able to lose themselves in the heavy traffic of the San Diego Freeway.

There was silence in the car. They were immersed in similar painful thoughts. Sandy felt like weeping; Jeff, like screaming. Was there no end to this killing? Every place they went death followed them like a mad scepter. This is what my Tami is part of now, Sandy told herself. And that dentist was our only hope. . . .

Rader struggled with the realization that he had put a bullet into still another human being. So easily. Where is this taking us? All at once, though, he breathed deeply. Resolution: Wherever it leads, there's no way off the path. I'll see it through now—for Murray . . . for Tami . . . for Danny Baliston. He looked at Sandy and saw her concern even in her profile. A sweet, warming emotion touched him. But mostly, he told himself, for her.

He still had the gold necklace in his hand. He looked at it now. There was a small, paper-thin disk attached to the chain. It was as large as a quarter and made of a metal he couldn't identify. It wasn't gold, he was certain, although it resembled gold. Perhaps there was a bit of copper in it. It seemed to have that burnished quality. He studied the object more closely. There was no inscription, no character of any kind. But radiating from the center were six hairlines. All irregular. Two with caterpillar humps; three with the jagged edges of lightning; one with the crenelated angles of a castle wall. It was as though the disk had been tapped internally at its radial point, and it had shattered. Yet it was perfectly smooth.

"What is it?" Sandy asked, noticing the way he had been examining it.

Jeff sighed. "I don't know." Then he thought of the man who had owned it, of the obvious anger with which he had hurled it, of his killer taking an insane chance to retrieve it. He murmured, "It's important, though. Somehow it's important." A thought struck. A connection? "Could you make out what Einberg was screaming after he threw this thing, just before he was gunned down?"

She shook her head. "Something about a father and a vacation."

"No, that was 'convocation.' For some reason, I could understand that. But are you sure about the rest?"

"Uh-huh."

"Sounded like 'bother,' to me."

"No, he yelled, 'The father . . . the father' and then what I thought was 'vacation' and then 'Get the father.' "

Rader let the words sink in. "The father," he murmured, testing their sound. "The father . . . convocation . . . get the father." They drove in silence for a mile or two.

"What do we do now?" Sandy finally asked.

Jeff felt her helplessness. The dentist had been so close! They could have had answers if he hadn't been killed. Now all they had were more questions: Why was he killed? Who was the killer? What was this disk? And was there a connection between it and the dentist's last words?

Then a light blazed suddenly within the darkness of his thoughts. He turned in his seat so that he was facing Sandy directly. He smiled comfortingly. "What do we do now?" he repeated the question. "Well, first we're going to find out exactly what this thing means." He dangled the chain and disk from a finger. "Then we're going to find out if there is a father in all of this. And finally we're going to find out just what Einberg meant by 'convocation.' "

"And do you really know how you intend to do all that?" It was asked so simply.

Jeff's smile deepened. His head bobbed slowly and evenly. "Indeed, I do, lady," he said. "Indeed, I do."

10

Blood.

It was running from two wounds: one in the side of his chest, the other in his leg. He could actually feel it sloshing inside his shoe as he moved. He tried to sit perfectly still. It was impossible; the mere act of driving required movement, and the slightest shifting of his foot renewed a sharp awareness of the sickening wetness.

Pain was commencing, too. The initial shock was wearing off.

He was slightly north of Santa Barbara now. The Pacific stretched at his left in glasslike serenity, a sardonic contrast to his own turmoil. He didn't even glance at it; his attention was entirely on his predicament. He had to get home safely. He was resolved not to pass out before his brothers and sisters could help him.

A flat, hot blade seemed to burn into his side now. He bent over in a paroxysm of pain. It brought bubbles of sputum to his lips. He clutched his side, and his hand turned wetter and a brighter crimson. The car veered dangerously, but he brought it under control again quickly. Despite the circumstances, though, he was confident he would reach home—but first his report. He had to make his report.

He pulled the green sedan onto a shoulder overlooking the ocean. His was the only vehicle there. He turned the ignition key; the engine stopped. Then he fumbled at the dashboard for a hidden release. He found it, pressed it, and dropped his hand as a section of the dashboard sprang open. Another spear of pain pierced through his side and twisted his body. When he could control himself again, he reached into the compartment and withdrew an object unlike anything in commercial use, so sophisticated, in fact, a stranger would have been totally incapable of identifying it as a telephone. He then removed a chain from around his neck. A small, thin disk, very much like gold and about the size of a quarter, dangled from it. This his blood-covered fingers finally slipped into a circular depression at the base of the instrument. He pressed the disk and turned it counter-clockwise ninety degrees. Instantly the telephone came alive with a gentle, undulating whine and soft, sibilant clicks. The sounds traversed a frequency band yet to be discovered by the general scientific community.

In a lonely, barren region of land, an eighty-foot pencil of gleaming metal rose slowly through a mountain crevice to catch these signals. Once it was in place, a strong, firm hand touched a button and established contact.

"Pedabine One."

The voice was gentle, rich with confidence.

"Father . . . it's Jesse."

"I've been waiting."

"Father, I've . . . been hurt."

A slight intake of air, a pause—and then: "What happened, Jesse?"

"The journalist . . . Rader . . . shot me."

Now an edge of knifelike coldness cut the air: "Are you hurt badly?"

"Yes."

"Did he escape you?"

"Yes . . . I didn't recognize him . . . until after."

"Can you reach safety?"

"I . . . think . . . so . . . ." The words disintegrated within a spasm of strangling pain.

"Your assignment, Jesse, was it completed?"

"Com . . . pleted."

"And the Majus X, where is it?"

"Here . . . on the seat . . . near me."

"That must not be found, Jesse."

"It won't be, Father."

The rich voice of Pedabine 1 warmed and softened again. A note of affection sounded clearly in words that were almost like a benediction: "Be careful, my son. Remember, we need you for the completion of The Game."

"I'll be careful. . . . Don't worry, Father."

In the green sedan, Pedabine 32 removed the disk from the instrument and replaced the chain around his neck. After this, he returned the telephone to its secret compartment. He closed the dashboard cover. Then he reached to his right and with a clawing motion drew the strange-looking detonating device closer to his side.

He opened the car door and eased himself out. Bent over slightly to lessen his pain, he carried the detonator to a large oak tree at the edge of the shoulder. There he knelt and unscrewed a yellow cap on the box's facing. A small red dial was exposed. He twisted this a half revolution. Then he stuffed the device within a split at the base of the tree.

Back in the green sedan, he started the engine and quickly pulled the car onto the highway again. He was five miles away when the device, the tree, and the surrounding vegetation were all instantly reduced to minute particles within a strange, roiling pillar of purple flame.

Far away from this scene, Pedabine 1 sat perfectly straight in his high-backed chair. He is one of my dearest children, he thought. Slowly, resolution squeezed his mouth into a cruel, hard line. His hands trembled on the chair's armrests. The Game is being threatened, he told himself. This *must* stop. He leaned forward and touched an intercom switch on the small table before him.

"Yes, Father," a man's voice responded.

"Emergency Primary Council meeting . . . in one hour," he stated. "The Imperative: Immediate Disposition of the Wilkenson/Rader Obstacle."

11

Jeff and Sandy pulled up before a small, nondescript diner east of Ojai. They had passed two others. This one looked right, though. There were no outside newspaper dispensers to flash their pictures before early breakfasters; it was seedy enough to discourage a more fastidious and alert clientele; and it seemed large enough to provide a pay phone.

They entered.

They were pleased by what they saw. The pay phone hung on the wall near the entrance and, in addition to being empty of customers, the place was serviced only by a Chicano short-order cook and one teenage waitress.

"Order something," Jeff murmured, going straight for the phone as Sandy slid into the first booth.

The waitress put aside her movie magazine and crossed from behind the counter with two soiled menus. "Hi," she chirped. "Want some breakfast?"

Jeff heard Sandy return the greeting and start to order. His attention then went completely to the slip of paper that he held in his hand as he dialed.

The instrument on the other end rang twice before it was answered: "Hello."

"Hello, Mr. Gavin?"

"That's right."

"I'm a friend of your brother. He gave me your number and told me I could reach him through you."

"Are you the kid?"

Jeff felt his heart ease with relief. Bless Michael Gavin, he thought, he's prepared thoroughly. "Yes," he answered.

"Good. He called once this morning and said he'd check in every half hour through the day. Where are you?"

Rader scanned the pay phone's number and recited it, reversing the last four digits as Michael had instructed.

"Stay there," he was told. "I should be hearing from Michael any minute now."

"Thank you, Mr. Gavin."

"My pleasure."

Until it was actually placed on the table, neither Jeff nor Sandy gave much thought to the breakfasts that had been ordered. Their conversation, in subdued tones, had been solely about Michael Gavin and their next moves in Los Angeles. But the sight of the eggs, the bacon, the hash-browned potatoes, toast, and coffee—and the accompanying heady aromas—aroused such intense waves of hunger, they attacked their food almost like ravenous animals. For a while, all talk stopped.

As Jeff was downing his final mouthful of coffee, the telephone rang.

They both jumped at the suddenness of the harsh jangle.

The young waitress at the far end of the counter looked up from her movie magazine and wrinkled her nose in annoyance.

Sliding quickly from his seat, Jeff mollified her with a brief: "For me."

She smiled and went back to her fantasies.

"Michael?" he asked softly as he lifted the receiver.

"How are ya, kid?" the gravel voice growled.

"Still alive."

"Well, let's keep it that way. Where are ya?"

"About an hour out of L.A."

"Tell me, was that you at the London house when he died?"

"Yes."

"I was afraid of that."

"Do you have anything?"

"A friend in the County Medical Examiner's Office told me London died of a massive coronary."

"No way."

"He also said there was a foreign substance in the body."

"What was it?"

"He doesn't know. Before it could be isolated and identified, it disappeared."

"What do you mean?"

"It dissolved. It was absorbed completely by the body."

"How could that be?"

"That's what's driving my friend up a wall, kid. It was an entirely new experience for him. It could have been a poison."

"It was."

"Then it's one that can induce an instantaneous massive coronary because that's what killed the man."

Jeff Rader was silent for a moment. "Do you have anything else?" he asked.

"Spoke to Anthony Duello, the detective who was originally guarding Sandy at the hotel. The two guys who relieved him? They were legitimate. Real Secret Service men. And I found out later, the one who went out the window had a missing finger joint, too."

"I expected that," Jeff responded.

"Mother of God," Gavin expostulated, "what is this all about?"

"Tell me"—Jeff lowered his voice and cupped the mouthpiece, turning his back to the waitress—"does the word Pedabine mean anything to you?"

"What?" An odd little hitch twisted the response, as though something special and long-buried had been touched.

Rader caught it. His stomach twitched. "It *does?*"

"Pedabine?"

"That's right."

"I-I don't know, kid. . . . There's something . . . I've heard it before, I know, but . . . wait a minute . . . wait . . . wait. Oh, sweet Jesus!"

"What is it, Michael?"

"I think I have something, kid. I'll be damned, I think I do! But I have to check it first." The old editor's words were rushing now. "Where are you going to be? What're you going to do next?"

The fervor was contagious. Jeff's pulse raced. He had difficulty keeping his voice low and controlled. "We're coming back to L.A."

"Are you crazy?" Gavin cut in. "The whole Los Angeles police force is looking for you."

"I know."

"All right, then, listen to me," the gravel voice insisted. "I'm driving a rented car. I want you to have it."

"Why?"

"A lot's happened to you since I saw you last—isn't there a chance someone's seen you in my Chevy?"

Instantly, Jeff thought of the events at the Seagull Manor. He remembered what Sandy had recounted of the manager's anger and surmised the old man could have informed the police, offering descriptions that would certainly have included the car. "That's right," he acknowledged softly.

"Then you be especially careful until twelve o'clock," Gavin advised somberly. "Around that time, go to the shopping center on Pico and Overland. You'll find a maroon, '84 Ford LTD in the center parking row, facing the supermarket. Leave my Chevy there and take the rental; the keys'll be in the ashtray."

"Thanks, Michael."

"No thanks, kid. We've gotta minimize risks if we're ever going to get to the bottom of this mess."

Jeff felt a flush of affection. The seriousness of the editor's statement had been tempered by the pronoun *we*. Michael Gavin was reaffirming his commitment.

"Gotta go now, kid," he rushed. "Keep calling."

"As often as I can."

They hung up simultaneously, each imbued now with a spirit of excitement: Gavin was onto something, something undoubtedly important, and Rader was equally certain about his own next move.

Jeff smiled faintly as he stood by the table and waggled fingers at Sandy in a "let's go" gesture.

She saw the look of expectancy in his eyes; her lovely face broke into a warm and eager grin.

Sandy turned the Chevy for their approach to Interstate 5.

"I want you to tell me about Tami," Jeff said suddenly.

She glanced at him quickly before returning her attention to the execution of the turn. The request had come as a surprise; they had hardly mentioned the child since Sandy had first begged his help. Now he was asking about Tami at the very instant that she,

Sandy, was thinking of her. For a moment it made her feel even closer to him.

"What would you like to know?"

"From what you've already told me—the way she played in the hospital, the vocabulary she used—I suspect she is an exceptional child."

It didn't escape her: she recognized Jeff's use of the present tense. She smiled appreciation and touched his hand. "Yes," she agreed warmly, "she is."

He took her fingers and rubbed them. "That's not a mother talking, is it?"

"No"—she grinned—"she really is. She started to speak full sentences when she was one and a half; she could read on the fifth-grade level at three, and at four, just before she was kidnapped, her IQ tested at one seventy-eight."

Rader absorbed the information silently, nodding his head in short, slow movements.

"You said she was going to school in Washington. It couldn't have been a public school; she was too young at the time."

"That's right. It was the Pestalozzi Day School for Gifted Children."

"And is that where her IQ was tested?"

"Yes, why?"

Jeff raised a hand, waving off the query. "Why did you send her to the Pestalozzi Day School? Why that particular one? There are certainly other private programs in Washington for the gifted preschooler."

"It was highly recommended."

"By whom?"

Two words. Two simple words, but they were like a random shot that inexplicably hit dead center. Sandy gasped with sudden realization; Jeff looked at her, his eyebrows raised.

"The dentist," she said in mild shock. "Einberg, the dentist."

"Now, that's interesting," Rader murmured. "All right, let's see where this goes: When did Tami first visit him?"

"About nine months before she was kidnapped."

"How many visits in that time?"

"Five . . . six."

"In only nine months, isn't that odd?"

"I-I don't know. He said she had problems."

"Why did you take her to him in the first place? Had she been complaining?"

"No, it was for a checkup."

"And why Einberg?"

"His practice was exclusively with children. I was told he was a magician with children."

"By whom?"

Again, bull's-eye!

Sandy's reply was like a short fuse on a bomb. "By . . . Everett Frazier," she whispered.

Jeff Rader jerked as though he had been hit. "Everett *Frazier*?" he repeated incredulously.

She had just named the Vice-President of the United States.

When the dust of surprise had settled and they were both able to breathe evenly again, Jeff continued his probing in more somber, cautious tones. "How did it happen? How did the Vice-President of our country come to recommend a particular dentist? What was it, a casual reference to a group he was addressing? A general remark? Or did he make the recommendation to you personally?"

"We were at a small State Department dinner. The Vice-President was there," Sandy began. "Adam and he had met at a briefing a week earlier, so they knew each other. I was introduced, and we exchanged only a few words at the time. But later that evening, while Adam and I were talking with Senator Ferguson, he came over and joined us. The conversation was very light. I remember the Vice-President saying he refused to discuss anything of governmental importance that night. And we all laughed and agreed. So we talked about everything else—the Kennedy Center, restaurants, traffic on Pennsylvania Avenue—and eventually the conversation got around to children. He had just become a grandfather for the second time. He was very proud. Like most grandparents, he was sure his grandchildren were the most beautiful, the most intelligent girls in the world. Well, Adam couldn't let that go by, so he told him about Tami."

"Did he seem particularly interested?" Jeff interrupted.

Sandy thought for a moment and then recalled: "Not at first. At first he merely laughed and exchanged boasts." Her tone changed. "But he did become interested when Adam bragged about Tami's reading ability. Then he stopped talking about his grandchildren for a while and began to ask questions about her."

"Like what?"

"Oh, like whether she's creative, what kind of vocabulary she has, if she's interested in a wide range of subjects."

"How did the dentist's name get into the conversation?"

"After a few of these questions, he switched the topic to the importance of good health in a growing child and what his son and daughter-in-law were doing along that line for their children. And then, come to think of it, he more or less steered us into the subject of dental health, telling us about an extremely insidious form of mouth disease that can have consequences almost like spinal meningitis. I remember now—he stressed the fact that four-year-olds were particularly susceptible to it, and that his granddaughter had recently begun a program of preventive dental care with a man who was a magician with children. Then he urged us not to take chances and to make an appointment with the man immediately."

"Einberg."

"Exactly."

"So you and Adam became anxious and took Tami to his office, and he eventually sent you to the Pestalozzi school where her exceptional intelligence was confirmed, shortly after which . . . she disappeared."

The implication was startling.

Sandy glanced quickly at Rader, her brows puckered with incredulity. "Jeff," she said, "are you suggesting that Tami was kidnapped because she's a gifted child?"

Rader bobbed his head. "Look at it this way," he suggested. "Tami is now with the Pedabines; they chose her, and they're improving her, we were told. Well, who are these Pedabines, at least those we know so far? Harold Durkin, police commissioner of Los Angeles; Arthur Marquand, publisher of the *Los Angeles Voice*; Myra Macon London, leading feminist; Milton Einberg, dental specialist; Arturo Hernandez—who, according to the news we heard on the radio after we left Myra's house, was the youngest multimillionaire in Mexico; and now, quite possibly, Everett Frazier, Vice-President of the United States. All outstanding, all brilliant people in one way or another. And I'll bet they're interested only in outstanding, brilliant children."

A thought struck him suddenly with an impact that only the force of understanding can have. "That's it! That's what Pedabine *means*! Don't you see? *Pedagogics:* the science of education;

that's where the *peda* comes from. And *bine* means bringing things together, grouping, like in com*bine.* That's it, that's *it!* *Pedabine* is the grouping of brilliant people for the purpose of abducting and educating brilliant children!''

"What about that killer in my house? And the two agents in the hotel? And whoever else has been doing the killing over the years? Are these murderers brilliant?''

"Maybe there's a wing of goons just for the dirty work,'' Rader shot back. "Or maybe they were brilliant, too, and just assigned to the dirty work by the organization. We don't know; it's possible, though.''

"I suppose so,'' Sandy conceded. She felt excitement welling. "All right, let me try something: We went up to Santa Barbara to look for Einberg. He had no way of knowing we were coming, yet there he was at our cabin early in the morning. How did he know we were there? How did he find us before we could even get started looking for him?''

"I'm listening,'' Jeff prompted.

"Well, if what you're saying about Pedabine brilliance is true, isn't it possible that he could have done it just by thinking? Just by sitting in his house and thinking?''

"What do you mean?''

"You know, like a twentieth-century Sherlock Holmes. . . . Couldn't he have figured out what we intended to do and exactly where we were without budging from a chair?''

The question was astonishing. If the answer was *yes*, they were up against people with truly awesome capabilities. Neither one uttered that frightening thought.

Silence.

In time, Sandy spoke again: "All right, he found us. But why was he there? Why did he go through the trouble? Certainly not to speak to us. If he'd wanted that, he wouldn't have run away. So he was probably just checking us out—checking to make sure we were in that cabin at all. But for what reason? And for whom?''

Their probing, an unbroken volley of questions-answers-questions-answers, soon resembled a sizzling tennis match. They didn't know why the dentist had been killed, but they recognized that they were in conflict with an organization whose disciplined members not only destroyed themselves, as that hit man had done in Sandy's house, but killed their associates as well. Life, apparently—even of their own kind—was of secondary importance to some "higher" purpose. To the organization itself? To its leadership? To some goal? Or perhaps to all three?

One thought suggested another, and they went back to their narrow escape from the Century International. There was something else.

"I've been troubled," Jeff confessed, "ever since I killed that agent in the hotel."

"I know," Sandy commiserated.

"Not only by the fact that I shot him," Jeff hastened to add, "but by the fact that he didn't shoot you."

Her expression shaped a question.

"Consider this," he explained. "There he was, wounded, trying with his last strength to hurl you through a window. But he had a gun. Well, if he wanted you dead, why didn't he just shoot you?"

"Because he'd probably been ordered to use the window—"

"Exactly," Jeff cut in. "Apparently these people follow orders. They follow them slavishly, regardless of changing circumstances."

"Thank God they do," Sandy breathed.

Jeff grinned and agreed with alacrity. "No argument from me there." But he tucked that Pedabine conclusion into a corner of his mind, feeling that it just might come in handy soon.

12

Morning
Friday, February 3, 1984

Morning
Friday, February 3, 1984

Pedabine 1 had left his room shortly after calling the emergency meeting of the Primary Council. There was something he wished to investigate personally before joining his council colleagues. He walked with long, quick strides down a wide, brightly illumined, tubular corridor. Soft, padded slippers muted his footsteps on the steel deck. His velvet robe rustled gently over the subliminal hum of air-control machinery.

He was a man of only average height, but he appeared much taller. His posture was straight; his leonine head with its mass of wavy gray hair sat securely on a sturdy, erect neck; his body was lithe and strong, and he moved with a quickness and certainty that belied his age.

Electric beams slid corridor doors open before him as he walked; trusting them completely, he never slackened his pace.

Whoever he passed greeted him with warmth and great deference: "Good morning, Father . . . Be well today, Father . . . Good wishes, Father . . ." Though there was absolutely nothing of a religious nature to the environment, the salutations had a ring of the clergy to them. And he always smiled and bobbed that impressively maned head in respectful acknowledgment.

He had made turns at intersections, taken an elevator to another level, climbed a half flight of stairs. Now he reached a thick glass wall at the end of a short hallway. A section of the wall consisted of a swinging door. Near the top of the door in blue-and-gold lettering was the legend A-7. Under that in slightly smaller print were the words RUDIMENTARY PHYLOGENESIS.

He stopped, clasped his hands behind his back, and studied the room on the opposite side of the wall.

It was a square room—thirty by thirty feet—with a high ceiling, radiant but soft lighting, an admixture of lively colors, and a strange compatibility of sterile machines and warm furnishings. Lining the walls were computers, word processors, audiovisual communication devices, and electronic duplicating instruments of all kinds. But in the center of the room, small armchairs, tables, and desks formed an oasis of irresistible charm. It was called the Meeting Place. Students and teachers hurried there to relax and to share their discoveries.

They were there now: six children between the ages of four and ten, jabbering animatedly among themselves and to their two instructors before starting their morning studies. All were too preoccupied to notice the presence of their Father.

Pedabine 1 observed their activity. A smile pulled at the corners of his mouth. So much energy, he thought, so much joy. Then he moved toward the wall, severed the electronic beam, and sent the glass door gliding open.

A chime rang as he entered the room. All eyes went in his direction. Immediately students and teachers jumped to their feet and faced him, grinning shyly, waiting respectfully.

"Good morning, children," he breathed when he stood before them.

Even the teachers joined the unison response: "Good morning, Father."

He smiled at a boy of ten. "And how are you today, my son?" he asked.

"Excellent, Father." The boy beamed.

"Good! And what are you working on, Pedabine 426?"

Soft laughter rippled through the group.

Pedabine 1 raised his eyebrows. His quizzical gaze went from one grinning face to the next.

"He's 424, Father," a seven-year-old angel finally offered with a marvelous chuckle.

Pedabine 1 reacted with playful exaggeration. "Really?" he gasped. Then, turning to the ten-year-old again, he apologized abjectly. "Oh, I'm sorry, I truly am." He sighed. "I must be getting old. I can't remember all of my children anymore."

Everyone laughed, including the teachers.

"Oh, you're not getting older, Father," the ten-year-old smilingly protested. "You'll *never* get old."

Pedabine 1 grinned and stroked the boy's hair. "Well, neither will you, my child," he said. "Neither will you."

The teachers beamed at this exchange. "Tell Father what you're considering now, 424, go ahead," one of them encouraged.

The boy grew instantly serious. "Spatial conceptualization, Father."

"Do you have a project?"

"Yes, sir. I'm trying to relate existing black hole theories to concepts of interdimensional reality."

"And are you happy with this project?"

"Yes, Father."

Pedabine 1 glanced at the teacher who had encouraged the boy to speak. The instructor nodded confirmation. Pedabine 1 grinned and showered the boy with a pleased "Good for you, child. I'm sure you're going to make a marvelous contribution someday."

The boy seemed to grow inches in that approbation.

"And you, little one," Pedabine 1 said, suddenly turning his smile upon the seven-year-old angel who had corrected him earlier. "I don't remember your name either. Will you please help your aging Father?"

The angel's eyes narrowed.

The smiles disappeared from the faces of the teachers.

There was a pendent silence.

"Well?" Pedabine 1 coaxed.

"You mean, you really don't know?" the angel asked, looking at him sideways through slitted lids.

"I'm afraid not." He sighed. "Let's see, you'r-r-r-re . . ."

Silence again. He hunched his shoulders in a cute shrug of helplessness. That did it.

"431," the child exploded with a laugh.

Everyone in the room joined her laughter. However, the teachers' sounds were tinged with something else—the quick release of apprehension.

Pedabine 1 straightened with satisfaction.

"And are you studying spatial conceptualization, too?" he asked the little one.

"No," 431 answered, "I'm working on my languages first."

"Wonderful! What are you studying?"

"French, Italian, and Spanish—but I'll be studying Hebrew soon, too."

"That's excellent, child."

Everyone was pleased.

The youngster's eyes twinkled happily as they narrowed again for a chirrupy question: "You knew my name all the time, didn't you, Father?"

The answer was warm with reassurance. "Of course I did, 431. I was only playing." He beamed now at the entire group. "Well, I must really let you get back to your studies, young people. It's not a holiday, you know."

"Good-bye, Father," they purred in unison. "Thank you for visiting us today."

"Good-bye, my children," he responded. "Enjoy your minds." He left with a nod of approval toward the teachers, a gesture that brought a flash of satisfaction to their eyes.

Pedabine 1 went directly to his emergency session with the other six members of the Primary Council.

"The child is progressing well," he informed his colleagues as he opened the meeting. "She has relinquished her former identity and is evolving satisfactorily under rudimentary phylogenesis instruction. She is integrating into her new history; she has accepted me as the Father and is able now to laugh with other children and to enjoy the pursuit of her studies. I perused her skill reports: She reads now on Omega Level, Phase A; her retentive powers have already been increased to Medial Range, Third Quadrant; and in Integral and Correlative Perspectives she has scored at the Eighty-Third Degree. She will be a credit to the world someday. That is one reason we must dispose of her mother immediately. The recovery of a child of this caliber by a natural parent would be a disastrous loss to mankind."

A murmur of agreement riffled through the council members.

"But an even more important reason for disposing of her," the Father continued, "lies in her tenacious determination to locate the child. This has led, as you already know, to a situation of jeopardy in respect to our principal objectives, a situation, I must admit, that becomes increasingly threatening with each passing moment." He sighed and continued a bit sadly, "Unfortunately, Sandra Wilkenson has never been assigned Stellar Directive status.

In that respect, I believe we've erred. Had that determination been made earlier, she would surely have been exterminated years ago, and four or possibly five of your brothers would still be alive."

"Five?" a council member asked in alarm.

The Father nodded somberly. "Pedabine 32 reported this morning. He has been injured seriously by the journalist, Rader; let's pray he can reach safety."

The information produced pained and angry mutterings.

"A call for Stellar Directive status for Sandra Wilkenson," one of the members pronounced, raising a hand.

Arms went up and a chant of "aye" greeted the proscription.

Stellar Directive was Pedabine's highest execution priority. It was rarely implemented, but whenever it did pass the council, it focused the full attention of the organization upon the assassination of its subject. Usually murders by Pedabine were superintended by the Division of Clearance; under Stellar Directive, however, the Primary Council itself mandated and supervised the method and the act of killing from its conception until the very end.

"The call, of course, must include the journalist as well," another member stated. "It's he who's been more directly responsible for the loss of our brothers."

"And it's he, really, who encourages the Wilkenson woman."

"Agreed."

"Then Stellar Directive is to include Jeff Rader."

"Aye." In chorus again.

Pedabine 1 was pleased. "The council must now be particularly inventive," he coached. "Both subjects are in hiding. Our first task is to ferret them out."

"Suggestion," a member responded. As attention went her way, she offered, "The child . . . if we use the child as a lure, the woman is sure to respond."

The murmur of agreement that greeted this, however, was quickly suppressed by the Father. "I'd rather not involve 431. If for any reason she should become aware of her part in the project, reactivated memories and their accompanying emotions would undo all the wonderful progress we've recently made with her. We might have to dispose of her, too, then—and that would be a sad conclusion to the entire episode."

The council members nodded understanding.

"Besides," another pointed out, "the journalist is actually our focal point. Without him, the woman was relatively helpless; if we were to take him first, the woman, being helpless again, would undoubtedly follow.''

"Good." Pedabine 1 championed the thought. "Make the thrust of your considerations the man. I believe you're right—capture him and the woman will follow." He rose and, with what seemed like a conditioned reflex, all six members of the council stood as well. "The matter will be governed now only by your inventiveness—and by my hope that it can all be concluded before the start of our convocation," he added. "Good-bye, my children. Good thinking."

"Good-bye, Father," they chorused.

He left in a rustle of velvet robe.

13

They reached Los Angeles at 9:30. The Golden State Freeway had ingested them; all the way into the city, they were woven into a protective cocoon of cars. Traffic had raced, and they had been swept along in safety.

They left the Golden State and swung east on the Pomona Freeway, getting off in time to pick up Whittier Boulevard. This took them past the "District of the Dead," right between the New Calvary and Home of Peace cemeteries, and deep into East Los Angeles. There they turned left on Atlantic Boulevard and pulled to a stop behind two parked trucks. They were down the street from a complex of grimy, four-story, red brick buildings.

It was a dangerous place for them. Crime and violence had aroused the concern of local businessmen, and the police department had responded with increased patrol surveillance. On the freeways, Gavin's car had been just another vehicle. But in the close and littered streets of this Los Angeles area, there was the possibility that it could be as noticeable as a birthday cake on a dungheap.

Jeff cautioned Sandy. He urged her to stay close to him when they left the car. He wanted to be away from the Chevy and into a specific building quickly, just in case a squad car should suddenly cruise this particular street. A little precaution, that's all. He had no way of knowing with certainty if Mike Gavin's

Chevy had been reported by the Seagull Manor's manager. But the mere possibility that it had demanded the utmost circumspection.

They closed the doors and headed back toward a narrow passageway between two of the aged lofts. It was little more than an airshaft.

As they neared their goal, a patrol car eased around a corner and onto the street. Neither Jeff nor Sandy saw it.

But one of the two officers in the cruiser spotted them.

"See that?"

"What?"

"That guy an' broad duckin' in the alley."

"No—what about 'em?"

"I dunno. There was something familiar about him."

The driver guffawed. "That the kind o' people you know? Guys who take their broads into alleys?"

"Pull up there, Benny . . . that break between 'em two red buildings."

The driver headed the patrol car toward the indicated place.

"You sure you saw somethin'?" he asked as he braked to a stop at the entrance. "That's a very narrow alley—"

"I saw 'em, I saw 'em."

"Now why should a guy an' a broad be goin' in there?"

"Beats me."

"An' you say you know the guy?"

"I dunno; for a second there, he just looked familiar, that's all."

"Well, let's take a look, okay?"

They left their seats and unhitched the leather flaps over their guns.

Jeff had led Sandy through the litter and around a corner by the time the officers reached the entranceway. They were now in a wider area, large enough for small-truck deliveries at rear docks. They hurried past two more buildings, cut across the cobblestone road, and vanished down three tall steps into a basement alcove.

Their pursuers, though, had cleared the alley just in time to see them descending the stairs.

"Went in that building . . . third one down."

"I saw."

They walked toward the grimy structure, one sweeping a disdainful gaze over the dismal surroundings, the other keeping his

eyes fastened on the small, dark gap into which Jeff and Sandy
had disappeared.

On reaching their goal, the two cops paused to consider the
situation. The three tall steps broke into a dank cubbyhole; at the
end of it could be discerned the paint-splotched face of a heavy
metal door; above the steps, bolted into the brick of the flat arch,
was a faded sign: META-CHEM TESTING LABORATORIES. All decidedly unattractive—but all perfectly innocuous and legitimate-
looking, too.

"Whew!" the cop called Benny mumbled, wrinkling his nose.
"Christ, this place stinks."

An acrid stench of chemicals hung in the air.

"C'mon," he urged, "there ain't nothin' here. It's a lab'atory,
can't ya see? They got some business t'do in there, that's all."

"Yeah, but why didn't they go in the front? Why alleys an'
the back door?"

"What's a matter with you? Back doors are supposed t'be
used, too. That's why they're there, y'know?"

Silence.

"Yeah . . . well, maybe you're right."

"Let's get out o' here. My nose is sendin' signals to my
stomach an' my stomach's startin' to argue with my breakfast."

They turned and retraced their steps to their patrol car.

"Still . . . it don't seem right," the originator of the action
protested. "An' besides, I still say, there was something familiar
about the guy."

Behind the thick metal door, a dimly lit hallway led to a
labyrinth of corridors. Jeff led Sandy unerringly through the
maze. Past storage rooms, toilets, and an occasional gopher-hole
office. Soon they stopped before a green door with a panel of
mottled glass, across which the shadowy outline of a figure
suddenly passed.

Jeff paused, one hand on the doorknob, the other raised in a
cautionary signal. His head was cocked as he listened intently.
Seconds passed. Silence. Finally satisfied, he eased the door
open and entered.

Sandy trailed, close behind him.

It was a large, windowless room. Well lighted, though, and
properly ventilated. It walls were lined with workbenches and
shelves; all were packed to overflowing with beakers, tumblers,
test tubes, and other laboratory testing paraphernalia, and one

corner was dominated by a huge instrument not unlike an X-ray machine. A crowded room. A busy room. Yet nothing had been haphazardly placed. It was as though every inch of space had been considered, logged, and pressed into service when needed. An incredible display of organized clutter. And every item was deeply relevant to the life of the little old man now hunched over a microscope in a corner.

"Hello, Mr. Morganvelt." Jeff announced their presence.

The semibald head jerked away from the viewer. The startled expression switched suddenly to recognition, from recognition to pleasure, pleasure to concern.

"Jeffrey . . . Jeffrey, my boy . . ." He swung off his stool and hurried toward them. "What are you doing here? Are you all right? The police are looking for you. You're in trouble. What happened? Why is your picture all over the papers?"

"It's all right, Mr. Morganvelt . . . I'm fine, really, I am." Rader grinned further reassurance. "I'm sorry I startled you, but—"

"Startled?" the old man interrupted. "Who cares about startled? It's you, my boy. What's this *mishegoss* on the news? They're saying such terrible things about you and—"

"This lady," Jeff stopped him. "Sandra Wilkenson. Sandy, this is Mr. Isaac Morganvelt, the very best metallurgist on the North American continent."

"Mr. Morganvelt," she acknowledged warmly.

"Charmed." He smiled, dipping his head gallantly once in a sign of acceptance. "He exaggerates since the time I know him as a boy." Then, not to be diverted, he swung anxiously back to Jeff. "They say you've *killed* people, Jeffrey. Is that true?"

Rader's grin dissolved. "Am I a murderer, Mr. Morganvelt?" he asked simply.

"I—I never thought that, my boy." He looked at Sandy. "A *boychick* who couldn't step on a bug." He turned to Jeff again. "But what's this all about? Why are the police looking for you— for the both of you?"

"We're working on a story, Mr. Morganvelt, a special one. And there are some people who don't want us to dig any further, that's all."

"But the police—"

"Someone there, too, sir."

Grunting once, the old man slapped a palm to his cheek and slowly shook his head in amazement and dismay.

"We need your help, Mr. Morganvelt."

"Of course, my boy, but what could an old man like me do for you?"

Rader dipped a hand into his jacket pocket and extracted Ralph Watson's necklace. He offered it to the metallurgist. "What is this thing?" he asked. "What's it made of? Is it cracked or are those lines meant to be in it? Tell us everything you can about it, will you? It's important, sir—very important."

Mr. Morganvelt held the object lightly in the palm of his hand, only inches from the end of his nose. His eyes squinted behind his heavy glasses. His head bobbed speculatively. "You'll be needing this?" he asked softly.

"I think so."

"Then I'll be very careful not to damage it," he murmured as he shuffled toward a workbench. He stopped suddenly and looked at his visitors. "Such an analysis will take a little time, you know." It was an apology.

"That's all right," Rader said gently. "We'll wait."

"Good. You'll be safe here," Mr. Morganvelt vouched. "Nobody ever comes down this way."

But Mr. Morganvelt had no way of knowing about the two police officers who had followed Jeff and Sandy to his building. No way of knowing that one had continued to be nibbled by doubts. That back in the patrol car and a full twenty minutes away from the Meta-Chem complex, he'd experienced a flash of memory. He hadn't met the man, but he'd seen him, all right, and it was at *precinct headquarters*. The suspect had been there—and not too long ago either—talking to the lieutenant about a closed case. The Baliston case, yeah, that was it. He's a reporter. And then another connection: Jesus Christ, he's the one they're lookin' for! Rader . . . Jeff Rader!

It was exactly 11:28 when Isaac Morganvelt placed his palms on the edge of his workbench and shook his head in respectful wonderment. He was impressed. Deeply. He lifted the necklace and stared at its swaying disk. Amazing. Simply amazing. Picking up his pad, he glanced once more over his notes. His head bobbed. A grunt, soft and almost inaudible, passed through his nose. "Beautiful," he murmured as he turned toward Jeff and Sandy. "Absolutely beautiful."

They had been waiting in silence throughout the examination, seated behind him, immersed in private thoughts. Now both heads jerked up expectantly.

"I've been in this business a long time," the old man began. "Fifty-five years. That's a long time. And this is the first time I've seen something like this."

Their interested expressions were a cue for him to continue.

"It's an alloy." He returned the necklace to Rader. "Let me explain first. There are two kinds of tests—a wet test and a dry test. The wet test uses chemicals. For the dry test I use that machine over there. It's called a quantometer. Maybe you saw me go to it? I did a dry test because the wet one takes longer, much longer, and you're both in a hurry, I can imagine. But even with the machine, there's just so much I can tell in such a short time."

"We can appreciate that, Mr. Morganvelt," Rader encouraged him. "Whatever you can tell us will help."

"Well, what you've got there looks to me like a very unusual mixture. There's tantalum, zirconium, hafnium, gold, copper, nickel, and iron. Now, that in itself is not so strange. I mean, any kind of alloy is possible. But what is different is what we call the purity and the balance."

"What do you mean?" Jeff asked.

"I can't tell for sure in such a quick examination, but there don't seem to be trace elements—that's the leftover stuff—none at all. Always there are minor elements mixed in with the major ones, but here there seems to be nothing. Just the seven major elements I mentioned. Now that makes it a perfectly pure alloy. And I've never heard of such a thing. And what's more, all the elements seem to be exactly equal in percentage. I mean by that, there's exactly the same amount of each one. A perfect balance. And I never heard of that neither." He compressed his lips and nodded. "Beautiful," he breathed.

"The necklace, too?" Sandy asked.

"The necklace and the disk are the same alloy."

"What about the cracks in the disk?" Jeff urged.

"They're not cracks. They're wires."

"Wires?"

"Like hairs. Thinner than hairs. They all meet in the center.

They come right out to the edge. You can see that only under the microscope.''

"Would it have been difficult to make the object?" Sandy inquired.

"Well, let's say *I* don't know how it was done—first, how a perfectly pure and homogeneous alloy was created and, second, how such delicate wires were included in the process without being damaged in the heating and cooling. And they're arranged in a special way. They're in a special design." There was a moment of silence. "If you could leave it with me, I could analyze it much better and maybe tell you more—"

Jeff interrupted, "Like what?"

"Oh, I don't know. There are some very faint scratches on the disk, around the edges, like it was used for something."

"Used?"

"I'm guessing. They don't look accidental. They seem to have a pattern. Like they've been rubbed in by a specific contact."

"Wires . . . use," Sandy offered. "That makes sense."

Jeff nodded thoughtfully. "But used for what?"

The old man shrugged. "What for, I don't know. But the disk probably slips into a circular depression."

"A circular depression," Rader repeated in a murmur. He was filing the information in his memory bank.

"I wish I could help you more, my boy," the old man sighed.

Both Jeff and Sandy grinned appreciation at his sad and gentle concern.

"You've helped us considerably, Mr. Morganvelt," Jeff said with sincere warmth as he stood to leave. "And I can't thank you enough."

"For you, *boychick*, anytime." He took Jeff's extended hand and drew him closer.

They embraced like father and son.

"And good-bye to you, too, young lady." Isaac Morganvelt smiled at Sandy, offering his small palm after stepping back from Jeff.

She took it. "Good-bye, Mr. Morganvelt."

"That's a nice girl you've got, Jeffrey," he told Rader with an appreciative smile. "You take good care of her, you hear?"

"He's doing that, sir," Sandy said softly, "and very well, too."

"Good." Then he became perfectly serious. "Watch out for the *mamzarim*. Both of you. Be careful, yeh?"

They left him near his workbench.

Twenty-eight officers of the L.A.P.D., including one fully equipped SWAT contingent, were now strategically located around the Meta-Chem building. As soon as that troubled patrolman had connected Rader with the recently issued top-priority APB, he had called in and triggered a fully-organized operation—one just waiting for its signal to spring into action. And evidently one so special that it commanded the personal involvement of the police commissioner himself. Yes, Durkin was there now supervising everything. His orders had been clear: Jeff Rader and Sandra Wilkenson were suspects in the deaths of three officers—one on assignment to his own department—and they had been involved, as well, in a violent incident at the home of a prominent public figure. "So," the commissioner had insisted, "I want them alive. I want to interrogate them, understand?" Then he added significantly, "*However*, don't forget they may be cop killers, and I don't want anyone here joining Lieutenant Fried and those Secret Service men. If they're armed—as we have reason to believe—and they resist apprehension, I'd much rather have you, and not them, come out of this operation alive."

The message had been plain: Sandy and Jeff were to be taken, but no one would really weep if their bodies were to be brought in dead.

A carte blanche for killing.

Now, suspecting nothing, Jeff had a palm against the thick metal door that led to the street.

"It's almost twelve," he was saying. "We have to get over to that shopping center next."

The door swung outward sluggishly.

Sandy stepped into the dark cubbyhole; Jeff was right behind her. His thoughts had been on the switch of cars that was to take place. The safety of Isaac Morganvelt's laboratory was behind them now; the threat of the streets lay ahead. His senses were finely tuned again.

That's why he saw it as he stepped into that dank alcove behind Sandra Wilkenson.

A glint. Tiny. Quick. A ripple of light in an otherwise shadowy alley. A slip of rooftop metal catching the morning sun? No, that wouldn't have flickered—that would have glared. Glint meant movement. But movement from what? Metal or glass stirring in a breeze? Maybe. But then again, maybe not. Maybe metal or glass and a person. Here? Above? In this line of filthy-windowed, grime-streaked buildings? If so, who? And doing what?

The whole series of thoughts had flipped through his mind in an instant. He touched Sandy's shoulder, stopping her. "I saw something," he murmured. He could feel her tense under his hand. "Don't look around."

The door was still open. He was almost out from behind it. "Let's play it safe," he suggested softly. "Inside." He started to pull her back.

That's when the bullhorn blared.

"Hold it right where you are!"

Sandy and Jeff jerked in the direction of the sound. They saw nothing.

"The building's completely surrounded," the bullhorn grated. *"All the exits are covered and there are marksmen on rooftops and fire escapes. You're in telescopic sights right now. So don't do anything foolish, and come out of that alcove with your hands clasped tightly behind your heads."*

Bullhorn distortions notwithstanding, the voice was recognizable. Durkin, here? Jeff thought. Pedabine's taking no chances. "Is that you, Commissioner?" he called, still holding Sandy's shoulder.

She felt his fingers scooping and grasping her blouse. The action was telling her something. She held perfectly still, tensed, poised for anything.

"That's right, Rader," the acknowledgment shot back. *"You do exactly what I said and everything'll be fine. We just want to talk to you about the shootings at the hotel and what happened last night in Mandeville Canyon."*

Jeff's stomach was quivering with apprehension. Marksmen. Telescopic sights. Surrounded. There was death in a wrong move. Then maybe that was the answer! No wrong moves. Simple surrender—and then an exposure of all that he and Sandy had learned about Pedabine so far. *Defense through exposure.* Once everyone knew about Pedabine, there'd be no further reason for the organization to kill them.

But even as the thought entered his mind, he visualized both of them cold in the morgue. Victims of poison-induced massive coronaries.

His grip tightened on Sandy's blouse.

She readied herself for his move.

"All right, Commissioner, I'm coming. No shooting, okay?" Jeff shouted.

"The woman, too," Durkin ordered.

"Right . . . but first you order your men to hold their fire."

"Move up those stairs, Rader."

"Not until we hear you order your men not to shoot!"

What's he doing? Sandy wondered.

The answer came as suddenly as the question was framed.

"All right, men," Durkin's bullhorn rasped, *"they're coming out. Hold your—"*

It was all Jeff Rader wanted. Diversion for a second.

His door hand lashed out. The heavy metal groaned open another foot. At the same time, he yanked with all the power in his arm at Sandy's blouse.

Fabric gave. But she'd been ready for something. She moved with his action. Twisted. Slammed into the wall and spun off it back into the hallway.

Jeff collapsed as she jumped. A body-ball. Curling toward the ground in the semidarkness of the recess. A minimal target for bullets that were sure to follow. And they did. They plowed into the walls, the door. Ricocheted off the top step, the archway. Puffs of red brick. Zinging beads of lead.

But that fragmentary split of time for which he had played was all Jeff Rader had needed. His drop toward the ground had been forward, toward a small side of the archway. He'd gone feet first. He'd caught it six inches off the floor, twisting his body on contact, feeling the soles of his shoes flush against its surface. And then he was a spring. The balling, the curling had wound him. He kicked hard at the wall, snapping open like a swimmer in a racing turn. His body knifed for the narrowing gap of the doorway. He was through it. Crashing into Sandy. Sprawling her over the floor. Tumbling, rolling, spinning around, he was on his feet in an instant. He charged back to the door. He tugged wildly at its huge metal handle, fighting to shut it quickly, to lock it tight—as bullets tore into its outer casing.

But it wouldn't lock for him. He fumbled frantically at the bolt lock. The door needed special jarring for that bolt to ram into place. He pulled. He lifted. He slammed the palm of his hand repeatedly against the heavy rod. Nothing. And time had been wasted. He heard the gunfire stop. Heard orders being shouted.

"Damn!" he spat and turned away from the stubborn lock.

Sandy was on her feet again, waiting for him, her face contorted.

"Come on," he snapped. He raced past her, down the long hallway.

Holding hands now, they ran through passages, down inclines, up steps. Occasionally a face peered timorously from a doorway. They ignored it. When Jeff did think of anything but escape, he blessed his dead father for having been such a close friend of Isaac Morganvelt and for having brought him along on so many of his visits to the old man's laboratory.

Then he stopped dead in his tracks. Despite all his efforts to lose his pursuers, he had heard a door open around a corner and the bark of an official order.

Sandy had heard it, too. Tendrils of fear fanned through her body. She gasped.

Jeff clamped a hand over her mouth.

Her eyes blinked. She jerked her head to signal control.

Removing his hand, he hurried to the corner. He flattened his back against the wall and fought to stifle the rasping sound of his breathing.

Sandy inched behind him.

Footsteps. Up ahead. Running closer.

Jeff tensed at the edge of the corner.

And they were there.

Now he shot into view. He saw three from SWAT. Two with automatic rifles, one with a handgun, closely grouped and right on him. He fast-dropped to a knee and knuckle-punched a deadly arc. The lead man was caught at belt-line. He pitched forward, his rifle skidding along the floor.

Rader was on one foot now. His leg snapping high, his hip swinging in for greater power. The kick slammed the head of the second man against the wall. His eyes clouded, rolled upward. He slid down the wall like a glob of grease.

The last man had a moment to recover from the surprise of the attack. His rifle came around in a looping curve. But Rader was on him as the gun chattered. Bullets flew wildly, chipping the floor, barely missing the two SWAT figures lying there. There was no time for anything more. The heel of Jeff's palm rammed into the man's face, caught him on the point of his jaw, snapped his head back. He staggered. He felt an elbow slamming into his side, a foot crashing behind his knee. The rifle clattered to the ground. The man buckled. He went down clawing, grappling, clutching at Jeff's clothes. It was a mistake. Closeness was all Rader needed. His leg came up sharply. He grabbed the man's head and slammed it downward. The crack of face-on-knee was an ugly sound. The man moaned as he slid into unconsciousness.

Jeff pulled the handgun from the limp fingers of the second man he had aced. He signaled Sandy.

She stepped over and around the bodies.

They went for the door through which the SWAT men had come. Slower now. Much more cautiously. If they could be surprised once when they believed they had been ahead of their pursuers, there was no telling what else could lie before them.

They came to a fork in the hallway. Jeff recognized it. He chose the right branch. He knew where it would take him, though he didn't know why he should be going there. It was stupid. Needless endangerment of a dear old man. In seconds they were once again in the large laboratory.

Isaac Morganvelt had heard the gunfire. And the moment he saw them—their expressions, Sandy's torn blouse, the gun in Jeff's hand—he understood and was moved to action. "Thank God you came this way,"· he said. "Come, fast." Grabbing a flashlight from a shelf, he darted back into the hallway.

They followed without a word.

He took them into another room near the end of the corridor. It was a storeroom. Musty. Filled with ancient equipment. In a corner of the room, he located a door hidden behind a tall, empty crate. This, like the back door of the building, was bolt-locked. Wagging a finger at it, he stepped back to allow Jeff to work the bolt free. After considerable tugging and twisting, the rod gave with a pull, the door was creaked open.

"Here," Mr. Morganvelt said, offering the flashlight. "All these buildings were constructed in 1927. The owner was a *meshuggeneh* from New York. He couldn't believe there could be a place without cold and snow. So he had them all connected. Then he could go from one to the other and not freeze outside. You go down those steps, you'll be in a passage. It branches into all the buildings, but if you'll go straight, it goes all the way to the last one—that's two blocks away. They're not looking for you there. Hurry."

They hesitated a moment, only to look at him with clear expressions of gratitude.

"Go, go," he urged, his hands waving impatiently.

Jeff started down the steps.

Sandy pressed her cheek against the old man's face as she squeezed the back of his hand. Then quickly she followed Jeff into the passageway.

Isaac Morganvelt closed the door. He bolted it again as well as he could and jiggled the empty crate back into place. Except for some dust disturbance, everything was as it had been before. Swiftly, he returned to his laboratory. He reached it only moments before a contingent of heavily armed guardians of the law charged down the corridor in the direction of his room.

He was standing in the doorway.

"Down there," he cried frantically, "a man . . . a woman . . . that way."

The hunters raced away from the location of the storeroom.

Beneath the buildings, Jeff Rader and Sandra Wilkenson hurried through a vile and narrow tunnel. Unused for years, it seemed to contain still, dead air thick with a putrid dampness not unlike that of a sewer. Breathing was difficult. Sandy buried her nose in the crook of her arm, the sleeve of her blouse acting as a filter. Jeff worked his mouth in short, rapid inhalations. They found themselves panting, gasping, wanting to retch and vomit. If they didn't get out of there soon, the stink would suffocate them.

At one point Jeff tripped and fell into a pile of broken bricks, the flashlight flying from his fingers and crashing to the stone floor. Near panic. Only once was there a respite from that clawing, clutching stench. A brief patch of coolness as they approached the end of the corridor. It brushed Sandy's hair. Fresh. Quick. A touch of life.

They came to steps exactly like those they had descended to get into the passage. Up. Five. Six. Eight. Another door. Heavy. Metal. *Locked*.

"Oh, *Jesus*," Rader groaned as his hands pressed against the barrier, "why didn't I think of it?"

"What's the matter?" Sandy asked from behind him.

"Of course," he muttered, "it would have to be locked . . . just like the other."

Sandy felt her knees give. She sagged against a wall. "And Mr. Morganvelt's probably closed the one at his end, too," she whispered.

The impossibility of their situation almost overwhelmed them. Sealed in. In darkness. In suffocating stench. Trapped to die.

Then out of desperation, a remembrance.

The touch of life. The quick, fresh, cool air that had brushed Sandy for a moment. "Jeff," she offered hopefully, "back there about thirty feet I felt something. There may be another way out."

Rader leaped down the stairs two at a time. He backtracked the passageway with Sandy running close behind him. The beam of his flashlight played across the walls.

There it was: a gap, no more than two feet wide. And cleaner air filled it slightly to overflowing.

Jeff poked the flashlight into the opening. A cluster of electrical conduits leaped out of the darkness. He traced their course. They reached to the ceiling of the shaft before curving into the wall. But there at the top, just where they curved, was the source of that wonderful fresh air—a small rectangular grill. Obviously an opening that had permitted work on the wiring of the building. Rader handed the flashlight to Sandy. "Watch how I do this," he advised. He sidled into the opening. Then, gripping the pipes with his left hand, he pressed his back hard against one wall, his shoes against the other. With slow, careful hitching, he inched his way up the recesses until his feet were straddling the grill. He had to kick only twice before the thin metal gave and fell away from its frame. Then he eased himself down again to rejoin Sandy.

"Can you make it up there the way I did?" he asked.

"I think so."

"Good."

He had her put on his jacket before starting—a cushion for her back and a cover for her blouse.

She was apt and strong, and in no time at all, with a little assistance from Jeff, she had eased herself smoothly through the aperture.

Reclaiming his jacket, he joined her quickly.

They were in a small, empty, darkened room now. It had only one door.

Rader placed his flashlight on the floor. He opened the door.

They stepped into a corridor identical to the one that had led to Isaac Morganvelt's laboratory. They followed this through twists and turns and, eventually, they came to the building's side exit. Looking at each other once and smiling with a mixture of triumph and trepidation, they stepped outside.

They were free. Grimy and filthy from their ordeal, but obviously beyond the perimeter of Police Commissioner Harold Durkin's stakeout and raiding details.

They saw no one as they left the building.

They headed away, farther east, toward Atlantic Boulevard. Rader chose to avoid Michael Gavin's Chevy. Going back for it would have been far too risky. No, they would have to reach the shopping center by taxi or bus. Of course, this was chancy, too. But the odds were far better despite the grubby appearance that made both of them more than a little conspicuous.

14

Michael Gavin had been a busy man.

Just as Jeff and Sandy were turning toward Atlantic Boulevard, he was cutting the ignition of his rented LTD in the parking lot of a shopping center on Pico and Overland.

Minimize risk. That's what he had insisted when he spoke with Jeff earlier that morning. Well, he had done everything possible to accomplish that objective. It was all in the trunk of the car—all except one last item, and that would be acquired very shortly. Then—*then* he'd be free to investigate that astonishing recollection. Pedabine. Jeff had asked him if he had ever heard the word. Well, indeed he had. But so long ago. Another age. Another lifetime. Amazing. And missing finger joints—he knew when Jeff first mentioned them that he'd heard of that, too. The connection—Pedabine, finger—was there in his memory. But he'd forgotten too much over the years. He'd need more. The details. *All* the facts. And he could obtain them again only by searching. Well, now he was free to dig. The morning had been busy and productive, but it would be nothing compared to the afternoon.

He pulled a pad and pen from his jacket pocket.

"Go to Bel-Air," he wrote. "Bellagio Gate. Take Roscomare Rd. almost to University Heights Hospital. Left on Linda Flora Drive. 83116A. Key under second flagstone near door. Empty trunk of car. Contents yours. Wait for me. Important. Michael."

He tore the sheet from the pad, wrapped it around the car keys, and slipped the packet into the ashtray. Then, closing the tray, he slid quickly from behind the wheel.

''Got a helluva lot to do now, Michael m'boy,'' he growled aloud, rubbing the palms of his hands together, ''and you're not a man to dawdle when things are getting hot.''

15

Two new gas stations glitter at Atlantic Boulevard and Hewlett Street like sequins in the armpits of an aging stripper.

But to Jeff Rader and Sandra Wilkenson they were mansions in a desert, a welcome touch of Disney-in-a-Slum.

Business was slow at the nearer one. The attendant was isolated in his locked change booth, staring at the screen of a portable TV set.

Skirting his line of vision, Jeff and Sandy ambled toward the restrooms. They reached them without being seen. The doors were open. They eased inside and snapped their respective locks.

Ten minutes later, they emerged vastly improved in appearance. Sandy had even done something magical to conceal the tear in her blouse, and her short hair had been easily finger-combed into place. Jeff now held his filthy jacket folded neatly over his arm. While it no longer carried the strange chain that had brought them to Isaac Morganvelt (this was now fastened about his neck, tucked under his shirt), one of its pockets held the gun he'd taken during his struggle with the three SWAT men. Of course, they weren't immaculate. But they were decidedly more presentable. Far less noticeable. They were ready.

Now they had to get to that shopping center. But how? They paused behind a stand of bougainvillaea at the edge of the station.

Sandy offered a suggestion: "Maybe we ought to split up. Get there individually. They're expecting us to be together. Separately we may stand a better chance."

Rader looked into her eyes. "That's quite a suggestion," he breathed. "Doesn't it scare you?"

"Out of my mind," she admitted, "but it makes sense, doesn't it?"

He grinned at her in admiration. He nodded his head and said, "You're right. It makes sense, but we can't do it. If someone should spot you, you might need my help. So let's separate but let's stay together."

"I don't understand."

"I think we ought to keep clear of taxis. Cab drivers notice too much. But bus drivers rarely even look at their passengers. Let's get to the bus and board it separately. Bury your face in a newspaper once you're seated—we'll get a couple down the street. And stay mid-bus, near the exit, just in case we need it. We'll play it like we're strangers, but I'll be nearby."

Now it was her turn to feel the warmth of admiration. She grinned at him and bobbed her head once in agreement. Then, stepping smartly from behind the bougainvillaea, she strode toward the bus stop on the next street.

Jeff followed about seventy feet behind her.

Only once was special attention given to them. That was by a middle-aged man who studied Sandy with disturbing intentness. When he actually made his move, he caused Jeff, six seats away, to tense and to prepare himself for trouble. Rader's concern proved to be unnecessary; Sandy managed her "suitor" with marvelous aplomb. As he sat beside her and smilingly opened with: "Excuse me, I couldn't help noticing what an attractive woman you are; are you in films?" she merely looked at him in wide-eyed amazement and gasped, "Oh, my God, what a shock! Whoever you are, you look exactly like my dead father." Then she buried her head in her hand and proceeded to fake soft and wrenching sobs.

The aging lover left the bus at the next stop.

At Pico and Overland, they converged on the shopping center from different directions.

Sandy approached at a slightly slower pace. This was to enable Jeff to locate and to start the LTD alone. Her reasoning: If the car was being observed, no move toward it would be made until she and Rader were together. Then, with the car's engine already running, their chances of escape would be improved.

The car was clear, though. No one had followed Michael Gavin. No one as yet suspected his connection with Jeff Rader and Sandra Wilkenson.

They left the parking lot, heading for Bel-Air, following Gavin's brief instructions.

Jeff glanced at her. She was sitting erect, looking straight ahead, her hands in her lap, her brows creased in concentration. He understood her gnawing need. They had proved that Tami was still alive, out there somewhere, but where? He reached over and placed his hand over hers.

The contact made her look at him.

He smiled. "We'll find her," he murmured. "We'll find her."

She relaxed perceptibly, a soft, warm grin pulling at her mouth. "You read minds in your spare time, too, I see." She sighed.

If Mandeville Canyon is countryside within a city, then Bel-Air is another land. A short distance from where homes of the famous and affluent snuggle into luxuriant vegetation or jut precariously from stony hillsides, deer abound and hawks can be seen swooping into valleys.

The rented LTD whirred over Roscomare Road, taking them deeper into this lush wonderland. On Linda Flora Drive, they turned left and backtracked through even denser and more spectacular foliage. A serpentine road, it curved and coiled and dipped. But, always, it rose higher into the hills.

The small stake was situated at the side of the road. So unobtrusively placed, they almost missed seeing it. An unpainted rural mailbox perched jauntily on its top. The side of the box had been painted with the legend 83116A. No name, just the numbers and that single capital letter. Near it, a narrow dirt road cut deeper into the countryside. Though it was only as wide as the car, the path was fairly smooth and even. They traveled it with ease.

Soon it rose over a hillock and curved into a small clearing. Jeff braked the car to a stop before a small but magnificently designed house.

All about them was nature-silence: small insect sounds, a soughing breeze, the gentle dialogue of leaves, animal rustlings.

The key to the front door was under the flagstone, just as Michael had said. Jeff used it to open their way to a blending of elegance and informal comfort.

"Ve-ry nice," Rader approved softly.

"Lovely," Sandy agreed.

"Wonder how Michael Gavin comes to have a place like this."

"Think it's his?"

Jeff grinned. "I wouldn't be surprised." He shook his head in affectionate admiration. "I've known that beautiful buzzard more than twenty years now, and he still surprises me."

"What do you think he left in the trunk of the car?"

"More surprises."

They went to the car trunk and unlocked the lid. What they saw was a cornucopia of boxes and bags.

They were puzzled.

As they carried the packages into the house, they could see that half of them were filled with food. But the remainder—what were they about?

They opened them and dumped their contents upon the long, deep sofa before the living-room fireplace. The items were about "minimizing the risks." Sprawled across the couch were pants, socks, shirts, stockings, blouses, sweaters, undergarments, a half-dozen sunglasses, eyeglasses with an assortment of frames, wigs of varying shapes and colors, mustaches and sideburns for Jeff, spirit gum, cosmetics for Sandy—in short, a small wardrobe of loose, comfortable clothes of ordinary fashion and a small mound of simple, effective articles of concealment and disguise. Obviously, to Michael Gavin minimized risks simply meant unencumbered movement and underplayed deception.

They checked clothing sizes and found them to be completely accurate. The old journalist's powers of observation were truly amazing.

Not since the start of their danger had Jeff Rader and Sandra Wilkenson enjoyed such ease and safety. Rader couldn't help uttering a thought he'd had when he talked with the editor's brother that morning: "Bless Michael Gavin."

To which Sandy breathed a heartfelt "Amen."

As they waited for their friend and benefactor, they examined their options. Jeff knew what his next move would have to be. It was more risky, more difficult than anything he'd ever in his life undertaken. But it was the only course of action open now—unless Michael Gavin had some information that would alter everything.

The afternoon went by swiftly. Some of it was spent showering and getting into their new clothes. The rest was used putting things away, listening to tapes of Pavarotti, Sutherland, Sinatra, and Streisand and just idling around. Cozy activities. They created a homey climate. The effect wasn't lost on either of them. For a moment they were like a well-paired husband and wife. Casual. Comfortable. Contented.

Michael Gavin arrived at 6:15.

The hum of a car creeping over the dirt path jolted them out of their reverie. True, they were expecting a friend, but there was no way to be sure their visitor wasn't a Pedabine instead. Jeff jumped for the gun; Sandy rushed automatically for the living-room window to peer around the edge of its shade. They relaxed only when they could identify Gavin's familiar figure.

Michael was excited. "By God, we've got it, kids," he declared the moment he saw them coming through the doorway to meet him. "The whole bloody picture!" He waved a large manila envelope over his head.

Words poured from all three of them. Nothing could be understood. And they all laughed suddenly when they realized it.

"Inside," Jeff urged. "C'mon inside."

Sandy rushed ahead. "I've made coffee."

"Bless you, Sandra m'girl," Gavin called after her. "Black for me." He entered the house ahead of Jeff, murmuring softly as he glanced about, "I love this place. I dearly do."

"Is it yours, Michael?"

"No, kid. Wish it was. My brother Sean's. Calls it his weekend retreat. Lord knows, he deserves it. Worked hard enough all his life. But don't worry, m'boy, he won't be using it until I tell him it's all right. I made sure of that." He looked suddenly at Jeff. "See you're wearing the clothes I bought. Fit seems to be okay."

"Perfect."

The old city editor quipped, "Ahhh, Gavin, you've still got your eye, all right."

By then they were in the kitchen, taking places around the

table. When all three were seated, Jeff asked, "Whose car are you driving now?"

"Another rental." He grinned. "One more, I become a member of the board, and Avis'll be Number One." Then his manner became sober. He patted the envelope lying before him. "Got quite a bit, kid," he said. "But it'll keep. First, you two. What's been happening?"

Once again they brought him up to date. Everything that had happened to them since they had last seen him at the Eros Lodge—events at Myra London's house, the experience with the dentist, their morning at Meta-Chem Laboratories. Jeff showed him the necklace and explained Isaac Morganvelt's findings. They even described the startling conclusions they had reached about the Pedabine name and character.

When they were through, he sank against the backrest of his chair and breathed, "It fits. I'll be damned, it all fits. . . . There are some pieces of the puzzle still out there someplace, but we've got enough of them now to see what this picture of madness is possibly about."

Then Michael Gavin began his story:

"This takes us close to the turn of the century, my young friends. Of course, I wasn't very socially conscious then, being born in nineteen and ten, but I became interested in that period when I was still a lad. And the *why* of that is part of the story, too. The starting point is a murder—in the year 1912. It was a bad one, and it involved one of the richest men in the country. He owned iron, copper, gold, silver, lead, and coal mines; he had interests in the young oil industry and considerable investment in the important lumber industry. He was one of those men we call robber barons. And as for the murder—well, it wasn't the man himself who was killed. No, it was his son. Crime of the Century, they seemed to call all murders in the old days. But this one was pretty terrible, even from the jaded position of a present-day newsman. The boy was nineteen. His name was Kendral. Nice, huh? He was absolutely brilliant. The pride and promise of doting parents. He enjoyed everything a great fortune of that day could offer. Including attendance at a college so exclusive only the most gifted children of the spectacularly wealthy were accepted. And he was killed by three upperclassmen. A scientific killing, they called it. Something like the thrill-killing of the Leopold-Loeb business later on. But because they were all such bloody geniuses, the style of the murder was much more imaginative and gruesome. Y'see, the boy was stripped naked and hung upside-down in a dry, abandoned well; his hands were bound behind his back, a blindfold saturated in lye was placed over his eyes, and a cup of red army ants was secured over his genitals. The idea was to see how long he would last. To see if the fright and agony would cause a heart attack or if he'd just expire slowly. To see if he'd retain his sanity or go bananas. It was all very scientific. The killers kept notes, they did—very careful notes on everything that happened.''

Sandy shuddered and Jeff winced.

Gavin continued. ''Well, the murderers were brought to trial, and they were found guilty. But the judge, in his infinite wisdom and mercy, put them all on three years' probation. That's right, they went free. Not a single day in a cell. Maybe big money got to him, who knows. Maybe he was paying back a debt. At any rate, it was their first offense, the judge explained, and they were all properly contrite and remorseful, and all so intelligent that imprisonment or death would deprive society of the good that such wealthy, bright, conscience-stricken young men could—and, he was certain, *would*—do.''

''How did that affect the father of the murdered boy?'' Sandy asked.

Gavin nodded gravely. ''Thank you, m'darlin'. You bring us right to the point now. The man was devastated. He saw the sentence as a breakdown of the legal structure; he saw brilliantly schooled killers as the corruption of educational philosophy; he saw murder in a Christian nation as the failure of organized religion. Notice: breakdown, corruption, and failure in law, education, and religion. And since he also saw these three areas as the foundation of good government, and good government as the instrument of social order, he was sure that nothing in this entire world was working properly—or *could* work properly without an entirely new societal approach. So he formulated one. An approach that would create a perfect little society based on law, education, and religion, one that would provide its members with safety, order, and every possible opportunity to develop their intellectual and creative spirits. And since his own boy had been so brilliant—''

''Wait a minute, wait a minute, Michael.'' Jeff stopped him.

He was astonished. "Are you saying the father of that murdered boy was the founder of the Pedabine organization?"

"You've got it, kid." Michael Gavin nodded.

"But—but how do you know that? I mean, what's the connection? Why this particular crime and Pedabine?"

"Right after the trial, the father wrote some articles for a magazine. All of his bitterness and disenchantment with society came out in them. Now, we have to jump—sixteen years later. That's 1928. I was with my first newspaper, the *Des Moines Sentinel,* and there was a big scandal going on about a local judge who was on the take. The trouble with the case—in a news sense, I mean—was that it had been dragging on so long, it was losing its steam. Well, I was eighteen then and full of piss and vinegar. So I begged the editor to let me try a new slant. He agreed, and I went about linking our judge's indiscretion to a history of legal corruption in America. There was research, of course, and that's how I became interested in that murder case. It was fascinating. So fascinating I couldn't let go. Dug into it for months—even after our own judge was booted out and put away."

"But that still doesn't do it, Michael," Jeff insisted. "That's not a connection. How do you know that specific murder case was the start of Pedabine?"

Michael Gavin smiled faintly and looked steadily into his eyes as he intoned: "Because there were three big things I'd learned in all that research years ago. One: The murdered boy had had a little accident when he was a child, and the result of that accident was a missing finger joint—left hand, last digit, amputation on a bias."

Sandy gasped.

"Two: The word *Pedabine* was used in an article describing the way the man would structure his perfect little society."

Jeff grunted.

"And three," Gavin concluded almost in a whisper, "the man's name was Avery Wesscoze. . . . He was the father, and his name was Wesscoze."

The significance of that last point hit Rader like a thunderbolt. "Wesscoze," he echoed, "the father. Je-sus, that's what that guy who swallowed the poison meant when he was dying! Not 'farther up the west coast,' as I thought, but *Father Wesscoze.* He was identifying his leader, his lord and master!"

"But the man can't still be alive," Sandy objected.

"Of course not," Rader agreed. "Let's see, he was how old at the time of the murder?"

"Forty-seven," Michael answered.

"Forty-seven in 1912," Sandy calculated swiftly. "That would make him one hundred nineteen today."

The excitement of Gavin's information had gripped all three of them by now. "Let's see, let's see," Jeff thought aloud. "The dentist screamed 'Get the Father,' and that suggests someone who's alive—"

"Not necessarily," Sandy cut him short. "It could also mean: Destroy the memory of the man and you'll destroy the organization."

"Or," Michael added softly, "it could just be an indication of orderly succession."

Sandy's quizzical expression called for clarification.

"Each new leader is called Father in honor of the founder."

That made sense. They liked it. They were certain they'd locked another little piece of the Pedabine puzzle neatly into place.

"Tell us more," Sandy prompted Gavin.

"What happened to the killers?" Jeff asked.

"They never fulfilled the judge's expectation. Never did a damned thing with their lives except play polo, booze it up, and whore around."

"And the boy's father?" Sandy asked. "What happened to him?"

Michael Gavin's big, square face took on a distant expression. "That's another mystery that fits right into this Pedabine craziness. He disappeared."

"Disappeared?"

"That's right, m'girl. Vanished. But not for a while. Soon after the trial, he started to sell off all of his holdings. Got rid of his mines, every single one of them; sold his interests in oil and lumber; cut his ties with his European connections; sold his yacht—got rid of everything, except his big house on the lakeside of Chicago. That he kept until his wife died."

"Ohhhh"—Sandy was saddened—"his wife died. . . ."

"Three years after the boy's murder. She was a basketcase from the day the body was found. He buried her with his son."

"Where?" Jeff asked.

"Chicago. In a family mausoleum."

"Which he, himself, never came to use," Jeff said.

"Right. As soon as she died, he sold the house and disappeared."

Sandy was puzzled. "I don't understand how a man of such prominence could just vanish. Wasn't there an investigation?"

"Absolutely," Gavin answered. "A big one. But nothing was ever discovered that could lead the authorities to him."

"And his fortune," Jeff asked, "what happened to that?"

"No one ever found out."

"Probably used it," Sandy concluded, "to start his whole program of kidnapping and murder." It was said almost as a murmur, but it had the power to round out the discussion. A brief, heavy silence now filled the small kitchen as the three probers considered the implications of everything that had been revealed so far.

"It's quite a thought." Jeff finally spoke for all of them. "Somewhere on this planet there's a functioning society of geniuses who come out once in a while to mingle with the rest of the world. Its citizens are probably all kidnapped children who grow up with such dedication to the memory of the founder that they're willing to kill themselves, their own citizens, and everybody else in defense of his principles. And they all become this way because their perfect little society gives them meaningful law, special education, and something or someone to revere—all, according to the original Father, the basis of stable, effective government and a fulfilling life."

"A criminal life," Sandy corrected.

"Only by our laws, not theirs," Jeff observed.

"A society of monsters," she insisted.

Gavin added, "Depends on which end of the telescope you're lookin' through, some people say."

She stared at him, a shadow of confusion clouding her eyes. "Do you believe that, Michael?" she asked quietly. She was thinking of her Tami.

"Oh, no, that's what others might say," he answered, touching her hand. "Michael Gavin believes that only the terribly young or the terribly twisted are foolish enough to buy a lie such as that. Our telescope was meant to be used in only one way; says so right in the Manufacturer's Handbook, and anyone who looks through the wrong end is going to see nothing but distortion, no matter how seriously he insists the view is better that way.

There are some things in this world that thinking will not make so, and right 'n' wrong is one of them.''

Sandy smiled.

"And after that sickening exhibition o' philosophizing"—he grunted as he stood—"I'd better be taking my leave.''

Sandy jumped to her feet. "Stay, Michael, please. We haven't had dinner yet. I'll make something for the three of us.''

"Sweetest invitation I've had all week"—he grinned—"but the answer's gotta be no, thank you.''

She seemed puzzled.

"He wants to take some precautions, Sandy," Jeff explained somberly. "They must have found the Chevy near the Meta-Chem buildings by this time and the Secret Service man's gun that I had hidden under the driver's seat; Durkin'll make the connection with us. They'll be looking for Michael, too, now.'' His eyes hadn't left the old editor's for a moment.

Gavin grinned and winked at him. "Gotta find a place," he said, offering a handshake.

Sandy was worried. "No, you don't," she urged. "You can stay here with us.''

"She's right," Jeff agreed, holding his hand.

Gavin responded with: "Well, maybe she is. But I'll get a room. Change motels every night. There's a lot to be done yet, and I'll be able to do it better on my own. There's nothing to be concerned about. Believe me.'' Though spoken gently, the words had a finality to them that ended discussion.

Jeff understood that, too. "Okay, Michael—just be very careful. Please.''

"Oh, I intend to, kid, I intend to be just that.''

He had left the envelope on the kitchen table.

While Sandy began preparing something for them to eat, Jeff removed the envelope and took it into the living room, where he sank to the couch. Now to find out what Michael Gavin had prepared for them. He lifted the flap of the large, brown envelope. Along with a sheaf of photocopies of magazine pages—six articles dating back seventy-two years—there was a perfectly uniform, neatly bound bundle of money. Jeff sat up straight. He riffled the stack four times before he actually counted it. Hundred-dollar bills. Fifty of them. And folded and tucked into the wide paper band that held the packet together, a neatly penned note: "Credit cards are probably no good by now, so your checks will be worthless, too. You're going to need funds. Cash minimizes risks. Stop objecting; you'll pay me back when this mess is over.''

Jeff Rader sighed and smiled. He sank back into the softness of the couch again. He was deeply relieved. One of his major concerns had been swiftly eliminated by the crusty old editor's foresight.

Jeff put the money aside. He'd tell Sandy about it later, over dinner. The articles, first. What else did they have to reveal? He found his answer in the first one he scanned, the one headed ''A Pedabine Order.''

It was a philosophical treatise. A neo-Platonic vision of *The Republic*. It considered justice. It established the morality for a very small and select state. It created an ideal world, an uncomplicated society of clearly defined principles and codes. It was shockingly prophetic.

''Listen to this,'' Jeff said as he and Sandy sat down to dine. He read a passage, with grudging admiration: '' 'It is not difficult to see into the future: Our society will grow prodigiously; affluence will be extended to the masses; greater numbers of people will succumb to the opiate of mindless pleasure; the nation will suffer an atrophying of intellectual and cultural purpose; educational institutions will then flounder hopelessly, steadily capitulating to the demands of the mediocre; the ability to think logically will wither; behavior will express feeling rather than reason; there will follow, on a monumental scale, the commission of heinous crimes, devoid of compassion and an appreciation of their legal consequences; our judicial and penal systems will be taxed far beyond their capabilities; the courts will make concessions and, in doing so, weaken further the effectiveness of law enforcement agencies; this, of course, will generate intense fear within the citizenry; good people will become blind to the travail of their neighbors; many will seek safer environs, but the evil will spread everywhere; the social structure will develop ever-widening cracks until, in an effort to save the nation, leaders will once again create the unifying involvement of armed conflict with a foreign foe. Eventually science will provide the means by which all social order may be destroyed. And what of the cloth? Throughout this steady decline into the abyss, organized religion will do nothing more than moan and plead with its customary impotence for an amelioration of mankind's sordid condition.' ''

Jeff stopped. He looked at Sandy.

''May I see that, please?'' she asked softly.

He handed the article to her.

She studied the page. ''This is quite a prediction,'' she murmured. ''He's foretelling a country of 230,000,000 people, a corrupted middle class, escapist entertainment, watered-down education, the Johnnies who can't read, write, or speak, our present crime rate, mass murders and terrorism, plea-bargaining, beleaguered police forces, a frightened society with a don't-get-involved mentality, flight to the suburbs and the Sunbelt, the spreading of violence to those areas, too, political efforts to create foreign scapegoats, and the possibility of nuclear war.''

''And that was written in 1912,'' Rader reminded her. ''The man was a modern Isaiah.''

''And Pedabine was his Jesus.''

''Not exactly,'' Jeff corrected the statement. ''More like his Essene haven in the wilderness. He describes a sanctuary where the righteous can study without interference. To Avery Wesscoze, although the intellectually blessed are not all righteous, the righteous should all be intellectually blessed. And in his monastery, special training and strict obedience will produce a spiritual immunity to social illness. An elitist religion, in a sense: Salvation from the madness of society lies in an insulated environment where the superior soul can be developed to its full potential.''

''His son's murder was more than he could handle.''

''He was brilliant, though.''

''Maybe, but insanity's no bigot, Jeff; it's willing to make love to anyone.''

Rader erupted happily. ''Great!'' He laughed. ''I like that!''

Sandra Wilkenson flushed with pleasure like a schoolgirl. She realized suddenly how important it was for her to be appreciated by this particular man. She dropped her glance and toyed with a breadcrumb on the tablecloth.

Jeff Rader, too, was affected by the moment. He recognized the happiness within his laughter. Despite the killings, despite the danger and violence, he felt better than he had in months. Knowing Sandy Wilkenson was making him well again. Just sitting there with her made him feel incredibly alive. I'll be damned, he told himself, she's got me thinking like a love-sick kid. But he enjoyed the idea. And it caused him, too, to drop his gaze in charming embarrassment.

There was a feeble effort at small talk.

He asked how she had learned to drive a car as she did.

She explained. "When I was a freshman in college, I had this mad crush on our local racing hero. I had my license before we met, of course, but he really taught me how to drive. I went to all the meets with him. Eventually I even drove in three of them." Her eyes were sparkling, and she looked perfectly delectable.

He had to restrain an impulse to reach for her.

She asked him how he felt about being a successful journalist. Wryly he joked:

> "Breathes there a newsman with soul so dead
> Who never to himself has said:
> 'I'll write a book yet, a literary crown,
> A novel to turn this old world upside-down?' "

He was grinning with engaging diffidence.

The remainder of the dinner and most of the evening became a hopscotch of insignificant conversations and increasingly significant silences. And though they knew what was happening, neither Jeff nor Sandy could slow the steady crumbling of their reserve.

It was almost ten o'clock when their gazes locked and final resistance evaporated. Eyes drew faces closer. Lips touched lips. Tenderly. Timidly. The taste of mouth was explosive. Their breaths caught, their pulses quickened, their bodies tensed and quivered. Small suppressed sighs tumbled from their throats.

They pressed their mouths together hungrily, reaching into each other. Sandy whimpered once in longing; Jeff choked back a matching response.

She placed her fingers lightly upon his cheek and slowly drew away. Her heart was pounding furiously now.

He gazed into her eyes. His breathing was hoarse, constricted.

They'd been sitting on the sofa until this moment, treating themselves only to the taste of their mouths. Now Sandy stood and looked down at him. He watched her closely. Her hand went toward him. He took it and stood by her. They were both trembling with anticipation.

They moved toward each other. Slowly they embraced, and

this time locked themselves in a kiss of unrestrained ardor. He felt the wonderful press of her breasts; she felt the full hardness of his manhood. They gasped and squeezed even closer.

Only the bedroom could serve them now.

They separated and looked at each other, knowing where they were meant to be.

"Come on," Jeff said in a choked, tremulous whisper.

She longed so badly to love him her teeth chattered and her body ached. This was the man she had been wanting ever since Adam's death. This was the fulfillment of her repressed needs, the filling of the vacuum. She had been denying herself male company for more than three anguished years—but she understood now that her denial had been designed to bring her to this very special man. However, an ugly worry suddenly sprang to life. It had been so long since Adam, and she had been his faithful wife. Could she satisfy another man? Would she please this new love? She wanted to voice her concern, but she didn't know how to do it without appearing to be disappointingly inexperienced.

"I-I . . . have to tell you something. . . . I may not be . . . very good at this," she heard him confessing in quiet embarrassment. "It's been a long time since I've wanted a woman as much as I want you, and . . ." His voice faded into a touchingly helpless murmur. He's apologizing, she thought with relief. He's as worried as I am. The love she was feeling welled in her throat so fully, she thought she would cry. She touched her fingers to his lips. She whispered, "Those were exactly the words I was going to say to you."

In the bedroom, soft shadows were limned across the bed by a winter moon. There was light enough to see clearly, darkness enough to cover shyness. Slowly they removed each other's clothing. They stood naked in a silent embrace, thrilling to the pressure of flesh against flesh. He traced a palm down her neck, across her chest, and gently cupped a firm breast. Air quivered through her parted lips. She trailed a hand down his side and lightly clasped his rigid, pulsing shaft. A soft moan rumbled deep in his throat. They stood that way in stirring silence, each becoming exquisitely familiar with the other. Then they sank to the bed and gave themselves to a wantonness of loving. His mouth and fingers searched her body, and she writhed in ecstasy;

she kissed him everywhere as though each pore of his skin was a source of life.

Then when it seemed as though one more second of their joy would be a moment too much, when their beings were burning with longing, they coupled and drove each other to glorious climaxes.

They didn't separate quickly. They pecked at each other. They murmured endearments. They spoke with eloquent silences.

No question troubled either mind now. No doubts. Jeff knew he loved this woman as he had never loved another. And Sandy saw him now as the one man without whom life would be incomplete.

Later, his arm about her shoulder, her head upon his chest, they drifted into gentle sleep.

Kidnapping and murder had ceased to exist—for a while.

16

Morning
Saturday, February 4, 1984

They were outside the house. Two of Pedabine's best soldiers, assigned to implement the Stellar Directive of the Primary Council. In the darkness before dawn they had inched their car to a clear spot only twenty-five feet from the front door. Then they had silenced the engine and scrunched down in their seats, patiently watching for their moment of action.

They were young men, both in their late twenties. There was something about them that screamed energy. Coiled springs. The keenness of attack dogs.

It was 8:30 now. A weak sun was up, and the sounds of daytime cracked the Saturday morning silence. Down the street a garage door opened. A four-year-old rolled from its recesses on a low-slung tricycle. "Don't go far," her house-coated mother called as the heavy door swung into place again. At the other end of the block, a motorcycle kicked in and soon sputtered into the distance.

"Should be soon now," one of the Pedabine soldiers muttered.

His partner grunted agreement.

Then, as if on cue, the front door of the house opened. A bathrobed man hurried out to scoop the morning *Voice* from his lawn. His name was Stanley. Stanley Kroft. And he was the husband of Jeff Rader's adoring sister, Annie.

"Our pigeon," the killer in the driver's seat whispered.

"Right."

They sat perfectly still.

Stanley Kroft barely glanced at the street. He saw the white van at the curb, but he gave it no thought. Some kind of vehicle was often parked in front of his house. Even business vans. The name printed on this one read PARADISE TELEVISION. He never even noticed it. All he knew was that his pregnant wife had become intensely distraught since her brother had started making news instead of reporting it. He hurried back into the house, opening the paper in a greedy search for new information about Jeff and the attractive woman with whom he was evidently on the run.

They waited until the door had closed behind him. Then the one on the passenger's side got out and crossed toward the house. He was dressed in corduroy pants, a blue workshirt, a light, partially zippered jacket, and sneakers. On his head he wore a service attendant's peaked cap and in his hand he carried a clipboard with standard order forms.

He pressed the buzzer and stood there chewing gum and humming.

The door opened. Stanley Kroft still held the open newspaper.

"Morning." The Pedabine agent smiled. "Paradise Television."

Perplexed, Stanley stared at him.

"Mardelin?" the killer asked. "James Mardelin? I've got a television delivery—"

"Got the wrong address, buddy. No Mardelin here. Sorry." The door began to close.

"Wait. Hold on a minute," the Pedabine agent pleaded with a troubled frown. "Thirty-six thirty East Palmaire, right?"

"Right address . . . but wrong customer. Sorry."

"Jesus Christ, not again! That's the second time this week. Damn it, I don't know where the hell to deliver this thing now. Say, I hate to bother you any more, but could I please use your telephone?"

Stanley Kroft hesitated.

"Only take a minute, I promise," the agent begged. "We got this new girl in the office, an' she don't know what she's doin' half the time. My order form says installation before nine thirty." He grinned. "Probably kids in the house waitin' for their Saturday cartoons."

A beat. Then Stanley Kroft smiled in return. "Sure," he said, "come on in." He swung the door open invitingly.

The agent entered, shaking his head and muttering something

about stupid office girls who couldn't be counted on to write their own names correctly.

"Phone's in the living room," Stanley offered. "On your left there." He closed the front door. When he turned around again, he was looking into the bore of a .38-caliber automatic, eye level, three feet from his face. His heart jumped into his throat.

"What do you want?" he asked, struggling to be calm.

"Where's your wife?" The voice was soft, clipped, tight now with purpose.

"You don't want her. Leave her alone, please, she's pregnant—"

"Get her."

Stanley hesitated.

"Get her, God damn it, or I'll kill her the second I find her!" Stanley Kroft's mind was a vortex of agony. If he called Annie, she might be harmed; if he didn't, this animal would find her anyway and murder her. "Don't hurt her, please," he pleaded.

"Call her, you son of a bitch, or she's dead!" It was a mad growl, and it terrified Stanley.

"Okay, okay. Just don't hurt her, okay? . . . Annie . . . Annie, there's some more news about Jeff in the paper. . . ."

She came in quickly from the kitchen, waddling behind the protuberance of their hope. "What is it?" she was asking. When she saw their intruder, she stopped with a gasp.

"Come in here, lady. Move, damn it, or I'll blow his fucking brains out right in front of your eyes!" he ordered.

Annie Kroft rushed to her husband's side as fast as she could move.

"Now"—the Pedabine agent smiled—"everything's going to work out beautifully." His entire manner had changed. "You cooperate and you'll both be all right."

"What do you want?" Stanley asked, his arm around his trembling wife.

"Good," the answer came back. "That's being sensible. Your car's in your garage, right?"

"Yes, why?"

"I want you to drive it out and park it at the curb where the white van is, and then come right back into the garage, understand?"

"Why?"

"Just do as you're told." He stabbed the gun menacingly into Annie Kroft's abdomen.

Stanley did exactly as he was told. After the garage had

disgorged the VW Rabbit and the driver of the white van had
swung his vehicle deftly into the smaller car's place, Stanley
walked up the driveway and lowered the door behind him.

Now, hidden safely within the house, the two agents implemented the first phase of Pedabine's Stellar Directive. They
placed a wide strip of adhesive over the mouths of both husband
and wife, and quickly blindfolded and separated them. Inside the
white van, one of them taped Annie's hands behind her back.
Then he strapped her legs together at the ankles. After this, he
placed a gauze filter cup over her nose. The gauze of the cup had
been treated with a completely odorless, fast-acting anesthesia.
Annie Kroft was unconscious in a matter of moments.

Meanwhile, in the bathroom of the house, her husband Stanley
was being murdered and methodically dismembered.

The Stellar Directive was clear: "Ann Kroft is to be taken and
held until Jeffrey Rader and Sandra Wilkenson are in Pedabine
hands. Her husband, Stanley Kroft, is to be eliminated. The
elimination is to be accomplished ruthlessly, brutally, to empha-
size in the clearest possible terms the danger in which the hostage
is being placed."

After completing Phase One, the agents got into their van and
drove away. No one saw them; no one noticed them. But a note
had been left in the bathroom. A small square of white paper. In
the upper left-hand corner, in neat script, one word: *Rader*. In the
center of the square, in large block form, one letter: *P*. Nothing
more.

From Harold Durkin's reports, Pedabine knew that Jeff was
now aware of its existence; Myra Macon London had revealed
that much in her house. As a loving brother, the reporter could
not possibly ignore the meaning of this Pedabine action. He
would soon reveal himself for his sister as surely as Sandra
Wilkenson would have revealed herself for her child.

17

Morning
Saturday, February 4, 1984

Morning light filtered through the diaphanous bedroom drapery.

Rader was lying awake. His internal alarm had shattered a dream of Sandra Wilkenson. Very sensuous. Very enjoyable. But it couldn't last. The mechanism clicked exactly at 6:30, jarringly, as though his pleasure had been trying to slip one over on his brain and his clock was having nothing to do with it. He experienced momentary annoyance. Then he heard Sandy's even breathing and he willingly relinquished dream for reality.

He turned on his side and watched her for a good half hour. He felt extremely fortunate to have found this woman. Fulfilled, actually. He thought about that for a while. It made him consider the nature of love, the marvelous completing character of it. All at once, though, another idea unsettled him: What would happen if they were unable to locate Tami? What would happen if they managed to escape the Pedabine dragnet, managed to survive in hiding but failed to find the child? Wouldn't there always be a void in Sandy's life? A love vacuum? One that even his own feelings could never completely fill? Would she ever really be happy then?

She opened her eyes and saw him watching her. She smiled dreamily and reached for him.

His questions were forgotten and their morning lovemaking was as moving as the night's.

Later, at breakfast, he was describing what their next moves would probably be. The radio was playing softly, an unobtrusive background to their dialogue. Neither was listening to it. Neither would have noticed—

. . . murder . . . Los Angeles . . . grisly crime
. . . Stanley Kroft . . .

It was the name that crashed through Rader's concentration. The name. He stopped in the middle of a word. His head jerked as though he'd been hit.

. . . body . . . bathroom . . . dismembered . . .

He flew from his chair. Pounced upon the radio. Twisted the volume dial with such force, the knob was torn from its shaft. He threw it aside, bent his head forward to devour the words.

A set expression of fear and horror darkened his eyes.

Sandy had gasped in shock at the suddenness of his outburst. Now as he leaned over the radio and the grotesque details poured into the kitchen air, her shock gave way to deep concern. "What is it, Jeff? What's the matter? What is it?"

He didn't respond. His head dipped lower as though he were trying to crawl into the speaker. A soft, agonized groan sounded through his nostrils.

Her hand went to her mouth. She watched, she listened in silence.

. . . the body was found as a result of a telephone call placed directly to Police Commissioner Harold Durkin. A hysterical woman, identifying herself as Mrs. Ann Kroft, wife of the victim, confessed to the killing and dismemberment of her husband. Mrs. Kroft's whereabouts are presently unknown, and, according to the commissioner, she adamantly refused to surrender herself to the authorities. This homicide is apparently related to the recent killings at the Century International Hotel and the home of Myra Macon London, charismatic leader in the Women's Rights Movement. Police are still trying to locate Jeffrey Rader and Sandra Wilkenson for questioning in those deaths. Commissioner Durkin has said the manhunt for Jeffrey Rader will now be intensified since the award-winning columnist for the *Los Angeles Voice* is also the brother of self-confessed killer Ann Kroft. Most puzzling to the police is a note found in the severed hand of today's victim, Stanley Kroft: It is a small square of white paper bearing only the last name of the newspaperman—Rader—and the single letter P.

For more up-to-the-minute news, stay tuned to station KN . . .

The call letters died midword. Rader had torn the radio from its socket.

"I didn't know you had a sister," Sandy whispered.

"They've got her," Jeff murmured. His insides were knotted. "They're using her. That's what the note means. They're telling us she'll die if we don't surface." His eyes filled with tears. "Poor Stanley. Such a sweet man . . . he wanted only good for everyone . . . could hardly wait to be a father. . . . *They cut him apart!*" His voice broke. "Oh, God, Sandy . . . they cut him apart. Now Annie." He tossed his head like a caged lion.

She watched him, her eyes brimming with tears. He seemed ready to explode, and she knew there wasn't a thing she could do to help. She yearned to touch him. She wanted to comfort him, but he was going through a torment so personal she didn't dare intrude.

He paced the kitchen. His thoughts were muddled and he was struggling to clear them. His breath came in choked gasps. A rage of incredible intensity was shaping within him. But he didn't lose control. Instead, he seemed to cross a threshold of agony and to settle into another mood. His breathing evened. His arms relaxed. His pacing stopped. He turned slowly and looked at Sandy with an expression so piercing it sent a chill of apprehension up her spine.

"What are we going to do, Jeff?" she whispered.

His answer came in a strange evenness. "We're going to see Annie, we're going to see Tami—and we're going to do that very, very soon."

Silence followed those measured words.

That's when the telephone rang.

Sandy leaped out of her chair at the suddenness of the sound. Jeff merely glanced at the instrument. Then he strode quickly toward it. He lifted the receiver and put it to his ear. Sandy watched and waited.

"Kid, is that you?"

The familiar voice sounded even rougher with concern.

"Yes, Michael."

"I just heard the news. You all right?"

"Yeah . . . fine, now."

"You know what it means, don't you, kid?"

"Where are you calling from?"

"A pay phone. We can talk. What're you gonna do?"

"Reach them."

Gavin was stunned. "You mean, turn yourself in?"

"That's what they want . . . but that's not what they'll get. They're insane, Michael. Killing comes as easy to them as breathing. If they had me and Sandy, it wouldn't help Annie in the least. They don't want her beyond using her to get to us. And once they have Sandy and me, they'll slaughter all of us without a second thought. I know that. Crazy as it sounds, she's actually safer while the two of us remain hidden. But we've got to move fast now because there's no telling when their patience will run out. The only way to help Annie—to help all of us—is to find them."

"You have a plan."

"We're leaving Los Angeles."

"When?"

"Soon as I put down this receiver."

"I don't have to know where you're going. Just remember I'm with you wherever you are. Stay in touch. I'll be digging into Durkin, Marquand, and London all day, and I should have something for you tonight."

"I'll call around nine."

There was an awkward pause. Both men wanted to express their deep affection; neither knew quite how to do that without causing embarrassment.

"Take care, kid," Gavin finally murmured.

"You, too, Michael," Rader answered softly.

Rader replaced the receiver. He turned his head slowly and looked at Sandy. There was something different about him now. Something cold. It didn't affect his warmth and tenderness for her. Not in the least. But it was there beneath the surface: another dimension of determination.

18

**Evening
Saturday, February 4, 1984**

They had moved fast. Time was now a major factor.

They had changed their appearances. Jeff wore a bushy brown mustache, a brown wig, and heavily framed glasses. Sandy's hair had become shoulder length and blond; skillful makeup had altered her skin tone and accented other features; her eyebrows, arched now in harsher lines, peaked above tinted, oversized glasses.

They'd used the streets and freeways of Los Angeles without incident.

Once, a motorcycle patrolman confirmed the effectiveness of their disguises by nodding amiably at Sandy as he pulled beside their LTD at a red light. But he was only one casual lawman. Since the surveillance teams throughout L.A. International Airport would certainly not be that casual, Jeff had decided to leave California by way of Burbank. A little time had been lost getting there, but considerable safety had been gained.

Before going to the Burbank airport, though, they'd stopped at the Ski Chalet in Pasadena. There they'd purchased short, heavy, reversible coats and two overnight bags into which they stuffed their other articles of clothing and disguise.

In Burbank they'd left their locked car in a long-term parking area. Then they'd boarded Republic's 10:30 flight to Phoenix. Arrival time: 12:30 P.M. This had allowed them ample time to make their 3:06 American Airlines connection to Chicago.

Now they were fastening their seat belts for their landing at O'Hare International.

The Father. The Father. It had all started with the Father. He had lived in Chicago. Avery Wesscoze. Mad Avery Wesscoze with untold millions and a scenario for his own little kingdom. Vanished. But to where? He had to have found a place, established some kind of headquarters somewhere. After all, the horror of Pedabine was now an incontestable fact—and Chicago had been the starting place.

It had happened so long ago, though. The earliest years of the century. Would there still be records? Would there be something that could actually be seen? Details about the Wesscoze interests, the Wesscoze way of life, were needed. Somewhere within the dim history of that mysterious man there had to be a lead, *something* that could be followed into the present and to the whereabouts of Tami Wilkenson and Annie Kroft.

Jeff saw no other way to approach the problem.

Certainly he couldn't corner Durkin, London, or even the *Voice*'s publisher, Arthur Marquand. They were all undoubtedly on guard now against surprise. Even if he were able to isolate one of them, even if he could pressure or threaten one of them for information, he'd get nowhere. His experience had taught him that Pedabine character would surely choose death before disclosure.

A clue had to be in Chicago. That's where the taproot had taken hold. That's where something of that root had to remain. Now his task was to dig—speedily, efficiently—to dig and to pray that his reporter's instincts and skills wouldn't fail him at this critical time.

It was a bad night. The Chicago wind whipped at them from the moment they left the terminal. It was cold. Biting. They shrank into their warm jackets, grateful they'd had the foresight to stop at that ski shop before leaving California.

A cab took them from O'Hare into the city. They traveled the Kennedy Expressway, past Harwood Heights, up to Montrose Avenue. They remained silent during the entire trip, drawing no attention whatsoever to themselves. The plane had landed on schedule at 7:42. By the time they'd reached the Dorset hotel near Western Avenue, it was a little past eight.

At the airport they'd called two places before locating accommodations. Their reservations were waiting for them. They registered as Mr. and Mrs. Wayne Castner. So far everything had gone smoothly. Now they'd soon learn whether this Chicago effort was justified. Everything rested on just how accurately Jeff had assessed the character of a very volatile little man. Time had made this gamble necessary. Time. They dared not waste it. There was no way to dig into Avery Wesscoze's history without assistance—not if they expected to make the most of every precious hour remaining to them.

Jeff had met the man he was after years before when he, Rader, had been a speaker at a national meeting of the American Journalists' Association. He'd come up to Jeff after the speech and said, "You're dead wrong, Rader. Reporters aren't worth a shit. Their words die faster than a rosebush in a Montana blizzard, and nothing they write ever changes a fucking thing."

He was Walter P. Able, owner, publisher, and sole writer of the prestigious bimonthly *Walter's Report*. His "newsletter" was a model of trenchant editorializing. He hated reporters and their cold, factual journalism; he loved opinions and the controversy they could stimulate. Politicians feared him, editors respected him, underdogs adored him. Illinois was his hunting ground; Chicago, his lair. Thirty-seven thousand subscribers lapped his words like bear cubs going after honey. *Walter's Report* hadn't made him a rich man, but he felt it had made him a successful one because no one owned Walter P. Able. No one told *him* what to think or write. And though he'd been offered the managing editor's job of almost every leading paper in the country—including *The New York Times*—he preferred to beat his own drum in the band-pit of Chicago.

Jeff had liked him from the moment of that opening insult. They'd even gone out for coffee to discuss the role of the reporter further. Although no friendship had ever developed, Rader had marked him as an honest and trustworthy man.

In the quiet of his room, Jeff placed the all-important call.

"Hello."

"Walter P. Able?"

"Speaking."

"Able, this is Jeff Rader."

Silence. Not one of puzzlement. Rather, one of recognition. Then a sharp exhalation crackled through the instrument, followed by: "Are you in Chicago?"

"Yes."

"Why?"

"That's what I want to see you about."

"You're a wanted man!"

"Is that the sound of caution, Able?"

There was a beat. Then: "You have my address?"

"Yes."

"Ring the buzzer twice."

"See you."

"When?"

"As soon as a cab can get me there."

He left Sandy at the Dorset. She protested, but he convinced her that her presence would accomplish nothing. In reality, he was protecting her. He had no way of knowing if this move would succeed. Walter P. Able had impressed him years ago as a true independent, a person who was totally unafraid of hardship and danger—but there had been something odd in his behavior just now, something inconsistent with Jeff's memory of the man. It would be safer if Sandy remained in the hotel room. Needless risk would be folly, and this was no time to be foolish.

In the darkness of the cab on the way to Richmond Street, Jeff Rader wondered if he were walking into a trap. What if Able were no longer the courageous person of yesterday? What if he had notified the authorities of Jeff's call? What if they were there now, waiting for him? What if, what if, what if— He removed his glasses and rubbed his eyes. There was no way of actually knowing, he realized, and what-ifs could strangle him. He sighed and relaxed. It was a risk that had to be taken. It made no sense to torture himself. He'd find out soon enough.

The building was an eight-story affair. Flat-faced and gray. There was no doorman. Rader paid the cabby and hunched against the wind for the warmth of the entrance.

Inside he scanned the tiny white nameplates on the wall: Harvey 1A . . . Gebring 1B . . . Preble 3A . . . Duerkopf 5A. There it was—Able 7B. He pressed the intercom buzzer twice. There was a pause. Then a long, rasping response sounded in the door's lock until he pushed against the frame and entered the lobby.

A walnut-paneled elevator took him slowly and silently to the seventh floor. As it did, he removed his wig, mustache, and glasses and stuffed them into one of the capacious pockets in his jacket. There was no need to surprise Able with his disguise; no need to reveal that he was even using disguise.

The door slid open and presented a cubicle only slightly larger than the elevator itself. A richly stained door occupied each of its walls. The one directly ahead, 7B, swung inward exactly as Jeff stepped onto the alcove's thick red carpet.

"Come in," a small, fleshy man greeted him.

He entered the apartment wordlessly and followed Walter P. Able into a book-lined room of surprisingly large proportions. Magazines, books, newspapers, and notepads lay everywhere. Coffee mugs, ashtrays, and pens covered tables and desks. Paste-ups, layouts sprawled over the floor. An impressive disarray. The workroom of a dynamo. Jeff took it all in, but he was also looking for something else: the presence of something unusual within the disorder, some indication of another person, the possibility of betrayal.

"You're nervous," the little man muttered as he indicated a chair.

"You're different," Jeff responded suspiciously.

"You're right." Able nodded. "But you're also safe."

Rader stared at him for a moment, evaluating. Yes, something had changed in Walter P. Able. But close-up, Jeff could guess that it probably wasn't a threat to him. He settled into the offered place.

"Coffee?"

"No thanks."

"Booze?"

"No—just information, Able."

"What the hell are you doin' in Chicago, Rader?"

"I'm on a story."

"You're on the run."

"That, too—but they're connected."

"Did you do those killings?"

"What do you think?"

"I think you would if you had to."

"There's too much to tell, Able."

"Why'd you call me, Rader?"

"I need your help."

"I'm listening."

"I want to find out about a man who lived in Chicago at the turn of the century."

"Go to a library."

"No, I need deep things—his interests, holdings—details."

"Big man?"

"Right."

"No biographies?"

"I don't believe so."

Walter P. Able sank further into his chair. His elbows were on the armrests. His cathedraled fingers formed a megaphone around his mouth. His lips barely moved when he asked, "How big is this, Rader?"

Jeff eyed him and answered softly, "Incredibly."

"And obviously very dangerous, too, right?"

Jeff affirmed this with silence.

Able dropped an arm and rubbed his bottom lip with the middle finger of his right hand. The gesture spoke for him. It said "I'm worried. . . . I don't know if I want to get involved in this."

Rader heard that silent statement. He leaned forward. "What is it, Able?" he asked quietly. "You've changed. We were never close friends, but I thought I had you right. Where's the fire? Where's the anger?"

"None of your fucking business, Rader."

"Like hell it's not," Jeff shot back. "If it stands in the way of your helping me, it becomes my business!"

In the silence that followed, Jeff Rader caught the nervous flicker of Walter P. Able's gaze. He reached out and touched the little man on the knee. "Come on, Walt," he said gently. "What is it?"

Able studied Rader's face for a few seconds. He sighed. "They're doing it, Jeff," he said. "They're finally doing it."

"What?"

"Cutting off my balls." He grunted once. "It comes from years of making enemies in high places." He stood and started to pace the room. "They're clever. They're using the law to kill me. Litigation. I'm being sued to death—so many suits, I don't have time to breathe. Money doesn't mean shit to them. They don't even care if they win. They just want to keep me tied up in the courts until I dry up financially and blow away. I don't have time for research anymore, I can hardly write, and I certainly can't publish. The newsletter's falling apart—*Walter's Report*, the only thing in this world that means anything to me—and I'm hanging on only by my God-damned fingernails. They're waiting. Man, are they waiting! One move—one wrong move, that's all—and they'll pounce on me like jackals going after a dying bird. People have been trying to get me for a long time, Rader. But it looks like this group is finally going to win the prize.''

"What's this got to do with me?"

"You're a wanted man, for Chrissake! I'm crazy even to be talking to you! If they find out I so much as know you, that could be the wrong move they're waiting for. They'll make me an accessory to whatever the hell you're tied into. They won't only close me down then, they'll put me away and melt the God-damned key!''

"Who're 'they,' Walter?"

"A whole pack, but it's really only one guy. And he doesn't even live in Chicago! He's the one directing the whole thing, though, I know that.''

"Who is he?"

Able paused for a moment. His gaze met Jeff's directly. "Arthur Marquand," he murmured.

It was like a blow on the head. "Marquand?" Jeff repeated incredulously. "The publisher of *my* paper?"

Walter P. Able nodded.

Jeff was stunned speechless. "But . . . how . . . ?"

"How could any publisher try to silence the press, huh?"

"Right."

"I don't know. But the son of a bitch is effective because he *is* a publisher. Lots of experience, that's it, and I know the man's done his homework. When it comes to libel action, Arthur Marquand seems to know every legal maneuver in the book.''

"Why, though? What did you ever do to him?"

"Nothing. But I've been rubbing some other skins raw, and apparently they belong to his friends.''

Friends! My God, could Pedabine be in Chicago, too? Of course it could. It was in the capital of the nation as well as L.A. Why not Chicago? And then who knows where else? Jeff's heart was racing. He could feel it in his throat. His words trembled. "Able," he whispered, "who are these friends?"

"Why?"

"Name them, damn it, name them!"

The force of that demand was more than Walter P. Able could ignore. "Joshua Clayton, president of Global Mining; Alexander

Durwell, president of Century Dynametrics; Stanford C. Waymark, president of International Telesystems. You want more?''

"How many more are there?"

"Three, but your publisher's the arrowhead. That's another reason I hesitated seeing you. I had this quick flash that maybe he'd sent you for . . . well, I don't know. It was a paranoid thought because obviously, since the police want you, you're not going to waste your time hounding poor ol' Walter P. Able.'' The words were accompanied by a wan smile.

Jeff barely heard the explanation; he certainly didn't notice the smile. His mind was centered almost entirely on his next question. "Able, think carefully—please. Do you know if any of those friends has a piece of little finger missing from his left hand?"

Able's brows knit. His head jerked. "That's the craziest damned . . . ! Why do you want to know a thing like that?"

"Please!"

Able paused and reflected. "Yeah," he groused, "as a matter of fact Clayton does, and Waymark, too. I remember a photographer once mentioning the coincidence to Clayton and his laughing it off. Why? Does that mean anything? And you'd better not bullshit me now, Rader!"

"I need your help, man."

"Oh, you do, huh? Well, I'll tell you what—apparently you know something I don't, and I've got a feeling it may help me get Marquand and his pack off my ass. So if you tell me what it is, you've got yourself a partner, my friend. And if you don't, you're on your own."

It was a cold and simple trade-off. Jeff weighed the wisdom of telling what he knew. For one thing, there was a facet of this he didn't quite understand: If Pedabine killed with impunity, why were Marquand and his friends pulling Walter P. Able through a legal wringer instead of silencing him quickly with a bullet? For another, Jeff was sickened by the possibility that he might be responsible for more killing. If the owner of *Walter's Report* should indeed be associated with him, whatever restraints there were that kept Marquand and his cohorts from killing Able would disappear quickly. Their objective would become more than legal harassment or imprisonment as an accomplice. It would surely become death. Jeff didn't know if he could live with the murder of still another innocent. He had already involved Mike Gavin— and fears about the old man's safety gnawed at him constantly.

He wanted to leave without saying another word, but the face of his sister suddenly sprang to mind. Her life was actually hanging by a short string in the hands of this irascible little man. Annie's death was a certainty without his help; Able's death was still only a probability. That settled the matter. In the next few minutes he revealed most of the pertinent details behind his reason for being in Chicago.

Able listened in stunned silence, but by the time Rader had finished, the banked fires in the troubled man had flared. He saw a way out of his dilemma now: It was through Jeff Rader. There was a chance, however slim, that the whole filthy Pedabine story might be uncovered. If that happened, it could free Able's cherished newsletter once and for all from the financially crushing pressure of endless court action. He rose wordlessly from his chair. He strode across the room to the telephone. He dialed quickly, and when the connection was made, his voice conveyed a warm and friendly urgency. "Leland? . . . It's Walter P. Able. . . . Fine. How are you? . . . Good. Leland, there's a friend of mine doing some research on Chicago at the turn of the century. I've told him you're the man to see. . . . I only speak the truth, my friend. . . . His name's Peter Stewart. You'll like him. . . . Good. We have a problem, though. Not a big one, but it'll inconvenience you, I'm afraid. He's from New York, and he just got a call telling him he's needed back there tomorrow. Can he get into the archives tonight? I know it's terrible of me to ask you to leave your home on a night like this and to open the archives just for a friend. . . . You really don't mind? Thank you, Leland, thank you very much. He'll meet you there. That's another one I owe you, my friend. . . . Stay well. . . . Okay, 'bye.''

He turned toward Jeff and explained, "Leland Mimler, curator of the Charles G. McClintock Archives. McClintock was one of the early settlers in Illinois. Wheeled and dealed in everything and became a force in the state. He had a sense of history so he kept records—not only of his own activities but of everyone else's as well. When he died, his papers became the basis of the McClintock Archives, and the material's grown steadily ever since. A small place, but the best damned collection of intimate historical details in the country. If you don't find what you want there, it doesn't exist.''

He had crossed to the desk as he spoke and scrawled something quickly on a random sheet of paper. "The address. Good luck, Rader," he said abruptly as he proffered the page. There was something new in his manner. New and yet old. He was Walter P. Able again. No longer the toothless lion. A man once more with a flicker of hope. He even pulled a corner of his mouth back into a familiar grudging smirk. "I once told you reporters are shit and their words never change a fucking thing. Well, make me wrong, Rader, make me wrong."

Guardian of the Past.

Leland Mimler looked so much like Hollywood's concept of a curator, he was almost a living caricature. Small, thin, and balding, with soft eyes behind rimless glasses, he seemed to flutter as he walked. And when he spoke, the reverential tones of his voice conjured images of great and ghostly struggles. Donald Meek in Historyland.

He welcomed Rader with warmth and interest.

In his wig, mustache, and heavily framed glasses, Jeff suggested something of the scholar. He sensed the impression and augmented it by responding to Mimler's respectful manner with a deference of his own.

After the usual amenities, Mr. Mimler became a model of assistance. Yes, he had heard of Avery Wesscoze. . . . Of course there were records of his life in Chicago. Indeed the McClintock Archives would be able to help Mr. Stewart. Undoubtedly he'd find exactly what he was looking for. . . . What exactly *was* he looking for? A record of Mr. Wesscoze's holdings? Lumber interests? Mines? Oilfields? Information concerning his habits, his pastimes? Well, those particulars shouldn't be too difficult to locate. After all, the McClintock Archives library was noted for the exactitude of its filing system. And if one merely knew where to look, one always enjoyed immediate success. (Soft chuckle.) Of course Mr. Stewart was rather fortunate to have the curator himself as his aide since—and he hoped this didn't seem too immodest—there was not another living soul who knew more about the archives' records than Leland T. Mimler. Indeed, they would have the necessary material before them in only a few moments. "Just a simple matter of knowing precisely where to—ah, here we are . . . Avery Wesscoze, tycoon, financier, empire builder. My, my, a little dusty there, isn't it? Goodness, I'm so embarrassed. Please forgive me, Mr. Stewart—it's just that some of our files have lain dormant for so many years, and—well, I'm sure you understand, being a scholar yourself and, therefore, another denizen of bibliographical nether regions. (A sly little smile.) I'll leave you now, sir, and if you should need me, I'll be just outside this room in my office. . . . Don't hurry. Take your time. I have work of my own, and since I'm here, I fully intend to remain at my desk until well past midnight. So rest assured, sir, you're not imposing upon me in the least—and besides, I'm only too happy to be of service to a friend of Walter P. Able.''

Jeff thanked him. He watched him leave. Alone now and sitting at the edge of his chair, he felt his pulse begin to race. The pallid spill of a desk lamp was the large room's only light. Heavy silence, its principal grace. Before him lay the all-important box, fat, musty, bound by soft black laces. Its contents could reveal the main secrets of the Pedabine mystery. He pulled a lace end, releasing the bow. The box's cover sprang open.

Packets of fragile, yellowed papers were revealed. Eagerly, he spread them over the table. He was delighted and relieved. He had hoped to find the material in some kind of order—by chronology or by subject matter—but the efficiency of the McClintock Archives' staff went far beyond his hopes. Each bundle showed a cover sheet; each cover sheet identified the year to which the papers were related; each year was followed by an itemized list of the packet's contents. And all the little parcels were arranged in perfect sequence. Ideal! It couldn't have been better if he had done it himself. He sent a silent thank-you to Leland Mimler.

Quickly, he studied the information on the cover sheets. Every time he saw a promising item, he placed the entire packet aside. In almost no time he'd separated eleven bundles from the mass of Wesscoze papers. Then, attacking the parcels in chronological order, he dug hungrily into their contents.

At first the particulars seemed to be disconnected. Acquisitions everywhere. Small ventures. Partnerships. Growth investments. Buyouts. Development projects. Flyer investments. Consolidations. Liquidations. New purchases. A maze of business dealings that seemed to lead only to confusion. But Jeff reached for the long legal pad and felt pen that lay on his table. He began to list the transactions in two columns. The first he headed PURCHASES; the second, SALES. It took a while, but eventually he produced an orderly record of Avery Wesscoze's financial affairs. After this, he began a process of elimination. He ran a dark wavy line

through each purchase and its corresponding sale. Soon all purchases and sales were inked out—that is, all but two. He was left
with two acquisitions for which he had no sales records. Strange,
he thought, everything's so incredibly accurate. Why should
there be two items left over? If Wesscoze meant to liquidate
everything before disappearing, why should two disposals not be
accounted for? Error? Loss of records? Or is it possible he didn't
get rid of them at all—that he kept these two after he'd vanished?

He went back to the packets. He searched them carefully again
for the missing documentation. He was looking for anything that
could shed light on this mystery—certificates, contracts, memos,
letters—anything. But there was nothing. And the words remained there on his sheet, two pristine titles staring up at him.
Islands in an ocean of wavy lines. ARDEN FOREST and THE RED
CONDOR MINE.

Interesting. Arden Forest, the Red Condor Mine. He tapped
the table impatiently. Within the consistency of such clerical
detail, why should there be the inconsistency of omission? Over
the years, researchers had collected this material with persever-
ance and thoroughness. How could they have missed two sales
transactions when they hadn't missed all the others?

Something was wrong here.

He turned the page of his yellow pad to a clean sheet. At the
top he printed ARDEN FOREST. Halfway down the sheet he added
THE RED CONDOR MINE. Then he attacked the pile of papers once
more for any information whatsoever about either of the two
titles. Forty-five minutes later he'd listed only three points under
the first and a scant two under the second. Arden Forest had been
purchased on Tuesday, April 2, 1895; it was a hundred-thousand-
acre spread of redwood and fir in northern California; from its
start, it had been a very prosperous timber operation.

The Red Condor Mine had been acquired on Friday, April 16,
1915; on that date, Avery Wesscoze had bought out his two
partners and taken sole ownership.

There was nothing else. Rader scoured those eleven packets
again and again, but he could find nothing to add to that meager
information. He looked up in exasperation. His eye caught the
dim presence of the wall clock above his table. He shot a glance
at his wristwatch. Where had the time gone? Almost midnight!
Nearly two and a half hours had passed. He had uncovered
something very troubling. It had raised questions, and unan-

swered questions had always been a rock in his gut. He was certain nothing more could be found in the packets he'd already examined. But what about the other little bundles? Could one of them contain some slip of data that might explain what had happened to Arden Forest or the Red Condor Mine? The only way to tell was to look through them. However, to do that he needed more time. And just how much he could presume upon the kindness and patience of Leland Mimler was something that needed answering first. He pushed his chair back. He rose. He headed for the lobby and the librarian's office.

The smiling curator was behind his desk. He was watching the doorway for Jeff's appearance. He had heard his footsteps clacking hollowly in the empty, marble-floored foyer.

"Come in, Mr. Stewart," he said brightly. "Find what you're looking for?"

"Partly," Jeff answered.

"Maybe I can help you further."

"Thank you, Mr. Mimler." Jeff slipped into the leather chair opposite the librarian's desk. "Actually, I'm a little puzzled, that's all. You see, the Wesscoze records are so meticulously filed I can't believe the material I'm looking for isn't really there—and I need a little more time. That's why I've come to see you, to find out when you intend to leave the building."

"Oh, my, don't let that concern you, Mr. Stewart. As you can see, I'm quite busy." He waved his hands over a mound of papers on his desk. "I'm really indebted to you." He grinned. "Your presence has forced me to complete something about which I've procrastinated for weeks. Take as long as you wish. By all means, as long as you wish."

Jeff grinned in return. "You're more than generous." He edged forward to rise but stopped short as a thought came to him. "Mr. Mimler," he said, "I'm working on Avery Wesscoze's business interests now, but I did hope to get into his personal life later. Maybe we can save some time. Do you know anything about his habits or pastimes?"

"Indeed, sir. He was a sailor of sorts. He entered summer regattas on the lake. He adored theater. Once he even guaranteed a Chicago performance of *Hamlet*, starring the great French actress Sarah Bernhardt. He was an outstanding chess player. And he loved to eat. 'Good dining,' he was credited with saying, 'is one of man's principal obligations to God.'"

The information prompted another question from Jeff. "Mr. Mimler, when I first told you I was here to research the Avery Wesscoze history, you responded without hesitation. And now you've enumerated little personal things about him as though you're an authority on the man. Was Wesscoze so important to the growth of Chicago or the State of Illinois that his name and habits should be well known?"

"No, no. Avery Wesscoze was a very successful man, to be sure, but there were many moguls of the period who contributed much more to the development of this region and our nation than he. Of course, there's no telling what he might have done had his family not suffered a horrible tragedy, and he himself had not disappeared so precipitately—"

"I know that part of his history, sir," Jeff interrupted gently and then pressed on. "Tell me, please—if he wasn't someone who would ordinarily be remembered quickly like one of the Morgans, Vanderbilts, or Astors of America, why is his name so readily familiar to you?"

Leland Mimler grinned. "Mr. Stewart," he said, "you're a scholar. You must be informed on many lesser known historical facts. I, too. Furthermore, I pride myself in knowing something about all the records in the Charles G. McClintock Archives." He chuckled. "However, to be perfectly candid with you, I'd probably have paid much less attention to the name of Avery Wesscoze were it not for the fact that a descendant of his sister is a principal patron of the library."

Jeff sat upright. "May I ask who that is?"

"I'm sure you've heard of him. Joshua Clayton, president of Global Mining, Incorporated?"

Jeff nodded slowly. "Yes," he breathed, "I've heard of him." And only hours ago, he remembered—one of Arthur Marquand's "friends," according to Walter P. Able. Another one with a missing finger joint. Another Pedabine in a high and powerful place. President of Global Mining. Then it struck him. Global Mining—the Red Condor Mine! Is there a connection? Is that where it could be now? *Still owned by Pedabine?* His thoughts veered in another direction. "Mr. Mimler," he said, trying to keep the excitement out of his voice, "may I see a copy of *Who's Who*?"

"Why, certainly," Mimler agreed, smiling broadly. "Are you interested in our benefactor now?"

"Well, he's related to Avery Wesscoze. Maybe I ought to know a little more about him, too. *Who's Who* should be a good starting place—unless, of course, the library has a special biography since he's one of your patrons."

Something happened to Leland Mimler's smile. Something small. Something not even perceptible in the partial lighting of the room. "Mr. Stewart," he cooed, "why don't you tell me what you'd like to know about Mr. Clayton? I'm sure I can locate it immediately for you."

But Jeff didn't know exactly what he *was* looking for. He had the name of a mine purchased over seventy years ago with no record of resale; he had the name of a Pedabine who headed an international mining corporation. That was it. Just that weak connection. But he also had a very strong feeling: If Avery Wesscoze had actually held on to the Red Condor Mine, and it was now part of Global's holdings, and Global's president was a Pedabine, it meant that Pedabine may have retained ownership for more than seventy years—and, damn it, that could be important!

"I don't really know what I want," he confessed to Leland Mimler. "Just looking. Certainly Mr. Clayton's biography will help, and if you could tell me where to find something about his corporate activities—"

The librarian grinned. "That shouldn't be too difficult, Mr. Stewart." He nodded. "Let's see now . . . the best reference for you would not be *Who's Who* but the most recent edition of *America's Corporations*. Detailed information about our country's giant industries and industrial giants." He chuckled slyly. "That is, all the information our business leaders are willing to divulge to the Internal Revenue Service."

He had come from behind his desk and started toward the main library room. Jeff followed closely. They clacked across the marble floors of the lobby before their footsteps were hushed by the rich carpeting of the library itself. Leland Mimler found the reference book quickly. He handed it to Jeff with shy little protests at Rader's expressions of appreciation. "Now you just take your time, Mr. Stewart," he reminded him pleasantly. "I still have considerable work to do. Tomorrow is Sunday, and I'll be able to rest all day."

Jeff settled into his seat again. He tore the sheets of notes from the legal pad. He folded them and slipped them into his rear pocket. Then he cleared a space on the desk and opened the volume of *America's Corporations*.

Leland Mimler, meanwhile, had gone back to his office where, after a troubled pause, he lifted his telephone receiver and dialed the private number of Joshua Clayton, president of Global Mining, Incorporated.

There were five rings before a sleep-slurred voice answered with some irritation: "Hello?"

"Mr. Clayton?"

"Yes. Who is this?"

"Mr. Clayton, it's Leland Mimler of the McClintock Archives. I hesitate to disturb you at this hour, sir, but you did request that I telephone you in the event of an unusual inquiry into the Avery Wesscoze files. . . ."

Irritation became interest. "Yes, Mr. Mimler?"

"A Mr. Peter Stewart is here now. He's a friend of Walter P. Able, and he's researching your ancestor—"

"At this hour?"

"That's what makes it unusual, sir—that and his not really knowing about a particular reference book, though he led me to believe he's a scholar."

"What does he want to know?"

"Right now he's reading about you and your business activities."

"I thought you said he's interested in the Wesscoze files."

"I did, sir, but he knows you're a descendant of Avery Wesscoze and—"

"What does he look like, Mr. Mimler?"

"Tall. Sturdy. Dark-brown hair. Mustache. Heavy-rimmed glasses. A pleasant-enough chap, and he does look scholarly, sir."

"Did he say why he's interested in my ancestor?"

"No, sir."

The voice softened. "It was very thoughtful of you to call, Mr. Mimler."

The librarian breathed relief. "I didn't know if I should disturb you at this hour—"

"I'm grateful you did. Do something else for me, will you, please?"

"Certainly, sir."

"I'd like to meet this young man. Find out where he lives."

"Somewhere in New York, Mr. Clayton. He'll be leaving Chicago in the morning."

"Oh?" He paused. "That makes his research even more intriguing, doesn't it? Now I know I should meet him. I'm sending my chauffeur for him, Mr. Mimler. Don't tell him that, please. And if he should prepare to leave before my man arrives, I'd welcome any effort on your part to detain him."

"Certainly, Mr. Clayton."

"I appreciate this. The library may expect another little contribution in the mail next week."

"Mr. Clayton, without your generous support, the McClintock Archives would be in dire circumstances, indeed. Thank you, sir, thank you very, *very* much. Good night."

Leland Mimler replaced the receiver in its cradle. He breathed a satisfied sigh. He had done the correct thing. A patron's wishes had been respected; the library would benefit again from its curator's diligence.

Inside the main room, Jeff Rader pored over the complicated history of Global Mining, Incorporated. Working fast, he had jotted significant details onto his yellow pad. By the time Leland Mimler had finished talking to Joshua Clayton, an interesting picture had begun to emerge.

Global Mining was much more than its name implied. It had subsidiary holdings in the areas of alternate energy, timber, electronics, and chemical research. It had offices in almost every Western country. It was a conglomerate of awesome dimensions.

Rader was thunderstruck. If this represented Pedabine control through Joshua Clayton, and Clayton numbered among God knows how many other powerful Pedabines, then the extent of the organization's influence over the life of almost every living soul on this planet was absolutely mind-boggling. He studied the information before him. He saw names, figures, places. He knew he could lose himself in them. The temptation to learn everything he could about Global Mining was strong, but there wasn't enough time for that. He drew his attention back to his main interest—the Red Condor Mine. And nowhere could he find a single clue to the disposition of that property.

There were mines everywhere—in Pennsylvania, West Virginia, Kentucky, Arizona, Utah, Nevada, Colorado, Alaska—in almost every state of the country, as well as in dozens of foreign locations. He felt swamped. However, it suddenly occurred to him that the names of the operations were leads in themselves. Foreign words for foreign mines, English for domestic. The Red Condor Mine . . . he concentrated on American locations. The Red Condor . . . Condor . . . let's see, a condor is a vulture and vultures are most prevalent out west. Wesscoze wouldn't have named an eastern mine after a western bird. He pulled his earlier notes from his pocket and ran his eyes quickly over Avery Wesscoze's eastern holdings: Yorktown No. 1 in Virginia; Mohawk Shaft in Upper New York. Yes, Wesscoze had a propensity for regional terms. Then the Red Condor Mine had to have been out west.

He searched the record of Global Mining operations again. This time, for western mines. That narrowed his list down to eight locations. Then he was stuck. Where, where among those eight—*if* the Red Condor Mine was being hidden—was the missing, unaccounted enterprise? He couldn't find it. There were no other leads. Disconsolately he stared down at the open pages of *America's Corporations*.

They seemed to blink at him: eleven innocuous letters. A single dark word. *Shakespeare*. He looked at it. How odd. What was Shakespeare doing among all those hard business titles? And why hadn't that seemed strange to him before? Was it because he had been concentrating on a mine and not on timber? Probably. Shakespeare . . . Shakespeare. Jeff Rader's heart suddenly leaped to his throat. Of course, there it is! Shakespeare—timber—*Arden Forest!* The other unaccounted transaction! What was Arden Forest? Where did the name originate? In a play . . . *Shakespeare's* . . . and Wesscoze was a lover of theater? He'd even brought Bernhardt's *Hamlet* to Chicago! That's it! Jesus, it fits!

Excitement surged through Rader like electricity going through water. He grabbed the book. He read the full name of the item: *The Shakespeare House*. His eyes raced greedily over the details—a private club near Atawan, California.

He jumped from his seat. Atawan, California . . . Atawan, California . . . where the hell is Atawan, California? He charged to a wall near the entrance. He had noticed map racks as he'd left earlier to speak with Leland Mimler. There was a lamp above the racks. He snapped it on. He pulled at the maps, looking, searching. Western States . . . Western States. There. He had it. He snapped off the rack light and rushed back to his table. He threw the map under his desk lamp. Atawan . . . Atawan—it's in northern

California, right in the middle of redwood and fir country! He pulled his earlier notes to him again. *Arden Forest*, they read, *100,000 acres of redwood and fir in northern California.* He had it! It was right! Avery Wesscoze had never disposed of Arden Forest. Maybe that's even where he had hidden back in 1915. Certainly! Deep in a forest. Away from all civilization. Nursing his insane scheme. Building a private utopia. Killing. Stealing children. Teaching. But why had the name been changed from Arden Forest? And Jeff speculated: To hide his identity completely. He had bought the property as Avery Wesscoze. It had been a successful timber operation. If he wanted to vanish on his own land, he had to have posed as a new owner. He probably closed down the lumber camps and renamed the property. And today his Pedabine still owns it through Global Mining. *The Shakespeare House—a private club.* Not a business. Not a part of Global's activities. More like—*a Pedabine headquarters.*

Jeff Rader felt the blood rushing to his head. His ears rang with the intensity of his excitement. He had to get back to Sandy. He had to tell her. They were close. Closer than ever before. They had a fix on a specific place. It felt right. It *was* right. They'd find Annie and Tami now. They'd find them. He knew it!

The sounds came to him through his euphoria. Light, sliding sounds. Footsteps on the marble floor outside the main room. At first Jeff thought they belonged to Leland Mimler. He looked toward the entrance expectantly. He listened. Something was wrong. The steps were too light. As though they were being softened intentionally. What's more, they were being made by two people. Danger was something Jeff Rader was now able to smell. The odor at that moment was putrid.

He moved quickly. He stuffed his notes into his rear pocket again. His glasses went into his jacket. The jacket was dropped on the table. He snapped off the desk lamp. The library was plunged into darkness, and only the dim light of the antechamber could be seen through the entranceway. Jeff waited. He crouched. His breathing quickened. His hearing sharpened. He tensed himself, ready for the worst.

The first figure appeared. A tall man in silhouette. He seemed to be hiding behind the right pillar of the entrance, only part of him visible.

Jeff ducked under a table.

The second figure balanced the first, shoulder and arm breaking the straight line of the left pillar.

Jeff slipped from under his table. Crouched, he circled behind
desks, a crab scurrying soundlessly for the stacks. He reached
them quickly. He stopped. He stood and peered through a pali-
sade of books.

The faint spill of entrance light was broken by the swift movement of the intruders. Each held a gun in his hand. They had
peeled around their respective columns like fleeting shadows. And
they were swallowed quickly by the blackness of the main room.

Jeff held his breath. The man on the right was coming his way. He
listened for the soft brush of his step on the carpet. There it was—
cautious yet steady—the tread of someone familiar with stealth.

"I know you're in here. I saw the light go out." The voice
was only yards away.

Jeff felt his viscera tightening. He opened his mouth for more
air. He held perfectly still.

"Don't be afraid. I'm not going to hurt you." The voice had
drawn nearer.

*Why are they working in the dark? Why don't they put on the
lights? They must think I'm dangerous. Do they know who I am?
Who the hell are they?*

"I work for Joshua Clayton. Mr. Clayton wants to talk to you,
that's all. Come on out. Don't be afraid."

*So that's it. Mimler called Clayton. But why? Is he a Pedabine,
too? Didn't notice his finger. No, he couldn't be. Wouldn't have
let me work this long if he were. Clayton's a library patron.
Mimler's just playing it safe.*

"What kind o' work you doing, Mac? Something for college?"
He was on the other side of the stack now. Only feet away.

*What's he doing? He's armed, using the dark, being careful,
and yet he's telling me where he is. Why? Why don't they—THEY!*

The flashlight beam caught Jeff Rader at the exact moment that
understanding flashed in his brain.

"DON'T MOVE, MAN, OR YOU'RE DEAD!"

He'd been suckered. Pulled off guard. Forced to think of only
one person while the other had circled the room and found him.

"Don't shoot! Please, don't shoot!"

Jeff's hands flew over his head. His face collapsed into a mask
of fear. His jaw quivered and spittle bubbled at the corners of his
mouth.

"Don't shoot. I won't do anything."

The talker had charged around the stack. He flanked Rader's right side now, stabbing a second beam into his face. "Don't move a finger, Mac," he warned.

"I won't," Jeff whispered earnestly.

And while the talker pressed a gun into the back of his head, Rader felt the partner's hands run expertly over his body.

"He's clean," the partner announced.

"Good," the talker replied. "Now you're coming with us, and you're going to be a good boy, right?" It was an ominous question.

"No trouble, believe me," Jeff promised.

They were between stacks, starting for the main aisle. The partner was leading; the talker was prodding Rader's back with the barrel of his gun.

And now he had *them*. Together. Suckered by his apparent fear. Believing he was helpless. Thinking mainly of leaving.

He pitched forward. Twisted on his right foot. His left leg snapped up and out like a mule's. A *Yoko Geri* kick. It caught the talker under the chin, and the force of it instantly crushed the man's windpipe. The gunman flew backward in the narrow passage. He clawed at the air. Tore books from their shelves. His gun went off. The bullet plowed wildly into the plaster ceiling as a strangled, wrenching scream ripped through his battered throat.

His partner had spun around at the first sound of movement. But he saw nothing—nothing except the flash of the gun and sudden, dancing lights. Because Rader had come up fast. Lunging forward. Swinging blindly in the blackness, his fingers curled tightly into a *Seiken* forefist. He had connected. Low. To the side. And flesh above the man's pelvis had collapsed almost up to Jeff's wrist. But the gunman didn't go down. He leaped forward, grappling, clutching, trying for a hold. It was a mistake. Jeff grabbed the man's coat. He fell backward, pulling him along. Right leg cocked. Foot in his gut. And when he sprang the leg, the force drove his enemy high over his head, flipping, flailing like a spastic diver. He smashed into the shelves. Crashed down on the talker. They tangled in a web of desperation and agony, thrashing, straining to get to their feet again. The talker making ugly gargling sounds, the partner screaming in rage and pain.

Jeff wasn't waiting, though. He'd rolled quickly to his feet. He was charging now for the main aisle. He whipped around the corner of the stacks. The entrance and the foyer were only yards away. Then suddenly the lights of the library blazed on, and Rader was caught in the open with only a long, heavy table between him and the men behind the shelves. The suddenness of illumination jerked him to a stop. For a moment he thought that Clayton had sent more than two men. It was Leland Mimler, though, his hand still on the wall switch, bewilderment and fear on his face. He had heard the gunshot, heard the crashing sounds of struggle, and he'd rushed in to investigate. Now he stood frozen at the entrance, staring at Jeff.

A thudding sound turned Rader's head around. Books. Books were flying from a shelf.

Mimler gasped in dismay.

But Rader gasped from pain.

The partner could be seen through the open shelf now, his gun in front of his face—spitting, cracking out death.

Jeff had been hit. He felt the searing path of a bullet in his shoulder. He dived for the floor. Rolled. Came up under the long, heavy table, lifting it like a shield and driving it toward the stack. The impact had the force of a battering ram. Books spilled everywhere. The shelves toppled. The gunman went down under the heavy weight of wood and metal. But it was more than that—it was a domino chain as a half-dozen stacks fell quickly and spilled their contents over the carpeted floor.

Leland Mimler stood transfixed. His library . . . his books.

Clayton's messengers lay unconscious within the chaos.

Jeff staggered to his feet. His shoulder ached fiercely. Blood ran down his arm, dripping off his fingertips. He was panting like the winner of a hundred-yard dash. He scooped up his jacket and wove toward Leland Mimler at the entrance.

The librarian shrank back.

"I hope his next check is a big one," Jeff mumbled hoarsely. He walked past the trembling little man into the frigid blast of Chicago's wintry night.

He breathed deeply. The air braced him. It cleared away cobwebs and snapped him erect.

He knew exactly what had to be done now. Though he was sure he'd seriously injured one of Clayton's goons, he also recognized the possibility that the other might regain consciousness quickly and free himself from his prison of books and shelves. Even if he didn't—even if he were out for a long time—there was still Leland Mimler. Recovering his composure, the timid curator would surely rush to the telephone for Joshua Clayton or the police. If it were Clayton, there was the possibility that no action would be taken tonight. But if it were the police, a description of him would be out in minutes. The safest course was to imagine the worst.

At that hour of the morning the glare of streetlamps spread an eerie cast over sections of Lincoln Avenue. Silence reigned. Only an occasional blast of wind and the crunch of his shoes in the brittle ice and snow told Jeff he wasn't on some long-dead planet. If the police should look for him, they'd spot him in a second. He had to change his appearance and get out of the area quickly. He turned the corner of the street and ducked into a doorway of a store. He removed his wig and mustache and stuffed them into his jacket's large pocket. So much for identification. Then he remembered the jacket—it, too, would be described. He pulled its reversible sleeves inside out, congratulating himself on his foresight. Before putting it on, though, he washed his bloody hand with some snow. He didn't want some alert cabby remembering blood. He tried to see his shoulder to determine the extent of the damage, but there wasn't enough light. All he knew was that the pain was like a spear drilling through to his fingertips now and that the entire arm was becoming useless. He grabbed more snow and packed it around the wound. It would slow the bleeding. Then he slipped into his jacket, readied some money in an accessible pocket, and stepped once more into the wind of the lonely street. He was a hunched figure in a frozen world.

If I can just make it to a hotel entrance, he prayed. He thought he'd be able to find a cab at a hotel hackstand even at this hour.

Four blocks from the library his thought materialized. Not in the form of a hotel hackstand; in the form of a taxi itself. It came tearing down the street, its driver hell-bent for home.

Rader stepped into the gutter and waved his good arm. The cab passed him. He groaned and spat his disappointment. But halfway down the street the car came to a fast stop and jerked into reverse. Jeff's spirits soared. He knew he loved this driver, whoever he was.

He was a beefy middle-aged black whose first words were "Saw tomorrow's headlines—'MAN FREEZES WAITING FOR CAB'—

an' shit, I got enough trouble without havin' *you* on my conscience!''

Jeff laughed along with him.

"Where to?"

"Courtney Hotel." The Courtney was a block away from the Dorset. He was taking no chances. If a police check of early-morning fares should be made, this cabby wouldn't lead the law directly to him and Sandy.

"Hey, man, what the hell you doin' out this hour, in this weather?" the driver asked, making conversation.

"My lady threw me out," Rader joked. "Said she'd been abused, confused, and definitely not amused."

Joviality. Leland Mimler must have noticed the bullet wound and the blood. They would be in a report, too. Levity would never be expected from a wounded man. Just another touch to mislead investigators.

They reached the Courtney. The trip had been a steady run of badinage and laughter. Jeff tipped the driver generously and watched him race down the street in a swirl of exhaust. Then he dashed into a doorway near the hotel entrance and donned his wig, mustache, and glasses again. The night clerk at the Dorset may have seen him leave. He had to return with the same appearance. He didn't reverse the jacket, though. He knew that blood had slicked the inside of the sleeve.

The walk to the Dorset was fast; entrance into the hotel, easy. But at his room, he suddenly lost the last of his strength. He sagged against the jamb, scratching weakly on the door.

Sandy had the latches free in an instant, and he stumbled into the room. She helped him toward the bed where he collapsed with a groan. Her first inclination had been to cry out. She'd stifled it, though. Quickly. Now she moved with the certitude of a general. She unzipped his jacket and rolled him on his side to draw a sleeve from an arm. That was when she saw the blood. Her heart tripped. A terrible whimper sounded through her nostrils. But the anxiety only sharpened her movements. Off came his jacket and shirt, and she straightened him on the bed. Then she rushed to the bathroom for towels. She dipped these into ice-cold water. She returned quickly. She bathed the arm. Again and again. His entire arm was a bloody mess. At first she couldn't even determine the source of the blood. But soon the affected area was clean enough for her to study the wound. She broke to the telephone.

"Is there a bell captain on at this hour?" she asked the night operator.

"No, ma'am."

"Get me the desk." The connection was made. Her voice became pleasantly suggestive. "This is Mrs. Wayne Castner in fifteen oh six. I know the bar and room service are closed at this hour, but I wonder if there's anybody down there with you who can get me and my husband a bottle of Jack Daniel's or Cutty Sark or anything, actually, so long as we can continue our little honeymoon party up here."

She heard the desk man's regrets.

"Be worth a twenty-dollar tip to us, honey," she answered oh-so-pleasantly. "Why, thank you, sweety, and don't forget a large bucket of ice with that, will you?"

She went back to Jeff; he was slowly regaining some of his strength. "What happened?" she whispered as she dabbed a cold, wet facecloth at the torn shoulder.

"Bullet," he answered. "Tell you later." But despite his exhaustion, despite his desire to remain perfectly quiet, he couldn't help adding "I think we've found Tami and Annie" just to see the joy and excitement spring to her eyes.

Her breath caught. Her lips compressed into a tight line of happiness. Tears brimmed. She leaned forward and kissed him warmly on the mouth. "Oh, God, I do love you," she whispered.

That was the best of all medications.

After the grinning desk clerk had been sent on his way, she cleaned the wound with the Jack Daniel's he'd brought and stanched the flow of blood with a steady application of ice.

In time, Jeff came to himself again. The pain had eased to a dull throb. Movement was returning to his arm. He studied the damage in a mirror. He sighed with relief. The deltoid muscle had been torn badly, but fortunately the bullet had passed through the shoulder. No bones smashed. Nothing major destroyed. A flesh wound, that's all. Bloody, painful, and incapacitating, but far, far better than it might have been.

They left Chicago that morning.

Sandy had treated and dressed the wound with supplies she'd purchased at a nearby supermarket pharmacy.

They avoided O'Hare International, believing the Chicago Midway Airport to be better for a safe escape.

19

Sunday, February 5, 1984

Jeff Rader had wondered about it: If Pedabine killed so easily, why was Walter P. Able being destroyed in the courts and not by a bullet? The answer was simple: Able was merely a new Pedabine game. He had challenged some of its members with his editorials. The challenge had been accepted as another opportunity to test Pedabine power and expertise. Marquand and his friends were enjoying themselves. But the moment Able learned of the organization's existence, the moment he aligned himself with Jeff Rader, his status changed from game to threat.

After Jeff had left the archives, Leland Mimler, in a state of panic and near shock, called Joshua Clayton. He babbled about devastation, violence, and bloodshed. Clayton finally calmed him. He assured the librarian all damage would be corrected well before Monday's opening hour. He urged him not to call the police until he, Clayton, had had an opportunity to question his men. He promised swift and terrible punishment for their actions. Bewildered and childlike, Leland Mimler placed himself and the matter entirely in the hands of his library's principal benefactor. He was terrified, but he was also relieved that he wouldn't have to undergo police interrogation. And the realization that Joshua Clayton's intervention would undoubtedly keep the shocking events out of the press pacified him even further.

His shaking fingers replaced the telephone receiver. Suddenly he heard sounds coming from the main room. *The man with the gun*, he thought. He ran to his office door. He locked it and turned off the lights. Then gentle Leland Mimler spent the rest of the night in the dark, sitting in rigid fear behind his desk.

Broken and battered, they made their way back to Joshua Clayton. One needed immediate medical attention; the other made his report.

It caused deep concern. Who was this mysterious researcher? What did he want from the Wesscoze files? Why did he fight so viciously to escape?

According to Leland Mimler, he had been sent by Walter P. Able. Why? Did Able know about Pedabine?

In the dead of night, long before Jeff and Sandy were preparing to leave Chicago, Walter P. Able had visitors. They were strange people. Cold. Earnest. They didn't have to do more than cock a gun at his ear to convince the owner of *Walter's Report* that his brains would decorate the walls if they didn't get fast and clear answers to their questions. He tried to sound defiant, but he was scared. He told them everything he knew. For his cooperation, he received a bullet in his ear. It tore away the top of his head and splattered his brains on the ceiling.

His body was found at 11:00 A.M.

Death was later recorded as a suicide. Probable reason: acute depression over legal reverses and professional failure.

Joshua Clayton reported the extermination of Walter P. Able directly to Pedabine 1.

"Father."

"Speaking."

"Your instructions have been followed."

"How did he learn of us?"

"He was in league with the reporter and the mother of 431."

"The reporter!"

"He was the researcher. He was wounded, but he escaped again."

An unspoken ferocity was evident in the even cadence of the Father's next words. "He is a very dangerous man. He's beginning to tell others about us. We have to know to what extent he's revealed our existence. He must be located quickly. He must be captured and brought to us alive. Evidently he doesn't believe his sister is in danger. He must be shocked into making a mistake. Ann Kroft is to be terminated immediately.''

''Are you instructing me to supervise her termination, Father?''

''No, it will be effected by someone at the Shakespeare House. You will be needed at the convocation. When may we expect you?''

''I expected to leave today. But I have to see to the repair of the library now and to the pacification of the librarian.''

''You mustn't miss the Grand Meeting.''

''I won't.''

''Good. Your brothers and sisters have been arriving steadily. They'll be pleased to see you again.''

''And I, them.''

''Until Tuesday, my son.''

''Good-bye, Father.''

20

Sunday, February 5, 1984

They arrived in Burbank at 5:30 P.M.

They had spoken very little during the flight. There had been a third passenger in their row and they hadn't wanted to risk being overheard. Jeff tried to sleep; his throbbing wound had permitted only five- or ten-minute snatches. However, brief as they were, they had helped.

It was a gun that had brought them back to Burbank. Rader had left it in the trunk of Gavin's LTD. It was the one Jeff had taken from Durkin's man in the tunnels of Meta-Chem Laboratories. Airline security checks had mitigated against his carrying it to Chicago. Now he wanted it, even though he had to go into the lion's den to get it. His damaged shoulder made his karate effectiveness uncertain. He needed something to adjust the odds, and he didn't know where to find another gun in California without revealing his presence there.

They went directly to the parking lot for their car. They tossed their overnight bags into the trunk. Then Jeff removed the all-important gun from where it had been hidden and eased it into the waistband of his pants. Now they had to get moving—fast.

They gassed up at a service station where Jeff also bought a road map. He knew Atawan was located north of Eureka, but he hadn't known exactly what roads would get them there. Sandy took the wheel. They were on Interstate 5, heading for Redding. At Redding they would take 299 to Willow Creek and then switch to 96 until they'd hit Somes Bar. After Somes Bar, it

would be a side road west to Atawan. A simple trip—but a long
one. Fifteen hours! Jeff's apprehensions increased with each passing minute. Annie's life was dangling on a thread of time. He'd
have preferred to fly from Chicago to San Francisco and to rent
another car there. That would have saved seven hours. But that
would also have left him without his gun. Its handle was pressing
under his rib cage. He touched it. He thought of Annie. He
wondered if he'd made the right decision in going back for the
weapon.

Sandy sensed his concern. She glanced at him. "Isn't there
anyone who can help us?" she asked.

He shook his head. "I once thought of writing this up and
mailing it to twenty or thirty of my friends on different newspapers
around the country. I figured exposure might destroy Pedabine's
effectiveness. If not destroy it, then at least weaken it. But I
decided I couldn't take the chance. That would be twenty or
thirty more lives I'd be putting into jeopardy. Walter P. Able's
life is probably over now because of me."

"We haven't heard anything."

"We will. I understand them now. By this time they've found
out who sent me to the archives. Mimler's told them. And
they've probably visited Able."

"Then you think he's already dead?"

He nodded. Quiet filled the car as he thought of himself: What
was he going to do if he should outlive this nightmare? How
could he adjust to the knowledge that he was now a killer and
that he'd also been responsible for the deaths of innocent people?
The silence was broken by a shuddering sigh. "And then there's
Michael—"

Sandy gasped. "You don't believe they've harmed him, do
you?"

"I can't say. They realize you and I know about them, or they
wouldn't have put a letter *P* on the note they left at Annie's
house. Myra London probably reported the fact that she'd mentioned Pedabine to me. After Chicago, they have to know we've
made the connection between them and Avery Wesscoze. And if
they link Michael to us—thanks to the Chevy we left near the
Meta-Chem buildings—then his life won't be worth much either.
They seem to want to silence everyone who knows about their
existence. So we're alone, you see? Nobody can help us because
I can't place anyone else in that kind of danger."

She reached over and touched his hand. The aloneness, the isolation from the rest of the world weighed heavily upon both of them. It made Sandy think the unthinkable. "What will happen if we do save Annie? What if we do free Tami? Pedabine will still be everywhere. It'll never stop looking for us."

"True."

"What will we do?"

"I don't know. That's the future. We'll think about it tomorrow. Tami and Annie are today."

She squeezed his hand.

He smiled at her.

"How's your shoulder?" she asked.

"Fine," he lied. He loved her concern. He brought her hand to his lips and he kissed it.

They drove all night. They worked in three-hour shifts. One slept while the other was at the wheel. That Monday at 8:00 A.M. they rolled quietly into Atawan, California.

Atawan is a small town. Population 4,600. It's near the juncture of the Klamath and Trinity rivers, east of the Redwood National Park. At 8:00 A.M. on that Monday, it was barely stirring. Jeff knew, though, what business would be awake. He had Sandy stop at the street pay phone of a service station. The directory hung on a chain under the telephone. He checked it. Good. Atawan had a newspaper: *The Atawan Signal*. Address: 18 Central Street.

They found it easily.

It was a storefront publication. Tiny. Two small rooms. Only one person could be seen through the window. She was studying some negatives.

"Morning," Sandy chirruped as they entered.

"Good morning," she responded with equal pleasantness. She was in her fifties, alert, ebullient.

"My husband and I were just passing through. Name's Seeliger. I'm Janice and this is Jerry."

"Why, hello there." She rose and crossed to them. "Elsie Olmstead. What can I do for you?"

"This your paper?" Sandy asked with bright interest.

"Lock, stock, and creditors."

All three chuckled.

"Elsie," Jeff said warmly, "we're on our way to Eureka. To

be honest, Jan and I are house nuts. We're absolutely crazy about interesting old houses—''

"Oh, you'll see a lot of them in Eureka, all right."

"Everybody tells us that," Sandy bubbled.

Jeff added quickly, "We were told Atawan has a unique place, too, and we thought we'd just take a peek at it before leaving."

"You must mean the Shakespeare House."

"Right."

"Beautiful place. Best example of Victorian architecture in the state. But you can't get in. It's a private club. Owned by a big eastern company. They use it as a recreation resort for their bigwigs. Got a big iron fence all around the property."

"How long has the fence been there?" Jeff asked.

"Long as I can remember, and I was born in Atawan."

"Can the house be seen from the road?"

"Barely. Although there's one spot where the trees thin out a bit and—"

"Where is that?" Sandy asked eagerly.

"Near the south end of the lake. You take Central Street out to the 89A intersection, go west until you get to the railroad crossing, then follow the first road on your right. It'll curve around to the south end of the lake, and you'll get a pretty good view of the house from there."

"Thank you, Elsie"—Sandy beamed—"thank you very much."

"Don't mention it." She smiled. "I've been inside a few times, but that's only because I run the paper here. It's a beautiful thing to see, all right. Too bad they won't let you in. You'd love it."

Sandy shrugged. "Well, the outside's better than nothing."

Before leaving Atawan, Jeff had Sandy stop at the service station again. This time he purchased a thick, heavy-duty towing cable.

On the way they considered their strategy: first, a quick look at the house and grounds; then, based on what they would learn, the approach.

They were there in fifteen minutes.

From the south end of the lake they saw a huge, sprawling building, green and brown in color, with ornately carved pillars, gables, and cupolas everywhere in perfect symmetry. It sat resplendently on a magnificent knoll, commanding a glorious view of the lake. Carefully manicured grounds ran to the edge of the surrounding forest and straight down to the water. A towering wrought-iron fence guarded the property. It was a storybook picture, something from another age.

"Amazing," Jeff breathed.

Sandy nodded agreement.

"The fence is the problem," he noted, getting down to business. "We certainly can't go driving up to its front gate. Have to go over, around, or through it someway. It ducks into the trees in places. See? I'm betting it goes all around the house."

"Probably," she agreed. "The only open space seems to be lakeside."

"That's where I'll get in, then."

"*You?*"

"You're not coming with me, Sandy."

"Jeff—"

"I don't have the faintest idea what to expect in there," he cut her off.

"Death, maybe," she said quickly.

"Right, and—"

"And if you go without me and that should happen, what do you think I'd do all alone, without you, without Tami? Just waiting for you to come back to the hotel in Chicago nearly drove me out of my mind."

"Sandy—"

"Without you I'd be dead anyway."

He looked searching into her eyes.

"If you leave me here, I'll only go in after you," she whispered. "You may need me."

He shook his head slowly in admiration. He smiled faintly. "All right," he relented, "but you have to do exactly as I say."

She leaned over and showed her agreement with a kiss.

The third floor of the Shakespeare House was an architect's dream. It was reached by means of wide stairs of gleaming redwood. They curved gracefully up to an elaborately arched hallway. Crystal chandeliers sparkled from an exquisitely patterned ceiling. There were eight bedrooms off this hall. Each had a door of heavy, white primavera wood. All had intricately carved facings. All were outstanding examples of delicate art and genteel taste.

Behind the second door on the left, Ann Kroft lay on her back in the center of a large canopied bed. She was still bound, gagged, and blindfolded. She was alone, she was awake, and she was terrified. What had happened? Where was she? Where was Stanley? Was he all right? Why was she being held? Who were these people? The questions tumbled in her brain.

They had taken her from her home straight to the Shakespeare House. She had been kept unconscious until yesterday afternoon. Then an antidote to the anesthesia had been administered. It had brought her to her senses quickly. She had been fed and allowed to use the bathroom. After that, she had been interrogated mercilessly. The questions had all been related to her brother— his habits, his interests, his friends, his haunts, his women. She had told her examiners nothing. After each question, she had begged for an explanation of her position and the whereabouts of her husband. Her appeals had been consistently ignored. Her blindfold had never been removed. The questioning, the isolation, the darkness, had merged into a swirling nightmare of confusion and uncertainty. All of this, coupled with a growing concern for the welfare of her unborn child and the safety of her husband, had turned her apprehensions into sheer terror.

Now she lay perfectly still, as though one wrong twitch would incite the hungry monsters of her mind. She felt lost, overwhelmed. She whimpered, and behind her blindfold, tears filled the sockets of her eyes.

The ground floor of the Shakespeare House held a small auditorium, meeting rooms, a well-equipped kitchen, a dining room with a breathtaking view of the lake, music rooms, a billiard parlor, two art rooms, and a small library.

They were in the library. Two men and a woman. They were arguing about a recent directive.

"If we kill her now, it will *not* violate the Primary Council's orders," the woman was insisting.

"I don't see it that way," the older of the two men said. "Our instructions are to hold her until ten A.M. and to question her every hour until then. Now, ten is not nine in my book—"

"You're wrong, Nick," the younger man interrupted strenuously. "The instructions require us to make the time adjustment. The Council uses its own time—ten o'clock there is nine o'clock here."

"No, no." The older man shook his head. "I've received instructions from the Council before and they've never required modification."

"So have we," the woman pressed, "and we've always made the adjustments."

"It's eight forty-five now," the older man said, looking at his watch. "We'll question her until nine. And then, I say, we wait another hour to question her again. After that, she should be extinguished. Suppose we were to kill her at nine, and for some reason she would have supplied us with valuable information by ten? Can't you see what we would lose?"

"It's not a matter of losing anything," the woman fumed. "It's a matter of orders. She's supposed to die at nine!"

"Let's call the Father and settle this," the younger man snapped.

"No!" The word came simultaneously from the woman and the older man. Both knew that such a call would certainly produce a solution to their problem—but both knew it would also produce pain and sorrow. Pedabine rewarded handsomely for accomplishment and punished severely for error. One of them would have to pay if their disagreement were made known. Neither was willing to take that chance.

"Then we vote—like the Council," the younger man insisted.

The older man knew he had lost. He looked from one to the other. "All right," he finally agreed, "she dies after the next interrogation. But if it's ever discovered that she was killed at nine instead of ten, understand this: I will not be subjected to the Council's questioning alone."

The woman nodded agreement. She rose. She crossed to a table in the center of the room. A small brown box lay at one end. She opened its lid extracted a small hypodermic syringe. After drawing a tiny amount of clear fluid into it from a sealed bottle, she turned and looked at her associates. She smiled strangely. "All right, let's go up and question our closedmouth lady one last time."

Outside the Shakespeare House, Jeff and Sandy were easing their LTD over uncertain roadless land. They had pulled into a tree-glutted area fringing the lake. They were skirting water now, edging closer to that iron fence. Jeff had studied its course around the house as it dipped in and out of the woods. He had concluded that it probably ran right down into the lake. And when Jeff crouched and examined the barrier itself, he had been momentarily shaken. Each of its closely spaced bars was over an inch in diameter. They spiraled upward twenty feet, curved outward, and ended in deadly barbed points. They were connected by heavy iron plates, and their main posts were imbedded in giant slabs of concrete. An awesome construction.

He followed it, though, to the water's edge. He saw how it was hidden among trees, extending into the lake for more than thirty feet. He saw how razor-wire had been heavily coiled around the trees as well as the fence—all the way to their end. He saw, also, that any boat attempting to circle those trees would be in clear view of the house's occupants. And then he saw what he had been looking for—rust. He squatted at the water's edge. He plunged his hand into the lake. Grabbed a bar. Felt the crusty oxidization of iron against his fingers. He picked at it. Particles peeled away. He studied the bar, trying to determine how high the lake had risen in past years, how much of the bar had been affected by immersion. What he saw satisfied him. He got back into the car.

"There was a little clearing about twenty yards back," he reminded Sandy. "Back up to it, turn around, and then back up to this spot again."

She didn't question him.

When they were close to the fence again, Jeff hooked one end of the cable he had purchased earlier to a rusted bar and the other end to the LTD's chassis.

"Now," he breathed, "if the ground will only stay firm enough to support us—" He nodded at Sandy. She eased the Ford forward. The cable went taut. She pressed the accelerator harder. The rear wheels began to spin and to sink. "Hold it," Jeff ordered. "Too soft. We'll dig ourselves in that way." He studied the situation. He sighed sharply. "When I say the word, gun it. The jolt'll either break the bar or the cable. We'll just have to gamble. Okay, get ready."

Sandy tensed.

"Go!"

Her foot slammed the pedal. The car leaped forward. The cable jerked into a straight line. There was a dull groan below the surface of the water, and a foot of the bar curled up and out like a pin-hook.

They were elated.

They did this to the three adjacent bars. There was a gap wide enough for them to squeeze through.

They left the car where it was, hidden among the trees, and inched through the opening. Then, gun in hand, Jeff led the way through the heavy foliage. They were wet and chilled, but they paid no attention to themselves. They were intent only on making the fastest progress possible. They crouched and raced toward a spot where the brush and trees were closest to the building, the lee side of the house. It offered the least clearing to cross, and soon they reached a point where they could see garbage cans. That heartened them. It might be where the kitchen was located. There would be a door there, and there would be activity. Activity meant work and work meant diverted attention. That would be their entrance. But they were too intent on their approach. They had ignored their rear.

It came out of the woods like a blur. Compact. Heavy. All muscle and hatred. It was a full-grown rottweiler, trained to kill. Its snarl was ferocious. Its charge powerful. It caught Jeff at arm level, and his gun went flying. But he gave with the impact, fell, rolled, and was on his feet in an instant. The dog had gone down as well, thrown by the evasive move. But it too, was up in a moment. It charged as Sandy went diving for the gun. Rader sidestepped the leap and hammered a fist at the animal's head. The crack of the blow was a mallet on a slab of meat. Pain exploded behind the animal's eyes. It had been trained to kill, though, and pain enraged it further. Growling, it rushed again. Jeff feinted. The attack was fractionally diverted. Enough for a mighty *Kanzetsu* kick. It caught the soft underbelly of the beast. But still it came on with demonic insistence. Rader stepped back. His foot twisted on a fallen branch. He went down. The animal was on him in a second. They lurched so wildly Sandy couldn't sight the beast with her gun. The dog lunged for Jeff's face. Snapping. Slavering. Jeff's weak arm came up for protection. Powerful jaws clamped on his forearm. He felt razor-teeth cutting for the bone. Only the padding of his ski jacket prevented maiming. He twisted. He fought to get to his feet. But 125 pounds of ferocity, with the attack power of twice that weight, drove him back to the ground. They thrashed. They rolled. Jeff made it to a knee. He drove a fist into the animal's rib cage. He felt the ribs break. He made it to his feet while the beast held on, its sounds becoming even wilder. Another fast blow went straight to the beast's testicles. A third to its throat. The dog's eyes glazed. Jeff felt the attack weaken. He slammed the flat of his palm hard over those glazed eyes, and the dog went blind. The viselike jaws opened. As the crazed animal dropped away, one final deadly kick caught it under its jaw. It lay on the ground now, panting, tongue lolling, beaten. The entire fight had taken only minutes. Rader's sleeve looked as if it had been shredded by a saw. He glanced at it. If that had been my throat—! he thought.

"Jeff!"

Sandy's warning came too late. The mate of the first dog was on him from out of nowhere. It hurled him to the ground. He went to his back. The animal straddled him. Snapping. Lunging. He couldn't get to his feet without exposing his face. He felt teeth sink into the naked hand of his bad arm. He felt flesh rip.

A shot cracked through the struggle.

The beast jerked once and then collapsed across Jeff's chest.

He pushed away the heavy dead weight. He rolled to a knee. He saw Sandy's arm dropping from a firing position. He looked around quickly, expecting another attack. He waited. Nothing happened. Sandy was only two feet away. He looked up at her and exhaled sharply.

She grinned weakly at him.

But their relief was premature. That shot had been clearly heard inside the Shakespeare House.

The questions were the same; the technique was different.

"Where's your brother, Jeff?"

"I don't know."

"Where does he go to get away from things?"

"I don't know."

"Does he have a special woman in his life?"

"I don't know."

"What does he do to relax?"

"I don't know."

"Who are his closest friends?"

"I don't know. I don't know!"

This time the questions were being spat like steady gunfire. No single shot was meant to hit a target. They were all aimed solely at intensifying Ann Kroft's confusion and fear.

She began to cry. "Where's my husband?"

They ignored her. "Where's your brother, Jeff?"

"Where's Stanley? I want to speak to him. Let me speak to him!"

"Where does he go to get away from things? Does he have a special woman in his life? What does he do to relax?"

"STANLEY!"

"Who are his closest friends?"

"STANLEY!"

A signal. The younger man suddenly fired, *"Your baby is going to die."*

Annie gasped as though she'd been burned.

That's when Sandy Wilkenson's shot cracked like an exclamation mark. They hadn't heard the sounds of Jeff's struggle with their killer dogs; they'd been too involved, and the distance and woods had muffled the snarls and growls. But the crisp explosion of Sandy's gun couldn't have been clearer if it had been fired inside the house.

The questioning stopped abruptly. All three interrogators were well acquainted with the sound of gunfire. They looked at each other. "Keep at her," the younger man snapped. He broke and rushed from the room. The older man looked oddly at the woman. He nodded sharply once. She turned to Annie again.

"You'll be dead in five minutes if you don't answer the questions."

Annie moaned in panic.

"That means your baby, too," the man drilled.

Annie cried out and thrashed away from the voices.

Outside the house, the younger man looked suspiciously over the lake. He saw nothing but the soft mist of morning. He cocked his head like an animal and listened. Again, nothing. He circled the house, scanning, searching. Near the kitchen entrance he stopped and suddenly called, "Baron! Pharaoh!" He waited expectantly for a sound, a flash of movement. When only silence answered him, he turned quickly and ran back into the house. He took the curved stairway as though he were flying. He broke into the room. "Something's wrong," he panted. "The dogs don't answer."

The older man didn't lose a moment. He rushed for the door. "Come on," he spat.

The younger man hurled an order at the woman. "Kill her if we're not back in five minutes!" Then he turned and raced out.

"You hear that?" she asked.

Annie whimpered helplessly.

Downstairs, both men pulled out .38-caliber revolvers. The older man directed, "Take the south side all the way to the lake; I'll take the north. Two shots if you spot anything strange. Be here in five minutes if you don't."

Quickly they touched timer buttons on their wristwatches. Then they darted in opposite directions.

Jeff and Sandy were on the east side of the house. They watched their pursuers charge toward the woods. As the Pedabines reached the edge of the trees, Jeff signaled suddenly to Sandy. They were fifty yards from the kitchen entrance. They ran in a semicrouch, breaking from one clump of bushes to the next, holding to no spot for more than a few seconds. They covered the distance quickly. Flattened against the wall near the kitchen door, they paused and listened. Silence. Jeff scanned the stairs on the outside of the house. They went from floor to floor, each flight ending on a wide veranda. He didn't know how many people were within the house or where they would be located. The outside seemed safer from that standpoint. But he and Sandy would be so exposed there! He decided quickly to take his chances inside. He turned the doorknob. The door opened. He slipped silently into a large immaculate kitchen with Sandy at his heels. They worked their way around stainless steel counters. Jeff's chewed hand was now wrapped in a bloody handkerchief; Sandy still carried the gun. They came into a small hallway. On their right they saw a large, windowed dining room. On their left, a short passage leading to the stairway. They started for the steps. The sounds of their movement were faint taps on a bare expanse of the redwood floor.

A door opened. They froze for a moment and then darted into an alcove. They heard footsteps. They waited. The air hung heavy with expectation. A woman's voice called from above: "Nick? Larry? That you?" They ducked into the room behind them. It was the library. They pressed against the wall. Soon they heard footsteps retreating and the shutting of a door. The closing sound had a sense of urgency to it. They exhaled and realized only then that they'd been holding their breath. Jeff turned his head. He glanced quickly around the room. He was sizing it for windows, exits—anything. He saw the easy chairs, the shelves, the desks. For a moment he thought of Leland Mimler. The image passed quickly, though, because an object had caught his attention. It was a tall glass display case. Somehow it looked out of place. Too prominently situated. As though its importance transcended that of the books. It drew him. As he approached it he could distinguish its contents: glass boxes—marvelously cut glass boxes of all sizes, on little, finely wrought gold legs, with intricately fixed gold hinges for the delicate lids. The case was filled with them. Each one contained some pebbles or sand or mineral. Each one included a cleanly engraved nameplate at its base. Jeff stared at them. One in particular dominated the display. Up front. Eye level. The largest and most beautiful box. It was filled with powdery sand so bloody in color that it startled. He read the inscription: *The Red Condor*. His heart leaped.

At that moment, a scream pierced the quiet of the house.

Sandy jerked at the sound; Jeff's hair rose on his neck.

It had been a word: *STANLEY!*

He had never heard it screamed before, but Jeff knew that voice, all right. He tore from the library like a madman, Sandy racing right behind him. The scream came again and again. It filled the house. It reverberated off the walls, a cry of desperation and sheer terror. It was a beacon, and Jeff followed it with all the speed his body could generate. Around the corner. Up the stairs. Two, three at a time. He reached the third floor in seconds. The screams had become sobs. They pulled him like a huge magnet to the second door. He went into it. Slamming his good shoulder against it. Smashing it open. Almost tearing it from its hinges. The scene was a nightmare: Annie—half on, half off the bed, her legs and arms still bound, her face and shoulders pressed grotesquely against the floor; the woman—standing over her, hypodermic in hand, head in his direction, a look of stunned horror on her face. She spun toward Annie. The needle swung up.

He moved without thinking, without even feeling the pain in his shoulder and hand. Before the woman could bend, he swept up a nearby chair and hurled it furiously. It caught her high on her shoulder and on the side of her head. She went sprawling. The hypodermic flew from her fingers. Jeff broke for the bed and pulled his sister off the floor.

Annie started to scream and struggle.

"It's all right, honey. It's all right, Annie," he shouted. "It's me, Jeff. I'm here. It's okay! It's okay!"

The words broke through her terror. She began to sob almost uncontrollably.

As he pulled at the blindfold, the woman on the floor scrambled for the syringe. He saw her move and went for her, but her fingers closed on the deadly instrument, and she swung around and leaped to her feet before he was two steps from the bed. He was blocking her way to Annie. She was facing him now, a look of such evil twisting her features that for a moment he thought he was looking into the hatred of Myra Macon London again. He knew instantly that needle meant death.

"Shoot her!" he shouted.

Sandy's arm came up.

The woman jerked her head in Sandy's direction.

"Shoot her!" he repeated.

The sound of the hammer cocking was like an anvil being struck in an echo chamber.

"FOOLS!" the woman screamed. And before the hammer could fall, she raised her hand and plunged the needle into her own forearm.

Two shots exploded. They came from a distance, though. The younger man had found the dogs.

The woman pitched forward, dead, exactly as the shots were heard.

It took a fraction of a moment for Jeff and Sandy to grasp what had happened. Then the distance of the sounds registered, and they realized they had forgotten their hunters. Jeff returned quickly to his sister. He ripped off the tape that bound her hands and feet. All the while he mumbled soft, reassuring words—words that, nevertheless, still retained a driving sense of urgency.

When her hands were free, Annie threw her arms around his neck.

He let her hang on for a moment, understanding her need, feeling her painful relief. When he released her hold, the movement triggered a plethora of questions. "Who are these people, Jeff? What do they want? Why are they looking for you? Where's Stanley? Where's Stanley?"

"He's not here," he half lied.

"Is he all right?"

"Annie, is there a little girl in the house?"

"What?"

"A little girl—her name is Tami, Tami Wilkenson. This is her mother."

"I-I don't think so."

Sandy Wilkenson's heart sank. She felt like groaning. But she recovered quickly and went to the door.

"There were only two men and that woman," Annie's words raced. "There were others, but they left and these were supposed to join them later."

"Where?"

"I don't know. Jeff, is Stanley all right?"

"Annie, we've got to get out of here fast. Come on." He dodged the question, pulling her to her feet. He yanked off his jacket and had her slip into it, rushing her, conveying the peril of their situation.

Sandy's back was against the jamb of the door. She was facing the stairway. Revolver ready. Every nerve in her body alert.

"Can you walk?" Rader asked his sister.

"Yes."

"Can you run?"

She spread fingers over her bulging abdomen. "I'll try."

Alone and uninjured, Jeff might have faced his enemies. There were only two, and he had a gun as well. But the safety of the women was preeminent in his mind. Given his present condition, he couldn't risk confrontation. Escape was the only sensible course of action open to him. He led them into the hallway. The Pedabines would be there in minutes. They'd come up that stairway. The safest route for him and the women, then, was down the stairs outside the house. He ran down the carpeted hallway, Annie and Sandy following like kite tails. When he reached the end, a ninth door faced them. The symmetry of the Shakespeare House had been obvious from the outset. Now in the hall, hand-carved doors opposed each other. Four on a side. If the second was a bedroom, Jeff reasoned accurately, the others were probably bedrooms, too. That meant the ninth door, the one at the end, had to lead to the veranda and the outside stairs. He twisted the knob. The door swung inward. They barged into a small anteroom with tall, curtained French windows. They pushed them and ran out onto the gallery. As they did, they heard a door slamming wide and the sound of running feet. The Pedabines were inside the house again.

Jeff broke for the stairway. Annie was gripping his hand. Sandy followed closely.

Annie's condition was holding them back. She knew it. She tried desperately to run the flights. It was impossible, though.

Soon she was panting. The knowledge that she was slowing them increased her frustration and eventually drove her to recklessness. They were almost at the bottom—on the last three steps. She jumped them. Her knees buckled. Her body lurched forward. She pitched into Jeff and collapsed to the ground. She felt something pull inside her body. She gasped in sudden pain.

Jeff and Sandy were kneeling, flanking her. "What is it?" Sandy asked anxiously.

"Nothing," she lied.

"You sure?" Jeff insisted.

"I'm all right."

They helped her to her feet. She fought to conceal the pain. "What do we do now?" she asked as subterfuge.

"This way," Jeff urged. He headed them directly for the break in the fence, straight for the car. There was no hiding this time. No caution. They had to make the woods before their hunters spotted them. They were exposed now. The distance to the trees was a clear breadth of tended grass. Time. Speed. These were their only security. They ran as fast as they could.

Each step was torture for Annie Kroft. Something was happening. Something terrible and dangerous. It twisted and pulled her in agony. It made it almost impossible for her to stand erect. Nevertheless, she drove herself mercilessly, intensifying her suffering, worsening the condition of her body.

They reached the edge of the trees.

Shots rang out.

Jeff glanced back. He saw the Pedabines on the veranda, arms raised. He saw the men turn swiftly and dart for the stairway.

The fence, the car were only yards away.

"Come on," he snapped, doubling his effort.

They charged into the woods. They were ducking branches now, dodging obstacles.

Annie cried out in torment. A sudden tearing within her abdomen brought more pain than she was able to mask. It came from everywhere. Quick. Stabbing. She felt as though she were losing her intestines. She sagged. She gasped and tumbled toward the ground.

Sandy leaped for her as she went down. Caught her just in time and saved her from smashing her face against a large rock.

Jeff was at their side in a moment. He knelt. "Annie, what is it?" he panted. "Can you stand?"

"The baby . . . ." she moaned. "Something's happened. . . ."

Without another word, he dug his arms under her body and lifted. He felt the torn muscles in his shoulder pull. He felt a knife race down his arm and into his fingers. But he held her. He swung around quickly. The fence! There it was. He could see it! He stumbled toward the opening. Sandy raced ahead. She squeezed through it. Jumped into the car. Started the motor for a fast getaway.

At the fence, Jeff suddenly realized he had blundered. Oh, Jesus! The opening—*it was too small for his pregnant sister!* He wanted to scream in self-hatred. He glanced behind him. The Pedabines would be coming any minute! He placed Annie on the ground. He dived for the bars. Jammed himself through. He ran for the car and the cable on the backseat. Frantically he hooked one end to the chassis. Tied the other to the next iron rod. "Go!" he shouted at Sandy.

She hit the accelerator. The car leaped forward. The cable pulled. There was a dull snap, and another bar curled into a pin-hook. Two more. He would need two more! He wrapped the cable around the next shaft. "Now!" he yelled. Again the car lurched. Again a bar curled upward. One more. One more! He worked like a demon. The cable went around the iron. "Go!" he ordered. Sandy hit the pedal. The LTD jumped. There was a sharp crack. The cable—the cable! *It had snapped.* Jeff's stomach turned. There was no time for repair. No time for adjustment. The Pedabines would be on them in moments. He went through the opening again. He was at Annie's side. She was conscious, but she was moaning and gasping.

"Annie," he begged, "Annie honey, I need your help."

She looked at him. Her eyes were going vacant.

"Come on, Annie," he pleaded. "Don't give up now. Come on, baby, hold on. Hold on!"

She seemed to hear him. She moved with him toward the bars of the fence.

He pulled his ski jacket off her shoulders. She was still wearing the light housecoat she'd had on when she was abducted. And under that her short nightgown. He pulled off the housecoat. He sat her in the water. He thrust her arms through the opening.

Sandy was standing on the other side. Waiting. Looking desperately toward the woods behind them.

"Help me, Annie, help me," he urged.

She moved herself forward. Water washed over her face. Went

up her nose, down her throat. She gagged. She coughed. Still she squeezed herself hard against the bars. Her shoulders were through. Her breasts. Her back. But her swollen abdomen caught against the cold metal and stopped her like a cork in a bottle.

Sandy had her by the hands, pulling.

Jeff was kneading her stomach, pushing, inching her forward. "Pull in, Annie, pull in!" he ordered.

She sucked her insides into a knot. She kicked at the mud under her feet. Jammed herself against the iron. She was moving. Whimpering and moaning, but she was moving.

Suddenly a shout shattered their concentration: "Nick! This way! Nick, they're over here!"

Sandy dropped Annie's hands. She went for the gun in her belt.

Jeff and Annie worked in a frenzy.

A shot! Ground puffed near the car!

Sandy fired twice in response. She knew she'd miss, but the returning fire might slow the Pedabines if only for a few moments.

It did. They ducked behind trees. They dodged from cover to cover.

Meanwhile, Annie forced herself against the bars with one last Herculean effort. She twisted. She squirmed. She fought to keep from drowning. She slithered. She tugged. And finally she was through.

Jeff came right after her. He pulled her from the water. Half carried, half dragged her to the car.

Sandy was behind them, covering. Firing at the Pedabines who were now in the open, shooting and running for the fence. Lead was kicking up ground all around the car. Sandy had left the doors open. Jeff and Annie tumbled into the rear seat.

Sandy leaped behind the steering wheel. The engine was still running. She gunned it. She slammed the shift into gear. The Ford sprang ahead like a greyhound from a starting gate.

They crashed through brush. Toppled small trees. Jounced over rocks and deadwood.

Bullets plowed into the trunk of the car.

But they made it to the highway. They made it. And they were free!

They had no specific destination. They'd hoped only to put as much distance between themselves and the Shakespeare House as a day's driving would permit. However, the impossibility of that hope became obvious in just a few miles: Annie twisted and moaned on the backseat. Her soul-wrenching cries erupted with every jarring movement of the car. Hot lances stabbed through her uterus. Blood wet her thighs. First a trickle. Then the frightening gush of hemorrhage.

"The baby!" She wept. "Jeff, the baby . . . it's dying!"

They were at the outskirts of Atawan again.

"Find an open store—any one!" Rader ordered Sandy.

The car swept instantly into a sharp turn.

Annie screamed.

Jeff comforted her. "It's okay, Annie. . . . Hold on. . . ."

He'd made a decision. He knew it was a dangerous one. His sister needed immediate medical assistance. There was no going past the town. They'd drawn a good lead on the Pedabines; so strong, they were well in the clear. He was sacrificing this advantage. He was exposing them.

He knew this much: If their pursuers were still after them, they'd have to enlist help to find them—the local police to hunt for "trespassers," townspeople who might have seen the car. The Shakespeare House was certainly reputable enough in the eyes of Atawans to guarantee local assistance. Someone would surely see them. Someone was bound to respond. Their only safety lay in distance. But that was not to be.

Sandy pulled up to a hardware store.

Jeff was out almost before the car had stopped. "A hospital," he snapped at the startled clerk. "Does Atawan have a hospital?"

"Uh . . . yes. The Orie Reed Memorial—"

"Where?"

"Huh?"

"Where, for God's sake?"

"Andover Street—three blocks down, turn right, and a mile out. . . ."

He was back in the car before the clerk had dropped her arm.

They covered the mile in record time. They screeched to a stop before the emergency entrance. Jeff rushed into the small building. "Get a stretcher—fast," he told an orderly. "She may be dying."

The urgency, the suggestion of death, spurred immediate action.

Annie was inside the hospital and under a doctor's care in moments.

Jeff and Sandy huddled in the waiting room.

He had fabricated a story for the registering nurse. "We were up along the Trinity River near Somes Bar—my wife here, my sister, her husband, and me. We got us a little trailer, an' we were gonna spend a week just toolin' around. Stan—that's my sister's husband, Stan Craft . . . C-R-A-F-T, like in aircraft— well, Stan called home yesterday, an' there was some kind of emergency. Business. So he went back to take care of it. He's supposed to meet us in Redding on Friday. Then we were all gonna go home together next Sunday. Home? That's in Sacramento. Eighteen thirty-seven Archer Place. My sister's name is Frances. We call her Franny. Thirty-six oh two East Windsor . . . that's right, Sacramento. Her doctor said it'd be okay to take the trip. She's not supposed to deliver for another three weeks yet. But then a little while ago, she slips an' falls into the river. Craziest God-damned accident! She comes out o' the trailer to say good morning, she's still in her bathrobe and nightgown. My wife an' me are standing on this big flat rock, getting in a little morning fishing. Franny comes up to us on the rock, says hello, an' then all of a sudden she slips. We got her out right away, but she was hurt bad. Bleeding. Crying. My name? Zeff. Zeff Dullea . . . D-U-L-L-E-A. No, I don't have any credit cards or anything on me. Left everything back in the trailer. What? No, I'm sorry, I don't know her Sacramento doctor's name."

He had created close-sounding aliases as a precaution. He hoped to avoid suspicious questions in case Annie had used their names. Big differences would cause problems; minor discrepancies could be attributed to her weakened and dazed condition.

Now he and Sandy spoke very little as they waited.

After what seemed like an eternity, the doctor appeared. He seemed tired. "We were fortunate." He sighed. "A little more bleeding and we'd have lost both of them."

Jeff's breath caught. "My sister," he asked fearfully, "is she all right?"

"She's asleep now. Will be for hours."

Sweet relief swept over Rader.

Sandy touched his arm. She sighed and smiled tremulously.

Their happiness couldn't be pure, though. Obviously the infant had died.

"What was the baby?" Jeff asked softly.

"What do you mean 'was'?" the doctor asked.

"I thought—"

"No, no. I said, 'A little more bleeding and we *would* have lost both of them' not 'we would have lost *both* of them.' The baby's fine. A beautiful girl. Six pounds three. Like to see her?"

Sandy's mouth dropped. Tears danced in her eyes.

Jeff was finding it difficult to speak. He gripped Sandy's hand. After a while, he finally croaked, "We'd like that very much."

The child was a miracle. Perfectly formed.

They stood in silence, just holding hands and grinning. Deep within Jeff, though, a worm of sadness writhed. He felt it. He even knew its reason for being. Stanley. The baby's father. How he'd have loved this moment with his daughter. How happy and proud he would have been.

A quick thought. That's all. It brought the entire Pedabine nightmare flooding back again. And with it the hunger for revenge that had been growing steadily since Murray Fried's death.

He stared at his niece, and his smile dissolved slowly.

Sandy sensed the coldness returning. She understood what it meant. She waited now for something that would signal their next move. It wasn't long in coming.

He turned from the child abruptly.

"I have to make a call." He addressed the attending nurse. "Where can I find a pay phone, please?"

She grinned. "Want to inform the baby's father, right?"

In answer, he merely nodded.

Michael Gavin's gravelly tones were a frosty fusion of complaint and relief: "Where have you been, kid? You were supposed to call me at nine o'clock two nights ago."

"Michael, we found Annie. We have her."

Nothing could have been more eloquent than the gasp that greeted this revelation. Undiluted joy reached out hundreds of miles and embraced him and Sandy. A lump rose in Jeff's throat; tears welled in his eyes. "She's had the baby," he said quickly. "A lovely little girl."

"Glory be. Where are you?"

"Orie Reed Memorial Hospital, Atawan. It's upstate."

"How'd you find her?"

"That has to wait. I'm going after them, Michael. Do you have anything for me?"

"Maybe. I did a check on Durkin, London, and Marquand. They have some interesting things in common. For one thing, they all came on the scene with a splash when they were twenty-one. For another, they all graduated from very small colleges around the country—Durkin from one in Kansas, London from one in South Carolina, and Marquand from one in North Dakota.''

''That doesn't jibe with Pedabine philosophy.''

''Kid, *none of the colleges is listed or registered anywhere*.''

Jeff tried to digest that.

Gavin's voice went on: ''I suspect they're sheltered until they're twenty-one and then given histories when they join the regular world.''

The implications of this were astounding. If Pedabine didn't release its members into the mainstream of society until they had reached an old-fashioned majority, and if abductions had been going on for decades, then the sheer number of Pedabines being prepared at any one time plus the staff required to care for them could be so large that the necessary facilities would be virtually impossible to conceal. Unless—

He couldn't hide his excitement. His voice vibrated. ''Michael, have you ever heard of the Red Condor Mine?''

''No, why?''

''I think I've uncovered their headquarters.''

''A mine?''

''It wouldn't be a mine anymore.''

''Where is it?''

''I don't know, but I'll find it.''

''Well, you'd better do it fast, kid, because something's up.''

''What do you mean?''

''They're gone.''

''Who?''

''Durkin, London, and Marquand.''

''Where?''

''Nobody knows. I've spoken with secretaries, associates, wives, and children. Zero. All three left word they'd be out of town for a few days, and because they didn't want to be disturbed, they didn't want anybody to know where they would be staying.''

''Did they take their cars?''

''London did. Durkin and Marquand had their secretaries book flights for them.''

''To where?''

''Durkin went to Phoenix. Marquand went to Denver. And by the way, I called a friend in Washington and learned that our illustrious Vice-President, Everett Frazier, is on a mysterious vacation, too.''

Convocation.

The word flashed in Jeff's mind. Einberg, the dentist, had shouted it. That's what he'd meant! They were all gathering now. That's why the Shakespeare House had been nearly empty. That's what Annie had meant when she said they'd all left and the remaining Pedabines were supposed to join them.

The convocation!

But why had Durkin gone to Phoenix while Marquand went to Denver? A ruse. Simple as that. An effort to mislead. A method of keeping the actual meeting place secret from any chance discovery of their mutual destination. Then where was the meeting place? Where was Pedabine's central headquarters?

''Michael, it's the mine,'' Jeff breathed. ''I *know* it.''

''What's the name again?'' Gavin asked.

''Condor—the Red Condor.''

''Funny name. Condors aren't red.''

It struck with all the breathtaking force of sudden sight to a blind man. There it was: *Condors aren't red.*

Gavin heard his sharp inhalation. ''What happened?'' he asked quickly. ''Everything all right?''

Jeff wanted to laugh. He wanted to pound something. But he controlled himself with great effort and murmured very evenly, ''Everything is perfect, Michael. I know just where they are.''

''Where?''

Rader didn't answer the question. Gears had shifted. He was speeding again. Rushing. Pulling things together for his final move. He had found the Pedabine hiding place. He was sure of that. What he'd do when he got there was still a mystery. But get there he would, and that couldn't wait.

''Sandy and I can't stay around this hospital too long,'' he explained quickly. ''Someone's bound to recognize us. Besides, Annie's safe now, I know that. They're all gathering for their convocation, and nobody's going to be looking for her here when he thinks we're still running and he should be at that meeting. Still, I don't want Annie to be alone—especially after she learns about Stanley. Michael, can you get up here? Can you stay with her?''

''I'll try.''

The response stopped Jeff cold. What did that mean: ''I'll

try"? It wasn't like Michael Gavin to hedge. Something was behind that answer. It portended trouble. "What's happened, Michael?" he asked.

"Nothing we didn't expect." The old man laughed. "The police found my car. They've linked me to you. There's an APB out on me, too, now, and they could spot me before I get out of the city. That's all it is, kid. I'll try to make it to Atawan. So far I've been lucky. No reason why my luck shouldn't hold. Tell Annie I'll see her tonight."

Glib. Casual. Bright. There was much to the answer, though, that was unsaid: Gavin could be apprehended at any moment; since the order had come from Harold Durkin himself, Michael would surely be consigned to the commissioner's department; true, the clan was gathering at the Red Condor Mine; however, just one lingering associate could mean the editor's death. It would be safer for him to stay in hiding another day or so. Only long enough to assure the departure of all Pedabines for the convocation.

Jeff voiced the thought.

Gavin brushed it aside. "She's had a rough time, hasn't she?" he asked in tones that were more like a statement.

Jeff knew he was speaking of Annie. He answered, "Very."

"Then we can't have her feeling alone and threatened. I'll get there the fastest way possible. You take care of yourself, kid."

"Michael—"

The telephone clicked. The old man was brooking no arguments. He had hung up.

Jeff tapped the receiver against the face of the coin box, distressed by Gavin's situation. But there was nothing he could do for his friend now. As long as Michael was unwilling to discuss the matter further, there wasn't even a way he could be reached. He had freed Jeff for action. Rader slammed the instrument on its hook and moved decisively to engineer the next steps of his search.

First, he wrote Annie a brief but intense letter:

Dear Annie,

When you read this, I'm going to be miles away. The people who held you captive are the same ones I'm looking for now. They're vicious. They've been responsible for every kind of horror you can imagine. But they're not invulnerable. You and my beautiful niece are proof of that.

I've registered you at the hospital as Frances Craft. I gave Zeff Dullea as my name. Keep things that way. Don't even tell them the name of your doctor in L.A. I don't want the police to find us yet. Everything will be corrected soon. I promise.

Some bad news, my sweet sister. There's no way to convey it in a note without seeming brutal so I'll write it quickly and cleanly: Stanley's been killed. The people I'm after did it.

If I were with you now, I'd hold you until your tears were dry. Try to feel me. Know I love you and that sweet, wonderful child you have brought into the world.

I'll be seeing you soon. Don't worry. Until then, you won't be alone. Michael Gavin is on his way from L.A. He'll tell you the whole terrible story.

> Thank you for my niece.
> Love you,
> Jeff

He'd have preferred to be there when she awakened. To tell her face-to-face about her husband. To comfort her in what he knew would be a devastating moment. But there was no telling how long she would be asleep. The doctor had said hours. He couldn't wait. He felt he had to move now, or he would be losing some kind of advantage.

Besides, Annie would not be alone.

Thank God for Michael Gavin.

What Jeff Rader didn't know, though, was that a lingering Pedabine was still in the office of Police Commissioner Harold Durkin, and Michael Gavin would never make it to Orie Reed Memorial Hospital.

21

They were in their car again. Another long trip stretched before them. Over twenty hours this time. Once more they were working in shifts. Three hours on—three off.

They had selected fresh clothes from the overnight bags still in the trunk of the LTD. The colors were bright and upbeat. Also, their appearances had been altered again. New wigs. New sunglasses. He was blond now; she, auburn. His shirt concealed his shoulder wound, and he was careful to keep his bandaged hand in his pants pocket whenever they left the car. To the unsuspecting stranger, they were anything but hunted hunters. All very innocuous. All very safe.

Their trip could have been shortened to ten hours if they had flown part of the way. But it had been 11:30 A.M. when Jeff completed his letter to Annie. A ten-hour trip would have had them arriving at their destination by 9:30 that night. Much too late and far too dark to accomplish anything. The longer trip, on the other hand, would bring them near their site by 8:30 A.M. No risk of being seen in a motel, no time wasted in locating other transportation. A good hour, too, for whatever they'd have to do next. All things considered, it had made more sense to drive all the way.

The Red Condor Mine.

When Michael had said ''Condors aren't red,'' Jeff Rader had been stopped by an image of a box beautifully wrought and prominently displayed. It had been in the library of the Shakespeare House. The contents had come from Avery Wesscoze's special mine. The nameplate said as much. And the contents had been red. Blood red. That was the answer to the mystery then. The *mine* was red, not the bird! Certainly! Wesscoze had consistently named his holdings after their environments. Well, if the condor could identify a region of the country, then the redness of the earth would locate the mine within that region.

In the strange way of insight, Rader's thoughts had fallen marvelously into place. There were only three places in the nation where the earth had that vivid carmine coloration: northern Arizona, southern Colorado, and southern Utah. He remembered his archives notes: Global had listed eight western holdings; among them, one in each of these states. But which of these states hid the Red Condor? *Which one?* The answer became clear in a moment: Durkin and Marquand were en route to a convocation, the location of which was a secret of such magnitude that Pedabines killed for it. Yet Marquand's secretary had booked a flight for him to Colorado; Durkin's, for him to Arizona. Deception. Deception. If they were trying to guard their secret, they would never have identified their final destination so blithely to their secretaries. Furthermore, they were going to the same meeting place, but they had headed for different cities—additional proof of their deception. Yes, they were protecting their headquarters—and the fact that they had avoided the third state, the fact that they had hidden its identity, now clearly pointed to Utah as the site of the Red Condor Mine.

In the car, Jeff had studied his notes again. They confirmed his conclusion: Avery Wesscoze had purchased the property in 1915, three years *after* his son's murder, even as he was writing essays on his elite society and divesting himself of all other holdings. Obviously this acquisition had not been intended for disposal. Evidently he'd planned even then to use it as some kind of headquarters for his community. And here was Global Mining today, with a Pedabine president and chairman of the board, in possession of the Red Condor. Oh, Global had it, all right. He saw that now. And cinching his conclusion was the fact that although the company ran operations in Arizona and Colorado, neither of these mines was actually situated in the red-rock areas of those states! There was only one property in Jeff Rader's notes that was located where the earth bled. It had been recorded simply as "Wilderness I, near Lodeville, Utah—For Future

Development." It was the Red Condor. No doubt of that. The name? Another device, that's all. Just as Arden Forest had been concealed through a name change to Shakespeare House, so the Red Condor Mine was now being hidden behind Wilderness I.

They arrived in Lodeville on schedule.

The car had behaved beautifully. The trip had been uneventful. Their shifts at the wheel had allowed them time to sleep. They were rested and eager to pinpoint the object of their search. There was only one personal worry: Jeff's wounds. Although he'd made light of them, Sandy was troubled by the stiffness of his arm movement and the festering of his hand. At Orie Reed Memorial Hospital, he had refused medical attention. He'd feared that one close look by a doctor or a trained nurse would immediately identify the causes of the lesions. Then dangerous questions would follow. Better to avoid that. Later he'd allowed Sandy to treat the wounds. They were now covered by clean bandages that had been brought with them from Chicago. A helpful measure, no doubt, but one that did nothing to mitigate Sandy's concern.

In Lodeville, Jeff stopped at a small general store. He picked a container of orange juice and a couple of plastic-wrapped sandwiches from a cooler shelf. As he paid for the items, he smiled pleasantly at the pretty young girl behind the counter.

"Good morning."

"Morning. Will that be all?"

"Of food. I'd like a little information, though, if you please." She smiled brightly. "Sure. What do you want to know?"

"Two things. One, what's the population of Lodeville? And two, who's the town's oldest citizen?"

"The population? I think it's two forty or fifty. Something like that. Why do you want to know?"

"And the oldest citizen?"

"Oh, that's easy. Mr. Yantis. He must be ninety-four now."

"Was he born here?"

"I think so."

"Where can I find him?"

"Last house on West Pioneer Road."

"Thank you. You're as helpful as you are beautiful."

She blushed. Leaning across the counter as he left, she called, "You have a nice day."

They found the house with no difficulty. It was an ancient clapboard building. Small but neatly kept. It had no paved streets around it. No formal driveway. No artificial landscaping. It just sat on the ground, two miles from its nearest neighbor, looking as indigenous to the environment as some nearby rocks.

Jeff and Sandy pulled right up to it.

The sound of the car's engine brought Mr. Yantis to the tiny porch.

"Mr. Yantis?" Jeff called.

He didn't answer. He merely watched them approach. He was a thin, stooped man in faded jeans and a plaid shirt. He had old leather moccasins on his feet and a battered, sweat-stained hat on his head. His face and hands were so age- and weather-wrinkled he looked even older than his ninety-four years.

"Mr. Yantis?" Jeff asked, looking up at him.

"That's right." The voice was surprisingly clear and spry.

"Mr. Yantis, my name is Eric Murdock, and this is my assistant, Cheryl Paine. I'm a television producer. May we talk to you for a few minutes?"

"Why?"

Jeff grinned. "We're doing some scouting for a show on this area, and a man your age probably knows more about Lodeville than anybody else in town."

"What kinda show?"

"Documentary. Want to show the history of mining in the Great Southwest."

"You from California?"

"That's right."

"Figured. Saw your license plate."

"Can we talk?"

"Come on in."

They entered a close but well-furnished room.

"You want some coffee?" he asked.

"That'd be nice," Jeff accepted.

As the old man prepared the brew in the adjacent kitchen space, Sandy queried, "Understand you were born here, Mr. Yantis?"

"Nope."

Jeff's hopes sagged. He needed someone who had lived in Lodeville for decades, someone who knew the history of the area.

"Born in Salt Lake City. Father came down to do some mining when I was two."

Hope surged.

"Then you got here shortly after Utah became a state, right?"

"Right." He brought the pot of coffee and three mugs into the living room. "What're ya lookin' for?"

"Oh, just stories," Jeff answered casually. "We plan to cover the mining industry of Utah, and of course we'll have to start with the old ones. Ever hear of an operation called the Red Condor?" He held his breath.

"That goes way back," Mr. Yantis muttered, pouring the coffee.

Jeff stole a glance at Sandy. Her head had jerked; her eyes had widened.

"Never was successful," the old man continued, sitting. "Finally shut the whole thing down in 1915."

So, Jeff thought, Wesscoze had purchased a failing mine that could be closed down without arousing suspicions. Smart.

"Where was it located?" Sandy asked.

"Eighty miles or so due west."

"Desert?"

"That's all there is around there, little girl."

"*Red* desert," Jeff stressed the word.

The old man looked at him. "Like blood," he murmured.

They had it. Their hearts were racing.

"Any roads to the place?" Jeff asked.

"Probably not. No one's mined out there for almost seventy years."

"How could we find the mine if we wanted to see it?"

"What d'ya want to see that for? More interestin' old shafts right around here."

"Oh, we'll look at those, too, Mr. Yantis," Sandy hurried to explain, "but CBS wants some pictures of the Red Condor area, and it wouldn't be good to go back without them, you know what I mean?"

He drooped the corners of his mouth and bobbed his head like a ball on a rubber string, as though he fully understood the imperatives of network production. "Desert's rough," he advised. "A few people's got themselves lost an' never come out again. Get yourself a Jeep."

"Good idea," Jeff agreed readily. "How do we get there once we've found one?"

"Go back into Lodeville to Benson. That's the main street.

Only goes a few hundred yards, but at the end you'll see the lumberyard. Turn right an' follow yer nose.''

"How far before we run out of road?"

"Can't say. I told ya, nobody's been out that way in years. All that land—thousands of acres—belongs to a big eastern company now an' they keep it very private.''

"Is it guarded?"

"Well, there ain't no fence around it, if that's what you mean, but yer still gonna be trespassin'.''

"How'll we know when we get there?" Sandy asked.

"Be a big, lone rock on the horizon. Eighty, ninety feet high. Nothin' near it. See it from a certain angle an' it looks like a giant bird. The old Red Condor used to be at the base o' that rock.''

They were fifty miles west of Lodeville.

They had been traveling for almost two hours. The road had become a rough, narrow path. Sometimes so slender it resembled little more than a walkway. They'd even encountered places where it gave out completely. The Ford, though, was holding up beautifully. Jeff had never intended to search for a Jeep. He doubted that one could be rented easily in a town the size of Lodeville without stirring unwanted interest. He'd agreed to Mr. Yantis's suggestion merely to encourage the old man into divulging directions to the mine. Now, deep in barren wasteland, Jeff started to become concerned. Could Yantis have been wrong about the directions? Could he have been babbling? After all, ninety-four years—there had to be some senility there. Had he and Sandy jumped too quickly? Had they allowed their eagerness to override good judgment? It might have been better to double-check the old man in town and risk revealing their interest in the Red Condor Mine. He fretted for a while over this, but then he checked himself. It really didn't matter. They were too far away from Lodeville to do anything about it. Yantis had said eighty miles. Well, they'd just have to take it the rest of the way and see what happened.

Sandy seemed to be sharing his apprehensions.

She murmured, ''I read somewhere that while the elderly can barely remember yesterday, they can always recall the remote past with an accuracy that would shame a camera. I hope that's true.''

The statement was only slightly reassuring.

Seven miles farther on, they saw their first sign, a small weather-beaten placard with faded letters:

TURN BACK
PROPERTY OF GLOBAL MINING, INC.
TRESPASSERS WILL BE PROSECUTED

They breathed easier.

Five miles more and the clear, straight horizon suddenly developed a pimple.

They watched it grow as desert dropped behind them. Arresting. Imposing. It stood alone, angry red in the morning sun. Steadily, however, it assumed another form, a vague but identifiable shape—a craggy bird, a huge, perching, mountainous condor.

They passed other signs. All weather-worn. All increasingly threatening.

"DANGER!"

"WARNING!"

"INTRUDERS WILL BE SHOT!"

Six miles from the object of their search, Jeff signaled Sandy to stop. The LTD idled thunderously in the desert stillness. They sat for a few moments without speaking, just staring at the hulking shape that loomed so near.

Six hundred feet beneath the surface of the Utah desert, the Grand Meeting was now in progress. It had commenced promptly at 11:00 A.M. Kendral Hall was filled with 702 Pedabines, every member of the organization from every corner of the world. All activities in the Red Condor Mine had been suspended. All stations had been left unattended. This was a convocation of momentous significance, and no Pedabine had been allowed to miss it.

The subject: The Game.

It had commanded Pedabine attention for almost seventy years. Every action the organization had ever undertaken had been executed with only one objective in mind: victory in The Game. Not partial success, not temporary success, but complete and permanent victory. Now The Game was almost over. Victory was at hand. Only the final moments of play remained to be planned and considered.

And this was no time for carelessness. Despite mandatory attendance, despite unattended stations, caution prevailed. For the period of the Grand Meeting, all alarm systems in the Red Condor had been temporarily circuited to Kendral Hall.

Over the dais, a two-foot panel of frosted glass stretched the length of the ceiling. It consisted of three sections. It seemed to be only a large but simple lighting fixture. It was more.

On both sides of the stage, the rich redwood paneling was latticed in intricate design. It seemed only to decorate the proscenium walls. It did more.

Pedabine 1 had been addressing the group. He'd been happily delineating a picture of its glorious past and preparing a picture of its glorious future. He'd just boasted of Pedabine successes in the field of medicine when the first of the panels above his head suddenly glowed yellow.

A troubled murmur rose from the audience. He saw the direction of their gaze. He turned and looked up. Then he smiled at the concerned faces before him and calmly pressed a white plastic square on the top of the lectern. On both sides of the stage a segment of the latticed panels slid open. Two enormous screens were exposed. The Father immediately suspended his remarks while he and his congregation sat and waited.

Desert sensors had detected Jeff and Sandy's car twenty miles from Condor Rock. Relays had been triggered. The warning light had been activated.

When they had driven to within ten miles of their objective, the yellow light above the stage gave way to an angry orange glare. Simultaneously, the two large blank screens flashed on, and a clear picture of the distant Ford suddenly appeared.

Silence reigned in Kendral Hall. No one moved.

Six miles from their goal, as Jeff pondered the seeming absence of Pedabine security, he and Sandy were the objects of very intent observation. Their faces still could not be discerned. The car's windows were up. The interior darkness hid them, but the persistent approach of the Ford was a matter of quiet and deepening concern.

The LTD's engine rumbled.

Jeff removed his sunglasses and the rest of his blond disguise.

Following his actions, Sandy did the same to hers. She didn't speak. She just watched him stare into the distance at the huge rock that represented the end of their search.

After a few moments, he spoke softly. "Shut off the motor, Sandy."

She reached and turned the key.

The desert silence was deafening.

Jeff suddenly exhaled sharply. He turned to her. He took her hand. "Here's where we stand," he explained. His voice was subdued, warm. "If that's the place we want, then that's where all of them are . . . and that also includes Tami." He felt her fingers tighten around his hand. He continued. "If they're all there, then at least one of them's had to detect our presence by now or they're all fools. Well, we know they aren't fools. So that means they know we're here. Now, there may be other ways to get into that mine, but the only one we're aware of is—or was—at the base of that rock. So, if we decide to go ahead with this, that's the only place for us to look, and if that's the only entrance to the mine, then we're going to be walking right into their web."

She studied him.

He waited for her reaction.

Her brows creased. "What do you mean, 'If we decide to go ahead with this'?" she asked. "I thought we'd come this far because we were determined to take it right to the end."

"I'm willing, Sandy," he answered quickly, "but I want to be sure we both understand the implications of this next step. If we walk into that mine, they'll be waiting for us. We may be dead very, very soon."

"I know that, Jeff," she said softly, looking directly into his eyes. "I also know that the trap is not just down in the mine. It's out here and everywhere we may try to hide. They're looking for us. The police are looking for us. And because of those two Secret Service men in the Century International, the federal government is probably looking for us, too. If we're caught anywhere, the Pedabines will get to us. There are no more places to run and nobody we can ask for help. There's really no place up here that's safe. Jeff, if I'm going to be killed, I'd just as soon die down there as anywhere else. There, at least, I may have a chance to see my daughter again."

"Aren't you scared?" he asked.

She nodded quickly. "Terrified." The admission was a short and tremulous croak. She swallowed. "But I don't see anything else I can do."

He studied her face. Warm flushes of love washed through him. It's unfair, he thought. I finally find someone as marvelous as you, and it's all going to end so soon.

He leaned over and kissed her warmly on her mouth. He felt the loving return of pressure. Their lips parted. The kiss lingered. Hovered. Settled. He drew his mouth away.

"I love you," she whispered.

He touched her cheek, his eyes echoing her words.

Then he pulled his gun from his belt, smiled, and murmured, "Come on. Let's see what's going on within their web." And they opened their doors to start their six-mile hike to the entrance of the Red Condor Mine.

Below them, the orange light went dark and the last panel flared a terrible red.

Their figures were very clearly imposed upon Kendral Hall's two huge screens now. Furthermore, they had been recognized. A gasp had escaped the few Pedabines who knew their faces.

The Father faced his audience. "For the benefit of the brothers and sisters who have not seen their photographs," he said, "these two intruders are currently Pedabine's principal adversaries." The announcement was made with an odd sense of pleasure. Then he signaled quickly and a young man in the first row rushed to his side. There were whispered words. The young man hurried to a group of children at the side of the hall. He spoke urgently to a little girl. She stood, and he ushered Pedabine 431 quickly from the room. The Father preferred not to have the little girl present while the group observed her natural mother and Jeff Rader.

They were within a hundred yards of the rock.

The red light above the dais began to pulsate.

Pedabine 1 reached over and touched another square on the lectern. Sound burst into the hall. The sound of footsteps on the desert earth above. The sound of clothes rustling. Even the sound of breathing.

Still, no one in the auditorium spoke. All watched and listened with total absorption as their enemies approached.

Jeff and Sandy were at the base of the huge rock. It reached above them, bloody in the bright sunshine, awesome in its grandeur. They paused, and looked about. Very cautiously, they started around the rock. They were searching for the mine entrance.

Rader had been troubled by a thought: If a convocation was truly in progress here, how had all the Pedabines reached this place without arousing the curiosity of Lodeville's residents? How had they passed through the town without being seen?

He found his answer on the opposite side of the rock. It lay at his feet: tire tracks—wide, heavy imprints of rugged truck tires. He could see they hadn't come through Lodeville at all. They had approached from the opposite direction. The Pedabines had converged on a few predetermined places where they had been met by large trucks capable of negotiating desert terrain. They had been brought here from directions that avoided contact with all outsiders.

He touched Sandy, then pointed. There it was: The tire tracks ran into a large split in the rocks, a jagged black maw.

They eased closer, tense, alert. At the edge of the opening, they hesitated. Listened. Peered into the semidarkness.

Thin shafts of sunlight pierced through cracks in the vaulted interior. Irregular contours were faintly discernible: projections, ledges, a ragged pile of boulders.

Silence thundered. The coolness of darkness attacked their skin as they sidled into the dusky cavity and worked their way toward a huge blank wall.

Six hundred feet below, Pedabine 1 touched the last square on his speaker's stand.

Instantly a heavy metal grating sealed the opening of Condor Rock.

Jeff and Sandy started for the entrance. A stiletto note whined from somewhere in the depths of the earth, stopping them in their tracks. The ground began to tremble beneath their feet. All at once they were plummeted downward. They pitched, jerked, swayed, fell against each other, collapsed to their knees. It was an insane drop, an elevator ride to Hell. It lasted only moments, but it forced the breath from their lungs, the blood to their heads. The stop was as abrupt as the start. It sent them rolling to their backs, reaching for each other, clawing as though they were slipping away into separate voids. When they realized the earth was stable, they struggled to their feet and drew closer for mutual support. Silence engulfed them again, but the darkness had given way to color. They were facing a tunnel—unlike anything they had ever seen. It was sleek, immaculate, and striking in design. Soft light seemed to make the entire tube glow a vivid green. A chromium catwalk hung from its ceiling. Narrow conveyor walkways sandwiched a steel road wide enough to accommodate a large truck or a bus. One of the conveyor sidewalks moved toward them; the other, away.

Sandy slipped her hand into Jeff's as they stepped on the moving sidewalk. It ran without a tremor. They hurried their progress by walking as it moved. But hurried to where?

They heard a voice. It seemed to come from somewhere ahead. They couldn't distinguish words.

The Father had resumed his address: "I shall soon be speaking with our uninvited guests. Now, though, we must not allow them to distract us from our purpose. Let us continue . . ."

Jeff and Sandy were drawn inexorably forward.

A hundred yards away, an intersection cut into the main artery. It was narrower than the principal tunnel, yellow in color, tubular in shape. The voice came from it, and it funneled the sound like a megaphone. Now they could understand the words. Someone was denigrating the past.

They followed the sound. Twenty feet into the vein, they were startled to hear a quick hissing release of pressure behind them. They turned sharply. Steel panels had slid swiftly from the walls to seal the passageway. They were locked into the area. They could only move forward now. They went toward the voice, constantly vigilant, expecting and fearing attack at any moment. There was nothing, though. Nothing but the strong tones of Pedabine 1 warming to the imagery of his own words:

". . . There is nothing on this earth that could ever justify such utter, pervasive evil. The structure had failed. Hope had withered, and society had doomed itself to a few more decades of mindless struggle before the inevitable and final cataclysm. Then Pedabine was born—Pedabine—and in this great birth came the first true hope for the realization of man's Historic Dream. . . ."

The tunnel ended at another steel covering.

Jeff touched it. Evidently it too had been moved into place. A safety shield, he told himself, doors to close off areas in case of fire or explosion. Now he and Sandy were caught, sealed in.

The voice of the Father continued:

"You are that hope, my children. You are everything the human race has been striving for. In your hands, in your minds, lies the future. You will bring peace and comfort and security to every living soul on this planet. You will bring order and harmony. . . .''

The words were coming from speakers at the top of the tunnel.

Suddenly the speakers went dead and, simultaneously, a section of wall opened. Now the voice came from this new passageway.

Jeff and Sandy moved toward it. He readied his gun. She was at his back.

The passageway was well lighted. They saw a short flight of steps ahead, ending at a door of clear glass.

The wall closed behind them.

They moved up the steps. The door before them was made of two-inch-thick plate. They were staring through it into a large room decorated with an oak desk, a grand piano, sculpture, paintings, carpets, armchairs—all the accoutrements of gracious living. It all seemed frighteningly out of place.

"Yours will be the glory of fulfillment," the Father was exhorting his children. "No one will ever again want for opportunity. No one will ever again fear for his safety. . . .''

Jeff reached toward the glass door. A beam was broken. The door swung open. He and Sandy entered the room. The door swung shut. Jeff broke toward it. He touched it. It was locked.

"Can you imagine what that means, my children? *You* will be the ones who will wipe out disease. *You* will be the ones who will eliminate hunger. . . .''

The voice swelled, exploded, glutted the air of the room.

Jeff and Sandy were drawn to the far wall. It seemed to be composed of black glass.

"*You* will eradicate congestion. *You* will end poverty. *You* will prevent suffering and *you* will even conquer death. . . .''

The glass was of ordinary thickness. A one-way observation window. They looked through it and down upon the spectacle of Kendral Hall.

"You, my children, you who are all the Pedabines in this world, *you* shall be the regulators, the masters of tomorrow!''

The eruption of Pedabine agreement was deafening.

Sandy saw youngsters in the audience. She could see only the backs of their heads. She searched the rows.

"The glorious moment is at hand," the Father continued. "The Game is almost over. For seventy years we have played our moves, fixed our positions, sharpened our strategy. For seventy years we have struck, countered, reevaluated. And finally we are ready for the last tactics of play. We are in key positions everywhere. We have gained the advantage. Everything is possible to us now. And once we have assumed the leadership of these United States—''

Both Jeff and Sandy jerked.

''—we shall move ahead to our inevitable victory. The death of the current President is a simple matter, my children. It has already been planned. He is to be assassinated in five days. Your brother, Pedabine 286—Everett Frazier—will be sworn into office minutes later, and The Game will then move swiftly into its final phase. The trophy is to be ours, my children. It is what we have hungered and struggled for—the prize of the gods. The trophy, my children, the trophy is this entire world!''

A storm of cheers and applause greeted this promise.

Jeff and Sandy turned to each other. Their faces were twisted in astonishment. So that was it. That's what Pedabine was all about. The killings. The training. The positioning of their intellectually elite. The dream of Avery Wesscoze had grown, expanded from that of a small secret society to one of total domination. Nietzschean. Hitlerean. But what of the humanistic projections: the end of poverty, the end of disease, the end of suffering? How could they be compatible with the organization's ruthlessness, its record of death and brutality?

Don't be so God-damned naive! Rader cursed himself for even entertaining the questions. He knew the answer: Every insane leader the world has ever known has wanted the perfect world, the heaven on earth—but only on his terms, only on his unwavering, inflexible, unrelenting terms.

Sandy felt a chill of fear rush through her body. Below them was an auditorium filled with accomplished people, all cheering wildly now for something so bizarre that only a diseased mentality could fail to see the morbidity of the goal. *And they had made that goal a possibility*. They ran major corporations. They controlled outlets of communication. They held key positions in law enforcement. Their ghastly history was proof of their cunning and their success. They could do it, Sandy thought with dread. As insane as this whole thing sounds, they could do it.

''There's the Father,'' Jeff murmured.

She nodded.

"I must leave you now, my children," they heard him quiet-ing his charges. "You are to start your group instruction immediately. Everything must be learned quickly and perfectly. Everyone must know exactly what he is to do when our fateful moment arrives. Remember, events will move swiftly once your brother is installed in the White House, and no breach of responsi-bility will be tolerated. So work hard, my children. Prepare yourselves. I shall be with you again before this session ends. I love you all. Adieu."

The entire audience rose to its feet.

Applause thundered as the Father left the stage.

Sound from Kendral Hall ended abruptly in the observation room. Jeff turned, sensing imminent danger. He could see through the glass door; the approaching hallway was empty. He crossed quickly to it, signaling Sandy to follow. The door was still locked, though. He pushed at it, rammed his good shoulder against it. It didn't even quiver. He ran his fingers over the door, looking for a catch, searching for a release. He found nothing.

A soft, whirring note sounded.

Sandy and he turned in time to see a section of wall open behind them.

The Father entered the room. He was followed by Jesse—Pedabine 32, the man whom Jeff had wounded in Santa Barbara.

Jeff's gun came up.

The Father spoke evenly: "Give that to Jesse. There's no escape, and if you should harm either of us, the little girl for whom you've struggled so heroically will be made to suffer grievously."

It was a perfect statement. A simple threat with all the shield-ing power of steel.

As he expected, Sandy leaped at the mention of Tami. "My daughter," she asked, "is she all right?"

"For the time being," he answered. His eyes were fastened on Jeff's. His meaning was clear.

Rader knew he was facing a man who didn't make hollow threats. He glanced at Sandy.

She flashed him an anxious look.

Jesse had walked boldly up to him. His hand went out. He gripped the barrel of the gun and twisted. The weapon slipped from Jeff's relaxing fingers. Jesse went to the oak desk with it, placed it in a drawer, and then resumed his position at the Father's side.

Throughout this, the Father's eyes never wavered.

"You're a remarkable man, Mr. Rader," he breathed. "You possess all the attributes of a Pedabine. A simple error by Myra London—one for which she will have to be punished later—led you to uncover our deepest secrets; a gantlet of obstacles failed to stop your progress to the center of our heartland. You have superior intelligence, outstanding resourcefulness, and extraordinary tenacity. If we had known of this when you were a child, you would be a Pedabine today. Your natural gifts would have been developed even further than you and your clumsy schooling have taken them."

He paused as though he expected a response.

Jeff remained silent.

The Father sank into a large, soft armchair. "Mr. Rader," he continued, "orders have been standing for some time now to apprehend you and to bring you before the Primary Council alive. You've made that apprehension easy. I thank you. From the moment our surface sensors detected your presence, you and Mrs. Wilkenson have been tracked, observed, and guided to this room. Though I've wanted to punish you for the pain and anguish you've caused us—though you had to be stopped because your progress was a growing threat to our purpose—I must admit I've also been intrigued by your apparent capabilities. You've come, as you know now, at a most auspicious moment. I wanted you to see our Grand Meeting, to hear our Grand Design."

Again he paused as though he expected a response.

And again neither Jeff nor Sandy said a word.

"Tomorrow is here," the Father murmured to himself. His voice simmered with passion. "The years of preparation have ended. The dream has become a reality." He looked at Rader again. "You've heard my address. You've heard the promise, the hope, the glory of a Pedabine life. Doesn't that excite you? Doesn't it stir you to know the millennium has come?"

Jeff watched him steadily. His voice was low. "It does, my Lord," he breathed.

The Father's eyes flashed wide in anger. "Don't mock!" he spat. "You're the first non-Pedabine to learn of our goals, the first outsider to see the inner workings of our heart. Your own intelligence should leap at what you've heard. I thought you'd understand. Don't mock!''

"Understand what?'' Jeff struck. "That you've slaughtered the parent and twisted the child—and for nothing but an insane dream?''

"Nothing?'' the Father snapped. He rose from his chair as though he were rushing into battle. "We are decades ahead of the entire world! We've already accomplished what ordinary society is now only dimly perceiving! We've mastered the sun for energy, created the true computer brain, developed mechanical marvels, controlled agricultural uncertainties, organized a peaceful society, and solved the riddle of the cell. Our knowledge is the knowledge of tomorrow, not today. Your futurists only dream of what we have made happen! Look at Jesse here. You shot him and almost killed him. We've made him well again in a matter of days. We've learned how life works. We can glue cells together. We can reconstruct genes. We can accelerate regeneration. We know how to increase intelligence, resist disease, regulate growth, and improve perception. There is no crime in our society, no want, no boredom. We've learned how to take the best in the individual and make that even better. No Pedabine ever doubts himself. No Pedabine ever escapes into drugs, alcohol, or mental disease. We are self-assured people. We can accomplish anything the human mind is capable of conceiving. And we're now going to offer that to the entire world. Nothing, Mr. Rader? Nothing? We have finally risen against indifference, against sloth, against lawlessness, against the degradation of mediocrity. In a very short while, this world will finally be organized as one human body. In a very short while, it will no longer know war and pestilence. In a very short while, it will have everything it has cried for from the beginning of time—unity, respect, order, and decency. And you call that *nothing*?''

"You've still killed—'' Jeff started.

"Far fewer than are killed by ignorance and with far, far better cause,'' the Father shot back. "And unquestionably there will be more—many, many more—until the nest is finally clean and all men can grow and soar like eagles. It will happen, Mr. Rader, it will happen. And we'll have peace. Peace everywhere—because although we have harnessed an entirely new and devastating explosive force, we've also developed the ultimate weapon of *peace*. That's right. You start. Is the idea so terrible to you? Is it so bizarre? Peace. It will finally come to mankind. When our brother is in control of this country, when our Pedabines are all situated in their respective positions of authority, we shall subdue the hostile, aggressive tendencies of the rest of the world with a new and wonderful weapon. Not a gas to destroy the lungs. Not a gas to attack the nervous system. No. Instead, a sweet, pleasant fragrance that can eradicate the most oppressive and vicious angers in the human mind. A gas of peace, Mr. Rader. No more fighting. No more suspicions. No more nuclear bombs, no intercontinental missiles or mobilized armies. Peace, Mr. Rader, blessed peace and the opportunity for every individual to become the very best that he or she is capable of being—''

''A beautiful picture,'' Jeff cut him off, ''but even Avery Wesscoze would have said you've taken his plan too far.''

The Father's lips spread into a sudden, broad smile. ''You weren't listening, Mr. Rader.'' He laughed. ''You weren't listening.'' Then softly he added, ''I *am* Avery Wesscoze.''

Both Jeff and Sandy jumped as though they'd been whipped with a naked wire.

''That's right,'' the Father continued. ''I told you we have solved the riddle of the cell, that we can accelerate its growth. Well, we can also arrest its growth and make it perform exactly as we wish. Mr. Rader, Mrs. Wilkenson, Pedabine has conquered aging—and, possibly, even the death that accompanies it.'' He let that sink in. The air hung heavy with the monumental significance of his words.

Jeff and Sandy looked at each other, dumbstruck. Was he lying? Was this actually Avery Wesscoze? Why, he'd have to be—

''I appear to be in the neighborhood of fifty-five, don't I?'' the Father asked rhetorically and not without a trace of vanity. ''I'll probably look forty-five in fifteen more years. We'll stop the regression then.'' He grinned. ''I don't want to go back to my infancy, you understand.'' He enjoyed their speechlessness. ''Don't look so stupefied. This is science. I'm telling the truth, I assure you. We've merely accomplished already what present-day researchers are on the verge of discovering. We did it sooner, that's all. In 1938, as a matter of fact, I was seventy-three then.'' He approached Jeff. ''Mr. Rader,'' he said softly and intensely, ''can't you appreciate the marvelous adventure on which the world is about to embark?''

Jeff Rader stared at Avery Wesscoze. After a long pause, he nodded. "I'm impressed," he said—and it was spoken very, very quietly.

The Father seemed to relax now, even as he became more excited. It was as though the approval of an outsider were the long-awaited vindication of his life's work. He approached Rader. He studied his eyes. He was smiling. "Once we've established our unified society," he said, "we shall enter the last phase of our strategy. Mr. Rader, all Pedabines have been rescued from their parents and trained from childhood. However, we'll soon be searching for and using the creative power of gifted minds everywhere and of all ages." He paused a moment. "Jeffrey," he murmured, "your presence in this room attests to your superior capabilities. I'm offering you amnesty for your crimes against Pedabine and the opportunity to become the first outsider to join us in our work."

Sandy was watching Jeff closely. He looked at Pedabine 1 and narrowed his eyes. "Are you really Avery Wesscoze?" he asked. He saw the smiling face before him nod slowly. "That could get me," he breathed. "Because if you are— Truthfully, I wouldn't hesitate a moment to become part of any venture that could offer the world a gift of immortality."

Avery Wesscoze slipped into another gear of relaxation. "You've been injured." He smiled. "We'll heal your wounds in a matter of days."

Jeff moved to Sandy. He put an arm about her shoulder. "If that can be done"—he grinned—"both Sandy and I will be more than willing to become your first converts."

Wesscoze's lips pursed. He sighed deeply. "Jeffrey," he said, "honesty is the spine of Pedabine character. Deceit only causes confusion and the weakening of commitment to ideals. Since you're going to join us, let me start with a demonstration of that honesty now. The offer I've just made was for you alone."

Wesscoze swept his attention to Sandy. "I'm sorry, Mrs. Wilkenson. In every way, you too are worthy of becoming a Pedabine. Unfortunately, your daughter's status precludes that possibility. Since her rescue, she's become one of our most promising children. Her conversion is almost complete. One day she'll become a leader. If you were to join us, you'd undoubtedly persist in your efforts to reclaim her. That would only create terrible problems and possibly destroy all the work we've done with her. I'm afraid that can't be risked. I have to ask you to go with Jesse now.''

It was a death sentence. As cold and final as a judge's gavel. Jesse moved in.

Sandy seemed confused, afraid.

Jeff turned quickly and faced her. His hands gripped her shoulders. "Sandy," he urged, "go with Jesse and don't worry. I'm sure Mr. Wesscoze is a reasonable man. I'll talk to him. Everything'll be all right, you'll see." It was said intensely, earnestly.

Jeff's movement and words had caused Jesse to stop. He was only three feet away, waiting for Jeff to conclude his advice. He barely saw the kick coming. It swung toward his head in a blur and caught him flush on the mouth. Teeth and blood clogged his throat.

The explosion of violence caught the Father completely by surprise. It was what Jeff had been playing for. Violence would paralyze this cultured and sheltered man. Immobility would keep him from sounding an alarm. There had to be no alarm!

Rader had misjudged Avery Wesscoze, though. Surprise could freeze him; violence was something he had nurtured. He snapped from his shock in a moment and flew toward his desk.

Jeff went spearing through the air to stop him. He hit Wesscoze two feet from the desk. They crashed to the carpet. Only the perfect soundproofing of the room kept the Pedabines below from knowing their Father was fighting for his life.

And a life-death struggle it was—because Jeff Rader was feeling the butchering of Stanley, the blasting of Murray, the slaughter of countless innocents, the anguish, the pain, the suffering that had brought him to this very moment. Here was the cause of it all. Here was the head, the font, the architect of unparalleled madness. To let him live would be the ultimate betrayal of mankind. Still, there had to be no alarm!

They tumbled across the floor, caromed off furnishings.

Soft popping sounds cracked through the struggle. It was Jesse. On one knee. His .32 swinging in Jeff's direction. His face a bloody atrocity; hideous guttural noises bubbling in his throat. The shots were wild. Hitting a lamp. Thudding into the wall. And Sandy was at him before he could straighten his aim. The statue in her hands came swinging at the back of his head. His

skull was split by the impact. He pitched forward, dead. She
went for his gun.

Wesscoze had rolled to his knees. The desk! An alarm was on
the desk! He lunged for it again. But Jeff had him, clubbing his
outstretched hand, spinning him around, swinging him to his
feet.

Wesscoze's foot shot up and caught Jeff behind his knee.
Rader's leg buckled. His hold slipped. He was going down. But
he managed one sweeping swing with all the strength in his good
arm before he collapsed entirely. The punch connected. It nailed
the Father squarely on the point of his chin. The crack of it was
like a pistol shot. The Father's head snapped back. His arms
splayed open. He flew up and hit the dark glass wall with all the
force of a catapulted boulder. It split asunder. And Avery Wesscoze
went hurtling and screaming to his death—twisting through seventy-
five feet of space into the astounded convocation of Pedabines
below.

Now it was a different picture. Rader had fought for the
advantage of silence. He'd had no idea what he and Sandy would
do after his attack. But whatever it would be, it would have to be
done in silence. As long as the Pedabine community remained
ignorant of its leader's death, Sandy and he would have a margin
of safety. Now everything had changed. That margin was gone.

The shattering of the glass observation wall had jerked all
attention upward. The sight of their Father flailing toward them
had filled every Pedabine in the hall with indescribable dread. It
was as though they were watching God fall from His throne and
all Heaven collapsing around Him. It was a moment of choking
disbelief. A frozen moment of terror. But when he struck, the
paralysis shattered. A scream of unimaginable agony filled
the hall. And over it, the president of the Primary Council
immediately assumed command: "FIND THEM! BLOCK ALL
TUNNELS! LOCK THE DOORWAYS! FIND THEM!" He was
pointing at one of the large blank screens. His logic had been
swift and certain: The Father's death had to have been an act of
violence; it was the first act of violence ever to take place within
the confines of the Red Condor Mine; Jeff Rader and Sandra
Wilkenson were the only new elements on the scene; they were,
in the Father's own words, Pedabine's "principal adversaries";
therefore, the violence had to have come from them. "FIND
THEM!" he was shouting above the din. "BRING THEM

HERE—ALIVE—RIGHT HERE BEFORE THE PRIMARY COUNCIL!''

Jeff heard the orders as he claimed his gun from the desk drawer. He sped past Sandy, signaling her to follow. It wasn't a matter of running to any particular place. He was sure they were going to die. It was purely an act of desperation. *Run. Get out of there. Find a better spot. Any spot. Hide there. Wait. Figure out what to do next. But, above all, don't die without a fight!*

They rushed into the opening through which the Father and Jesse had entered the room. They were in a narrow hallway. It stretched a hundred feet. They ran its length, expecting a stairwell, a door—anything. All they found was a blank wall. They were bewildered. Something was wrong. How did Wesscoze get to the observation room? He'd come this way. There had to be an exit!

Rader examined the walls. No cracks. He checked the corners. Everything seemed solidly joined. Angry frustration swept through him. It was here! It had to be here! He knew there wasn't time for further searching. Pedabines would surely be coming through the entrance—wherever it was—at any moment. *The room.* The observation room—if he could just break that plate-glass door! He started back.

Sandy was at his heels.

A soft pneumatic hissing stopped them.

They whipped about and saw a section of the ceiling dropping with a snap. Stairs. Their guns came up.

There was a person on the steps. Right hand outstretched. Palm showing. Fingers spread. A look of wild excitement in his eyes.

"Don't shoot!" It was a hoarse command. "This way! Hurry!" The hand jerked once in his direction. He turned and disappeared up the steps.

Jeff threw a quick glance at Sandy. They hesitated. Was it a trap? An example of quick Pedabine thinking in a moment of near-death danger? He was either getting away, or he was helping them. And if he was helping them—why? Jeff suddenly thought of the dentist, Milton Einberg, and of his suicidal run. He remembered his words, the tossing of the necklace. That had been help for some unknown reason. Maybe this was another weak strand in the Pedabine web. It didn't matter. Waiting meant certain capture. The stairs were there. There was nothing to do but take them. They did, and they saw them lift back into place as soon as they had reached the top.

They looked around. Shortly ahead, another opening waited. This one off the hallway, not in the ceiling. They ducked into it. The wall closed behind them. The new corridor was creamy enamel. The light all around them a crisp, clear blue. The air cool and silent. They hurried. They could hear their own footsteps, the sound of their breathing, the tortured wheeze of exertion. Nothing more. Their rescuer had disappeared. They raced to find him. They were running so fast, they almost missed it: a small, triangular porthole. Two feet high. A foot off the floor. Open. Waiting.

"Come on!"

It was their missing guide. His voice seemed to be coming from a cauldron.

Sandy grabbed the bar over the porthole and scooped into the opening feet first.

Jeff followed.

A cover closed the hatch, but they didn't notice. They were sliding. Shooting through a tube of smooth stainless steel. It arrowed downward. Dropping them. Pulling them at ever-increasing speed. Their breaths caught. They reached for support, for some kind of grip. It was futile. They slid wildly. And just when they believed a horrible bone-smashing collision was imminent, the course curved sharply into a blast of soft, warm air. It cushioned. It slowed their rush to a gentle stop, and they stepped safely into an immaculate, attractive receiving room.

Their guide was waiting. He gestured. Without a word he turned and passed through an open doorway.

They followed. They weren't running now. They were at a quick walk, their eyes on his back, his own strides setting their pace. They tailed him to another corridor. He signaled caution. They froze. He peered around the corner. Satisfied, he wiggled his fingers. They followed again. Only a few yards this time. He stopped at a section of wall, pressed his palm against it, and waited as it yawned. All three walked into a small but wonderfully furnished room.

He turned to them. "I live here," he said. "You're safe, but only for a while."

His voice was husky, rich, surprisingly deep and resonant.

Jeff stepped up to him. His eyes narrowed. "Why are you helping us?" he asked suspiciously.

"Later," the answer came quickly. He stabbed a finger sharply toward Sandy and then raised it in a wait-a-minute sign.

She looked at him quizzically as he opened a door and entered another room.

He was back in seconds.

Tami Wilkenson was walking before him.

The sight of her daughter sent Sandy's heart into her throat. She knew her instantly. The face. The eyes. The delicate curve of her mouth. Three years had passed since she had seen her last. Three long, torturous years. There was a new hairstyle. More height. Weight. A skeletal maturation from baby to little girl. But there was no doubt at all about the identity of this child. Sandy's breath quivered. Her eyes filled with tears. The years of hoping, of anguish and despair had finally made the dream come true. She wanted to rush to her, to hold her, to kiss her. But she simply stood there, fearful of Tami's response, a finger at the corner of her mouth.

Tami looked at her, then at Jeff, and then up at the Pedabine standing behind her.

"431," the rich voice announced, "this is your natural mother."

His statement was the final piece for the child. Earlier, before he had ushered her from Kendral Hall, she had glimpsed this couple on the stage's giant monitoring screens. Something about the woman had seemed familiar. Teased her memory. Awakened dormant longings. What was it? Who was she? Then in the isolation of these quarters, the feelings had writhed and wriggled to the surface of her consciousness. She had recalled scenes. Incidents. Snatches of conversation. But it was all so confusing. So upsetting. She looked at Sandy again. The information she'd just been given battered at the remainder of her Pedabine programming. Resistance crumbled. Memory flooded in.

"Mommy?" she asked timidly.

The word tore at Sandy's heart. Her tears overflowed. A long, quivering sob broke past her parted lips. She nodded her head.

"Mommy?" The word gained strength, conviction.

Sandy heard the change. Her face broke into a glorious, radiant smile. Tears raced down her cheeks. Her hands went out slowly. She sank to her knees.

"Mommy . . . Mommy!" Tami shouted, breaking to her,

leaping into her waiting arms, crying, sobbing, mingling her tears with laughter, kisses, and exclamations of joy.

Jeff Rader's throat ached, and his own breathing trembled as he watched the reunion. He glanced at their rescuer. He saw him smiling faintly, a pleased and yet strangely intense expression on his face. Jeff crossed to him. "Thank you for this," he said softly. "Even though we're all probably going to die down here, somehow you've made the whole thing successful."

"Why should you die?" came the startling response. He gazed directly into Jeff's eyes. "I'll get you to the surface."

Rader wanted to hope, but he realized hope was futile. Escape to the surface was no guarantee of safety. He'd reasoned it before: A death sentence had been placed on him and Sandy; as long as Pedabine let it stand, they would be hunted, found, and eventually murdered. Nothing had changed. It was especially true now that he had killed the Father. Of course, the recovery of a child believed to have been dead for three years would be startling enough to generate interest. But before the authorities would believe a seven-year-old's substantiation of Pedabine conspiracy and actually undertake an investigation, someone would surely reach the three of them. All it took was the touch of a needle. He'd seen that twice now. Nevertheless, if they could reach the surface, as their rescuer was suggesting, that would be another major success—and he would take their lives now just one success at a time.

He grinned at the offer. "Let's go," he said with an emphatic nod.

The Pedabine strode past him to Sandy and Tami. "431," he said, "you're going with your mother and this man."

Tami looked up at him. Conflicting emotions played across her features. "Did the Father say I should?" she asked innocently.

"Yes," he lied.

"Where are we going?"

"Where there are stars and trees and rivers."

"Are you coming, too?"

He shook his head. "I still have things to do here."

Sandy stood and faced him. "Thank you," she said. "I'll thank you every day of my life."

"She's a wonderful child," he murmured. "Guard her well." He traced a finger fondly across the girl's cheek.

Jeff's newspaper experience had taught him never to question assistance, but he found himself asking again, ''Why are you doing this? Why are you risking your life for us?''

''I'm doing it for myself as well'' came the cryptic answer. ''It's time to keep a promise.''

Rader's brows knit.

''They killed every member of my family. I've known that for some time. One night I sneaked into the records section; I ran my computer file.'' His voice deepened. He was remembering something special. ''When they took me, I promised they would be hurt.'' He looked at Jeff. ''It's time to keep a promise, that's all.''

Jeff nodded his understanding. ''What's your name?'' he asked simply.

''336.''

''Don't you remember your real name?''

''Oh, yes . . . Baliston . . . Daniel Richard Baliston.''

The shock that rattled Jeff and Sandy was almost too much to bear. They blurted sounds as though they'd just been roundly slapped.

Danny Baliston watched them questioningly.

Jeff's surprise gave way immediately to intense excitement. His words raced. ''I can't believe it. You're here. You're here! We know all about you, Danny Baliston. We know exactly what happened nine years ago. Why, you're even responsible for our finding this place.''

Baliston was puzzled.

''*This is perfect!*'' Rader exploded. ''Danny, you get us out of here—all of us, and that means you, too—and I'll *make* them listen! With both you and Tami to prove our story, they'll have to believe. We'll expose the whole Pedabine operation. We'll get them!''

The young man shook his head. ''You have to go without me.''

''You can't stay,'' Sandy protested. ''They'll know you gave us Tami.''

''Come with us,'' Jeff urged. ''It's the only way to destroy them.''

Danny Baliston didn't answer. A little smile pulled at the corners of his mouth.

''Come with us,'' Jeff repeated.

The young man seemed to hesitate a moment. ''We'll see,'' he murmured, "we'll see." Then he switched into another attitude, a quick, decisive one. "Let's go," he ordered. "We've lost too much time. They may even have organized the search by now." He turned away abruptly. He crossed to a wall and placed his palm against it. A panel slid wide. He entered quickly, without another word, without a backward glance. His stride was long, fast, and certain.

Jeff, Sandy, and Tami followed him as closely as they could.

He had led them into a bright corridor. The walls were pale yellow. Strips of chromium sectioned them at regular intervals. Light came through the partitions. Every fourth one glowed translucently.

They pressed through silence. Only the sounds of their movement could be heard. Muffled. Soft over resilient flooring.

He was taking them to an emergency escape shaft. The main elevator within Condor Rock would be guarded now. Access to it would be blocked. Since no one would suspect he was helping them, it would be assumed that Jeff and Sandy were ignorant of the escape routes. The emergency elevator would still be opened and operable, he believed.

They went from yellow passageways into pink. They were heading for the Red Area of Critical Evacuation. They still saw no one. They still heard nothing unusual.

But that wasn't to last.

Danny Baliston had just passed a palm over an innocuous-looking dividing strip. The wall had opened. They found themselves face-to-face with two Pedabines entering their corridor.

No one moved. It was a split second of suspended animation. Then understanding struck.

Jeff leaped past Danny Baliston. He had the lead man in an instant. He swung him around. He hammered his neck and drove the doubled figure headfirst into the wall. The Pedabine groaned and crumbled to the floor.

Tami screamed.

Sandy swept her up in her arms.

Jeff turned to face the second man. But he wasn't there. He was running. Crouched. Weaving. Shouting the area's color like a jammed Klaxon alarm. The words filled the hallway, echoing off the walls. The safety of silence was gone. Jeff dropped to a knee. He leveled his gun. He had to get that Pedabine, get him before he could reveal that Danny Baliston was helping them. They couldn't lose the advantage of that secret!

Rader squeezed the trigger. A section of lighting panel far ahead exploded. He'd missed!

The Pedabine dived into a wall. He was gone.

Jeff charged for the point of disappearance.

Danny, Sandy, and Tami came up behind him. Tami was shaking, her eyes wide in fear, tight choking gasps racking her little frame.

They had reached another triangular porthole.

"Transport tube," Danny snapped as he ran ahead.

The Pedabine had escaped.

Jeff realized what that would now mean: Their location was known; their direction would be assessed; their exits blocked. There was no time to waste. He scooped Tami from Sandy's arms, and the three of them went flying after Danny Baliston.

Alarms went off. Jarring, screaming sirens.

Their enemy had reached a control. Pedabines would soon be swarming into the area like locusts.

They burst into a new corridor. The color was red. They ran through it. Driving. Gasping.

Now a voice growled over the sirens: "Area Red! Area Red! Section Four! Section Four!"

Their escape shaft had been identified. Pedabines were being instructed to stop them there.

Ahead of them, Danny Baliston had cut into a narrow cleft in the wall. They rushed for it. But in the wildness of flight, Sandy suddenly tripped. She went sprawling. Her gun went skittering. She had been directly behind Jeff. He heard her cry and gasp as she fell. He stopped. He turned. His breath burst from him like air from an exploding balloon. *The passage was being sealed.* A steel panel was sliding between Sandy and him. He screamed her name. He dropped Tami, tossed aside his own gun, and leaped at the closing panel. His fingers caught the edge of it. He fought wildly to stop its progress. Sandy was scrambling to her knees. Tami was screaming, "Mommy! Mommy!" The panel dragged Jeff. Pulling him steadily. Forcing him closer to the wall.

"Hurry, Sandy, hurry!" he groaned.

Near the shutting point, Rader swung his foot up and braced it against the wall.

Sandy scurried on all fours for the narrowing gap.

He fought the force of the panel like a madman. He felt his wounded shoulder tear again. He felt his damaged hand slipping on fresh blood. *"Sandy . . . Sandy."*

She dived. Under his leg. Twisting her body through a space that was no more than a foot in width.

Jeff leaped away, and the steel door slammed shut with the clang of prison bars.

She was on her feet. "I'm all right, I'm all right," she repeated. The words were a blur, though.

Tami rushed at her, crying her fear and relief.

"Come on," Jeff urged. He had retrieved his gun. He was looking anxiously toward the cleft into which Danny Baliston had disappeared.

The sirens were still blaring. The area was still being identified by that growling voice. The child ran willingly with Sandy. Jeff was waiting at the opening for them. They reached him and followed him into it without a moment's delay.

It was a bare-earth tunnel. Narrow. Dark. Damp.

When they came to the end of it, they found Danny Baliston waiting impatiently. "Everyone all right?" he asked.

Jeff answered, "I could have used you."

"I jammed the last sealing panel up ahead, and I had to bring down the elevator. Follow me, we're almost there." He turned and bolted away.

They stayed right behind him this time. Up a flight of metal steps. Through a maze of darkened ways. And soon they were there. They'd run into a cell-like cubicle 15 feet by 15 feet. Dimly lit. Cold. Forbidding. It seemed like a dead end.

For a moment, Sandy and Jeff were perplexed. Then Jeff looked up and saw a flickering star a light-year away. He understood immediately. That pinprick of light was day.

Danny Baliston was moving swiftly. He had run to a far corner of the shaft and dropped to his knees. The elevator was a simple platform. It had no walls, no safety fencing, no grates. It was merely an earth-covered floor that would seem like actual ground on the surface of the desert above. Perfect camouflage. A Pedabine precaution against accidental discovery. Danny was sweeping earth away. Quickly he uncovered a small metal box. He pulled at it, and it swung upright on a two-foot iron support. "Stay in the middle," he ordered, running toward a passageway opposite the one from which they had just entered. "I switched routes and brought you into Section Six. They won't realize that for a while." He pointed at the metal control box. "Take off the cover and press the button."

"Where are you going?" Sandy cried. "Come with us."

He shook his head. "Have a promise to keep. Good luck." He was gone before another word of protest could be sounded.

Jeff had gone to the control box. "Get ready," he ordered. "Remember, stay in the center."

Sandy ran to the middle of the platform. She dropped to her knees. She pulled Tami close.

Rader tore away the heavy plastic cover. "What the—!" There were *two* buttons on the face of the box. What was the second one? He looked closer. No. It wasn't a button. It was a depression in the box—and under it were the letters EMER. POW. No matter. The one on the left was obviously the starting button. He punched it with his thumb. He heard the power go on. Felt the elevator vibrate under them. Gathering force. Starting to move. He leaped for the center.

And then suddenly, abruptly, everything stopped.

The gathering force, the vibrations, the movement—the elevator had gone dead.

Rader leaped for the control box again. He pressed the button. Squeezed it. Pounded it. The elevator wouldn't budge.

"Area Red! Area Red! Section Six! Section Six!"

They had been found. The power had been cut. Pedabines were being directed to them.

"Area Red! Section Six! Area Red! Section Six!"

The few dim bulbs in the wall of the shaft were still on, throwing their feeble light.

Jeff clawed at the metal box. Nothing was happening. But there was emergency power. There had to be. That's what the letters had to mean! He had to activate it. But how? The control wasn't even a button. It was just a circular depression, that's all, a circular depression. He heard the words as clearly as if Isaac Morganvelt were shouting them into his ear. Of course, *a circular depression*. . . Ralph Watson had died for it. . . . Jesse had risked his life for it. . . . It had wires in it, and Morganvelt had said it was used for something. It was a *key*, a Pedabine key, the means of getting through to their secret quarters! The necklace—the *disk*! He ripped Ralph Watson's chain from

around his neck. He fumbled the disk over the control spot. It
slipped in. It fit!

At that exact moment, Pedabines rushed from the tunnels.
Four men.

"Jeff!"

Sandy's shout brought his head up sharply.

His gun came into play immediately. One man fell with a
bullet in his side. Another took one in the chest. The two
remaining Pedabines, though, were on him before he could bring
them down. The gun was knocked from his hand. One of them
dived for it before Sandy could reach it. He had it! Meanwhile,
Jeff was battering the third senseless. He turned quickly. He was
facing his own weapon. Leveled. Pointing directly at his chest,
only four feet away. His heart almost stopped. He was a dead
man. But why hadn't the Pedabine fired? *Why isn't he blasting
me? I gunned his friend. I killed his Father. Why isn't he
shooting?* The answer was there as he was thinking the questions.
He had stored it away days ago, sensing even then it would be
important. *Pedabines were robots—slaves to command.* The Century International Hotel . . . a dying gunman trying to throw
Sandy out the window when he could have killed her with a
bullet. Why? *Because he had been ordered to do it that way.*
And this one had been ordered, too! Jeff had heard it himself,
immediately after Avery Wesscoze had plunged to his death:
"FIND THEM! BRING THEM HERE—ALIVE—RIGHT HERE
BEFORE THE PRIMARY COUNCIL!" They wanted Sandy and
him, but they wanted them *alive!* He wouldn't shoot. He *couldn't*
shoot! Jeff leaped at him. They went down. Tumbling. Grappling.
Rader's knee came up. It caught the man just under his sternum.
Air gushed as though his lungs had exploded. His eyes bugged.
His strength died. He lay there momentarily paralyzed. Jeff raced
back to the control box. The disk! The key! Why hadn't it
worked? He pressed it frantically. There would be more Pedabines
any second now. What was wrong with this thing? *What was
wrong?* Sirens still blared. The voice still directed: "Area Red!
Section Six! Area Red! Section Six!" And the elevator wouldn't
move. Then, still pressing it, he twisted the key. Slightly.
Accidentally. It seemed to grip in the depression. He jerked in
surprise. That was it—*it had to be turned!* He swung it
counterclockwise. Ninety degrees. Instantly the hum of power

filled the shaft. The control box automatically tipped back into its floor molding. The ground vibrated under them.

Sandy dropped to her knees again, pulling Tami to her lap, holding her tightly.

Jeff ran to the fallen Pedabines. He dragged them. Swung them. Threw them off the elevator. And not a second too soon. The floor started to rise. Slowly at first. He sprang toward Sandy and Tami. He wrapped his arms about them. It gained momentum. Faster. Faster. It became a rocket, propelling them skyward. The floor swayed wildly. The light above grew swiftly. They were flying into orbit.

Sandy began to laugh.

Jeff, too.

They pulled together, an ecstatic, tight knot.

Premature joy.

Abruptly the power stopped. The elevator halted so jarringly they were thrown to their backs. They were near the surface. Not there yet. But oh so near. Twelve feet. Only twelve feet.

Rader looked around quickly at the walls. The mechanism was imbedded, covered. There was nothing to climb on. "Sandy," he called. "Fast!" He knew their current had been cut in the mine below. He knew it would soon be reversed.

Sandy jumped at his words.

He bent his leg near a wall.

She understood instantly. She stepped on it, swung to his back, climbed to his shoulders. And when he stood, she reached for the surface and pulled herself free. Now she lay on her stomach and reached into the shaft again. Tami's fingers stretched toward her. Jeff had boosted the child. She wrapped her hands around Tami's wrists. She struggled to her knees. Lifting her. Pulling. And finally swinging her up alongside herself.

Meanwhile, Jeff was searching desperately for some means to join them. He needed height. Something to climb on. Some kind of step that would bring his reach to the rim of the shaft. The control box! It was on a two-foot support. He broke to where it lay flat in its frame. He pulled at it. It wouldn't lift. He planted his feet. Squeezed his fingers under the steel bracing. Tugged. Strained. Fought it. An agonizing bolt of pain ripped through his bad shoulder, but he tried to ignore it. He jerked at it. Once. Twice. There was a snap. It broke from its lock and swung upright again. Swiftly he stepped on the control box. He reached for the edge of the shaft. He was still a foot away. Then he felt it—a physical hum. The power had been turned on. *Reversed.* The elevator trembled beneath him. He lunged upward. Arms straining. Fingers reaching. And the elevator plummeted back to the depths below. He was clinging to the edge of the shaft. Dangling six hundred feet above certain death. His shoulder was almost strengthless. His hand a bleeding, slippery mess. But he held.

Sandy was pulling at him. Fighting to save him from the yawning black pit into which she was staring.

"Back away," she heard him say. "Back away."

She released him. She stood. She clutched Tami to her and watched prayerfully as the man she loved as much as life struggled with his last shred of strength to pull himself to safety.

He strained, he clutched, he heaved, and he drew himself slowly, agonizingly upward. Then with one last mighty effort, he hitched over the lip of the shaft and lay with his face in the desert soil, panting and virtually spent.

Sandy rushed to him and pulled his legs free.

He crawled away from the opening. He collapsed and rolled to his back.

Sunlight, rich clean sunlight, embraced him.

Air, sweet fresh air, bathed him.

Sandy was on her knees at his side, anxiously stroking his hair, his face, worriedly murmuring her love, her concern.

He gulped. He drank the air. It surged into his lungs, quickly reviving his body. He pulled himself to his feet. He swayed. "Come on," he croaked. "We're not clear yet." Then he turned to get their bearings.

Condor Rock rose in the distance. Area Red, Section Six, had brought them to the surface only one mile from where their LTD still stood. Their spirits leaped. In their condition, and with the possibility of pursuit, any shortening of distance was a Godsend. They went straight for the car. Jogging. Stumbling. Never taking their eyes off their objective. They reached it in minutes. They swung the doors open. They fell onto the front seat.

Sandy turned the key.

The engine started immediately.

Smiles broke on their faces for the first time since they had reclaimed Tami. They were free!

Then unexpectedly, the car began to shake, to sway.

"What the—!"

"What's happening, Jeff? What is it?"

"I don't know."

The ground beneath them was trembling, growling.

The Ford rose on a swell of earth. And suddenly, through their windshield, they witnessed a sight that took their breath away: Condor Rock disappeared within a long, roiling pillar of purple flame. They recognized the explosion instantly. It was the same kind that had obliterated Ralph Watson's house. Only more powerful now—a hundred, a thousand times more powerful.

"My God!" Sandy gasped.

"Turn this thing around!" Jeff barked. "Get us out of here!"

Her foot hit the accelerator like a driver's in a drag race. The car leaped forward. She whipped it into a tight turn and gunned the engine for all it could give.

The land was going crazy under them. Heaving. Exploding deep in its gut.

Rocks, boulders—pieces of the main Pedabine entrance—began to rain around them.

The Ford tore across the desert, swirling a cloud of dust like a demon tornado.

Rader looked back through the rear window. *The earth was disappearing.* The desert was caving in! Following them. Racing them. Trying to snare them and suck them into its vortex.

The accelerator of the car was on the floor. The engine was screaming. Sandy was hunched over the wheel, knuckles white, lips squeezed between her teeth. Jeff's arms were about Tami, holding her close, softening the jarring, jolting punishment of their flight.

And the collapsing land kept chasing them—gaining!

They saw the horizon shift. It was unexpectedly upon them. They were caught in the collapse. Sinking. Climbing uphill now. Sand began to slide toward them. The car fought it. Bucked it. Surged into it—upward, upward.

Then as astonishingly as it had begun, it ended.

The heaving became a ripple; the ripple, a tremor; the tremor, a calm. The roaring gave way to growling and then to rumbles and, finally, to silence.

The LTD topped the rise of its climb and leveled off on flat land again.

Rader looked back: A crater of enormous width spanned the car's rear window. And inside, deep, deep within its bowels, rested the threat of Pedabine.

They were safe now. Finally. Totally. Permanently. Safe.

22

Tranquillity.

Lush, verdant growth; clear, azure sky; clean, warm sand; eternal, rumbling surf. Tranquillity.

Mr. and Mrs. Jeffrey Rader had rented a lovely, rambling house off Leho'ula Beach. They had been "soaking sun" for months now, guiding the recovery of their daughter, Tami, and watching the healing of their sister, Ann Kroft.

The child had stopped having nightmares. She hadn't mentioned a Pedabine experience in weeks. She was dancing along the water's edge now, her feet playfully challenging the exhausted waves, slicing little impressions in the wet sand as she darted away. The laughter of her game was a delightful treble over the constant bass of the ocean. Child and nature. Pure music.

The woman, too, had shown signs of mending. When Jeff first informed her of her husband's death, the shock and sense of loss had been overwhelming. She'd cried long and hard. But her intelligence and basic emotional strength had ultimately allowed her to control her sorrow. Outbursts had stopped as if the care of her infant girl had become her only concern. She still found her eyes filling suddenly as a quick unexpected memory of Stanley flooded her mind. But lately even this had diminished. The beautiful baby, the surroundings, the loving attention of her brother and his new family were the best of therapies. Annie was sitting at the edge of a beach blanket now. Her legs were together, knees bent, feet planted in the soft sand. Her six-month-old daughter was nestled against her thighs, tiny hands holding her thumbs, little fat knees bouncing happily. She had named the girl Stacy, after Stanley, and she was now repeating the word playfully, drawing lovely bursts of laughter from the child. The sound was infectious. It caused her to respond with a happy melody of her own. Mother and child. More music.

Sandy and Jeff had married three months before. The ceremony had been simple and warm. They had held each other in a loving gaze as the binding words were spoken. Then their first kiss as husband and wife had been a sweet, gentle thanksgiving for the luck, the fate, the God, that had brought them together and seen them successfully through their ordeal. Jeff had given up his seventeenth-floor luxury apartment in Westwood; Sandy had prepared and closed the house in Beverly Hills for their long, relaxed honeymoon. Immediately after the wedding ceremony, they'd left with Tami, Annie, and Stacy for Jeff's dream spot— Hana Village.

Annie had protested at first that they should enjoy their first weeks alone together. But they had begged her to join them. The beach house they'd rented was enormous, they'd argued; they would have their own wing; she and Stacy would have one, too; the sun and sand would be good for everyone; this was no time for her to be alone in Los Angeles; and, finally, Tami needed the loving presence of her only aunt. An irresistible argument. Besides, Annie had been anxious about her sudden and inexplicable moments of depression. She'd allowed herself to be persuaded, and everything had turned out beautifully. Now Jeff lay on his stomach, his chin propped on the heel of his hand. Sandy lay on her back, her neck resting in the curve of his waist. They were both grinning, watching Annie and the baby, hearing Tami and the waves. A perfect audience for the perfect symphony.

For three months after their escape from Pedabine, there had been no sweet music. They'd experienced only the worst cacophony of anguish. There were deaths that had to be explained—at the Century International, at Myra Macon London's house, at Annie Kroft's. They'd had to clear themselves in Los Angeles and satisfy the government in Washington. They had told their incredible story to the law. All of it. And the first narration had so astounded their listeners that a lid of militant secrecy had immediately been clamped on the entire inquiry, and they had been swiftly and unceremoniously placed incommunicado.

Only three facts had saved them: one, that Jeff had the credibility and the reputation of a nationally recognized, award-winning columnist; two, that Sandy had been the wife of Adam Wilkenson, a murdered diplomat in the Department of State; and three, that Tami Wilkenson, pronounced dead, was standing right there beside them.

It wasn't that they had been believed immediately. On the contrary, the entire story had seemed so fantastic that it stretched the credulity of their original interrogators to the breaking point. Anyone else offering it would have been instantly booked, fingerprinted, and scheduled for psychiatric observation. But Jeff's and Sandy's backgrounds, and Tami's presence, were enough to give pause, enough to generate anxiety, over what course of action to pursue next. At first, their police questioners had even become angry. They'd believed that Rader was trying to hide behind an enormous fabrication, one too bizarre to be dismissed. In their thinking, Jeff was playing the odds of the Big Lie.

But then there was Tami. And she was fact.

It confused them completely; it created the unsettling need to dump the entire matter into more competent laps for a more authoritative study.

Until then—secrecy and isolation.

The questioning that followed had been a nightmare. Jeff, Sandy, and Annie had been separated. Two highly placed officials had conducted endless hours of repetitious inquiry. They'd cajoled, wheedled, badgered, insulted, and psychologically battered all three of them. The aim had been to produce discrepancies in their unbelievable story. After days of this, when none appeared, the official attitude had begun to change. It went from impatience and anger to doubt and concern. Then slowly, corroborative evidence had filtered in: a slight flap over the whereabouts of the Vice-President; a report that some corporate heads seemed to be extending their vacations without notification; a seismological interest in the Utah desert's minor earthquake activity. Individually, the points had seemed to be unrelated and of no major significance. Collectively, though, in light of Jeff, Sandy, and Annie's explanation, they became particularly frightening. Insidiously, the story had become plausible. It was no longer a simple matter of unresolved local murders. It had become a possible conspiracy of international dimensions. Obviously, too hot for municipal hands. In strictest secrecy, it had been referred to the highest levels of the federal government.

Henry Bayard was sent by the President himself to conduct the investigation. Only a handful of completely trustworthy people had been informed of Bayard's involvement. He had known Sandy in Washington. He had stimulated the District of Columbia's search for Adam Wilkenson's killers and the consequent destruction of Alpha 61. And he now undertook his inquiry with a vengeance. After a week of carefully checking every detail of what had come to be known as The Story, he reported to the President: "It's true."

Jeff had assured Bayard that all Pedabines had perished in The Condor Mine—that he had actually heard the Father say to his flock: "You, my children, *you who are all the Pedabines in this world* . . ." That information had eased anxiety of continued activity of the organization. However, it'd had no effect upon official concern about public reaction if The Story were ever released to the news media. The President and Bayard feared general panic, the loss of public confidence in the government, and a weakening of the American image within the international community. The coverup began.

Before they were released, an explanation was devised to absolve Jeff, Sandy, and Annie of all culpability in the already publicized killings. Reports that had linked them to the murders were labeled "false and malicious"; officials insisted that the search for the real perpetrators was continuing. All mention of Pedabine had been scrupulously avoided. Furthermore, everyone who had heard even part of the The Story had been cautioned never to breathe a word of it to anyone at any time. The disappearances of leading figures were allowed their normal media interest and study. Nothing of Pedabine involvement was ever unearthed by reporters. In time—a very short time—daily events crowded the missing persons into the background of history.

Eventually Everett Frazier's body was allegedly found in the wilderness of Wyoming, clawed beyond recognition by a grizzly bear; Harold Durkin was said to have died in a light plane accident somewhere off the coast of California; Arthur Marquand's decomposed body was discovered in a wrecked Jeep near a ghost town in Nevada. Apparent cause of death: dehydration.

The entire Red Condor Mine area was purchased by the Defense Department and quickly guarded from accidental or intentional probing.

All of this had taken three months. Three terrible months.

But now nature, time, and love were demonstrating their healing powers.

Laughter and pleasure were steadily replacing anguish and tears.

Of course, Pedabine would never be completely forgotten. All four would carry scars for the remainder of their lives: Annie would study Stacy and recall the features of her husband; Tami would become aware occasionally of the missing finger joint of her left hand; Sandy would embrace her daughter and remember her own three years of tortured searching; and Jeff would periodically and absently finger the bullet scar in his shoulder. All had reminders, but all would move away from the pain.

"The plane should have landed an hour ago," Jeff murmured suddenly, apropos of nothing. He was thinking of the interisland hop from Oahu.

Sandy didn't move. "Uh-huh."

Annie nodded and bounced Stacy into another wild giggle.

They were expecting visitors.

Mention of the airplane caused Sandy to think of California. "Jeff," she said, turning to face him, "how long do you want to stay in Hana?"

He groaned luxuriously and rolled to his back. "I could stay here forever," he replied.

"Why don't we?"

He raised his head and looked at her with a smile.

"Do you plan to go back to the *Voice*?" she persisted.

"No." The answer came fast. "That part of me is over."

"Then we don't have to go back, do we?"

"What'll I do for work?"

She smiled and whispered some words he had once spoken to her: "Breathes there a newsman with soul so dead . . ."

He chuckled. Her reminder, though, was something that had been teasing him for some time now: a book. A good, exciting book. Actually, if he were to start one, it could be written as easily in Hana as in Beverly Hills. More easily, in fact. Fewer distractions. And he'd be good at it. He believed that. Yes . . . a book. A new career. That sounded good. All right—he'd do it. Yes, he would!

"Hey, down there!"

The caller pulled their attention upward. It was one of their expected visitors.

"Michael!"

Michael and Sean Gavin had promised to spend a week with them, though both of them knew from experience what the tropical sun could do to their fair skin. And here they were now, descending the path to the beach, armed for battle with hats, shirts, towels, lotions, and umbrellas.

The greeting was an eruption of joy.

There was a day when Michael wouldn't have believed this meeting could have taken place. It was the morning he had received Jeff's call from Orie Reed Memorial Hospital in Atawan. He had hung up and left the house immediately to fly to Annie's side. But he had been recognized and stopped by a security guard at Los Angeles International Airport. A suggestion had been made to drive him to the police commissioner's office. He had argued vehemently against it.

So, Durkin's office had been called and notified of his apprehension, and Michael had been informed that an aide of the commissioner was leaving immediately to question him.

Gavin had been prepared to die if the aide turned out to be a Pedabine. However, if he was going to be killed, he had determined to make the job as difficult as possible. First, he lied to the security guards about a serious coronary condition, and he insisted on having a doctor in attendance throughout the questioning. Next, he concocted a tale about threats to his life for stories he had approved when he had been editor of the *Voice*. A contract was still out on him, he said, and the killer could be recognized by a missing finger joint on his left hand. He demanded, then, that anyone who professed to be from Durkin's office be examined before being allowed to question him. If a missing finger joint should be discovered, then the party should be held and the L.A.P.D. notified immediately. If, however, everything seemed legitimate, then he, Michael, would answer questions—but only if the security guards were at his side with the doctor and the questioner was never allowed closer than ten feet.

After developing this scenario, Gavin had then warned the airport officials of the grave legal and publicity consequences if